and style. The novel deals in science fiction, mythology, hyper-action, love, and mystery." —*Austin American-Statesman*

"In a novel that is simultaneously irreverent, gut-wrenching, satirical, and sorrowful, Gonzales demonstrates a fresh and varied voice, along with perfect comedic timing." —*The Kansas City Star*

"So fresh and so funny, the pacing is so fast and crackling, you won't be able to stop reading." —*Tor.com*

"Sci-fi freaks and magical-realist devotees will flock to this debut novel by Gonzales." —*Refinery29*

"A wholly invented world rife with satire, absurdity, and somehow love and even warmth. With this debut novel, Gonzales . . . proves himself to be both a wonderful addition to a proud literary tradition (that of Vonnegut, Borges, Saunders, Bender, and Barthelme, et al) and a true original." —*Lit Hub*

"I wanted to go for a ride and *The Regional Office Is Under Attack!* took me on one. . . . I was rewarded with pure satisfaction."

—*BookRiot* (The Best Books of 2016 So Far)

"You may not be familiar with the name Manuel Gonzales, but once you've had the pleasure of delving into one of his out-of-the-ordinary literary creations, you won't forget it. . . . In his debut novel, *The Regional Office Is Under Attack!*, Gonzales conjures a futuristic world of super-powered female assassins. . . . Gonzales's tale has something for every reader: Double agents! Secret romantic trysts! Conspiracy! Fight scenes! Friendships gone awry! At its core, however, *The Regional Office Is Under Attack!* is ultimately a tale of vengeance—one during which you'll find yourself struggling to choose a side." —*BookPage*

"You might want to get a firm grip on your socks before cracking open this one; otherwise, Gonzales is likely to knock them off. It's very difficult to categorize this mind-bending novel. . . . It's pure excitement. . . . A brilliant genre-blender."

—*Booklist* (starred review)

"A hyperkinetic sci-fi set piece along the lines of *Die Hard*, seeded with paranormal elements cribbed from half a dozen other franchises and the absent-parent grudges that fuel any number of teen novels. . . . Genre enthusiasts will love the spooky cyberpunk spirit at play here." —*Kirkus Reviews*

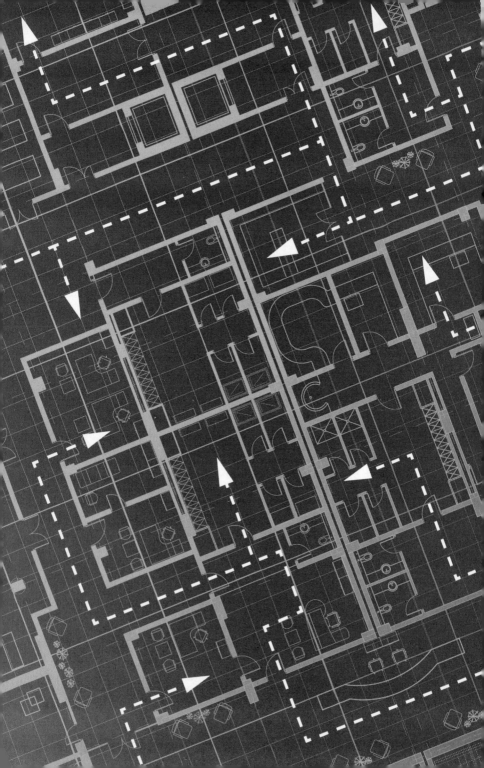

# Praise for *The Regional Office Is Under Attack!*

"A tour de force . . . Repurposes the devices of a genre specializing in fantasies of mastery into a portrait of chastened adults moving through a world where mastery eludes us all . . . What binds the whole thing together is a persistent, self-contradictory human desire to both be extraordinary and to fit in, finally, somewhere. *The Regional Office Is Under Attack!* sneaks up on you. It starts out looking like a heist yarn intertwined with a couple of origin stories, but it keeps coming back to the stuff people devour superhero comics and spy thrillers to escape: isolation, confusion, triviality, moral doubt." —Laura Miller, *Slate*

"An entertaining and satisfying novel. Like the best of the stories it satirizes so gently, it's rollicking good fun on the surface, action-packed and shiny in all the right places; underneath that surface, though, it's thoughtful and well considered. Gonzales has created a superheroic fighting force of the kind we've grown so used to through constant exposure to the Avengers and various iterations of the X-Men, and then he has turned out their pockets and flipped open their diaries."

—*The New York Times Book Review*

"Highly entertaining . . . Wonderfully strange and fun, Gonzales's novel follows both the women attacking and defending the Regional Office and how their lives intersect." —BuzzFeed

"A hugely entertaining read." —*Chicago Tribune*

"Like the writers he is compared to, Gonzales's stories' fantastic premises are always anchored in real-world conflicts that hold universal familiarity. The story nods to tons of tropes—from *Kill Bill* and *Charlie's Angels* to *Blade Runner* and *The Karate Kid*—but it frequently subverts those tropes and uses them to flesh out characters that dazzle." —*The Rumpus*

"The Regional Office really IS under attack! This is not metaphor! It is a wry and propulsive work of inventive fiction by a terrific young writer! Read it!"

—Jess Walter, *New York Times*–bestselling author of *Beautiful Ruins*

"Delightfully weird, weirdly delightful! Manuel Gonzales clearly has a labyrinth of a brain—all stuffed with monsters, trapdoors, and complicated heroes. Sign me up as a member of the fan club, please."

—Kelly Link, author of *Get in Trouble* and *Magic for Beginners*

"This book is a winged creation, and absolutely marvelous. Gonzales keeps turning the kaleidoscope to reveal the strangest, darkest, and most beautiful dimensions of human love, and the conversion of mechanical fury into living strength."

—Karen Russell, author of *Swamplandia!*

"The Regional Office, a shadowy organization of spooky oracles and superpowered middle-management misfits, isn't the only thing under attack in this tremendous debut novel. With exuberant prose and a corkscrew plot, Manuel Gonzales vanquishes artistic orthodoxies, tiresome genre boundaries, and every humdrum narrative convention in sight, leaving in his wake a riveting story of secrets, betrayals, and vengeance!" —Claire Vaye Watkins, author of *Battleborn* and *Gold Fame Citrus*

"Wild, visionary, ablaze with heart and riot, *The Regional Office Is Under Attack!* is unforgettable—an epic love story that confronts our future with a howl and fireworks." —Paul Yoon, author of *Snow Hunters*

"*The Regional Office Is Under Attack!* is wickedly subversive, suspenseful, and thoughtful, all at once—but most of all, it's just fun to read, from the first sentence to the last. Put down your expectations and pick up this book. It'll hit you like a lightning bolt." —Jess Row, author of *Your Face in Mine*

"A ridiculously fun story about love, as well as time and timing, both good and bad. And because of that, it's also timely. The ending—with its deft glimpse at a hypothetical future—is alone worth the wild ride."
                    —Hannah Pittard, author of *The Fates Will Find Their Way*

"When it comes to fiction it usually doesn't bring out the LOLs so much as me laughing on the inside. Which is why I was pleasantly surprised to find myself cracking up during some of the fight scenes and especially a bunch of the lines with curses while listening to the audiobook of *The Regional Office Is Under Attack!*"
                    —*BookRiot*

"Gathers up conventions of all genres—hot killer assassin teens, hostage-scenario nail-biter, supernatural mystery—without sinking into any of them, or letting them get stale . . . The emotional currents flowing beneath and through Gonzales's blockbuster action scenes are remarkably well rendered. I inhaled this book so quickly." —*The Guardian*

"Firmly establishes Gonzales as a practitioner of literary sci-fi . . . It's just so much fun to read. . . . A gifted writer who effortlessly pushes and pulls the reader through shifting timelines, and his smooth writing style sparkles with wit . . . A superb piece of high-tension storytelling." —*The Dallas Morning News*

"Cinematic, like a well-done graphic novel set in a tornado of timeframes—an inventive labyrinth with oracles, superpowered female assassins, and mythology . . . *The Regional Office Is Under Attack!* pushes beyond the average reading experience. . . . A surrealist Tarantino-esque adventure, more readily compared to *Pulp Fiction* in its plot and a Yves Tanguy painting in its mood, atmosphere,

# THE REGIONAL OFFICE
## IS UNDER ATTACK!

MANUEL GONZALES

RIVERHEAD BOOKS / *New York*

**RIVERHEAD BOOKS**
An imprint of Penguin Random House LLC
375 Hudson Street
New York, New York 10014

The Library of Congress has catalogued the Riverhead edition as follows:

Gonzales, Manuel, date.
The regional office is under attack! / Manuel Gonzales.
p.      cm.
ISBN 9781594632419
I. Title.
PS3607.O56227R44      2016               2015024640
813'.6—dc23

First Riverhead hardcover edition: April 2016
First Riverhead trade paperback edition: April 2017
Riverhead trade paperback ISBN: 9780399573217

Printed in the United States of America
1   3   5   7   9   10   8   6   4   2

*Book design by Lauren Kolm*

*For Anabel and Dashiell and, as always, to Sharon*

Get out, get out of my sanctum and drown your spirits in woe.

—Pythia, the Oracle of Apollo at Delphi

From *The Regional Office Is Under Attack:*
*Tracking the Rise and Fall of an American Institution*

If you were wealthy, but extremely so, and you were in
the market for a lavish adventurous getaway, one that
might require the retainer of Sherpas—in the event that
you came across a mountain you wished to scale—as
well as a hot-air balloon and balloon crew in case, well,
that came up, too, the desire, if you will, to hot-air-
balloon over the glacial formations off the southern
coast of Chile, then you could hardly do better than to
contact the staff at the Morrison World Travel Concern.
Located on the ground floor of an unassumingly expensive building on Park Avenue between Fifty-Sixth
and Fifty-Seventh, the Morrison World Travel Concern
catered to only the most lavish of vacations.

Although, in truth, if you were the kind of wealthy
individual who could afford the kind of service provided
by the Morrison Concern, more than likely, they would
have already contacted you. They had been known to do
this with an almost preternatural instinct for not just
the best way to find you but for offering you a vacation
package you didn't know you had always longed for
until it was offered. Then, once it was offered, you would

experience such a strong urge to take the vacation they had suggested that you would be practically unable to do anything else until you had.

The agents of the Morrison Concern once set up an illegal nighttime zip-line tour of the Manhattan skyline (for a prince of Saudi Arabia) and, a few years ago, handled the arrangements for a private, curated tour of the *Titanic,* led by the filmmaker James Cameron, the travelers exploring in retrofitted (for safety and comfort) nineteenth-century diving suits they then had the option to purchase as keepsakes (for a Canadian couple who wish to remain anonymous). There is a rumor that they once burrowed deep into the Perito Moreno Glacier and there constructed an elaborate reproduction of the interior of Sleeping Beauty's castle for a young girl's seventh birthday party, and another rumor that they once entertained but ultimately declined a young tech-industry billionaire who wanted to host a New Year's Eve party on a submarine as it sank into the deepest depths of the Mariana Trench.

How they obtained the resources to outfit such expeditions, no one knew, but outfit them they did, and with uncanny skill.

If, however, you were not wealthy, or even if you were, but were not particularly interested in the Mariana Trench or New Year's Eve parties, but were interested, rather, in the amassing forces of darkness that threaten, at nearly every turn, the fate of the planet . . . or, say, you were concerned with the fate of your mother, who was stolen from you when you were very young, abducted and then brainwashed and made into a triple or quadruple agent, only then to be killed in a firefight thousands of miles away, and you were seeking cold retribution for this . . . or maybe you had been told a frightening prophecy about your as-yet-unborn first child and you wished to have it confirmed or refuted by an oracle . . . or your daughter, your once-sweet little girl, had begun exhibiting problems at age fourteen or fifteen, or not problems but issues, or not issues but powers, had begun to exhibit unprecedented physical strength and mental willfulness that you hoped to have fixed, or not fixed but cured, or not that either (the word you were searching for, ultimately, was *honed*) . . . if these were your needs, then once again, there was perhaps no better place to start than at the offices of the Morrison Concern.

In which case, you asked for Kathy and then mentioned that you would like to book a trip to the Lost City of Atlantis. A few years ago, you would have asked to book a trip to Akron, Ohio, under the assumption that no one walking into these offices would have actually wanted to book a trip to Akron, Ohio, until shockingly enough, one particularly wealthy and eccentric older gentleman did, which led to any number of complications and a prolonged and messy bit of cleanup, and eventually, a protocol change. Regardless, mention Atlantis and Kathy and you would have been led by a woman not named Kathy—no one named Kathy has ever worked for the Morrison Concern—to a special VIP elevator, which would have delivered you nearly a mile belowground to Level B4, the only level accessible by this particular elevator.

At this point, you would have left the offices of the Morrison World Travel Concern and would have found yourself inside what was sometimes known as the Regional Office. Hopefully you would not have found yourself there by accident. In either case, when you arrived at Level B4 the elevator doors would have opened and you would have seen, stenciled on the wall in light-blue calligraphy:

*The Regional Office: uniquely positioned to Empower and Strengthen otherwise troubled or at-risk Young Women to act as a Barrier of last resort between the survival of the Planet and the amassing Forces of Darkness that Threaten, at nearly every turn, to Destroy It.*

Standing there waiting for you, most often, would have been a woman named Sarah, who (so it was rumored) had a mechanical arm, and she would have taken down your information, offered you a consultation, and then, most likely, sent you on your way with a promise to handle whatever situation needed handling, a promise that they would put their top people on the job, a promise that they would soon be in touch. On the elevator ride back up to the Morrison World Travel Concern, you would have been spritzed with a mist that wiped your memory of the Regional Office and everything you'd just witnessed.

On rare occasions, though, depending on your needs, depending on who you were, you might have been met by the director himself, a friendly and calming man named Mr. Niles, and ultimately, after answering a short survey, Mr. Niles would have entertained your particular needs, your desire to work for the Regional Office, or any other questions or suggestions you might have had in order to fight against said amassing forces of darkness, etc.

This happened infrequently, however. The Regional Office was finely tuned, equipped with its own protocols and devices to root out forces of darkness—the evil undead, alien creatures threatening earthly annihilation, superpowered evil masterminds—as well as potential superpowered warrior women who would be trained (honed, you might say) to engage in this never-ending fight. But should you suspect that the crack den in your neighborhood was less a crack den and more a den of werewolves, or a nest of vampires, or that your child's ninth-grade science teacher had more than the spring science fair on his agenda, had possibly developed (so you suspected) a chemical compound from which he hoped to extract world domination, or that your teenage daughter had grown into a young woman of potentially exceptional (and difficult) powers, the Regional Office was where you went. Mr. Niles was whom you should consult (consultations were free), as the services provided by him and his well-trained staff were unparalleled, or nearly so.

If you found yourself facing a problem, in other words, that did not appear to be easily solved, the good folk at the Regional Office were the ones who could solve it.

But not today.

Almost any day but today.

Because today, the Regional Office is under attack.

BOOK 1

# 1.

Or it would be, shortly.

In ten minutes, more or less.

Rose wished it would be less.

Less would be, Christ, less would be amazing.

Mostly because Rose was ready to get this thing started, but also because she was sitting quiet on forty well-trained and slightly antsy mercs in full combat gear who were also ready. Ready to storm out of their unmarked gray vans, their fake delivery trucks, their ATM vestibules, ready to invade and then take over this plain, unremarkable office building, ready to force their way a mile belowground and into the heart of the Regional Office and wage their full assault on it. Then, soon after that, if all went according to plan, ready to level the place, make the whole thing shudder to the ground.

Metaphorically speaking, that is, what with the Regional Office already located mostly underground and all.

Rose was ready for it to begin because she was seventeen and impatient and she was sitting on all of these men who were amped up on testosterone and protein power shakes. Superpowered, highly trained supergirl or not, Rose felt her control over these grunts slipping, ever so slightly.

And she had to pee.

But she had her orders. They couldn't move until seven forty-five. She didn't know why, but those were her orders. Hold the men until seven forty-five.

Rose checked her watch. In five minutes, the assault was a go.

She'd been practicing.

Like, in front of her mirror for almost an hour last night, practiced that fucking move. Twirled her hand in the air in that military circle fist-pump thing that she'd seen before plenty of times in movies but had always assumed was made up. Anyway, she was totally ready to do that thing, whatever it was called, and then, Jesus, finally, these assholes could rush out and go and the hired help would be out of her goddamn hands and on their way to the assault and she could get on with her own business, which involved ghosting her way a mile belowground, without an elevator, thank you very much, in search of the director, who, if these grunts did their job the right way, wouldn't know what the hell was happening until it was too late.

Not that she wasn't, deep down, feeling some small sense of pride in the fact that she had been given command of the mercenaries and put in charge of starting the entire assault. She was the youngest one on the team—didn't hit eighteen for another two weeks—and hadn't been what anyone would have called a model student at Assassin Training Camp or whatever the hell they wanted to call it. She'd almost quit after just a couple of weeks because she'd been a total spaz, so, sure, what a surprise that she would have risen in the ranks, etc., that this responsibility would have been bestowed, etc., it was an honor and a thrill, etc., etc., but really, if she were going to be totally honest about it, about leading the charge of forty grunts who were actually—no shit—grunting, like, all the time, she'd rather they'd just given her her job to do and not this management position because what a pain in the ass managing people was turning out to be.

She'd already had to separate, like, two of them because they got into a shoving match about a fucking seat in the fucking unmarked gray van, and she'd had to yell at them, like, Are you fucking kidding me, are you goddamned third-graders?, and then shove them both apart, almost knocking them both unconscious.

And she could tell, as she was yelling at these two assholes, she could totally see Colleen covering her mouth to keep herself from laughing, which only confirmed what she'd suspected all along: She'd only been put in charge of these assholes because being put in charge of anything was a shit job.

She checked her watch, again.

One minute. Jesus Christ, one more whole other minute.

Fuck it, she thought. Close enough.

She gave the signal.

# 2.

When Henry and Emma had first found her, Rose was running from a couple of assholes—Akard and Schroeder—who were in hot pursuit of her on their four-wheelers because they'd walked up on her pouring eye drops into the water bowls of their mangy yellow country dogs.

It was their own fault—Akard's and Schroeder's, not the dogs'—for spreading lies about her all over school after Akard cornered her late one night near the courthouse down on the square and told her to suck him off and she told him she'd rather do one of his sorry dogs before she did him, then she kicked him hard in his nut sack. She ran, then, too, pushed forward on adrenaline and an electric kind of fear, her heart *boundboundbound*ing inside her head. She was surprised not at what Akard had done—word was he'd been making the rounds of all the freshman and sophomore girls—but that she'd been able to think of something smart and mean to say in the heat of the moment, which she never had been good at really, and then for kicking Akard in his balls.

For a short time after, she mistook herself for the kind of girl who could take any shit dished out, and she sure as hell wasn't the kind of girl who'd let an asswipe like Akard go besmirching her good name, but just now, as Akard and Schroeder caught her eye-dropping their dogs and started coming for her, Rose had seen in their eyes a serious and unsettling look of anger, and worse, a kind of glee at the prospects of what they might do to her. This got her to running, fast and hard but not as fast or hard as she could've because her feet were hitting the pavement weird because of how, even in late September, it still felt like summer, and the pavement was hot and she had lost her flip-flops and the roads in her shitty town were, well, shitty and full of rocks and divots and cracks.

Not that running in the grass would've been better since there wasn't much grass, just more rocks and dirt, and the little grass that was there was sick with stickers and fire-ant hills.

She'd slowed Akard and Schroeder down with a couple of rolled trash cans and then by cutting through the Hunts' back-yard, but she could hear them behind her and now she was head-ing out of the neighborhood and around the next bend into open country—baseball fields, mostly—where she was pretty sure they'd have no problem catching up to her.

As she rounded the bend, she looked over her shoulder to see if she could see them yet, and turned her head back around just in time to see a pickup truck headed right for her.

If she'd had more time, she would have screamed, something along the lines of "Holy shit," or "Jesus fuck," but she didn't have time and so she dove to the right hoping the truck, if it swerved, would swerve to the left.

There was honking and squealing and swerving (left, thank God) and the truck came to a stop on the narrow, rocky shoulder, its front wheel almost tipped into the rain ditch. When the dust had cleared a little, the man driving—if you could call him a man, since he seemed just a few years older than Rose herself—rolled down his window, about to say something, probably along the lines of Are you okay?, but Rose got there first.

"Why don't you watch where the fuck you're going!" she yelled.

"Me? You're yelling at me? What the hell, kid? Why the hell are you running down the middle of the goddamn road?"

Except by the time he'd finished asking his questions, she'd walked herself to the passenger side of the truck, opened the door, and slid herself inside. Then she gave him her best smile—which was a good smile, she'd always had a good smile—and said, taking a deep breath, "About that."

She told him, briefly, sort of what she'd been doing and why and then she told him how it had been harmless fun and anyway they were assholes and they both got what was coming.

He pulled the truck back onto the road just about the time Akard and Schroeder came tearing around the bend, and Rose would be lying if she said she hadn't enjoyed the look of shock on their faces as they swerved hard to round either side of the truck and then spilled their four-wheelers into the rain ditch.

She rolled the window down quick and stuck her head out and yelled as loud as she could, "Fuck you, jack-offs."

Then she plopped herself back into her seat, smiled her good smile again, and turned to the guy driving, who she realized hadn't told her his name yet, and she said, "So."

He looked at her out of the corner of his eye. "How old are you?" he asked.

"Why? How old are you?"

He smiled and shook his head again and said, "Never mind."

She looked at him closely then. He wasn't ugly, exactly, but he wasn't good-looking, either. His features, when taken individually—his nose, his lips, his eyes, his ears, even—were nice enough, but put together they didn't seem to match.

Rose didn't care. She wasn't going to marry him. She was just using him for a ride.

"My name's Henry," he said. He waited for her to say her name; she could feel him waiting in the way he paused. Then, when she just looked at him, he said, "So. Where am I taking you?"

"I don't know," she said. She wasn't ready to give her name just yet, but she wasn't ready to get out of the truck yet either. "Where you going?"

He lifted his hand off the steering wheel and looked at the dash. "Well, in a second, I'm going to have to get gas, but after that, I'll take you back home. Sound all right?"

She shrugged. "Whatever," she said, and then leaned her head back against the seat and closed her eyes.

# 3.

Finally, she gave that signal and the fucking mercs were off, pouring out of their vans like weaponized roaches, and then they were gone, and Colleen, jog-walking right behind the mercs as they charged into the offices of the Morrison World Travel Concern, patted Rose on her ass and gave her a peck on her cheek and told her, "Nice work, kid," and then waved casually over her shoulder and called out, "See you on the other side" as she ran to catch up with the grunts, leaving Rose standing on the sidewalk feeling like she felt that one summer she agreed to help out with the pre-K kids at church camp, how relieved she'd felt every fucking day when it was recess and all those little shits had run screaming and hitting and shoving out of the multipurpose room and into the play yard and all she'd wanted to do was sit down and revel in the peace and quiet for one goddamn minute.

She took a deep breath. She let it out. She wanted to take, like, five hundred more, but there wasn't time. She had a suspicion today would be a day full of deep fucking breaths.

Rose sprinted into the parking garage where there was supposed to be an elevator that she couldn't take because where would be the surprise and fun in that? No, she had to find the vent because of course there was a vent. It was always the same with these fucking places: Something as stupid as a vent opened up the entire labyrinth of a place, no matter how secure the rest of the building was. And sure, there were measures set up to protect the vents, lasers and heat sensors and weight sensors and shit like that, but they'd been taken care of from the inside, from their girl on the inside. And sure, Rose knew that no matter how all-powerful and underground your organization was, you had to make it so the people working for you could breathe and shit, but, Jesus, when she was done with this line of work, she planned to find somebody good at making things, like an engineer or someone, and together they'd invent a way to ventilate air into a building without ventilation shafts and she'd make, like, a billion dollars in the secret agency business. Because if you worked hard enough at it, you could bypass laser sensors and shit, but no matter how hard you tried, you couldn't get down a ventilation shaft that wasn't there, and that was the goddamned truth.

Rose climbed into the shaft, hooked her cable to the edge, and taking a deep breath, started counting to five, and then, because she liked surprises and hated waiting, let herself drop at three.

Rose dropped twenty or thirty feet and then caught hold of the rope, threw her feet against the aluminum of the vent shaft, leaving deep boot marks in it, almost breaking the shaft off its column. She should have been wearing gloves. She hated wearing gloves, though, hated the way they constricted her hands, the way she couldn't grip things as well as she liked, not even with the grippy kind of gloves, not the way she liked to be able to grip into a thing when she needed to, and anyway, she hardly felt the burn of the rope as it burned in her palms. Still, she couldn't help but hear Henry's voice in the back of her head: Where the hell are your gloves, newbie?

God, though, she was bored. Bored of Henry's voice in her head. Bored of this assault, which felt to her like nothing more than a glorified training session.

What was worse was if everything went the way it was supposed to go, she'd be bored the whole time.

Well. Most of the whole time. Taking care of the director of this outfit might offer its own—albeit brief—distractions.

Rose wondered what Colleen was doing. She wondered how the grunts were doing. Rounding up hostages, leading the oblivious fools in the travel agency down to the real offices of the Regional Office. She wondered if the travel agents even knew who they worked for. Probably not. People are idiots. She wondered what Jimmie and Windsor were doing, how they were handling their teams, wondered if they were already done with their assignments. Rose didn't wonder if anyone had died yet—no one had but someone would soon enough and then others after that—because she hadn't quite caught up to the idea that people—strangers and people she knew—were going to die. She was only seventeen, after all. So far it all seemed like a game, like an elaborate, somehow less fun game of paintball she was playing with Andrea and Colleen and Windsor back at Assassin Training Camp, but then thinking of Windsor made her think of Henry, which always dropped Rose onto shaky, spazzy ground.

Henry wasn't even on the fucking premises. He was monitoring the operation from the rendezvous point, but as far as she knew, that meant watching *Point Break* on Netflix or some shit like that.

But at least he wasn't with Windsor. Tall, gorgeous, white-blond, blue-eyed, smart, funny, age-appropriate Windsor.

At least there was that.

At least she didn't have to waste time or brainpower trying to imagine or not imagine what shenanigans might've been going on with him and Windsor while she was stuck here in this shitty ventilation shaft.

Not that she cared.

Not that she gave two shits about Henry.

Not that she gave him another thought.

She stopped. Fuck. She'd missed her goddamn turn.

# 4.

Rose didn't know how long Henry had been driving around, how long she'd had her eyes closed. Not too long, of course. You couldn't drive around this town for too long before you were driving out of it, but with the windows in his truck rolled down, the hot air blowing across her face, Rose didn't feel any immediate urge to open her eyes, to see what the hell this stranger was doing or where he was driving her in his truck.

Then she became bored.

She opened her eyes just in time to see two girls she knew standing on the side of the road, looking over something dead on the pavement, giving it serious consideration.

"Hey, wait a minute," Rose said. "Pull over real quick."

Then she leaned out of her window. "What the hell are you girls doing?"

The taller girl, Patty, looked up, squinted, crinkled her nose. "Hey, Rose. We were coming to get you."

"What is that?" she said, nodding at the thing dead in the road, pretending like she didn't notice or care that fucking Patty had given Henry her name.

"Squirrel," the shorter, dark-haired girl, Gina, said.

"What's so goddamn interesting about a dead squirrel?"

"It ain't dead," Gina said. "Just smashed."

"Oh," Rose said, and then she slipped out of the truck before Henry could stop her. "Let me see."

It was a sad sight, that squirrel.

The back half of it had been flattened into the pavement by someone speeding down the two-lane road, but the front half of it was still moving, had managed to pull itself a good two or three feet. At that moment, it seemed to be taking a break. Then its front paws started moving again, and she tried to imagine it pulling itself across the road. Tried to imagine the pain—did squirrels feel pain?—and the effort. The confusion, maybe, of having just recently had back legs that worked, of once being quick and acrobatic, able to climb trees and jump branch to branch, terrorize blue jays and mockingbirds, taunt cats and dogs.

And now this.

Where did it think it was going?

Gina and Patty were chatting about something behind her and maybe one of them asked who was that driving her around and another one might've asked what had happened to her shoes, but she didn't pay them much attention, or rather, she listened to them just enough to know they were dead interested in who she was with and what she was doing driving around with this strange man, dead interested, in other words, in her, which was part of the point, wasn't it?

Making people dead interested?

The squirrel's chest beat rapidly, and Rose wondered if the beating was its lungs struggling to take in breath, or its heart struggling to pump blood into parts that were leaking that blood straight out again. Watching how fast its chest was beating, she felt that they should do something.

Then she heard the truck door open and slam and she turned to see Henry walking toward them. He was carrying a small hammer in his left hand. He nodded at Gina and Patty, and Patty smiled back because that's how Patty was and Gina took a slight step back because that's how Gina was. Henry got up close to the squirrel and said, more to the squirrel or to himself than to the girls, "What have we got here, buddy?" He dropped down into a squat. He pressed the hammer to the squirrel's head and Rose, suddenly sure of what was about to happen, sure and unhappy about it, said, "Hey, wait," but before she could say anything else, he drew the hammer back and tapped it sharply on the squirrel's forehead—if squirrels even have foreheads, Rose thought. The tap wasn't too hard, just hard enough that the squirrel collapsed and the rapid movement of its chest slowed and then stopped. Someone, Gina or Patty, gasped behind her, and she imagined the two of them flinching, turning their heads into their shoulders.

Pussies, she thought.

Henry gave a small smile, more of a grimace, and said, "There you go."

"How in the fuck," Rose said.

He shrugged. "Just a matter of where you hit it," he said. "Find the right spot," he said, "squirrels, birds, dogs, cats." He shrugged again, as if this were common knowledge, that there would be one spot on the skull just vulnerable enough that knocking that spot with a ball-peen hammer would do a thing in. "People, even," he said.

"Where?" she asked, standing up again. "On a person. Where would you have to tap a person like that?" she said.

"Oh," he said. "Well." Henry smiled at her. "Everybody's different, you know."

She knew where, though, knew exactly where you'd have to tap a person on the head in order to send him on his way. Or where you'd have to tap her, in any case. There'd been a spot on her own head that had been itching to be touched, deeply touched. She could feel where it might be with her fingertips but the spot that urgently needed pressing against was too deep inside her, covered by layers of skin and bone and whatever else it was that was held inside her head. She'd been feeling this for the past couple of days and had tried pressing hard against her head with the palm of her hand, and when that didn't work, had pressed her head against the warm glass pane of her bedroom window, and then the sharp corner of the headboard of her bed, and against her bedroom wall. She'd pressed the eraser points of pencils and the blunt end of a pair of scissors there, too, all to no avail.

She'd never considered the dull tip of a hammer, though.

"Right here?" she asked, pointing to that spot on her head, just at her hairline, straight up from the bridge of her nose.

He barely looked at her, where she was pointing, and then, flustered, focused his attention on the squirrel flattened on the road, and said, with a bit of a hitch in his throat, or maybe that was Rose's imagination, "Maybe, I guess, I don't know."

Then he said, "It's dead now, anyway."

Looking at Gina and Patty behind her, he said, "You want me to leave you here with them, then?"

Rose looked at the squirrel and then at Patty and Gina and then at the truck and Henry. She knew the right thing to say to the strange man who'd picked her up on the side of the road and had just killed a squirrel with a hammer. Yes, go on ahead, I'm fine now. But she was drawn. She wasn't sure what she was being drawn to but it seemed a hell of a lot more interesting than what she'd be left with if she let him go.

Gina, who'd been studying Rose out of the corner of her eye, spoke up. "She's fine with us," she said. "Right, Rose?"

But Rose shook her head. "Actually, you mind running me to the store? I told my momma I'd pick something up for her and I lost my flip-flops back there and don't want to walk barefooted." She said this and didn't look back at Gina or Patty, sure she knew what kind of look she'd see on their faces, Gina's anyway.

"Let's go, then," he said. And then as they pulled away, Rose looked back at Gina and Patty still standing next to that dead squirrel, Patty waving limply until Gina noticed this and grabbed her arm and shook her head, and then the truck turned a corner and Rose couldn't see them anymore.

# 5.

Rose had gone too far down the shaft. She didn't know how far too far, but too far, she could sense it.

Should've taken that left back at Albuquerque—that was her dad's saying, although Christ if she knew what the hell he was ever talking about. Whatever, though. It was Henry's fault, somehow, his fault for distracting her and maybe her fault just a little for being so easily distracted.

She pulled herself up, hand over hand, ten feet, fifteen, twenty. She was beginning to wonder when she'd get back to her turnoff, just how far below it she'd lowered herself, when she came to it, the opening—if it had been a snake, it'd have bit you, which was another one from dear old Dad—and Christ, how could she have missed it?

She swung herself to it, close enough to grab hold of the ledge with one hand. She was going to let go of the rope with her other hand, climb into the new shaft branching off to the left, and be on her merry way, but she stopped. She couldn't say exactly why she stopped, but she did.

Something felt . . . off. Told her, Hold on, now, what's wrong with this picture?

But then something else told her, Nah, this is it, go, go, you've got shit to do.

Except her arms weren't tired, and her legs weren't tired. Nothing was tired. And she was fifteen, maybe twenty minutes ahead of schedule, so why the rush, right? Let's figure this shit out. Let's use the Force, Luke, and all that other seeking-deep-within-ourselves-for-the-True-Answer bullshit she had been fed at Assassin Training Camp.

She let go of the ledge, held on to the rope, pushed herself off the wall into a gentle bit of pendulumming. She closed her eyes and went deep, went real fucking deep inside herself.

And here's what she saw:

A map, in her head, a detailed motherfucker of a map, not just of the ventilation shaft but of the whole ordeal: travel agency, director's office, training rooms, employee break rooms. Each girl had this same map stuck inside her head. Hell, if she wanted, she could pull up the secret compound in upstate New York, too. So.

Where was she?

A pinprick of light glowing hotly in the ventilation shaft.

Okay. Where was she supposed to be?

Same fucking light.

Good. All good, except, it wasn't right. She could feel it. Something was still wrong, with her or her map or the fucking shaft.

She felt this overwhelming urge to open her eyes, to just look around and see, Hey, there's the opening I need, but she wouldn't let herself. Whatever it was that was wrong, her eyes were in on it, she was sure. Her body—fingers, legs—in on it, too.

Devil's advocate: Security had been fixed by their woman on

the inside, or that's what she had told Henry and Emma, had told all of them, and Rose had made it this far—the others, too—without sounding off any alarms, so the intel seemed good enough. The opening was dead-to-rights right in front of her. She'd been on this rope for ages and was on a strict schedule. So what was her hesitation?

Counterargument: That she was hesitating at all was her goddamn hesitation. She'd never been one for thoughtful consideration of action and consequence, had been a headfirst, why-the-hell-not kind of a girl, and if anything made her pause even a little, well, fuck, that seemed suddenly enough to make her pause a lot.

Time ticked by.

She opened her eyes. The rope dropped out of sight and into the darkness below her. It stretched out of sight above her. She'd stopped swinging ages ago. Everything was pointless. She closed her eyes again, frustrated.

She had to do something. She couldn't just hang there.

Okay, just playing devil's advocate one more time: What if the whole thing is a setup? What if the whole point of this is to stop me in my fucking tracks? What if it all only feels wrong just to make me hang here, immobile and useless, until it's too late and the whole shebang is finished and I've fucked up the whole operation?

Counterargument: Fine. Fuck it.

She opened her eyes. The opening looked as real as it ever had. She swung her legs back and forth to get some momentum and then grabbed, finally, hold of the ledge. It felt as real as it had just five minutes ago. So far so good. She let go of the rope with her other hand and grabbed fully on to the ledge. And then everything she was looking at, everything she was holding on to, flickered like a hinky picture on a shitty cell phone, and then it was gone and she was holding on to the smooth, purchaseless side of the ventilation shaft, or, rather, not holding on to it, not holding on to anything, and she fell.

# 6.

The wind from the truck window caught hold of Rose's hair, pulling it out of Henry's truck. Henry wasn't doing much talking and she didn't feel like talking much, either. She watched the landscape pass by, familiar and dull, and only half listened to whatever was on the radio in the background.

"Those your friends?" Henry asked.

She had been biding her time, she realized. The last few weeks of summer, these first few weeks of school, sure, but even before that. These past few years. Maybe her whole life. Biding her time. She understood that now, and that here, even in Henry's truck, she was still biding her time.

"Not really, no," she said.

How was what she had been doing different from what Gina and Patty had been doing with their lives? she wondered.

They were biding their time, too. They just didn't know it. That was what was different. They would finish out high school, Gina still a virgin, Rose was sure of it, and then each go off to college, with maybe a stop-off at the junior college for a couple of years first, and then, degrees in hand or not, they would wind their way back to this dump of a town, their eyes set on Randall Thomas (Gina) or Clem Buchanan (Patty), or boys of their ilk, inheritors of their daddies' body repair shops or small-town construction firms. They might work for a couple of years, teaching kindergarten or managing one of the antique shops on the square, and then quit working once it was time to start pushing kids out of their nethers. It was an oppressive and frightening thought, picturing the two of them not much different from their bitter, hard-smoking mothers. But it was a thought she kept close to the surface, a reminder, a sort of anti-goal she'd set for herself, alongside, Don't wind up stuck here like your loser parents did, or, more simply, Don't turn into your loser parents, her dad a shiftless asshole who hadn't worked an honest day in his life (according to her mother), her mother a nagging, thickheaded harpy who couldn't see a man's potential, couldn't see past the tip of her blunted nose (according to her dad).

Henry turned the truck into the Stop-N-Go and she came out of her head.

"What are we doing here?"

Henry smiled his strange, uncomfortable smile. "I need to get some gas, remember?"

"Oh. Right."

"Won't take a sec."

She opened her door and slid out of the truck. "Since we're here," she said casually, tossing the words over her shoulder as she crossed the parking lot.

"Hey, wait," Henry said, but she wasn't listening.

She might as well get something good out of this shitty day.

Ian Honsinger had told her he'd be working the Stop-N-Go, and if she came by and she was nice to him, he'd get her some cigarettes. Whatever being nice meant. That she had wound up here, by fate or accident, made her feel better about heading out with Henry. Plus she could use a cigarette.

Honsinger was at the counter, like he'd said he'd be, but seeing him, and his leering smile, and his cheap haircut, she wasn't sure the cigarettes were worth the effort it would take to flirt with him.

"Hi, Rosie," he said, stretching out the "e." Then he looked past her and at Henry, and his eyes squinted and his mouth turned. "Who's that you're with?"

She looked casually over her shoulder, even though she knew Henry was the only other person at the gas pump. "Some guy. Henry, I guess."

Ian stepped out from behind the counter and there was something puffed up and threatening about him now. She noticed, then, how he hadn't stopped giving Henry the stink eye. "I don't know him." He looked down at her for a second. "I've never seen him before."

She wanted to get a pack of cigarettes and a Coke and then get back into Henry's truck, or maybe not that, either, maybe just the cigarettes and the drink and out of this gas station, which smelled strongly of Ian's body spray now that he'd started moving around, casting the scent of himself into the farthest corners of this tiny little place.

Why was everything in this fucking town so damn tiny?

"Whatever," she said. "Like you know everyone." Then she poked him in the chest. "You gonna get me those cigarettes like you promised or what?"

He stopped staring down Henry, who hadn't noticed anyway,

and looked at Rose, then grabbed her poking finger in that thick palm of his. "I don't know," he said, smiling his stupid smile again. "What are you going to give me for them?"

She smiled up at him, sweetly, innocently, then leaned in real close, and he leaned in close and draped his arms over her shoulders, and she could picture him at a school dance, homecoming or prom, maybe, his heavy arms weighing her down, his splotchy face too close to her eyes, and then she shook her head and almost laughed as she stuffed a five-dollar bill in his shirt pocket.

She'd been practicing this.

She'd seen something like it in a movie but was surprised she'd had an opportunity to actually try it out. She almost said, "How's this for your troubles, loverboy?" But she changed her mind and backed off instead.

Just in case.

"That," she said. "I'll give you that."

He threw the cigarettes on the counter without asking which ones she wanted. She thought she'd heard him say something when he pulled the wallet out of his back pocket, slid the five dollars inside it. *Tease,* maybe. Or *cock-tease.* But she couldn't see his lips when he said it, and it could have been her imagination.

She ignored him, anyway. "Thanks, Ian," she said, singsongy and sweet again.

He looked at her and then back at Henry, waiting in the truck now, tapping his hands to some song playing on his stereo. Then he looked back at Rose and said, "Better be careful the kind of folk you run around with, Rosie." He leered at her. "Strange man like that might look at a little girl like you and try to take advantage."

She rolled her eyes. She backed herself into the door and pushed it open with her backside and said, "Fuck off, Honsinger," and then did her best to flounce herself to Henry's truck, and when she saw Ian was still staring at her, or at the truck, or at Henry, even though he couldn't see Henry through her, she rolled her window down and flipped him off, and then they were gone.

# 7.

At least she wasn't just hanging there anymore, hanging in the middle of a ventilation shaft, pointless and bored.

There was that.

At least there was that.

Rose hip-checked the side of the shaft, tumbled ass over head and into the other side of the shaft. She scrambled to grab hold of the rope but had kicked it swinging and she couldn't find it in the near dark. Her headlamp swung the light hither and yon, but she was still too high up to see any semblance of a bottom.

Assuming, of course, there was a bottom. Colleen had jokingly told her to be careful down that ventilation shaft, that she'd heard the woman who'd founded the Regional Office had magicks enough to have conjured a bottomless pit that enemies of the Regional Office were thrown into. What better place to hide a bottomless pit than in a ventilation shaft, right?

Hardy-fucking-har-har, Colleen.

Fucking fuck.

The impact. Assuming there would be an impact, she was worried about the impact, but only because it would hurt like a motherfucker. But besides that, she'd survive the fall, and whatever parts of her didn't immediately survive would start to stitch themselves back together soon enough.

Getting out. She was worried about what would happen after she was dropped at the bottom of a shaft that was well over a mile belowground, but not so worried about this, either, because, well, she'd find some way out, by stealth or by force. She knew she would.

But the mission. God, those assholes had drilled it into her good. The fucking mission, she was worried about that, about missing out. That's what had her scrambling so hard to find the rope.

She closed her eyes and reached out blindly and grabbed hold of air and then grabbed hold of air again, and thought maybe she should just give up this plan, and then something glanced against her wrist, and she grabbed again and caught hold of the rope and held tight, for a second, for less than, jerked to a bounding halt, before her shoulder gave out as it jarred up against gravity, and she let go again, but flung herself this time, whipped herself with some small deliberation so she could land hard against the side of the shaft, so she might slide down it, maybe catch hold of a different ledge, first with her forehead and her chin and then, when that slipped off, her elbow, which didn't hold on much better, until finally her knee and calf and shin and ankle and then her boot caught, thank God for that fucking boot with its zippers and straps, its nooks and crannies, and then she held, for long enough, anyway, to pull herself up and in, and once she was in, she collapsed.

Now what, newbie? Henry, fucking Henry, pestering her inside her head.

You don't know where you are or how to get to the director's office, so, now what?

She'd figure it out, okay? Jesus.

But now what? Henry asked again, smug asshole. He knew the answer, of course, always knew the answer. Why else would he ask the fucking questions?

Just give a girl one goddamn minute, okay, a fucking minute to pull herself together, to take a fucking break, Christ.

She took a breath. She closed her eyes. Then she passed out, was out cold for at least fifteen minutes.

# 8.

Back in Henry's truck, she offered him a cigarette, which he took even though she could tell by the way he held it that he didn't smoke.

The lighter popped out of the dashboard. Rose took it and pressed her cigarette into it and then took a deep drag from it and then held the lighter out for him. He had been holding the cigarette in his left hand and took the lighter in his right, trying to manage some rigmarole with his elbows on the steering wheel so he could light his cigarette, but the road began to twist and bump, and he startled, swerved a bit, and managed to drop the cigarette into his lap and the lighter onto the floor.

"Christ in a basket," he said, glancing down and up and down and up, one-handing the steering wheel while he scrambled, hunched over, for the lighter.

"No wonder you almost hit me," Rose said. Then she said, "Here, relax." She placed her hand high up on his thigh and bent down, her body twisting just enough to give her scrunching room below the gearshift on the steering column. She could feel her tank top riding up her back and wondered at the peep show she was giving Henry, and hung down there a second longer than she needed to, and then she sat back up, the lighter held in front of her as if it were a diamond or some other gem she'd just pulled out of the earth. Then she said, "Here, gimme that," and she reached into his lap and grabbed the cigarette, which had fallen in between his legs. She brushed the zipper of his jeans lightly and he jumped in his seat, sending the truck to the left before pulling it hard back to the right.

"Sorry," he said.

"Jesus, Henry," she said, laughing. "Settle down, will you?"

Then she tipped the cigarette between her lips and lit it and then she took a drag off it, her own still lit in her left hand. She blew the smoke out of the side of her mouth and then leaned over and said, "Open," and then put it in his mouth, where he held it for a moment, not smoking, but breathing out of his nose and the side of his mouth, until he remembered his hands on the steering wheel, one of which he freed to pull the cigarette out of his mouth and hold out the open window.

"So. Which store am I taking you to?" he asked.

"I lied," she said. "I don't need to go to the store."

Then she took a breath and looked at him and said, "It's been kind of a weird day."

"Where are we going, then?" he said.

"I don't know. Home, I guess?"

He looked at her. He'd dropped the cigarette out of the window. "So, weird, huh?"

"A little, yeah." She didn't know why but she felt her voice hitch. Voice hitching wasn't a normal thing for her. Her sister, sure. That girl's voice hitched at the drop of a pin. At the first sign of trouble—the house was out of milk, their mother's cat had been sleeping on the kitchen table, Rose had borrowed her favorite sweater—you could count on that one for a tremble of the lip, a hitch of the voice. But Rose liked to think she was made of stronger stuff than her sister, and sure, she'd seen some strange look in Tyler Akard's eyes when he came chasing after her, and sure, the sight of that squirrel might've troubled her a touch, and maybe almost getting hit by a truck earlier in the day, etc., but Jesus Christ.

Pull yourself together.

"How old are you?" he asked again, catching her off guard, pulling her out of her head.

"Sixteen," she said, forgetting she'd wanted to keep that a secret from him. "Well, next week. I turn sixteen next week."

He sighed and in that sigh she thought she heard him mutter, "Too young," but she couldn't be sure. Then he didn't say anything and neither did she and then he turned onto Church Street and turned to look at Rose and smiled at her and said, "Just about there."

Only later—too late, in fact—would she realize how strange it was, what he said, when he said it.

Just about there.

They were, though. They were only a couple of blocks from her momma's house, and so she didn't think about it too much at the time, didn't let it register that she'd never told him where she lived, hadn't given him directions or an address. And then later still she would think how strange it was that he would have said that at all, said anything, in fact, to tip her off, to let her get her guard up, even if she hadn't.

Gotten her guard up, that is.

They pulled up to her house. She tried to open the truck door but it wouldn't open. "Hey," she said, just as he was reaching across her, maybe a little uncomfortably so, to fiddle with the lock, the handle, saying, "Sorry about that, it gets funny." He couldn't open it and something inside her hitched again. Then he opened his own and got out and she turned herself to climb over and he said, "No, no, stay there, I'll get it," and he closed his door and trotted around the other side and opened her door from the outside.

"I need to get that fixed," he said when he held out his hand to help her down from the truck.

"Yeah," she said. "Well, thanks, anyway, for the ride." She tried to let go of his hand.

"Here," he said, the flat of his other hand resting lightly against her back between her shoulder blades. "Let me walk you to the door, make sure someone's home for you."

She didn't say, There's no one home, which there wasn't, or that she had a key, which she did, or that it wouldn't matter on account of how her mother never locked the door anyway. Her chest fluttered but in no good kind of way and her palms started to sweat, and little unwelcome shivers shot out of her skin where his hand was pressed against her.

Well, hell, she thought.

What she would do would be simple enough, Henry behind her or not. Shove the door open, just enough to slip inside, and then shove it shut and lock it behind her.

Which she did, in one smooth motion, as much of a surprise to her as it was to Henry just how well that had worked. Henry yelled after her, "Hey, wait." He pounded on the door and she shook her head and thought, Fucking creep. And then she turned and stepped into the house and was ambushed.

# 9.

When Rose came to, she didn't know how far behind schedule she was. It took a second or two to figure out that she had made it across the shaft and into the next set of tubing.

The fall had shattered her piece-of-shit shatterproof watch, and don't think Henry wasn't going to get an earful from her about being such a cheap-ass on accessories.

She was enough behind schedule anyway (she could just feel it) that she said, Fuck it. Fuck the pain, fuck her weak legs, fuck her torn arm, and she jumped across the ventilation shaft to an opening just across from and above the opening she'd landed in. Don't think there wasn't a shitload of scrambling for some kind of hold, a lot of embarrassing kicking with her feet and grunting as she became frightened and then desperate to push through all that pain from the fall and grabbing the rope so she could pull herself up, because there was. That, and a heavy desire to go right back into unconsciousness that she almost didn't resist. But then she pushed her way blindly out of the shaft into what turned out to be an office, dark and unoccupied. She kicked the computer onto the floor while scrambling onto the desk from the ceiling, and then she hopped down after it.

She closed her eyes, took some deep, deep breaths (who would have thought all that meditation crap from Assassin Training Camp would have come in so useful), then recalled her map.

Two floors down, half a wing across from where she needed to be.

She snuck into the hallway and she ran.

The halls were empty. A good sign, she supposed. The rest of the plan must have been moving along smoothly enough. And sure, great, that was good to know, of course, but also that meant that if there was a wrench in this mechanism, she was it.

She found the stairwell, jimmied open the door, took the stairs three and four at a time.

Surprise. The whole point of this exercise had been surprise. Which, fuck that. No way the director of this operation didn't know that his world was caving in all around his ears by now. At worst, he'd found some way to sneak out of the fray. At best, he was sitting tight, arming the defenses in his office. And neither scenario was any good for her.

Wendy, their woman on the inside, the one who'd undone the main security system, had briefed them all. "I can't touch the director's office, sorry, it's on its own system, and he's the only one who controls it. But catch him off guard," Wendy had said, "and Mr. Niles won't have enough time to cue it all up."

At the time, Rose had wished Wendy would stop using the guy's name, would stick to the script and say *director*.

"Mr. Niles," Wendy continued, "from what I've been told, he's real twitchy about this sort of thing, didn't want any defenses in the first place, because he's always worried the system will screw up, won't recognize him one day, will decide it's time to weed him out, so to speak, and so he keeps it dark, the whole system, unless he knows he needs it. So if you do it right, you do it quick." She shrugged.

Right and quick. That was all it took.

Henry and Emma probably shouldn't have assigned the "right and quick" job to her then, the fucking spaz.

Two floors up, she kicked open the stairwell door, not even pretending to be subtle anymore. Subtle hadn't ever been one of her strengths, anyway. She flew down the empty hall and slid to a stop just outside the glass door that opened to the receptionist's desk and the receptionist who stood careful guard over the director and who was right then—Rose couldn't believe her fucking luck—working some kind of crossword or Sudoku bullshit on her computer. Caught completely unawares.

Rose ducked out of sight. She pulled herself together. She counted down from ten.

Then, at seven, she charged.

Or, she didn't exactly charge. She threw her momentum into this nifty slide across the tile, still out of the line of sight of the crossword genius, and didn't pop herself out of it until the very last moment, like she was sliding into third base, like she was one of those real fast base stealers who can pop back up to standing after a wicked slide but like they didn't stop, didn't even pause to think about stopping, and that was how she slid: At the last second, she lit herself up onto her feet and grabbed the door handle and shoved herself inside, and before the receptionist could even register what kind of hell was barreling down on her, Rose had her by the throat.

Or should have.

She should have had her by the throat. Or, rather, by the whole fucking head and neck, if you were going to be technical about it, her arm wrapped around from behind, squeezing the receptionist's windpipe shut, knocking her out cold, except that the receptionist wasn't even fucking there.

Nothing was there.

Not the computer, not the Sudoku, not even the goddamn desk, all of it some image or hologram, probably the same make as the image or hologram that dropped her down that fucking bottomless pit (yeah, now that she was out and away from it, bottomless, why the hell not?).

But who the fuck cared because whatever it was, hologram or magicks, what it also was was a trap, most definitely a trap.

# 10.

There were three guys waiting for her in her mom's living room, and they grabbed her and she screamed and one of them clamped his hand over her mouth and she bit, and then he screamed and let go, and she kicked back with her right leg and felt it contact something—his knee, maybe—felt something crunch, heard someone fall. She stomped another's foot, hard, and then yanked her arm out of his grasp, but the third one grabbed her free arm and pulled her to him by both her wrists and smashed his forehead into her face, and she saw stars, actual stars, little motes of light that swirled around in front of her eyes. And she heard him chuckle and say, "Jesus, guys, this was too easy," and then she kicked him in the balls and he crumpled and let go of her wrists, and she grabbed him by his shirt, and then fell backward, pulling him forward on top of her, and in one swift hard kick, she threw him over her head so that he landed hard on his partner, knocking them both down.

How she'd done this, she had no fucking clue.

The closest she'd come to a fight was when she'd kicked Akard in his balls.

She scrambled up, looked around, and found Henry leaning

against the door, his lips pursed, his eyes regarding her coolly. He nodded.

"That was pretty good," he said.

Then he said, "These guys, they weren't amateurs."

Then he looked around the room at them and said, "But they did underestimate you, didn't they?"

Said, "People always underestimate you, Rose. Isn't that right?"

She didn't ask him how he'd gotten inside, didn't ask him what he was doing there, what he wanted, who those guys were, didn't waste her time screaming, had let go of the hitch in her voice, that or had let it grow into something else, and instead she focused her energy on charging straight at that fucker, and then, as she was charging, then she yelled.

He watched her as she charged him and smiled and said, "But not me," though that could've been her imagination since it didn't feel like she could hear much of anything.

He stepped to the side and he grabbed her by her arm, pulled her in close like they were ballroom dancers, trapping her strong arm against her side, and then grabbed her by her neck with his other hand, so tight she couldn't breathe, and then his leg swept her off her feet and she landed hard on her back against the hard, thin carpet that reeked of her mother's Pall Malls, her free arm suddenly trapped under her own body weight and his weight as he bore down on her, and she could see his eyes, calm, blue eyes, and she could see his lips moving, but she couldn't hear him, there was too much noise already banging around in her head.

Then, as he choked her, as he tried to choke the life from her, she swung her leg, she didn't know how, but she swung it high and hard and kicked Henry in the side of the head, hard enough to throw him off her, hard enough to make him stumble, and she hand-sprung onto her feet and before anything else could happen, anyone else could pop out of the darkness and surprise her, she ran straight to Henry, ran at him as he got himself to his knees, though to her last dying day some part of her will always wonder why she didn't just run the other way, didn't just do what any sane person would have done, why she didn't push her way out and run like hell. She ran at Henry instead and delivered a swift kick to his side, and then another, and then she realized there were more parts to him to be kicked or scratched or punched and she was aiming her next kick for his face, his not-ugly, not-handsome face, when the lights in the house shut off and everything went dark, darker than normal when the lights were shut off, and Rose couldn't see anything, and a woman's voice called out, "Enough. That's quite enough."

# 11.

Training. Remember your goddamn training.

So the receptionist isn't here. So this is a trap. So what? She's been in traps before.

She jumps up—straight up like fucking Luke Skywalker in *Empire* when Vader tries to freeze his ass in carbonite—and then flips herself around to a) get a good look at the shit gunning—literally gunning—for her and b) push herself off the ceiling, which isn't that drop-tile bullshit but nice wooden planking, thank God for egotistical directors of demonic organizations and their urgent need for evil-lair trimmings of the fancy, Nate Berkus sort.

What she sees before throwing herself into the fray:

1. Gun turrets, five of them, already out and targeting her since probably as soon as her hand grabbed the door handle.
2. Some real *Last Crusade* or *Dr. No* shit, by way of blades, half as tall as she was, spinning vertically and horizontally across the room.
3. Strange-as-shit whirling-dervish-type miniature robots spinning round and round like some kind of hybrid of the gun turrets and the spinning blades, in that they're shooting out lasers (pell-mell enough that, in the nanosecond she took to

get her lay of the land, one accidentally took out a gun turret) and have spinning blades spinning out of their tiny
torsos and thin robot arms, Maximilian style. (*The Black
Hole*, Henry. Please do try to keep up.)

And last but not least:

4. Gas pouring into the room out of secret cubbies.

Jesus Christ, this Niles guy sure is a nervous fuck.

Take a deep, deep, deep breath and hold it.

Don't think about what kind of mess is waiting for you in his
actual office if this is what he has lined up for anyone who dares
approach his receptionist.

Don't think at all.

Pivot.

Shove.

Handspring.

Land.

In between handspring and land, of course, grab one of the
whirligig ones by the top of its whirligiggly head and throw it slic-
ing into one of the big spinning slicers, the side-to-sider, not the
up-and-downer, to cut the dervish clean in two, but which won't
quite stop the whirling, which will keep the laser-gunning head
going long enough to knock out another gun turret (that's two,
three more to go) and the bottom going just long enough to man-
gle one of the other dervishes.

She doesn't see this, not in real life, anyway, can only picture
it in her head before she leaps.

Land.

Throw.

Double back handspring.

Super jump with a backflip.

Land again with a kick to disable the other spinning-blade number, stop it cold, and turn it vertical to act like a shield against two of the gun turrets on her weak side.

Another kick to knock it off its spinny hinge-arm doohickey.

Henry would know the name of this shit. Hell, so would everyone else, but she could never bring herself to give a fuck.

Knock it off its hinge, catch it by its center before it sinks into the floor, and discus that bitch at two more gun turrets.

Round-off.

Spin-kick the head free from the last whirling-dervish bot and into the last gun turret and the body into the glass partition separating the hallway outside from the receptionist's office inside, cracking it open enough, anyway, for Rose to stick her head through and let a breath out and take one more big gulp of nontoxic air before twirling herself in and out and about and around the last three spinning slicers, which aren't so much to tackle once there aren't any more guns or spinning robots targeting you, and then she's at the door.

Shove yourself through, and there he is.

The director himself.

Mr. Niles.

And he's all alone and there are no whirligigs swarming around him in some sort of protective shell, and he's standing back against his desk, and there's a look in his eyes, a look that for a moment she mistakes for the kind of look you give when you're done, when you're finished with all of this, when you're ready to go home, or to cross over to the last frontier or whatever the fuck you want to call it. But then he grins and pulls around his left hand and it's covered in something she can't make out at first but that looks, well, his hand looks like it's covered in another hand, not a glove but a different kind of hand, and his grin grows wider and wider, and then Rose realizes, no, it's that he's coming closer and closer, and almost but not quite too late, she realizes he's coming right at her.

# 12.

The lights came back on, brighter somehow, and there was a woman sitting on Rose's mother's couch, a woman dressed all in red, sitting there not bored exactly but like she wasn't as interested as she actually was.

Then she stood up.

She stood up and up and seemed just so damn tall, beautiful and tall.

Rose didn't know who she was, didn't know her name, and only later would she learn about her connection to the Regional Office or what the Regional Office was, and about the personal war she was about to wage against it.

But that would be later.

At that moment, Rose only knew that here was this woman, stunning and calm and powerful, and that simply looking at her made that hitch in her voice come back.

The Woman in Red stepped up close to Rose and touched her finger gently to Rose's forehead, where there would be a nasty bruise soon enough, and in that touch Rose felt some living, pulsing, twitching memory shiver under her own skin, a thing that started at the touch, coursed through her down to her feet and into the earth, and then rose up from the ground all over again, up her legs and through her whole body to rush tingling up the back of her neck—she could feel it, could trace the shiver's path—up her neck and over and through her skull, where it landed, finally, on that spot, touched her the way she'd been desperate to be touched, and her body went limp. After everything that had happened that day, her body decided now was the time to give out, and she felt herself start to fall, and she hoped—deeply hoped—that the Woman in Red would reach out and grab hold of her, but she didn't.

Henry—where he'd come from she didn't know—Henry caught her, instead, and she looked up at his not-unhandsome face, and the feeling continued to move through her and seemed to grow out of her, seemed to want to envelop him, too.

She didn't push him away or struggle out of his grasp. She let him hold her and despite everything, she moved in, instead, for a kiss.

Her first.

Despite what she'd told Patty and Gina, despite all the things assholes like Akard and Schroeder said about her, her very first kiss.

When she's older, when she's back in this small town, when she's drunk and half-asleep in her car, having pulled herself over because even in this state she knows she shouldn't be on the road, and before the police pull up behind her with their bright flashing lights, and before she mouths off to them, before she tells them to go fuck themselves because for Christ's sake she's doing the right thing and not driving back home shit-faced unlike most people she knows, and before she resists arrest and struggles so strongly against the handcuffs that for the next week her wrists will be red and swollen, before she head-butts the window of the police car and cracks the window, and then tries but fails to smash the foot of one of the officers with her booted heel, before any of this happens, she'll be thinking about this kiss, which wasn't a great kiss, by no means was it a great or sexy or even sensual kiss, but it was her first real kiss, which made it memorable in and of itself, but also because of how she likes to joke with herself about that kiss and how fireworks lit the sky, right as they kissed, likes to joke with herself about how all hell broke loose with that kiss.

Which, in a way, it did.

Then the kiss broke and the room and her momma's house and the people in it and the Woman in Red all came back into focus.

Judging by the look on Henry's face and the sound of the woman's laughter, the kiss was unexpected. Henry stood her up.

"Are you all right?" the Woman in Red asked.

Before Rose could answer, Henry shook his head. "Nothing that won't heal."

The Woman in Red smiled. "That wasn't what I meant." Then she looked at Rose and then back to Henry. "Well? Your assessment."

Henry shook his head again. "You saw it all for yourself," he said. He paused and pressed his palm gingerly to his side. "She's strong." He looked at Rose. "Angry," he said. He didn't touch his fingertips to his lips but Rose will always imagine that he did when he said, "Passionate."

The woman smiled again, the look on her face so genuine and welcoming that Rose couldn't help but smile back and feel, for whatever reason, relief.

"Still," Henry said, and the smile on the woman's face wavered.

"Yes?" the Woman in Red asked.

"I think she's too young."

Rose thought she saw the Woman in Red roll her eyes. Then she took Rose by the hand and squeezed Rose's fingers slightly, playfully, and said, "She's ready." Then, to Rose, she asked, "Are you ready?"

"Ready?" Rose asked, surprised to find her voice there, just waiting for her but sounding not like herself at all. "Ready for what?"

She pulled Rose closer to her, close enough that Rose could smell what she thought was a light, citrusy perfume, but what she would later come to find was just the woman's natural smell, and the Woman in Red said, "Come with me."

She smiled her smile again and said, "I'm going to tell you a story."

From *The Regional Office Is Under Attack:*
*Tracking the Rise and Fall of an American Institution*

In order to grasp the full consequence of both the rise and fall of the Regional Office, in order to better understand where these women—both the Operatives of the Regional Office and their attackers—came from, what wellspring delivered them their mystical properties, how Oyemi and her partner, Mr. Niles, sought them out when these mystical properties manifested, why Oyemi focused her energies only on these women, in order to understand what had been lost when the Regional Office lost its way, one must know one's history.

When it comes to the history—the complete and accurate history—of the Regional Office, one might begin with the day Mr. Niles and Oyemi met, back in the third grade, back before their names were Mr. Niles and Oyemi, even. Or one might move farther along in time to the day Mr. Niles devised and drew up the plans for the Black Box, which was instrumental in guiding both Oyemi's mystical properties and the focus of the Oracles when seeking out new Recruits and which brought them Jasmine, one of their most successful early Operatives. Others endeavor to begin with the day Mr. Niles and Oyemi "recruited" the first Oracle, a young woman named Nell, whose recruitment sent ripples, far-reaching ripples, into the fate of the Regional Office. Some scholars focus their attentions almost entirely on the Golden Age of the Regional Office, on the exploits of the likes of Jasmine (for obvious and sophomoric reasons, her battle against Mud Slug never fails to find its way into almost every scholarly study of the Regional Office); and, before her, Gemini and her long-running battles against Harold Raines; on the missions conducted by Emma, on Emma's mysterious death, and so on, these authors favoring the flashier (but shallower) accounts of the Battle of Blanton Hill; on the capture of the interdimensional terrorist Regency; but ever failing to delve into the deeper history of the organization and the ramifications of choices made by the less visible operators.

This paper, hoping to offer a more nuanced and complete consideration of the Regional Office, will assign the beginning of the Regional Office to the accident that should have killed Oyemi but didn't. The accident that didn't kill her, but in fact imbued her with mystical properties. The accident that happened on a Tuesday, at or near IKEA.

Oyemi was shopping at IKEA, not because she needed anything but because she was bored. Mr. Niles had left town for a week and she had few other people—i.e., no other people—she called friends, and walking through IKEA killed more time than anything else she could think of to do. Not to mention, it was heated and she couldn't afford to run the heat in her own apartment.

In six months, she and Mr. Niles would graduate from Rutgers University. In two months, her great-uncle would die—aneurysm—and would, much to everyone's surprise, leave Oyemi the bulk of his sizable fortune. A surprise both because he and Oyemi had only met once, and because no one knew he'd amassed any kind of fortune, much less a sizable one.

People can be funny that way.

But at that moment, she was broke, barely paying her rent, arguing with financial aid to wrangle more money out of them her last few months of college. She could take the bus to IKEA for free with her student ID, could walk around for free, could bring a book and sit in a living room or a bedroom diorama and pretend she was home, although it felt perhaps more like she was in some strange zoo or amusement park, an exhibit for future generations to see: *Poor College Student (Circa 1993)*.

After a while she left the store.

It is possible she was asked to leave.

Feeling restless and unwilling to wait for the next bus, she decided to walk home.

Here is where most accounts differ, despite the fact that all accounts from this time are Oyemi's, namely because she was by herself when everything that happened happened.

Either in the parking lot or half a mile or three-quarters of a mile down the road, something happened: Oyemi was irradiated by an unseen alien force, or she was struck and subsequently irradiated by a small meteorite, or she was irradiated by an eighteen-wheeler that lost control of its cargo, jackknifed off the turnpike, and crashed, sending its oil drum of irradiated liquids spinning right at her and bursting open just before crashing over her, but no matter which story she told, each one ended with Oyemi irradiated, and, somehow, discovered in a small park near Rutgers University, twenty-three miles away from the IKEA.

A couple found her, naked and faintly glowing. They found her near a picnic table. The man called 911 while the woman looked for Oyemi's clothes or a blanket or anything to cover her with, but finding nothing, the woman walked quickly back to her car, where she kept a blanket for picnics, and draped this over the girl (if that's what this glowing, naked thing was)—only for the blanket to begin smoldering before catching fire and then burning to ash, which it did even before the woman could yell out to her husband, who was still on the phone with emergency services. This was also when the woman noticed that Oyemi, in a fetal position, lay in the center of a widening circle of bare earth, the grass and weeds on the outer edge of this circle shriveling into black tendrils and then to ash as the woman stood staring at them. Which was also when Oyemi woke up, opened one eye, an eye that glowed hotly, or no, not that, an eye that seemed a window, rather, like the window to an old furnace, so that the eye itself wasn't glowing hotly, but that the inside of Oyemi glowed hotly. Seeing this, the woman screamed and ran and grabbed her husband, made him drop his phone and run too, before whatever had happened to their blanket, whatever had happened to the grass and weeds and ground, before any of that could happen to them.

Nobody, not even Oyemi, could explain how she made it back home, how she managed not to set all of New Brunswick ablaze, although until just recently, if one knew what signs to look for, one could trace the path she took from the park back to her apartment—a melted metal pole, a tree trunk singed in the shape of a woman's handprint, a path of footprints where the earth had been burned to dirt that refused to grow back to grass for nearly twenty years—small markings of her passing that day.

Regardless of how she made it home, by the time she made it home, enough of the radiation had burned itself out of her that she could pick up the phone and call Mr. Niles and tell him to come back to New Jersey sooner rather than later before the handset melted around the pads of her fingertips.

Of course, a faction of scholars has formed under the shared belief that none of this happened, a faction that has, over the years, gained members and support and influence, which is why this piece of the history of the Regional Office often goes unmentioned, unexplained. And only recently, the faction itself has split into two separate groups:

Those who believe this never happened and that Oyemi always possessed the powers she possessed, who believe that she used this story as a way to reveal and contextualize these powers; and,

Those who believe she never possessed any mystical properties at all, possessed only the power to fool the powerful into following her lead.

If one chooses, one can seek out these theories on one's own, though the authors of this paper assure one that they offer little but speculation, biased and unfounded.

Regardless, while Oyemi waited for Mr. Niles to return, she fashioned a plan. This plan became the foundation for an idea of what she could do now that she had changed. The possibilities opened up inside her even as her mind and the mystical properties of her expanded, even as she began to sense and see the power of the girls and women she would seek out and train to be her Oracles and her Operatives. The Oracles would find the Operatives. The Operatives would do what, she didn't know, not at first. But while she waited and cooled, she began to think thoughts that became ideas that grew into what she and Mr. Niles would come to call the Regional Office.

# 13.

Sarah's time with the Regional Office had trained her to harbor certain suspicions, take few risks, set in place specific precautions, and so it was more than a surprise that there was an envelope waiting for her when she got home. It had been taped to the inside of her door. The locks hadn't been picked or forced. The small piece of black thread she set in the doorjamb every morning when she left for work hadn't been disturbed.

She'd once told Henry how she left her apartment every day before leaving for work—the thread, the locks—and he had laughed and he had told her she was too serious, that she worried too much, but see? She was right to be so cautious. Sure, her precautions hadn't kept anyone from breaking into her apartment and taping an envelope to her door, but still. At least she'd had precautions set in place.

In fact, she only saw the envelope when she turned to dead-bolt the door. In other words, she hadn't even sensed that someone else had been in her apartment. She should have at least sensed something, right?

Her name was written in black Sharpie across the front.

She stared at it.

Then she turned away and walked into her kitchen.

Ten minutes later, with a cup of tea in one hand, a cookie in the other, she walked back to the door to see if the envelope was still there.

It was.

She put the cookie in her mouth to free her hand and she pulled the envelope off the door. It peeled right off. She'd assumed it had been taped there, which had annoyed her because it was her experience that, no matter how hard you tried, the tape goo just never came off, but it had been hot-glued.

How considerate.

And strange.

She sat down at her breakfast table and opened it and slipped a file out of it and began to read what was inside.

This was at midnight.

It had been a long day. Mr. Niles had been acting strange. The Oracles had been unusually quiet. No one had seen Oyemi in almost a month. And Henry. Well. Henry had been acting a little strange ever since that last mission with Emma, the one that killed her. That had been two years ago now. She'd been covering for him, sure, because she was a friend, but still. They were going to have to have a chat. Enough was enough. They all missed Emma, but work was work. Sarah sighed. She stopped ranting in her head.

She would skim through the file, see what kind of serious trouble it might mean, call the head of security and leave him a message, maybe call Mr. Niles, too, and then she'd be in bed by one, one thirty tops.

Three hours later, her apartment was a shambles, or not a shambles, really, as the word itself—*shambles*—implies something with more charm and less total destruction to it. So let's say more than a shambles but shy of totally wrecked. And so: Her apartment was just shy of total wreckage. It's fair to say what she found in that envelope had made her upset, or rather, it's fair to say that upset was a far piece from what she was. Angry, let's say. Infuriated. That, too. But also clarified. What she had found in that envelope had given her a clear path forward. A sense of what she needed to do next. She picked up what was left of the file, stepped gingerly through and around the rubble of what was left of her apartment. She sighed. She grabbed her keys and her security badge. She grabbed her shoulder bag, turned, and looked one more time at the wreck of her apartment—the eat-in kitchen's table broken into thirds; the dishes smashed across the floor; the pillows and cushions torn, their batting ripped out—looked for perhaps the last time, and then stepped into the hallway.

She ignored the small crowd of neighbors who had gathered there and who had been banging on her door for, oh, twenty minutes, and pushed past them so she could go downstairs and head for her office.

# 14.

When Sarah first came to the Regional Office, the streets had been noisy and smoggy and the air damp and the day hot, made hotter still by the buildings, the concrete, the glass, the steel, which trapped all that heat and let it radiate out all day and most of the night. Sarah had missed the city, the heat and the noise and the smell, had missed it because she loved it.

She had thought moving to California would have been a good thing, moving away from home (everyone moves away from home, right?), moving away from the look that people in the old neighborhood gave her, even still, because she was the girl whose mother had disappeared. Moving away from all of that had seemed a good idea, but she didn't like California. The weather made no sense. The air, the sky, there was just too much of both. She hated driving, not that she had had a car out in California, but she had hated being driven around, too. The people were too easygoing, too smug for her tastes, and for a while now, she had wondered if the move had been a tragic mistake. It was good to be back in the city, anyway, even if just for a short while, and even if she didn't know exactly why she had come back home, what she hoped to gain by coming back.

Sarah had found the building and the office she was looking

for—Morrison World Travel Concern—almost half an hour ago. She stood outside it and then walked away from it and bought a hot dog and a pretzel and a soda. She sat on a half wall just down the street from the travel agency to eat and afterward walked back up to the front door and stared at the scripted name, the travel posters in the window, and wondered what the hell she was doing here, what she hoped to find here for herself. Sarah thought about taking the train and then the bus to her aunt's house. Her aunt would be at work and she didn't know Sarah was even in the city, but Sarah could surprise her. She could pick up some food or grab some things from the store, bake her a cake. Her aunt loved cake. That was what she should do. Go back to Brooklyn, where she belonged, and make this a visit with her aunt and not a complete waste of her time. When she had received the letter from the Morrison World Travel Concern inviting her—directing her, more like it—to come to their offices on this day, a first-class ticket included, she had assumed it was a scam or a high-priced piece of marketing that had been mailed to her by accident. But then she saw her mother's name in the letter and she read it more closely, and then read it again—information about your mother, etc., etc., unusual circumstances surrounding her disappearance, etc., etc.—and while she had no idea what a high-end travel agency could or would tell her about her mother, who was she to pass up a free first-class plane ticket back to New York?

Now that she was here, though, she felt uneasy about the whole situation.

She clenched her fists in resolve and nodded as if coming to a hard-won decision and half-turned to head back to Fifty-Ninth, back to the subway, back to a real life, but before she could change her mind again, she stepped inside.

A shiver ran through her, which she blamed on the air-conditioning.

A pretty, young receptionist smiled at her. "Good afternoon. Can I help you?"

"I'm looking to, um, book a trip to Akron, Ohio?" Sarah said.

Sarah had looked up the Morrison World Travel Concern before coming. She couldn't find a website for them but had read a number of stories—many of them in magazines like the *Aston Martin Magazine* and the *Robb Report*. She knew the kinds of vacations booked here, which were not the kind of vacations one took to Akron, Ohio. She expected the receptionist to frown at her, or to look at her blankly, or send her to Travelocity or something, or worse yet, to book her a trip to Akron, Ohio, where Sarah had no intention of going. Instead, the young woman held her pretty smile and said, "Great. I'll let them know. While you wait, can I offer you something to drink? Water? A glass of champagne?"

Five minutes later, another woman escorted her to an elevator and told her, "Someone will be waiting for you," and smiled at her as the doors closed and the elevator began its descent, which was a long descent, and then a few minutes after that, when the doors opened, there he was: Mr. Niles.

# 15.

It was almost five in the morning by the time Sarah made it back uptown, back to the Regional Office. She would've been at the office sooner if she'd taken a cab, but she didn't trust a cab—or much of anyone at this point. She could have called one of the Regional Office drivers. They were on call twenty-four hours a day, mostly for the Operatives, whose assignments often required oddly timed comings and goings, but she wasn't sure she could trust their drivers, either—their own drivers!—not to mention, calling for a car at this hour would have drawn unwanted attention, might have tipped off someone she didn't want tipped off. Not just that she'd received their envelope, but that she'd refused to accept their offer, which had been contained within that envelope, but not only that: She was preparing to take action against those who'd made the offer.

So she took the trains. The F train was murder. The 4 was worse. But the platforms and the cars, aside from the occasional drunk passed out on a bench, were empty, and she would see anything weird or out of sorts that might be coming for her.

Not to mention all the waiting, all the time she spent stewing, helped to clear her head, helped her relax.

Still.

What a drag.

Not what she'd had planned for her Tuesday morning. Or her Monday night.

She unlocked the first-floor office door and then punched in the elevator code, started the long descent.

No one else was in, at least. Even the cleaning crew had long since come and gone.

When she first started working for Mr. Niles, she came in early every morning, hoping (and failing) to impress him and the Operatives—Mr. Niles, if he even noticed, never said anything, hadn't cared, and the Operatives hazed her for it, but back then there hadn't been much that they hadn't hazed her for. She would come in before sunrise and use her key to Mr. Niles's office— which she had kept even after he had given her her own office— and sat at his desk and watched the sun rise over Manhattan through the three tall video screens that were built to look like windows, the pictures on them so vivid, so real, that there were moments when the rising sun would force her to shade her eyes, when sunlight seemed to stream into the room, when she almost forgot she was a mile, at least, belowground.

Those mornings, that sunrise, were the best things about working for the Regional Office those first few months. Better than all the fancy gewgaws and super-advanced technologies they used to find new Recruits, better than the training room with its hologram modules and Danger Room sessions, better than the advanced weaponry, better than Mr. Niles and what he'd done for her, and way better, so, so much way better than her mechanical arm made of a nearly impervious and unbreakable metal alloy and controlled by hyperadvanced nanorobots but disguised to look no different than her other, normal arm.

But back then, just about everything was better than that arm.

Not because she hadn't wanted the arm, though in truth, she hadn't asked for it, either, had been talked into it. The arm had been Mr. Niles's idea—if she wanted to avenge her mother, she would need enhancement, etc.—and sure, she appreciated it now, couldn't imagine her life without it now. But back then, she didn't know how to use it, how to control it, or why she needed it. Back then, what she had wanted from the Regional Office were answers, and when she was given those answers, what she wanted were actions—of the vengeful sort, full of violent retribution—and Mr. Niles had insisted, had promised that revenge would come, but before she could have revenge, she would have to take the mechanical arm.

Now she rubbed the key to Mr. Niles's office between her normal thumb and forefinger (she tried her best not to rub things between her mechanical fingers as that made her body twitch the way it twitched when she accidentally bit into a piece of tinfoil or handled those paper towels that were less paper and more towel). She thought hard about that sunrise, about setting herself up in that office in front of those big windows again, letting these newly arisen troubles take their own course. If she had known that Mr. Niles was already in there himself, had been there all night trying to figure out whether he should stay with the Regional Office or find some other thing to do with his life because he'd become tired, so tired of all the bullshit of working with Oyemi and her Oracles, she would have gone to him, and would have told him everything she'd learned reading that letter left on her door, and might have possibly changed the trajectory of not just this day but of her life, and not just her life, but the life of Mr. Niles, and maybe the life they might have had together, not as a couple, though maybe she wouldn't have minded that, but more as a globe-trotting, world-saving duo. Rogue demon hunters, and the like. A thought, she wasn't afraid to admit (to herself, horrified by the thought of admitting it to Mr. Niles or any other living soul), she'd pondered not a few times. But she didn't know he was there, and instead she believed—correctly—that the Regional Office was going to come under attack, and believed—incorrectly—that this attack would come in the next few days, the next few weeks, and that she was going to be the one to save the Regional Office, and that to do so, she had to stay down here and work instead of watch for a rising sun.

If only she had known that the Regional Office was already under attack, had been under attack, in one subtle way or another, for the past two years . . . but she didn't know, wouldn't know until too late. Not too late to save the Regional Office, which, let's face it, was done for, at least the way Mr. Niles and Oyemi had envisioned it. But too late to save herself.

And way too late to save Mr. Niles.

# 16.

"My mother disappeared," Sarah had told Mr. Niles at that first meeting, even though clearly he would have known this, since they had found her, they had invited her to their offices promising information on her mother's disappearance.

Still. Sarah believed in coming right to the point. People could be so awkward the way they danced around the topic of her mother.

"She disappeared when I was eight."

Mr. Niles had offered Sarah his hand and had led her off the elevator into an open office thrumming with activity. He'd introduced himself and hadn't bothered with the unnecessary *You must be Sarah* that she had expected. He'd offered her something to drink, something to eat, and when she had refused both, had taken her to his office, and that was where they were talking now.

Mr. Niles, who had short black hair that would have been curly if he'd let it grow out, and a soft, round face, and very little chin to speak of, smiled at her and told her, almost gently, "I know."

Sarah didn't know what to say to that so she didn't say anything. Mr. Niles tented his hands together and pressed the tips of his index fingers to the tip of his nose. He tilted back in his office chair and regarded Sarah with what Sarah took to be some skepticism.

"I know that she was abducted," he said, finally, "and I know a lot more than that." He dropped his hands into his lap and leaned forward in his chair and said, "What I don't know is if you're ready."

"Ready?" she asked.

"For the truth. About your mother. And about you."

She didn't know what truth there would be for her to find out about herself, but she didn't know why the Regional Office would have contacted her in the first place if Mr. Niles hadn't thought she was ready to learn what they knew about her mother. That was the whole reason she had come.

It was strange, though, being here, telling Mr. Niles the small piece of her story, waiting to hear what he had to say. Strange because she had long ago stopped killing herself trying to puzzle out what had happened to her mother. After her mother had disappeared and she had gone to live with her aunt, Sarah hadn't known what had happened to her mother, not even in the abstract. She only knew that her mother was gone, and that she missed her, and that she was sad because of this, but the other aspects of her life hadn't changed very much. She still had to go to school, still had to wake up in the mornings and go to bed at night at the same specified times. She still liked the same foods—not many of them—and still had the same friends—again, not many of them. What it meant that her mother was gone wouldn't occur to her until she was older, which was when she started to think seriously about the things that might've happened to her mother. And as a teenager, Sarah tortured herself—that's how Sarah liked to think of it—with all the possibilities. From: Her mother took an honest look at what the next ten to twelve years held in store for her alone in the city with a daughter she didn't fully understand and simply walked out, wiping her hands clean of that potential disaster, to: She was nabbed on the way home, forced to live in a basement in a building two doors down or the next block over, a sex slave, or worse. Sarah couldn't imagine what worse would look like, could only imagine that there could be worse.

There could always be worse.

She didn't know what Mr. Niles would tell her, or what would happen after that, but what she knew was that she was ready.

Ready for something, ready for anything, ready to move on, ready for the truth.

"I'm ready," she said. "I'm as ready as I'll ever be," she said, and this made Mr. Niles smile, maybe because he admired her confidence or maybe because he knew she was wrong.

# 17.

Sarah brewed a pot of coffee.

It was nice being in the office before anyone else. It was quiet, true, but that wasn't what was so nice about it. Late at night, after everyone else had gone home, it was quiet then, too. No. This was different. Desks were still cluttered and the mail room was still a mess and someone had left a dirty coffee mug and plate in the kitchen sink, but still, there seemed to be something fresh and untouched about the office. This early and as empty as it was, the office contained a well, or a bubble, a fragile bubble of potential for great work to be done, grand and fantastic deeds to be accomplished. That was it. That was the difference. By the end of any day, of every day, it seemed, all the day's potential had been undone by phone calls and meetings, e-mails and paperwork.

Plus, this early, with no one around, she could get to work without everyone scrambling to her with their problems, most of which weren't even her responsibility. She wasn't the office manager or the intern coordinator or the director of outreach or assistant to the regional manager. She worked directly for Mr. Niles, was his go-to, had been so almost from her first day working here, but without fail, every single day someone would come to her with some stupid question about toner cartridges or to complain about that idiot intern Jacob, or to hand her a list of supplies the office had run out of. But whatever. Let those nitwits send her e-mails about resetting their voice mail passwords; she didn't care. Not today. Today and in the coming weeks, she would be too busy saving their goddamn asses, so thank God no one else was around.

She poured milk into her coffee and looked out over the empty cubicles and told herself she would make a habit of this again—once this attack was thwarted—of coming in early, maybe not every day, but often.

Often enough.

But for now: the attack.

It wasn't explicit, the warning she had received, if that was what it had been.

The envelope had contained a letter, an offer letter of sorts. Someone trying to lure her away from the Regional Office. Not sent, though, from any kind of headhunter firm—not that there were many headhunter firms trafficking in the world inhabited by organizations like the Regional Office, but there were a few, and this hadn't been sent from any of them. This had been sent, or delivered, rather, from the organization itself. She didn't know which. Whoever had sent the offer hadn't specified.

And there was information, about the Regional Office, about Mr. Niles, about her arm. Information that had made her mad, violently and destructively mad. Information clearly, blatantly false. Damning and cruel, intended, she was sure, to turn her against the people she had come to think so highly of, to work so hard for, trust with her life and, quite literally, her limb.

Not that her anger had passed but had been refocused. She

had curbed her impulses and trained her anger on making whoever left her that envelope pay and pay dearly.

The question she had to answer, then, was: who?

By the time anyone else showed up at the office, Sarah had narrowed the list of suspects down to six. Six organizations or con-
glomerations or evil confederations or anarchist splinter groups
with a) any vested interest in the total destruction of the Regional
Office, b) the logistical and mystical support and backing and
training and time to carry out such an attack, and c) as her aunt
would have dubbed it, the brass fucking balls to even think of such
an attack.

Six of them. On a spreadsheet. Leadership outlined, strengths
and weaknesses enumerated, potential readiness for such an assault, earliest timeline for such an attack. That's as far as Sarah
had gotten when she heard, "Wow, you're here early."

It was Wendy. Thank God it was Wendy and not that idiot
Jacob.

If she was going to deal with one of the interns this morning of
all mornings, better it be Wendy.

She could not handle Jacob right now.

"Check your tablet, I sent you a spreadsheet just a minute—"

"Yeah, I got it, just now," Wendy said, scrolling through the
names. "This year's Christmas card list?"

Sarah was scanning the building schematics for the Regional
Office on her computer, looking for weak points, points of entry,
defense positions, and, frankly, she didn't have time for jokes. She
shook her head. "The Regional Office is under attack," she said.
"Or will be, soon, quite possibly very soon, so, if you don't mind."

Wendy smiled and then just as quickly stopped smiling. "Wait, what? Are you kidding?" Sarah stopped scrolling through the schematics to pause long enough to throw Wendy a look. "I mean, right, you're not the jokiest person I know, but, really? We're under attack? Guns a-blazing attack?"

"Minus the guns, yes, we're under attack, or I'm pretty sure we will be." She paused. "Actually, there might be guns."

"Cool," Wendy said, and then so she wouldn't get a second look or worse, said, "I mean, not cool as in 'awesome,' but." She paused. "How very interesting." She paused again. "So, is this new intel from one of the Ops?" she asked. "Or something from the Oracles?"

"Look at the list, will you?" Sarah said, ignoring her questions, not yet ready to mention to anyone else the letter on her door, the information inside it. "Keep it between you and me for now. I would prefer not to have people in a panic all day, and maybe if we work real hard at it, we can stop it before it becomes too interesting. Hmm?"

"Oh. Stop it?"

Sarah sighed, spun in her chair to look at Wendy, to make sure it was Wendy and not, who knew, Jacob in a Wendy outfit. "I'm sorry, but are you feeling okay? Yeah, I think we can all agree that we should stop the attack. Right? Stop it?"

"Oh, yeah, sorry, it's just that, well, you said we were under attack and I thought you meant, like, right now, that we were in the middle of it, that's all." Wendy cleared her throat. "Stop it, definitely. Stop the attack *before* it happens. That's definitely what we should do."

"Great. Glad we're all caught up. The names, please?" Sarah went back to the drawings. What was she missing, what had she missed, where were the flaws? She wanted it all narrowed down, the attack scenario and her counterattack options worked up and presentable before the end of the day, but there was something missing. She couldn't pinpoint what, but there was something. She could sense it.

Wendy hadn't moved. Sarah stopped and took a deep breath and rubbed one of her eyes with her thumb. "What, Wendy?"

"Should we tell Mr. Niles?"

"How do you know I haven't told him already?"

"Right, sorry. What did Mr. Niles say?"

Sarah's shoulders slumped. She couldn't feel the weight of her mechanical arm, that's how it had been designed, but this morning, she could feel the weight of it pulling her down, she swore she could.

"We'll tell him when we have something more concrete, how about that? We don't . . . storm into his office with six possible attackers and a probable attack." Wendy was nodding. "The list, Wendy? Can you focus on the list, please, and help me figure this out?"

"Right, boss," Wendy said. "I'll run probability reports for each name, create three—no, five—possible counterstrategies for each, get them to you by . . . what time is it now?"

Sarah checked the clock. It was almost eight. How had it gotten to be almost eight? Sarah stared at the clock.

"Whatever," Wendy said. "I'll have it all to you before ten?"

Relieved that Wendy was acting like Wendy again, Sarah smiled.

"Perfect, thanks." Wendy smiled back, was about to leave when Sarah said, "Oh, and"—she sighed, God, why couldn't she stop sighing—"I should probably bring Jasmine in on this. What time does she come in today?"

Wendy cocked her head not unlike a spaniel. "Oh, nine I guess?" she said.

"Never mind. I'll look it up," Sarah said. Wendy was usually on top of this shit, and Sarah didn't really have time or patience for her to come down with a case of the "interns," but whatever. She'd figure it out herself.

Wendy moved closer to Sarah, reached over her shoulder for Sarah's tablet. "Here," she said. "You're super busy. I can look it up for you, put her on your schedule."

Sarah held her tablet firm. "It's fine, Wendy, Jesus. I can take care of it."

She scrolled through the schedule. It took her a moment to realize something was wrong and another moment for her to recognize what that something wrong was. Wendy was still leaning over her and then she felt Wendy stand up, step one or two steps back.

Jasmine wasn't there. On the schedule. That was what was wrong. She was on a mission. Sarah didn't recognize the mission, but more surprising even than that—which was pretty damn surprising since Sarah approved and cleared every mission—was how no one else was on the schedule either. How every one of their girls was also on a mission. Against all protocol, every single Operative was gone, off-site, and in Jasmine's case, off-dimension.

"What the hell is going on?" Sarah said.

A creeping, slow-moving sense of what was going on crept and slowly moved into the pit of Sarah, and she was about to say, Jesus, we're too late, it's today, but then the client elevator dinged and that ding was followed by voices, unfamiliar, gruff voices, and those voices were followed by screams, which were followed then by more voices and gunshots and then more screams, and so, really, Sarah was too late to say even that.

# 18.

The day Sarah's mother disappeared (was abducted), she forgot to pack Sarah a school lunch. She promised Sarah she'd bring it to school before lunch, that she'd bring it right away, and later Sarah wondered if her mother had been on her way to bring that lunch to school when she was taken, or if she'd simply forgotten about the lunch altogether, which had happened before. Sarah always hoped that her mother forgot about the lunch a second time and was tootling around in their apartment or somewhere in the city, doing something silly and unrelated to Sarah or Sarah's school or Sarah's well-being, when she was nabbed.

Sarah would have been happy to know, for instance, that her mother had gotten sidetracked even on her way home from dropping Sarah off at school. That she had walked by a Duane Reade and remembered that her hair dryer had broken and that she wanted a new one, and that while in Duane Reade, she remembered other things she needed to get—makeup, a humidifier, Q-tips—and that she was grabbed as she was walking out of the store.

Sarah loved her mother and loved it when her mother did things that were motherly, which she didn't do too often, but Sarah would have preferred it if her mother had been taken away from her while doing something frivolous or ordinary, and not in one of the rare moments she exhibited any kind of maternal instincts.

Sarah's mother never came back, in any case, and Sarah's teacher shared some of her lunch with Sarah when it was clear there wouldn't be a lunch. She ate half an apple and half a ham sandwich, drank half a Tab. The rest of the day was normal. The entire day, in fact, felt normal. Her mother's forgetting her lunch—they were running late and her mother had almost forgotten her own shoes—the two of them running the last two blocks together, Sarah spacing out during most of the school day, running around the playground by herself, crossing two bars on the monkey bars before falling off, and her mother running late to pick her up from school. These all pointed to any ordinary day.

But then her mother was really late.

And then her mother was so late that the receptionist called the only other number on file, which was Sarah's aunt's number, because she'd already called Sarah's house four times and the receptionist had kids of her own, you know, and couldn't spend the whole night waiting there with Sarah.

"I wonder what happened to that mother of yours," her aunt said as they walked hand in hand to the subway. Sarah didn't mind at the time. She didn't suspect, in other words, that anything had gone wrong, and plus her mother never let her hold hands this long because it made their hands sweaty and Sarah's mother didn't like sweaty hands, so Sarah shrugged and squeezed her aunt's hand quickly and her aunt squeezed back.

They picked up pizza on the way to her aunt's apartment. Her aunt let her watch television while she called around looking for Sarah's mother. She gave Sarah a bath and gave her a T-shirt to wear as pajamas, too big and wonderfully soft and thin, and then she read to Sarah from *A Wrinkle in Time*—"One of my favorites when I was a girl"—and then she tucked Sarah into her big, fluffy bed and told her, "In the morning, guess what? You'll wake up in your own bed!" And as she fell asleep, Sarah thought to herself that she wouldn't be upset if she didn't wake up in her own bed, that it would be just fine, thank you very much, to wake up in her aunt's bed, which felt clean and lovely, but then she woke up and it was the morning and she was still at her aunt's, and she was surprised by how much this upset her.

Her aunt took a day off work and took Sarah to school and picked her up again in the afternoon, and the rest of the afternoon and that night, her aunt told Sarah things like, "She's probably just with some friends in the city and lost track of everything," and, "You know how your mother can be sometimes, like she's on a different planet," which was true, or had been true when her mother had been a younger woman. As a girl and into her teens, Sarah's mother had the habit of disappearing from the house for a day or two, crashing on the couches of friends in the city or in Brooklyn, or not sleeping at all, sitting in diners or cafés with friends or people she had just met, and then coming home to any number of punishments, which didn't bother her at all because she hadn't been a rebellious girl, just forgetful and thoughtless. When she had become pregnant with Sarah—she hadn't the slightest idea who the father was, or else convincingly pretended she hadn't—she'd changed, or if nothing else, she had stopped leaving the house and forgetting to come back, at least until now.

Another night passed, and then it was Saturday and there was no school, and her aunt said, "Hey, do you want to go to Coney Island today?" and Sarah said, "Sure," even though what she really wanted was to go home and for her mother to come back. But she didn't want to upset her aunt, who seemed more than upset enough, and she didn't want to say what was on her own mind, either, as she would only upset herself by saying out loud the thing she wanted to do but couldn't do. And so, fine, she would go to Coney Island with her aunt, except her aunt stayed home and Sarah went with a friend of her aunt's who also had kids, three of them, the oldest four years younger than Sarah, and for most of the day, Sarah watched her aunt's friend yell at her kids or caught her aunt's friend staring at her with a strange, sad, pitying look in her eye.

On Sunday, her aunt bought cookies and pizzas and cake and popcorn and closed the blinds and turned her apartment as dark as she could and ran movie after movie after movie, Sarah's favorites, which weren't many and which were mostly her favorites because they were the ones she had at home—*Labyrinth* and *Top Gun* and *Time Bandits*. When they ran out of movies, Sarah's aunt kept the apartment dark and the popcorn popped and they sat and watched whatever was on TV, and then, on Monday, the police came over. After that, a man and a woman from CPS came to her aunt's house, and after that, Sarah's aunt took her back to her mom's apartment, where they packed her clothes and her toys up, and Sarah asked her aunt if they couldn't just stay there.

Sarah's aunt told her, "Maybe, maybe we will, maybe we'll come back here and stay until your mother comes back," but they never did. One day while she was at school, her aunt moved what she could from Sarah's old apartment and sold the rest and what she didn't sell was left on the curb. And then time passed and Sarah changed and while she didn't know it, her mother changed, too, which was why when Sarah was older and she saw her mother week after week, year after year, she never once knew they'd been brought back together.

# 19.

Sarah stood up and pushed by Wendy and then stopped in the doorway.

She knew she should have kept going, should have barreled down the hall and into that fray, should have put her mechanical arm to the good use it had been designed for, but she didn't. She stopped instead. Not because she was afraid—she wasn't—or because she didn't think she'd do well in the fight—she would have—but because it wasn't her instinct to barrel into anything.

She was careful—had always been careful, even and especially as a child, even and especially when situations required bold action. She was a thinker, a planner. She thought through everything, the possibilities, the action and reaction, the cause and effect, the consequences of *therefore* and *but*.

People were screaming—not just people, but coworkers—and hostages were being taken, therefore she should put an end to it all, and the Operatives were missing, therefore she was the strongest and most skilled defender on site, and she should get to work defending, but then what? she thought. She runs down the hall wielding her mechanical arm, disarms and neutralizes three men, or let's be generous, let's say five, if you give Sarah the element of surprise, five men, neutralized, or dead, but how many are there in all? And so let's hope for the best but prepare for the worst and say there are twenty, no, forty men with guns, now down to thirty-five, and now she has lost the element of surprise, and all that's left to her is brute force, cunning, and speed, which she contains, not just in her mechanical arm, but contains in the all of her, but still, brute force and speed and cunning, set up against thirty-five men with guns and who knows what else. And Jesus—are there magicks involved? There would have to be magicks involved, otherwise how would they have conspired to push past security? How would they have managed to send all the Regional Office's own defensive team of Operatives off on missions so that not one of them was on campus? So, yeah, sure, let's throw magicks into the mix, too, and let's take away complete surprise because they would have to know by now that she was not on board with their offer, with the package that she had found that night in her apartment, that she would be, in fact, lurking somewhere to join in on this fight, so maybe not total surprise. Add to that technological wizardry, because who would plan an attack against an organization equipped with a semi-cyborg (although Sarah didn't love the word, *cyborg,* and liked to think of herself more as enhanced) and not come equipped with its own technology to counter? Which mostly takes away her brute force. Takes away brute force and leaves speed and cunning, which don't come into play as much when running headlong into an uneven fight. Leaving her only one real option: to *Die Hard* it John McClane–style, but with Wendy working with her, the two of them squeezing through air ducts and lurking in stairwells and plotting in empty offices, picking off these bastards in small guerrilla groups.

So it was settled.

She had her plan, not just the only but also the very best plan, contrived in a matter of seconds while she stood there in the doorway.

Not bad, O'Hara. Not bad at all.

She turned to pull Wendy along with her, down the hall in the opposite direction to the back stairwell and from there to the upstairs break room, but when she saw Wendy, Wendy had changed.

Sarah couldn't tell how. Not right away. Wendy looked at the clock and made a wincing smiling face and said, "They're a little early." And then she punched Sarah in the face. "But better early than late, right, boss?" And she punched her again, in the chest this time, so hard and so fast that Sarah couldn't react, couldn't think, could only fly backward, crashing through the glass wall of her office and into the cubicle right outside it—Wendy's fucking cubicle—and then things went dark and she didn't get up.

# 20.

"We will give you a mechanical arm, Sarah," Mr. Niles told her just before the men cut off her real arm.

"A mechanical arm so perfect," he said, "that not even your own mother will know which arm is the real arm and which is the mechanical arm."

He said, Not even your own mother, even though they both knew that her mother was dead, that she was killed by the very men whom Sarah had sworn to hunt down, with the help of Mr. Niles, and with the assistance of this mechanical arm. He said, Not even your own mother, but Sarah liked to think he meant, Not even the person closest to you, not even the person who might know you better than you know yourself, not even the person who reared you from infancy and has since gazed unflinchingly into the darkest depths of your soul and who, nonetheless, continues to love and admire and watch over you, not even this person will know which arm is the mechanical arm.

Of course, before he said any of this, before they prepped her for surgery, before she even knew about a potential for prepping for surgery, he sat her down in his office and passed a file folder across his desk. On the folder was a picture of her mother, and inside the folder a detailed account of what had happened to her after she was taken, which included more photos, confusing photos, disturbing photos, disturbing because they were so confusing.

Her mother with an AK-47. Her mother bent over what looked like a dirty bomb, her face turned to the camera, her eyes wide and full of mirth. Her mother in full camo, lined up with a group of similarly aged men and women also outfitted in camouflage, holding what looked like grenades over their heads, grenades as if they were flutes of champagne. Her mother in an apron leaned over a stockpot at an old white stove, the kind Sarah always pictured when imagining a life out in the country with a mom and a dad and land. Her mother looking in that photo more motherly than Sarah had ever remembered her looking, and to the right of her, a table of bearded men and limp-haired women, one looking at the camera, the others looking at a map or a roll of papers in front of them.

"A terrorist cell of anarchists working out of Damascus took your mother. They thought your mother had been imbued with gifts," Mr. Niles said as she flipped through the file folder, "gifted with special abilities, powers, you might say, and maybe she had been, and maybe not, that we cannot say, but that's why they took her." He sighed. "Why they brainwashed her, why they trained her."

Then he sat back in his chair and let a silence settle into his office as Sarah turned slowly, carefully through all of the pages in the file folder, and not until she looked up at him did he lean forward again and say, "I'd like to offer you the services of this office. I'd like to offer you a deal."

# 21.

The problem with having a mechanical arm nearly impervious and super fast and super strong, comprised of hyperadvanced nanorobot technology and looking no different than her regular arm, was that people always assumed just because Sarah had the ability to crush metal with her armored grip that, when faced with a situation not to her liking, her first reaction would be to crush something with her mechanical fist.

Or if crushing weren't possible, smashing.

The elevator control panel, for instance. People seemed to always be waiting for that moment when, impatient with the often glitchy elevator, she would throw her fist into the elevator control panel, or the glass wall of her office, or through one of the interns.

A number of people seemed to be waiting for her to throw her fist through an intern.

Jacob, perhaps.

Not many people in the office would have blamed her for throwing her fist through intern Jacob.

All of which was only made more frustrating and disappointing when you woke up one day to find all that potential squandered by time and inaction and an inability to risk losing what you loved to gain something more.

In other words: When Sarah woke up, she woke up and her arm was gone.

Her mechanical arm, that is, and not gone, not entirely gone, just no longer attached to her. It had been a day full of strange uncertainties, but if anything was for absolute certain, it was that her mechanical arm was no longer attached to her. Instead, it was on a metal gurney not more than five feet in front of her.

Sarah was tied up in a chair and her other arm burned with not a small amount of burning pain, and when she finally got the chance to look at her other arm, which wouldn't be until they pulled her out of that chair and carried her to where the other hostages were being kept, she would see the three-inch gash, down to what she'd think might be bone, and would think happily to herself, They couldn't tell which was which, either.

Would think, Mr. Niles will be so pleased.

But at the moment she wasn't thinking of her normal arm and hardly noticed the burning pain and was only barely aware of the idea of thinking of Mr. Niles or the Regional Office or what was going to happen to her next.

All she could think of was what was right in front of her. How she had wasted what was right in front of her and how all she could do now was simply sit and stare at it and let it all continue to go to waste.

Hell no.

She took a deep breath and jumped or did whatever that thing was when you were tied tight in an office chair to try to scooch it across the floor.

The back legs tilted but not by much and she didn't feel the front legs do anything at all.

Leverage. She had the wrong kind of leverage.

If she had her arm, boy, these ropes and this chair and this office wall and even the concrete floor below her, boy, they wouldn't stand a chance, and then the men outside, however many of them, the men scattered throughout the whole Regional Office, they'd get what was coming to them, too.

The real problem with having a mechanical arm that was etc., etc., ad infinitum, was that she never did: throw her metal fist through Jacob, the elevator panel, the glass wall of her office. It was her job, she thought, not just her job but her position, her responsibility, her role in the Regional Office, not to throw her fist around willy-nilly, mechanical or not, though now she understood that she had misunderstood her role in the organization, her value to Mr. Niles, and that she had held herself in check, had pulled everything back, had stilled herself—not just her mechanical arm but her regular arm, too, and not just that but everything—had stilled herself to the point of stillness by mistake and for the wrong reasons, and now the problem was she was going to be killed, was going to die at the office, not ever once having fully let herself go.

# 22.

When Sarah woke up from the operation, she woke up standing in the middle of a wrecked lab and operating room, fairly unconcerned about her arm, about either of her arms.

She was breathing hard. Her chest heaved. Her hands were clenched into fists. A red light was pulsing and a small series of sparks lit up the heart-rate machine to her left and then the machine collapsed into a heap.

For a few seconds, Sarah didn't know where she was, what had happened, how she had gotten there.

Faintly, Sarah remembered lying down on the operating table. She remembered a mask being placed over her mouth and nose. She remembered counting down from one hundred. She remembered becoming stuck on ninety-three. And that was all she remembered.

A heap of something in the corner of the operating room moaned and shifted.

The doctor. A heap of the doctor in the corner of the operating room moaned and shifted.

Then she heard Mr. Niles speaking to her, but his voice crunched and crackled, and it was too loud, everything was too loud, and she stuck her fingers into her ears, but carefully, she remembered, because one of the fingers might have been mechanical. She remembered that, she was beginning to remember that.

She looked around the operating room for Mr. Niles, but he wasn't there, and then she realized he was speaking to her over an intercom.

"What?" she said. "What's going on?" she said.

"We're opening the door, Sarah," Mr. Niles said. "It's okay. Everything's going to be okay. We're opening the door. Nothing's going to happen. Try not to hit anything or anyone."

Someone else in the intercom room with Mr. Niles said, just loud enough for the microphone to pick up, "Anyone else, you mean."

"What?" Sarah asked.

"Just rest your arm, okay? Just rest everything." Mr. Niles paused. "I'm coming inside now."

A hiss escaped the door and she realized she hadn't known she'd been locked inside, that the doctor had been locked inside with her. The door pushed open and there was Mr. Niles. She had expected him to be dressed in scrubs or in a hazmat suit, or, judging by the state of the room, full body armor, but he was wearing his normal office clothes, minus the jacket, his sleeves rolled up, his tie pulled loose.

He smiled. "Well. That was unexpected."

Two paramedics stepped cautiously into the room behind him and then crept over to the doctor heaped into the corner.

He stepped closer to her, closer than she felt comfortable with, considering. Considering what she must have done coming out of the operation, considering her own inability to remember any of it, considering the doctor, whose femur had been pulverized, according to the muted chatter she could hear from the paramedics.

Mr. Niles studied her, studied not just her arms, which would have been expected, but looked closely into her eyes, stepped around her in a slow circle. The paramedics lifted the doctor onto a stretcher. Mr. Niles came back around to look her in the face.

"Fantastic," he said.

"Fantastic?"

"I'd certainly call this a success," Mr. Niles said.

"A success?"

"You're alive. I'm alive." He looked around the room. "This is an easy cleanup, frankly. You should see what some of the other girls have done, the Operatives." He took a deep breath and let it out and placed his hand on her shoulder, her normal shoulder. Then he smiled at her again and placed his hand on her other shoulder and shook his head and said, "Remarkable." He took her by her hands and lifted them up and put her palms flat against his palms and her whole body shuddered, and she couldn't tell if she was afraid and shuddering or thrilled and shuddering, but her breath caught in her throat when he intertwined her fingers with his.

Then the moment passed and he let her hands go and he took her by the arm—her normal arm—and started walking her out of the ruined lab.

"Yes," he said, "yes, very much a success." Then he said, "I want you to remember this, though." He stopped and turned her to look at the wreckage. "Take a good look around you and remember this very clearly. Maybe back when you were just a normal girl, back when you were Sarah O'Hara, girl with two normal arms, this kind of outburst would have been okay. Uncivilized, of course, but otherwise harmless." He swept his arm across the damage she had done. "But now. We must demonstrate a modicum of self-restraint, mustn't we?"

She nodded. She opened her mouth to apologize, but he stopped her from saying she was sorry, that she didn't know what she was doing, that she wasn't in control of any of it.

"You'll learn," he said, shaking his head. "Soon enough, you'll figure it out."

# 23.

Sarah wasn't going to give up.

That was what they wanted, of course. For her to give up.

Or, rather, what they wanted was for her to be captured and neutralized and, apparently, they wanted to take away her mechanical arm, all of which they—whoever They were—had achieved without much, or any, difficulty, and so her giving up might have been, in Their minds, a rather moot point.

In anyone's mind, a moot point, actually, including hers. Especially hers.

Not giving up meant she was going to do what, specifically?

Scooch the chair inch by inch the five or so feet to the metal table where her mechanical arm now lay lifeless and possibly ruined? Fine, sure, okay, and then what was she planning to do?

Her arm. The skin—her skin—had been stripped from it in uneven patches. The circuitry showed through, sinewy and blood-smeared, and the joints and the skeleton made of steel, or rather, made of an alloy that was better than steel, unbreakable and nearly impervious.

So what if she could get to it? She didn't even know if it still worked, and even if it did, who the hell was going to reattach it?

Her?

Tied tight in this chair and not a doctor or a surgeon or a robotics engineer or whatever the hell she would have to be to reattach a mechanical arm, to herself?

She jump-scooched her chair another inch closer. Her forehead and her neck began to sweat. She jump-scooched another inch, maybe even two inches, and then the pain in her regular arm and the pain where they had pulled off her mechanical arm and the pain in her face and skull from where Wendy—that fucking bitch Wendy—had sucker punched her were all homing in on her, waking up to her, but she didn't care.

She jump-scooched.

She jump-scooched.

She jump-scooched.

Her foot, if her legs hadn't been tied down to this chair, her ankles hadn't been strapped to the legs, her foot could have touched the table now if she extended her leg all the way.

And now her ankle, she could have wrapped her ankle around the wheeled leg of the table and drawn it to her.

And now her shin, she could have touched her shin to the leg, and her leg, she could have kicked the table over by now, or better yet, she could have thrown her foot onto the tabletop itself and brought the whole thing crashing down to her if she wanted, if she'd been able.

Jump-scooch. Jump-scooch. Her knee tipped against the closest leg, shifted the table a hair. She could smell it now, her arm, the metal and the blood of her arm swirling together in a perfect storm of copper penny down her nose and into her throat.

She breathed in huffing gusts through her nose and her wide-open mouth. She had drenched herself in so much sweat that the dried blood from Wendy's punch had loosened, mixed, had run over her lips, onto her teeth and tongue.

But she didn't care.

She had made it, goddamn it.

And now what?

She could close her eyes. She could let her body shudder to a halt. She could faint!

She could do practically nothing she wanted!

In truth, she had harbored the notion that making it would be enough, would be trial and sacrifice enough, that the universe or her arm would recognize her effort, would reward her for it somehow—That's it, Sarah, you've done enough, you've done more than enough, let us take it from here—so she sat there huffing and sweating and wincing and concentrating, willing the arm to do some damn thing, waiting for the universe to right itself back in her favor, but nothing.

Not one damn thing.

She closed her eyes. She slumped her head—the rest of her, too, but the ropes wouldn't slump with her—and she would have sobbed, would have started heaving and crying, but then the door opened, and two men came inside, and she pulled her shit together.

# 24.

Mr. Niles and the doctor didn't show her the arm they'd cut off after the operation.

Sarah wasn't sure when or how she'd devised the notion that they would have, as if her now-detached arm were nothing more substantial than a pulled tooth, but she found herself asking about it, after the incident, after crushing the doctor's leg, wrecking his lab and the operating room, after Mr. Niles led her quietly to her room, where she could heal and recover and come to some sort of grips with everything.

"Can I see it?" she asked when Mr. Niles, just before leaving, asked if there was anything else she needed.

"It?" he said, although, even then, even that early in their friendship, she could read him well enough to know he understood her question just fine.

"My arm," she said. "The other one," she said.

She expected him to cough or lick his lips or fiddle with his tie or look to the left or the right, expected him to employ any number of stalling techniques that would give him time to figure out how to answer this delicate and weird and horrifying—even Sarah understood it was weird and horrifying—request, but he didn't deliberate. He didn't hem or haw. He said, "No, of course not." And then he nodded once and said, "Let me know if there's anything else," and then he was gone and she was alone with an arm that wasn't hers, that wasn't even human.

When it hung there at her side, her arm felt surprisingly just like any other arm. It didn't feel heavy or deadened. Her shoulder, where the arm had been attached, felt numb, but only for the first hour or so after the operation.

Her room was bare. She had expected a dorm room or a hotel room of some kind, with a kitchenette and a living suite, but it was gray and quiet and, but for a twin bed attached to the wall and a sink and a closet for her clothes, empty. The mirror over the sink was small, square, and only just large enough for her to see her face, her hair, her shoulders, the very tops of her breasts if she were naked, and nothing else, but she found herself staring at the mirror every morning and every night for hours on end.

She stared at her shoulders and the tops of her arms, at her biceps, or what she could see of them if she let her arms hang at her sides, or what she could make of them—or the one, at first, her real bicep, which was the only one she could lift and squeeze into shape. A tiny white line of a scar wrapped itself around her shoulder where they'd attached the mechanical arm, and another identical scar wrapped around her other shoulder, and the two arms looked so much alike that there were days when she could convince herself that she couldn't tell, either, which was which.

That first week and most of the second week, she couldn't move it at all, not by thinking, not by trying. What had happened in the operating room, the way she had torn it apart, must have been a fluke, Mr. Niles told her. "Muscle memory, or a knee-jerk reaction," he told her. "Like a chicken running around with its head cut off," he told her. Which didn't make her feel better, nor did it make any sense to her.

"It's a process," the doctor, crutched and timid in her presence, told her. "The internal operating system is still working out the best way to communicate with your own neurological system. And then your muscles and your synapses all have to be retrained. But it will work itself out. Leave it to its business and it will work itself out."

But she couldn't just leave it to its business. It was her arm, damn it. She couldn't not try. She tried the first moment Mr. Niles left her alone, even though he'd told her not to, not for a couple of days at least. She walked into her room and closed the door with her normal arm and then turned around and stared at the closed door in front of her and willed her mechanical arm to lift. She tensed muscles. She closed her eyes and imagined a reality. A reality that involved her mechanical arm lifting full of grace and fluidity to open the door. She pretended the arm wasn't even there, or was nothing special, that the last thing she wanted or needed was for the arm to make some movement, operate some simple machine. She tried to trick herself into using it. She let herself fall forward, tried to sneak up on the arm, jolt it into the action of catching her as she fell. She tried this sort of thing for what must have been hours, but none of it worked, and she was tired and sore and ready for bed. She struggled one-handed with her clothes and her shoes. Everything about her hurt and wanted to sleep. She sat down at the edge of the bed, winded and unhappy, only to remember she hadn't turned off the light. She debated lying back on the bed and covering her eyes with her normal arm and sleeping with the light on but she hated sleeping with the light on. She sighed and leaned forward to give herself the momentum to stand back up, but leaning forward, something else happened: Her mechanical arm swung down of its own volition and grabbed her shoe, and before she knew it, her arm had thrown the shoe, hard, so very hard, at the light fixture over her head, hard enough to smash the fixture and the bulb and to stick her shoe firmly into the ceiling.

And after that, all she could do was stare at it, even in the dark, stare at that arm and wonder what, if anything, it might do next.

# 25.

Their faces were masked. She could tell by the way they moved, by the way they walked and swung their arms and held their chests forward, she could tell by the look of them, they'd been trained by someone who had once worked for the Regional Office.

They stopped when they saw her, saw how close she was to the gurney, to her arm, and they looked at each other and then one of the men shrugged and the other shrugged back and then he glanced briefly down at the arm on the table, as if to make sure it was still there, that it hadn't left, hadn't sprouted legs and walked away on its own.

She didn't say, Where am I?

She didn't say, Who are you?

Didn't say, What have you done with Mr. Niles?

She didn't say anything except for with her eyes, which said, quite clearly and pointedly, *I am going to kill you,* to the man who'd looked down at her mechanical arm, but he didn't flinch or take on a concerned look or falter in his step or step backward in fear as she had hoped he might. Instead, he smiled at her and then looked at the other man and nodded at him and they laughed as if they'd just shared a joke, and she wondered if they were talking to each other, if they'd been talking all along but in a secret way, in a way that she couldn't hear. Telepathically, maybe.

The two men untied her and moved to lift her out of the chair. They weren't rough with her, and the one trying to pick her up by the armpit that wasn't an armpit anymore because it was a stump shied away a little bit at first, uncertain where to lift from. The other one had forgotten his gloves and was barehanded. He had soft, gentle hands. They concerted their efforts and lifted her up, and she saw the gash on her other arm, and thought, They didn't know!, and she ignored the burning, ignored the sight of her own bone, and she thought of Mr. Niles, and she did not panic.

She didn't panic at all.

She made a silent vow to Mr. Niles that she would not panic, that she would find some way out of this mess, a mess she imagined was of her own devising, and that she would find him, find him at least to apologize to him, and in her mind, she clenched her fist. She imagined herself standing in front of everyone who might stand in her way, and in her mind, she clenched her mechanical fist, ready to wreak havoc on all of the enemies of Mr. Niles and the Regional Office. As the two men walked her past the table where her mechanical arm lay useless and lifeless, and just before they yanked her out of the room, she looked at it and imagined her mechanical fist tightly clenched and full of its unimaginable power.

And that's when she saw the fingers twitch and jerk and then swiftly close, her mechanical hand, swiftly close into a powerful fist, and she felt a gasp rising in her throat, but then they hit her in the back of the head with something heavy and blocky, and everything went blurry, and they hit her again, and things went black.

# 26.

Once in a while, Sarah would get a call from Mr. Niles. He would bring her into his office. He would sit her down in the chair across from his desk. He would sigh. He would lean forward and smile and ask about her, ask about her arm, about the apartment he'd found for her, ask about her aunt, who he knew lived in Queens now and was very important to Sarah.

He did this every time, and every time, this ritual made her feel anxious. Or not anxious, but antsy.

She appreciated his attention but because she was barely twenty and had a mechanical arm and was desperately seeking vengeance, she really just wanted him to get to the point, which she knew would come only after she'd answered his questions, refused his offer for water and then for coffee, assured him that she was doing fine, thank you, and that she was ready, she was ready to see whatever he'd called her in to show her.

Namely, she was ready for the file on his desk, the name inside that file, the photograph, the last known whereabouts.

"We found another one," he would say. He would start to slide the folder to her. "I won't bore you with the details of how we found him," he would say. But then he would. He would bore her with the details. He told her how these men and women had changed their faces through major surgeries, had hidden themselves away in the farther reaches of Nepal, had quietly joined religious cults in western Colorado, had faked their own deaths in airplane tragedies, train derailments, house fires, suicides.

And she would wait, growing ever more impatient for him to finish and to give her the damn file, which he finally would after one last, "Are you sure you want this, want to continue this work?"

At which point she knew she was allowed to simply take the file, that she was almost expected to do so, that for whatever reason Mr. Niles preferred not to give her these things, preferred that they be taken from him almost but not quite against his will.

Then she would sit back in her chair and open the folder and look at the photograph, study it, study the face, study the other photos that might be in the file, and then she would read from cover to cover and then from cover to cover again. And then, having lost track of all time, she would look back up for Mr. Niles, who would have left his own office, left her to it so she could study the file alone, and find the room almost dark, the sun nearly set, and on the desk in front of her, a ham and cheese sandwich and a diet orange Fanta, which she would take—the sandwich in a few bites, the Fanta in two or three swallows—before she returned to the file, committing it to memory, all of it to memory.

What she didn't expect was how good she would be at tracking down and killing the men and women who had abducted and, ultimately, murdered her mother.

Although, really, if she was being honest with herself, she had proved to be good at so many other things that, in hindsight, she wasn't entirely surprised. Hunting down targets and eliminating them in secret simply happened to be just one more thing she had taken to, no different, really, than nanophysiology, or artificial subconscious dichotomy, which was what she had been studying in college before she dropped out in pursuit of the truth about her mother.

Not to mention that the Regional Office itself had done most of the heavy lifting. Less seek-out-and-destroy and more just destroy on her part.

Then one day she arrived in Mr. Niles's office expecting to pick up another file, go after another man or woman responsible for her mother's death, only to find Mr. Niles standing behind his desk empty-handed.

"That was the last one," he told her. He held his hands up, spread his fingers wide, and then clapped them together and smiled. "There's not one of them left."

"What do you mean?" she asked.

"I mean, you should be proud of yourself. You took care of every last one of them."

She didn't like this. "You should have told me," she said.

"I just did," he said, still smiling.

"Before. You should have told me before. I thought there would be more. There aren't more?"

"There was," he said. "There was one more, but there was an accident."

"An accident?"

"He got wind of our man following his trail, tried to run, stole a car, wasn't the best driver." He picked up a small envelope full of photographs. A car wreck. An oil-slick road. Burned wreckage.

"We checked it out," Mr. Niles said before she could say anything. "It's real. He's dead." He paused and leaned heavily against his desk. "And he was the last one."

Sarah held on to the photos and flipped through them but had stopped looking at them.

"And now what?" she asked.

Mr. Niles sat in his chair and shrugged and looked up at her and said, "Now you have your whole life, your whole life in front of you. Whatever you want." He looked down at the paperwork on his desk, began reading through memos. "You could go back to school, I don't know. The apartment is yours as long as you like it." He looked up at her again. "Don't feel in a rush to leave, in other words." Then he turned back to his work.

Sarah, having avenged her mother's kidnapping and murder at the hands of an anarchist splinter group, and not sure what else to do, and a little stunned, turned to leave his office.

"Oh, Sarah?" he said before she got to his door. She turned back to him, expectant, though she couldn't have said what she was expecting. To be offered a position, maybe. To be told she had proven herself the equal of any one of the Operatives. To be told how far she had surpassed anyone's small expectations of her and her mechanical arm. And later, she would learn from Mr. Niles himself that he had wanted to offer just that—a position as an Operative, his unfettered praise—but that Oyemi had very clearly said, "No, not Sarah. Operatives are Operatives, Oracles are Oracles, and everyone else is everyone else." He had cajoled, he had begged, and finally he had threatened to leave the Regional Office altogether, and had only been brought back from the brink—why, she would wonder, would he care so much about someone he knew so little about?—by Oyemi's promise that Sarah would come back, that the Oracles had made their prediction, and that he wouldn't lose her. But Sarah wouldn't know any of this for some few years yet, and so when she turned expectantly and he said, "I'm going to need those photos back, please," and shook his head, and said, "Record keeping, filing. You know how it is," and she handed the photos back to him, a troubling feeling of anger and disappointment welled up inside her.

"Don't be a stranger," he said then, as he went back to the work on his desk.

And she left, without so much as saying good-bye, and she stayed away for two days, until she couldn't stay away any longer. On the third day, she stormed back into the travel agency and down the elevator. She shoved her way into Mr. Niles's office, ready to yell, ready to rant, ready to throw her anger and frustration and confusion behind her mechanical fist and maybe tear his office apart, and maybe Mr. Niles himself apart, too, except that when he looked up from the papers on his desk, he looked so happy to see her, and said so casually, as if she hadn't left in the first place, "Oh, good, I was just thinking about you," that she forgot all about how angry she had been.

He handed her a file folder and said, "Take a look at that, tell me what you think. Serious threat? Think Jasmine could pull it off herself, or do we need a team?"

She took the folder and sat in the chair across from his desk and read the report. Together they argued out a plan of attack, the logistics, the fail-safes, and an hour later, Mr. Niles stood up, stretched, said, "Nice work, Sarah." Said, "I'll be in my office if you need anything," and then he patted her gently on the shoulder and he left, and it wasn't until then that she noticed the nameplate on the desk, and then outside the office, the newly stenciled name next to the door—both of which read SARAH O'HARA—and she had been there, for the Regional Office, for Mr. Niles, ever since.

From *The Regional Office Is Under Attack:*
*Tracking the Rise and Fall of an American Institution*

When looking through the literature describing the process by which Oyemi and Mr. Niles gathered together
not only their team of mystically inclined superwomen
but also the famed and dreaded Oracles, who at once
directed the movements and growth of the Regional Office and quite possibly predicted its downfall, one finds
little more than stark conjecture and bland assumptions.
In other words: One is faced with a wasteland of crackpot
theories penned by junior research assistants. Still, the
Oracles proved pivotal in the rise and fall of the Regional
Office, and no serious study of Oyemi and Mr. Niles and
their awesome accomplishments would be complete without some critical consideration of the acquisition of the
Oracles.

Evidence of this process, however, is not easily found.

Clearly, dangers lurk in the shadows and at the edges
for scholars who find themselves stretching beyond tan-
gible and reproducible pieces of evidence, reconstruct-
ing conversations, the physical movements of people long
gone, whenever they presume to obtain an understand-

ing of the thoughts of great and horrible figures from history. Scholarship is scholarship. Art is art. To shoehorn one into the other is to invite confusion and bedevilment, and yet, there are times when one must push forward, must offer a narrative if only because there cannot be a void.

Nature abhors a void.

And so: Oyemi's great-uncle died, money was passed down, and an office in Queens was illegally sublet. Then for six weeks, Oyemi and Mr. Niles sought out their first Oracle.

By whatever means—the reading of auras, probing the young woman's mind, trying to see into her future based on the pattern of freckles on her face, etc., etc.— Oyemi peered at, judged, and found wanting what must have been over five hundred young women in the first six weeks she and Mr. Niles hunted for their Oracle.

An advertisement was not placed, flyers were not posted all over the city, girls did not line up outside the offices of Oyemi and Mr. Niles, though what a lovely image, the line of them circling the block as if each girl were hoping to be cast in some strange and dark Off-Off-Broadway show, or to care for the Banks children before Mary Poppins swooped in and blew them all away.

But no. They walked the city together, Mr. Niles and Oyemi, as Oyemi cast her new mystical glance down dark alleyways, in brightly lit lobbies, at girls on the subway or walking through the Sheep Meadow, or in a coffee shop or in a library or hailing a cab or anywhere at all, really.

Everywhere, in fact. She looked everywhere.

By the end of each day, Oyemi had exhausted herself so completely that Mr. Niles had to carry her home—to conserve the money she had inherited, they had decided to live in the same office they'd rented—where she would fall asleep on the sagging, smoke-stained love seat they had found on the street the day they had moved in. She fell into a heavy sleep no later than six o'clock each evening, out of which she could not wrench herself until nearly ten the next morning.

She lost weight. The dark, unearthly sheen of her skin turned a sickly, lackluster pale green. At night, while she slept, her nose bled, so that she would wake with a face crusted over by her own blood and snot. Her eyes watered and her ears itched and she broke out in hives once or twice a day, and Mr. Niles told her to stop, begged her to stop, worried that she was draining herself looking for whatever or whoever it was she was looking for. But Oyemi would not quit, until finally Mr. Niles told her, "One more time, I will go with you one more time and then I'm done, tomorrow is the last time, and after that, I'm gone, and you can come, too, and we can do some other thing with the money and power, or not, I don't care about any of it, I care about you, but no matter what, this is the last time, because I'm not going to bear witness, not to this, not to the end of you."

The next day, they found Nell.

She was walking out of a Duane Reade.

The procedure, up until that point, had been for Oyemi and Mr. Niles to walk around various neighborhoods and wait for Oyemi to "get a feeling," and then Mr. Niles would approach the woman attached to this feeling and ask her questions—they had written a fake survey on the increased cost of living—with the idea being that Oyemi could then examine the woman unnoticed (despite how un-unnoticeable Oyemi had become), as all of the young woman's attention, all her psychological and emotional defenses, would be trained on Mr. Niles. Oyemi, then, could sneak up behind the mark and close her eyes and proceed however it was she proceeded and then a minute or so later, open her eyes and shake her head and they would move on.

It is safe to assume that Mr. Niles understood little of what was going on and that, to him, the entire procedure was slipshod and inefficient and doomed to failure. So when Oyemi spied Nell stepping out of the store and tapped Mr. Niles on the shoulder and told him, "Her, quick, her," he failed to notice the urgency in her voice, the heat from her hand when she tapped him.

Mr. Niles walked over to the young woman, smiled his charming, useful smile, and asked her if she would mind answering a few questions for his survey. The young woman barely had time to answer "Yes" or "No, thanks," before Oyemi clubbed her on the head from behind, catching her just as she fell.

"Don't just stand there," Oyemi said. "Grab her, quick. We need to get her to the office."

They brought the woman back to their building. Oyemi carried her into her office and laid her on the floor, still unconscious. Mr. Niles searched her purse, found a wallet, and in the wallet found a handful of receipts; a photograph of a little girl, which he tucked into his pocket; and a driver's license, which was how he discovered her name was Nell. He also discovered she was twenty-four years old (two years older than himself at the time) and lived on East Tenth.

It's unclear what Oyemi had done to the girl when she hit Nell over the head, how hard she'd hit her or with what. Regardless, Nell didn't wake for almost three hours, during which time Mr. Niles and Oyemi sat in the front room of their office, Oyemi quietly and expectantly on the couch, and Mr. Niles, unsure what to do or where to sit, pacing around the room.

It is safe to say he became increasingly nervous.

Then Oyemi perked up and looked at the closed office door and said, "She's awake. Finally." Then she rushed into the room, closed and locked the door behind her, and didn't come out.

Let us conjecture that, at this time, Mr. Niles decided to go, to leave, to go where? Anywhere, really, and to seriously consider whether he could ever come back.

When Mr. Niles first met Oyemi, the two of them had been children. Her name hadn't been Oyemi and his name hadn't been Mr. Niles; those were names they adopted to play a game, a prescient game in which they took over the world, or, rather, she took over the world. Oyemi, supreme ruler of the planet Earth, and her butler, Mr. Niles. Well, her butler at first, and then her superpowered butler, and then not a butler at all but her right-hand man, unless she was mad at him for any of a number of reasons that children become mad at each other, and then he was her butler again.

Mr. Niles didn't know what a butler was, so Oyemi pointed him to Alfred, from *Batman*, as a reference and that was who he pretended to be. Mostly, though, Oyemi had an odd sense of humor and thought the idea of a supreme ruler of the planet with a butler named Mr. Niles was funny, and while Mr. Niles didn't always quite understand, he played along anyway.

Then and until his death, he played along anyway.

But knocking a woman unconscious, kidnapping her, that was where the line was drawn, obviously. This is what he must have thought to himself as he walked out of the office, down three flights of stairs, onto the street. What he must have thought to himself as he looked left

and right, looked for signs of having been followed—
even then, Mr. Niles would have been, to some degree,
paranoid—looked for some piece of this world that still
looked familiar as he operated under a new understanding of Oyemi, of this project he had signed up for, of the
life forward he was staring at, and at his not unreasonable decision to leave it behind. But then something—the
sound of Oyemi crying out, perhaps, a deep-welled, anxious, mournful sound in her voice, maybe, or a crash of
glass and brick, or the welling up of some deep-seated
and unfaded and urgent love he had nearly forgotten—
called him back.

Often, it is at this point in the story of the Regional
Office that people ask the question: Was Mr. Niles in
love with Oyemi?

No one knows the definitive answer to this question.
Mr. Niles left no diary or journal, no hoard of love letters he had received from Oyemi, nor letters written but
never sent on his own part. Might he once have loved
Oyemi, might he once have adored her, might she once
have been his first true love, might he have been love-
struck in the third grade, when they first met? Certainly
any of this is possible, and it is possible he continued to
love her, to be in love with her, even after she suffered the
accident that should have killed her but didn't.

The far more interesting question, however, and the
question no one can answer but for oneself, is this: Is love
enough? Was love enough to justify or explain what hap-

pened next and then after that and then after that and then again until the end?

Mr. Niles turned. He rushed back upstairs. By the time he burst back through the office doors, everything had finished, and Oyemi's office door was open, and standing in the doorway was the girl, not Oyemi.

To those who ask, Where is your evidence? Your proof that Mr. Niles harbored doubts, that Mr. Niles left at all, that any of this happened the way you say it happened?

We say: How else could it have happened? Mr. Niles waiting patiently in the front office while Oyemi performed her administrations on the young woman, Nell? Mr. Niles with a newspaper or a magazine, or looking over the business strategic planning report for the Regional Office while whatever horrifying sounds might have been emitted by either Oyemi or the girl, or both of them, filled the small office? Mr. Niles brewing a pot of coffee because maybe it would be a long night ahead?

The authors of this paper leave it up to the reader to decide which scenario is most reasonable.

The girl looked fine, in any case, which surprised Mr. Niles. It is not difficult to imagine what he might have expected outside of fine. Ever since the accident that should have killed Oyemi but instead imbued her with mystical powers, a lot of things had been less and less right with Oyemi. The way she moved. Books could be penned simply about the way Oyemi walked after the accident, the fluid look of her as she stood up from a couch. The way she twitched. Her odd manner of speaking, the faraway look in her eyes, her smile, which grew ever more toothy. She flared her nostrils in the days after her accident, wider and wider. An affinity for raw meats, the nosebleeds, an ability to predict things five minutes into the future. It is not unreasonable, then, to assume that what he expected to find were the remains of the girl, her skin-covering perhaps, crumpled in the corner of Oyemi's office, the rest of her, the whole of her, sucked out of her skin by Oyemi, who would, after having feasted on the girl's immortal soul and whatnot, reemerge as a creature vibrant and shiny-new. At the very least, he must have expected the girl to be frightened or confused or beaten up, that the whites of her eyes would not be white anymore. Yet she looked so untroubled, so at ease, that it took a moment for Mr. Niles to see the one thing that had changed about her, which was her hair, which had been shoulder-length and a dull brown color, and now was entirely gone.

Not shaved, not as if it had been shaved off, but as if it had never been there to begin with.

Mr. Niles said something to her like, "Is everything all right?" but she didn't say anything back. She smiled serenely, not at him but through him, and then made her way to the window, where she stared out at the traffic and the other windows across the street from them.

Oyemi, stumbling out of the office behind Nell, looked the way Niles had maybe expected Nell to look. Scooped out. Pale, sweaty, exhausted, red-eyed. A smell wafted off her that made Mr. Niles self-conscious and uncomfortable. Oyemi struggled to get to a chair and then sat heavily down in it, and then she sighed, and then she smiled.

"Whatever you do, don't call her by her name," she said. "Her former name."

She closed her eyes and let her heavy head fall heavily into her shaking hands.

"She's in. She's agreed to come on board, to be part of our plans," she said.

With great effort, Oyemi pulled her head back up to look at the girl or maybe to look past her. Maybe she was looking at what Nell represented, the future that was even then being laid out before her because of this girl, or maybe she was looking at the same thing the girl was looking at, which seemed to be nothing and everything, and then she let out a long, ragged breath.

"She's the first," Oyemi said. "The first Oracle."

And then she collapsed.

BOOK II

# 27.

Something—electricity, blue magicks?—crackled out of the director's hand, the one that looked like it was covered by another hand, crackled in a way that reached out for Rose, for her face, for her neck. Like, there was this crackling fucking energy shooting out of the glove or hand or whatever and usually when you saw that shit in a movie or on a TV show, you knew, whoa, that crackling blue thing must be hot with some real fucking power, and sure there was some power there, she could feel it, but that wasn't the whole story with that crackling blue energy, she could tell.

That crackling blue energy was a living thing.

It had a hunger she could sense. It had its own goddamn desires. To touch her face, to wrap itself around her pretty neck. Like, the energy was whispering shit into her ear, trying to bring her closer so it could caress her cheek, tickle the sensitive, ticklish parts of her.

It knew all about her.

It was seducing her.

It was mesmerizing and pretty fucking convincing, say what you will about its being the inanimate blue energy of a severed hand.

And it almost grabbed her.

But then training and her own instincts shook through, and she ducked, rolled under the director's swinging arm, rolled out of the reach of the glove and its crackling blue wants, and was up on her feet behind the director.

Then before any more of that weird energy and its hocus-pocus let-me-nibble-your-ear shit could happen, she'd sweep the legs out from under the director, shove him forward, stand on his neck just hard enough and at just the right angle to snap it, and then leave for the rendezvous spot, and somehow, even with the delays, even with all that bullshit in the ventilation shaft and even with having to defeat spinning, twirling robots, she would find the rendezvous (and Henry) before Windsor did and fuck, why the hell not, she would grab Henry roughly by the collar of his shirt and pull him close to her face and whisper, "You guys suck at intel," and then give him a kiss, a real kiss, Jesus, finally a real kiss.

Except that when she swept the director's legs out from under him, he wasn't there to be swept.

He was in the air, flipping up and over her in a long, lazy arc, graceful, like he'd just dismounted the uneven bars.

Where the fuck was the intel on this? That's what Rose wanted to know.

The magicks in the ventilation shaft? All that shit waiting for her outside the director's office? And now this?

"What the fuck?" she said.

And then he kicked her in the face.

# 28.

Rose knew it was a drill, just a field exercise at Assassin Training Camp, but still, she couldn't help but feel nervous. Nervous and sweaty. Although the sweat bit of it had less to do with her nerves and more to do with the uniform—a cotton and polyester blend that didn't breathe for shit.

She looked down at Wendy, twenty feet below her, scouting around, seeking her out. This was going to hurt both of them, what she was about to do, drop down from her perch in that tree and land squarely on Wendy's shoulders, but it was going to hurt Wendy a hell of a lot more. And maybe a few weeks ago, she wouldn't have cared how much it was going to hurt Wendy, would have maybe relished the fact that it was going to hurt Wendy, but today, she felt a little bad about it.

But not bad enough not to do it.

She dropped. She knocked Wendy out cold even before Wendy knew she'd been dropped on.

Next up, Colleen.

It was Henry, she knew. Henry, watching her, watching all of this play out. He was making her nervous.

God, what a spaz.

She meant herself too, of course. She'd gladly admit that she was acting a total spaz, but Jesus. Sixteen- (almost seventeen!) year-old girls were supposed to be spazzes, weren't they? Wasn't that, like, some kind of God-given right?

What was Henry's excuse? That's what she wanted to know. What was his fucking excuse?

Sure, Henry might have been a martial arts expert, a demolitions expert, a hard-ass who pushed and pushed and pushed her and the other girls in their training and was damn good at it, too, but give him a kiss, a simple little kiss, and you totally fucked up his game.

Not that there was any kind of game, not that it wasn't absolutely fucking clear to anyone with half a brain in her head that Henry was totally, madly, absolutely in love with the Woman in Red. But still. A girl can dream, can't she? Not to mention, Windsor was all over that shit, especially now that Emma was off on some other mission, wasn't set to come back until it was time to attack the Regional Office. And if nothing else, it was Rose's responsibility, wasn't it, to make sure Windsor didn't fuck things up for Henry and Emma, even if that meant getting in the way of Windsor by trying to get closer to Henry and, well, Christ. Whatever.

No it didn't make sense.

No she didn't care.

Colleen was close. Rose could sense her. Too close for her to scramble back up the tree and get the drop on her the way she had Wendy. She stripped Wendy of her boots and heaved them high up into the trees. She was going to be pissed. Those were her favorite boots and it was cold out, but Rose couldn't have Wendy waking up and joining Colleen and the others. It was just a field exercise, yes, but it was a competition, too, and Rose wanted to win. For a lot of reasons, she wanted to win.

Still. Those were Wendy's favorite boots.

"I'll come back for them," Rose said. "I'll climb up there and get them for you, I promise," she said.

Then she slipped away, back into the trees.

# 29.

Four months ago, when she first arrived at the compound, she had been expecting things to be different.

She had been expecting it to be like *The Karate Kid,* maybe. Where she would be taken in by a lovable if befuddled and frail old man, who would, at a crucial point, reveal himself to be neither of those—befuddled, frail—but instead a subtle but powerful fighting machine and mentor, who would ultimately provide the love and wisdom of an otherwise absent parent. She would spend weeks performing a number of mundane, idiotic, useless tasks—sweeping the already swept floor, cleaning the pristine toilet bowl, making fried-egg sandwiches, which he would then refuse to eat ("I'm allergic")—which would reveal themselves to be mysterious but powerful kung fu poses. Sweeping the Floor, Cleaning the Toilet, Frying the Egg.

Or if not that, then like *An Officer and a Gentleman,* but without the gentleman bit. Her pitted against the hard-ass drill sergeant. She'd be the spitfire who constantly mouthed off and who would ultimately reveal herself to be pitted against her inner demons, not the drill sergeant at all, who would prove herself foolhardy but full of bravado, and in the process develop a bond with her fellow trainees, becoming in their eyes an example of what not to do, of how not to act, but also, in the end, by the end of boot camp or whatever this place was, becoming for them, also, an example of a hard battle fought and won with difficulty, tenacity, and through her indomitable spirit and unfathomable skill.

Hell. She would have taken *The Parent Trap*, even. Warring factions of girls at summer camp who were so similar in nature and looks, strengths and weaknesses, all of them hemmed in by a male-dominated world that strove to limit their power and strength, that their first instinct was to undermine the force they would have become if only they worked together, but finally they would be brought together by the threat of some other Big Bad outside of themselves—maybe something more threatening than a really bad thunderstorm, and more like a drug-dealing camp counselor or something, but whatever.

That.

She would have been happy to have experienced that upon her arrival at the compound.

What she hadn't expected, though, and what she couldn't quite handle, was the sense of overwhelming indifference that had been waiting for her when she arrived.

She had been the last girl recruited and no one had been expecting her and they didn't seem to care that she was there.

But then somebody must've cared, somebody must've wanted her since they'd come to her, had broken into her mother's house, had recruited her to the team.

The Woman in Red—her name was Emma but for a while Rose could only think of her as the Woman in Red—apologized for how long it had taken for her to pick Rose up, as if Rose had been waiting for someone to come get her at the bus station or the airport, bags in hand. She had only learned about Rose very recently, she explained. The Oracles, she said. Her weak connection to them, not to mention the physical distance and all the protective charms Oyemi had put in place, she said. All of it made the system, which was already imperfect and glitchy, practically impossible to manage. It was like driving at night through heavy fog with nothing but more heavy fog as your headlights, she told Rose.

"If you know what I mean," the Woman in Red said.

Rose had no idea what she meant or what she was talking about, but at the time, she didn't care. She just nodded and smiled. She knew things were about to change, her life was about to change, and she didn't want to risk fucking that up by asking questions.

"There's not a lot of time left," Emma said with a sad smile. Time for what, Rose didn't ask. "But you'll do splendid. I just know you will." Splendid at what, Rose again didn't ask.

Then, in Rose's mother's living room, Emma introduced her to Henry, formally introduced them. "This is Henry," she said. "Henry, this is Rose," she said. She said all of this as if Rose and Henry had never met, hadn't just moments ago altercated the way they had altercated, then kissed the way they had kissed.

"Henry's in charge of training and orientation," the Woman in Red said. "He'll take good care of you, I know." Then she smiled and said to Henry, "Won't you, Henry?" She said this in the way that Rose's mother would tell her, Best behavior, Rose, whenever they went to church, which was hardly ever, which was why she never knew how to behave at church, which was why she always failed the best-behavior test, and she wondered if Henry would do the same.

She hoped he might.

"She's in good hands," Henry said, and then shook his head and said, "You know what I mean."

"Quite," Emma said. Then she took Rose's hand again and they whisked her off.

# 30.

Rose saw the director's kick coming, or Spidey-sensed it. She didn't like to spend too much time trying to figure out what was training, what was mystical properties of herself, and anyway, did it even matter? She was moving, that was the point, moving backward even as his foot connected (with her chin instead of her nose, and another half second later, she would have back-bended clean out of the way, but whatever). She was thrown back into her own flip but not as hard as she could have been thrown, and jarred by this kick—way more than she would have expected to be by this overweight, soft-chinned desk jockey—but not so jarred she couldn't keep her wits about her enough to turn in the air and land on her feet.

"Do you like it?" he asked, holding the hand within a hand in front of his face, looking at it as if he were a little surprised, too, at how badass the glove was turning out to be. Then he flipped his wrist at her, like he was throwing an imaginary Frisbee to her, and blue bolts shot out of the fingertips.

She jumped out of the way. Just.

"It was a gift, you know. From the woman who sent you," he said.

So he knew, she thought. Knew who'd sent her, probably knew

they were coming for him, had known for how long? Days? Weeks? The whole fucking time?

Henry and Emma were going to get a fucking earful.

"Funny she didn't warn you about it," he said. "Maybe she forgot I had it." A flick of his wrist, a bolt of lightning. "Maybe she forgot about me altogether. What was it? Did one of the Oracles tell her? Remind her I was here? Is that why they've been so quiet? They've known all along and she's been waiting? Biding her time?"

She rolled herself to his desk, not sure what she would find there to help her defeat a crazed lunatic who had been waiting for her and who had a magical, all-powerful glove made out of someone else's hand and that gave him superpowers, but it beat sitting around dodging bolts of lightning.

"The Hand of Raines," he said as he arced more lightning bolts at her, scorching the desk and the air around her. "Maybe you've heard of it. Maybe not. Top secret, you know. When Gemini finally destroyed the warlock Harold Raines, all that was left was his right hand." He stopped and looked at the glove and then craned his neck to see if he could see Rose hiding behind his desk. "Oyemi magicked it—who knows how—turned it into a glove." He clenched the fist and then closed his eyes and then, for a moment, for two moments, floated inches off the floor. Then he dropped and opened his eyes and nodded his head. "I was supposed to test it out with her, you know. The two of us, together. Oyemi and me. Like always."

Rose crouched and tested the weight of the desk and then sprung up, lifting the desk up (use your legs, not your back) and flipping it log-roll style right at the director's head. He karate-chopped it, the way you karate-chop something in a cartoon, the way that would never really work in real life, but that gloved hand just sizzled through wood, solid oak or cherry, she didn't know, but a heavy fucker of a desk, she knew that much. The desk sliced into two pieces, fell harmlessly to the floor on either side of the director, and now she didn't have any good cover.

Fuck.

"But, you know how it goes," he said. "Or maybe you don't." He took a step toward her and then another. Unhurried. Unconcerned.

"She got so busy and then she had her Oracles and then they all moved out of the city, her and her Oracles and a few others she brought with her to her compound in the Catskills." He stopped and shook his head and sighed. Then he looked right at Rose, looked at her as if they were at a Starbucks, catching up over a latte, looked in her eye and gave her half a smile and said, "I didn't even know where it was for the first six months she was out there."

None of this made any sense to Rose but she didn't care all that much, either. All she could figure was that maybe he thought someone else had sent her, which, fine, what did she care. All that mattered was getting herself out of this, and if he wanted to go on and on about the woman who gave him this glove instead of using the glove and then writing a long, emotional blog post about it, fine with her.

For every step he took forward, she took one back, thinking that this would buy her a little time, that he wouldn't really notice anyway. He was standing between her and the door, but if worse came to worst, she could make her own door, get out of the immediate vicinity of this loon, and open the fight up, give herself breathing room, space to work, to improvise. This office was just too cramped.

Step, step. Step, step.

"So, fine, I understand, we were both busy," he said. "We were running the Regional Office, I get that, but"—he shook his head—"there was something else, too, I don't know, some distance between us. You know? Not that there wasn't. Not that we didn't." He paused. He sighed. "We've both changed, haven't we? But this, this seemed more than just normal growing apart." He had been walking toward her but not looking at her, had been looking at his hands or his feet, had been distracted by his own story, his own memories, but then he looked at her and noticed where he was, what he was supposed to be doing, what she had been doing. "No, no, no. Stop. Stop, just. Don't be an idiot. Don't think I'm an idiot."

"A distance," she said. "I've had that, like, with my best friends from school," she said.

"Don't patronize me," he said, and then he charged at her.

She kicked him, aiming for his nuts because, well, desperate times, etc., but he grabbed her foot, with the blue-crackling magical fire-hand, grabbed her foot and threw her up and over and God that burned, more than she could have imagined a burning sensation burning, and she flipped ass over head, and she thought, briefly, everything now flitting through her mind so damn briefly, about kids she remembered from when she was a kid. Kids with their dads at the beach or at the one pool in her shitty hometown, whose fathers would throw them high into the air, make them do these spectacular flips and falls off knees or shoulders or chests, and how jealous she had been watching those kids fly into the air and land graceless in the water, splashing and giggling and asking for more, for again, and how she wished she had some water right below her to land gracelessly into, instead of the cold, marble floor of the director's office, or worse yet, his waiting arms—how the hell did he move under her so damn quick? She made an adjustment, which she knew was going to hurt, was going to hurt more than just a little, but less than if she let him catch her however he wanted. She wrenched control of herself midair and aimed herself at the director's head, her fist outstretched, one leg stretched back, the other leg knee up, her other fist cocked and at the ready at her hip, like she was Supergirl, flying off to save the day, but aimed right at the director's head knowing full well that he would grab that fist, what else could he do, grab it with the Hand of Pains or whatever he'd called his glove, and he did and it burned—fuck it burned—but he could only grab one arm at a time, right?

No matter what else the glove could do, it couldn't grab more than one part of her at a time.

So while he had her by her wrist, burning the shit out of it, and while the burning pain leapt up her wrist and her arm, like it was shimmying up through her veins, heading, she was sure of it, toward her head and her heart, she punched him good on the bridge of his nose with her other fist, punched him as hard as she could punch, which was pretty fucking hard, she knew, having once punched an old VW Beetle onto its side after a particularly unfun afternoon of Assassin Training Camp. A VW Beetle she had assumed was Windsor's—because of course Windsor would drive a fucking canary-yellow classic Bug—except it wasn't hers, it wasn't any of the girls' at camp, but regardless: Her punch was a mighty fucking punch.

With that mighty fucking punch, then, she knocked this guy on the bridge of his nose, came down on him like her fist was the Hammer of Thor.

The whole of him shuddered. His legs creaked. The gloved hand let go of her arm, and she fell, and he sat down hard on his ass.

Finally. Thank God. At least a punch worked, at least something.

She sagged down to the floor herself and closed her eyes a second, just a second. That crackling blue light was no joke, man. Wisps of smoke curled up off her arms and her shoulders; she could smell them. She took deep breaths. She willed her body to stitch itself back in place as best it could. She stood herself up and opened her eyes again only just in time to see the director's gloved fist, or fisted fist, whatever, swinging right for her own face. She moved left. He clipped her ear, singed her hair, melted the earring she was wearing to her earlobe. She spun and kicked at him and maybe that punch had shuddered him enough to throw his head off play because he wasn't soaring through the air this time and her boot connected with his gut. He oofed and flew backward across the room and smashed into the bookshelf against the far wall, and they swayed, and books fell from the shelves, and the shelves swayed some more and she was waiting, holding her breath, waiting for them to crash down on him, do her dirty work for her, or at least slow him down enough that she could do her own damn dirty work just a little easier, but the shelves settled and held and the director pulled himself back up.

And no more close-quarters hand-to-hand combat for him, no sir.

He flipped his wrist and lightning flashed.

# 31.

Rose packed her bag—bag, not bags, despite her loud protests—
and packed it quickly. No one was home, but she didn't care—she
didn't think she cared—about saying good-bye. The Woman in
Red and Henry waited for her in the kitchen. The three guys who'd
ambushed her were out back smoking. With the Woman in Red in
the house, everything looked impossibly dingier and grayer than
ever before and all Rose wanted to do was leave.

After leaving her house, she had half-expected there to be a
helicopter waiting for them but was too enthralled with the
Woman in Red, with the idea of leaving behind her former self, to
be disappointed that what they had waiting for them was, in fact, a
rental car, an off-white Ford Taurus. She did her best to be not too
disappointed again when where they whisked her off to turned
out to be an abandoned office park just outside of Durham, and
again when she discovered that not only were there other girls
there, girls not much different from herself, but they had been
here for months already, six girls, an even bunch, paired up as
roommates, as training buddies, except for Rose, odd man out,
who had a room all to herself. "Lucky you," Henry said, as if he
meant it.

There were two of everything in the room—two beds stuck

out of opposite walls that could double as uncomfortable-looking couches, two sinks attached to the same wall on opposite sides of the door, two dressers and two closets next to those. In one of the dressers there were clothes for her, all the same black V-neck T-shirts, the same metal-gray cargo pants.

"Those are for training," he told her. "You'll get a uniform soon enough, and then when you're not training, you can wear whatever you like."

She didn't have much else to wear. The Woman in Red hadn't given her much time to pack. All she had with her, other than the clothes she'd been wearing when they'd come for her, was a yellow sundress—her favorite, though here, now, it seemed wildly out of place—and a pair of shorts and a T-shirt, her flip-flops, and a pair of wedge sandals.

Christ, what a spaz.

She pretended to look around the room. Henry handed her a folder.

It was strange being alone with him. She had been alone with him for an entire day, practically, and then he'd been truly a stranger, but that hadn't felt strange at all. That had felt natural, and she wondered if he had been putting on some kind of act or if he had felt that, too. Later he would tell her, Both, and she would believe him. But now that she'd kissed him, and that he'd kissed her back, it seemed that neither of them knew what to do but to stand awkwardly in her small dorm room and talk about anything but what had happened before. He was focused on trying to make her feel special about the fact that she didn't have a room-mate and that she'd come there late, and she was focused on trying to figure out how to say something to him about that kiss, about the spur-of-the-moment quality of it, about the first-time-ever quality of it, and she was trying to figure out how to apologize for having done it but also make it clear that she wasn't exactly sorry that it had happened and that she wouldn't be opposed to a second, less spontaneous go-around, and how old was he anyway, and did he make it part of his business to kiss people almost immediately after jumping them and trying to strangle them to death, or was it just her, and sorry, too, about how she'd kicked him in the ribs all those times.

It was all too much, the things she wanted to say, and while she knew now the jumping and the strangling had all been part of some plan, some kind of test, it had scared the shit out of her and she felt torn between these two feelings—scared shitless by this guy and urgently attracted to him—and she felt that saying something, saying anything, might help even all of this out, but where did she start?

So. He handed her a folder and she took it and opened it and pretended to read it. Inside was a set of schedules and rules and guidelines. They were straightforward and basic but he went over them anyway, pointed out breakfast and lunch and dinner. Lights out at ten o'clock.

"Usually," he said, "everyone's up by five thirty for a quick five-mile run together, but . . ." He paused, ran his hand through his hair. "Considering how much catching up you're going to have to do, uh, we're going to have to skip the run. And the midmorning yoga class." He said this as if he felt a little sorry for her, as if she were missing out on something, which, she would realize later, she was, missing out. Not on the yoga class. Not on the morning run.

Missing out on the team, on being a part of the team.

Then he said, "Well. Okay. That's the nickel tour." He said this as if it were time for him to leave her to herself, to organize her room, which didn't need organizing, or gather her thoughts, which he must have known wouldn't have been gathered any time soon. But then he didn't leave. He stood there. She stood there. She rocked herself forward. She remembered to say, "Thanks. For the tour."

He rocked himself back, just slightly back. "Training starts tomorrow," he said. "You might notice people packing things away," he said. "We're moving into phase two and we're shutting down this specific operation, and so we're all a little distracted," he said. "Don't take it personally," he said. "We're really glad you're here." He said this, Rose knew, to make her feel better. She pretended, for his sake and for hers, that it worked.

She waited. He waited. Then he said, "About before," and that was all she needed, it seemed, before she rushed into her own, I know, I know, I'm totally, well, not sorry, sorry isn't, anyway, I'm just, I just wanted you, I didn't want you to think, and she moved closer, and he moved farther back until he had the door open and had stepped out of the room, had crossed the threshold to the other side, and then he interrupted her.

"Look, Rose," he said. "I just needed to tell you. I'm kind of in charge here. I mean, Emma and I. We're in charge here. In charge of you and the others and your training and it's not like we're back in your hometown, right? Driving around checking out dead squirrels, right? It's not like that here. So, about before, that's not how it's like here, is what I'm trying to tell you."

"Oh," Rose said, feeling less and less sorry for all those kicks. "Sure. I get it."

"Do you understand?"

"I got it," she said. "I just said how I got it."

"Good."

"Better than good," she said. "Great. Perfect."

"It'll just make things easier."

"I like easier," she said, and then she closed the door on his face.

# 32.

Rose hid herself away behind a fallen log, some overhanging trees. If she squinted, she could barely make out Wendy's boots hanging from a tree branch in the distance. She listened for the sound of Colleen finding Wendy, though she knew Colleen wouldn't make such a blatant mistake unless she was trying to trick Rose somehow. Rose had left three trails behind her. An obvious trail that Colleen would know was not the real trail but was a dummy trail with a booby trap set along some part of it, and a second, much less obvious, almost invisible trail that Colleen would assume was the real trail, but which was also a dummy trail with a booby trap set along some part of it, and a third untrace-able trail, Rose was sure of it, that, just for shits and giggles, had a booby trap set along some part of it, too. The funny thing about that invisible trail was that if Colleen were to find and follow it, which she couldn't, she would be able to follow it to a spot in the woods that was just out of view of the booby-trapped spots of the other two trails but where Rose could wait and watch for Colleen to come down one path or the other.

Rose hoped that Colleen would come down the obviously false trail, not because she didn't think Colleen would be smart enough to know it was obviously false, but because she might outthink

herself and decide the obviously fake trail was made obviously
fake because it wasn't fake at all, but also because the booby trap
at the end of that trail wasn't quite as harsh as the booby trap
down the other, almost invisible fake trail she'd left, and she liked
Colleen, who was maybe a bit too type A but who meant well and
who had, a couple of weeks ago, tried to keep Rose from failing
out of superpowered-assassin school.

After nearly a month, the training had not been going well.
The martial arts instructor—not, to her disappointment, Henry—
spent hour after hour sweeping her feet out from under her and
throwing her over his shoulder and trying to explain to her poses
and moves and countermoves that she didn't understand at all
and whose names she couldn't remember. Lost Monkey, Wooden
Monkey, the Broken Faucet. None of those meant the first goddamn thing to her.

She was a disaster at languages and couldn't master even the
simple phrases she was asked to learn—Where is the gun hidden,
How do I get to the basement level of this building—and she was
fairly confident that if she were dropped into the wilds of Alaska
or some other equally feral place with nothing but a rope and a
hunting knife, she could survive there for a sum total of five minutes for all that she'd learned in survival training. The one thing
she could do, thanks more to her cousins and uncles who were
minor-league pyromaniacs and owned more empty land than was
good for them, was, in the parlance of her demolitions instructor,
blow shit up, if only basic shit and in the crudest and most elemen-
tal of ways.

She trained all day, before breakfast and through lunch and

then again after dinner, but she wasn't making progress, wasn't making any progress at all, it seemed, but not because she couldn't learn this shit. She was good at learning but generally didn't care enough about the shit she was supposed to learn in school—diagramming a sentence, proving geometrical shapes that had long ago been proved (of course it was a triangle, why in the fuck did she need to prove to anyone, let alone herself, that that was a triangle)—but here she was faced with truly interesting shit to learn and she'd hit a wall.

She told herself she didn't know why, but she knew why.

She was lonely, and she didn't like it here.

She'd met the other girls, if briefly. They nodded at her and smiled at her and shook her hand, firmly, too firmly, and welcomed her aboard, and maybe they gave each other looks, We do not have time for this bitch looks, or maybe that was her imagination. All of this happened a week after she arrived and in the five minutes in between when they had to leave for another extended field exercise and she had to leave for another unsuccessful martial arts training session, and after that, she saw them in passing, sometimes in the bathrooms, or in the hallway, usually as a group that seemed to have no room for one more. They were beautiful and older than her and looked very much like a unit, like a complete whole that functioned perfectly, thank you very much, without her.

Once, she ran into one of them on her own, the girl named Colleen, who often wore pink shorts and a yellow tank top and had a boyish haircut that made her look French, who, when she had first seen her, Rose had pegged as potential arch-nemesis material.

Rose imagined her, *Mean Girls*–style, at the head of the posse of other girls, terrorizing and torturing and humiliating newcomers, who would have them all throw their worst at Rose, only for Rose to stand strong against their onslaught, to show first through her unwillingness to back down and then through her unfathomable skill that she was a natural leader, that she was the star of this moment, but Colleen hadn't yet paid a lick of attention to her.

Rose ran into her in the weapons training module. Her weapons instructor had set up extra training time for her because she couldn't shoot for shit, which made no sense, none at all. Rose had grown up around hunting rifles, and the occasional crossbow (her uncle Artie), and while she'd never taken to hunting herself, she'd always been a decent shot and had never shied away from guns. But every time she held a sidearm, a rifle, a shotgun, a semiautomatic in front of her weapons instructor, she choked. She just, she didn't know, flinched, pulled left, thought too much about what she was doing. And out of the corner of her eye she could see the weapons specialist roll his eyes. She could sense him mentally counting down the seconds until lunch.

It was her time in the module but Colleen was in there already, shooting away. Colleen didn't seem to have noticed her coming in, didn't look like she would finish any time soon, but Rose didn't care, not really, and she was going to offer to let Colleen work with her, if she wanted, because it would have been nice to have the company, nice to talk to someone who wasn't yelling at her for forgetting the Chinese character for "dead in the bathroom stall," but as soon as Colleen saw Rose waiting outside, she shut her module down and packed her things and left, with barely a nod as she walked by.

The short of it was this: Rose was lonely, and it was affecting her work, and soon they were going to kick her out of assassin school, she knew it, and it was completely fucking stupid of her.

So she didn't have friends. So she hadn't seen the Woman in Red since the day she was brought here. So Henry turned and walked the other way whenever she saw him. So what? So what if the story the Woman in Red had told her had prepared Rose for something very different from all of this, had included words like *leader* and *hero* and *saving the world* and *fighting the Good Fight*?

She was a silly little girl, she told herself. She was a silly little girl and she should just toughen up. She should toughen up and stop thinking about home and her momma and daddy and sister, mean old Gina and dumb old Patty. She should stop missing the way she had thought of herself when the Woman in Red first pulled her aside, first told her all about what she could become.

She should stop all of this, but she couldn't.

# 33.

Rose was sitting on her bed thinking about this—again—when someone knocked on the door of her room. The entire time she'd been at this school, this place, no one had knocked on her door.

"Who is it?" Rose asked, hopeful and suspicious all at once. She didn't honestly care who it was, except in the back of her mind she did worry it might be someone come to make her go back home.

Colleen opened the door and poked her head inside and said, "Decent?"

"I guess," Rose said, and then, feeling a little put off by this girl, who had not only opened her door but who was now standing inside the room without an invitation, she said, "I guess they don't teach you to knock first in assassin school."

"I did knock," Colleen said.

"Well, I guess they don't teach you to wait for the hostess to invite you in at, oh, fuck it," Rose said. "What do you want?" She didn't mean to sound this way, pissy and upset and on the verge of tears, real fucking tears, but she couldn't help herself. Someone had come to see her in her room for the first time in nearly five weeks and she was fucking the whole thing sideways, she could tell, and she couldn't stop herself. "I thought I locked the door. What, did you just break into my dorm room?"

"The doors don't lock," Colleen said. "House rules."

"My bad. I must have misplaced my assassin school handbook."

"That's not what this is, you know."

"Whatever. They're going to kick me out anyway. Tomorrow maybe."

"Maybe," Colleen said. "It's possible. You wouldn't be the first." Rose, who had been looking at the dirt under her fingernails, looked up. "There were twenty to start," Colleen said when she knew she had Rose's attention. "In fact, it's kind of amazing that they brought you here at all. As far along as we are, that is."

"Yeah, it's been a fucking blast. I'm sure they're as happy about it as I am."

"Well. Maybe," Colleen said. "Look. I know we're not friends and you probably don't care what I think, but you're overthinking it. I've been watching you. You're trying too hard. You've got natural ability, or they wouldn't have brought you here. You've got it inside you but you're not letting it out and soon, you're right, soon they're going to send you home. If they don't think you can cut it, they're going to send you back. Soon, like, maybe tomorrow."

Rose turned to look away. Colleen opened the door again. Rose stood up and sighed and said, "You're right." Then she said, "We're not friends and I don't care what you think. So, thanks."

Colleen smiled. "Stick around and we will be friends. Trust me."

And then she left before Rose could say, "Doubt it," so she yelled it as loud as she could at the closed door.

Rose decided she'd be long gone before either of those could happen. Becoming friends with Colleen or being kicked out.

She knew, she could tell by the way they looked at her—her instructors, everyone—that maybe she'd been holding on by a thread but that that thread had snapped and any minute someone—that fucker Henry—was going to show up at her door and tell her to pack her things and then take her back home. So. That night, she packed her backpack and left her room. She'd never tried to leave her room after lights-out before, which was weird since she'd been sneaking out of her momma's house every night for the past three years, her mom's Pall Malls stuffed into her shorts, the whole shitty town her playground, though mostly she just walked around the quiet, gaslit downtown and smoked cigarettes and kicked rocks and enjoyed not being at home.

The hallway outside her room was dark and quiet. She assumed there would be video cameras monitoring the compound at night, but she figured that no one would be monitoring them actively. As she moved out of the wing of the building that contained the dorm rooms she realized that there might be guards standing at the gate. She hesitated, considered going back to her room, figuring out an actual plan, but she'd made her decision, and she'd have to either sneak past the guards or talk her way past them.

There weren't many men she couldn't talk her way around.

When she reached the guards, she didn't have to sneak past them or talk her way around them. They—two of them—were crumpled on the floor, unconscious (or dead), a trickle of blood running down the forehead of one, and at the sight of them, Rose stopped.

She moved to the guards, to see if they were alive, but then she saw the security monitor behind the desk, showing screen after screen of television snow, and she went there instead. It took her less than a minute to find and remove the device that was interfering with the signal. She shifted the screens from one wing and training room to another. The dorm rooms, too, including her own. The cameras were everywhere apparently. The thought made her shudder. But she didn't see anyone. In fact, she didn't see anyone at all. The girls' rooms showed screen after screen of empty rooms. Beds unmade, rooms left in disarray. They'd been taken. Each and every one of them had been taken, wasn't anywhere inside the buildings. Someone had invaded the compound, had disabled the guards, had abducted the trainees, had done all of this making hardly a sound.

They had done all of this and had left her behind.

Son of a bitch, she thought.

Even the fucking bad guys, whoever they are, don't know I'm here. Or maybe they knew and just didn't give a shit because of how much I suck. God fucking damn it, she thought.

She kicked the security desk hard enough to punch a hole through it with her foot.

Then she grabbed her backpack and stormed out of the compound and went looking for the assholes who had left her behind.

It wasn't an easy trail to pick up and follow, but she found it anyway and followed it almost ten miles. By the time she found the camp, it was after four in the morning.

She spotted three guards standing outside a large tent, and then another guard standing outside a smaller tent ten yards farther back. The large tent must have held the girls. She didn't know what was inside the smaller tent, but at the moment she didn't care. Then a fifth guard came strolling into the camp light.

They spoke, quickly and quietly. The boss was almost ready. The girls were secured. The truck was on its way. Fifteen, twenty minutes tops. Everything was moving on schedule, according to plan.

Only after the fact did she realize they were speaking Russian. Well, fuck. She could speak Russian!

Rose looked behind her at the path she'd taken to get here, considered how long it would be before she could get back to the compound; find Henry, or anyone else; and bring that person, or whatever army she could muster, back to the campsite. Then she thought of what she'd packed with her. Her dress. A couple of language books. Her wedge sandals. A clicker pen she'd stolen from one of the near-empty offices. No weapons. No gear.

It shouldn't have been left to her. Risking herself for these girls who hardly knew her, who could barely make the effort to smile at her anymore. This job should have been the job of someone else. Anyone else.

She sighed. She took a deep breath. Silently, she crept forward.

# 34.

The director's office had seemed a lot bigger to Rose before he'd started shooting lightning bolts at her. Although the lightning bolts weren't as bad as they could have been.

Not to say they weren't bad. Not to say they didn't singe and burn. Not to say they didn't hurt like hell.

Just to say: They should've killed her, but they didn't.

For one, she was quick. They barely grazed her—her calf, her shoulder, her boot—as she tumbled around trying to get herself closer to the director. Closer, that was where he had seemed most vulnerable.

And for two, she was protected. Of course she was protected. Emma and Henry, they wouldn't have sent her on a suicide mission. Or, sure, maybe they would have sent her on a suicide mission, but they wouldn't have done so without offering her some amount of protection.

They were assholes, but the kind of assholes who wanted to win this thing.

So. Runes, spells, counterspells. A little extra help in case her innate superstrength and superspeed and all the training they'd given her wasn't quite enough. Not that she believed in it. The magicks, that is. Not that she didn't believe in it, either. If there were women with superpowers and Oracles who could predict the future and a woman in a place called the Regional Office with a mechanical arm that looked like just any other arm, why couldn't there be magicks and spells and runes? Just that they sprung this voodoo on her right before she left and for all she knew, someone back at base could have lit a Virgen de Guadalupe candle for her, too. Not to mention that the way she imagined it, when they cast these spells over her it would have felt like a shimmery dome, except, really, it was like nothing had happened. She had expected it to be like that game kids play where they crack an imaginary egg over your head and it feels real, like egg yolk is really dribbling down your face, but she didn't get even that. Just, "So when are they going to cast these protective countermeasures?" and, "They already did. You're good to go."

Still. They weren't doing nothing.

Not to mention this polyester-blend bullshit they called her assault uniform. Sure, it didn't fit her right—too tight on the calves, because not everyone had the calves and ankles of a fucking gazelle like Windsor did, and too loose in her chest, because, well, she was seventeen (eighteen in two weeks) for Christ's sake, and not the most developed seventeen-year-old—and it didn't breathe at all, like, as soon as she put it on, she was cooking inside it, sweat dripping down her back and into her fucking panties, but as a flame and lightning and bullet and, who knows, a dragon-breath deterrent, it had its strong points.

But it didn't much matter—outside of keeping her alive—because she didn't know how long all this shit would stand up to the guy with the glove that had once been a hand, and the director wasn't letting her get close. He let loose with a barrage of lightning bolts and a whooshing of gale-force winds, and she wondered if all this glove could do was X-Men Storm-style shenanigans, or if there were more deadly uses that the director just wasn't smart enough or skilled enough to have figured out yet.

She also wondered what the hell happened if you cut that shit off his hand.

Like, would he be consumed by the blue flame of the glove's power latching on to the closest warm body as that power was released from the glove itself?

Or would he just be in a lot of fucking pain because she'd cut off his hand?

Was it even attached to him or was he just kind of wearing it?

Either way, it was bound to be a better situation than one in which he still had the glove and his hand.

Normally, the thought of cutting off his hand wouldn't have crossed her mind. Not like she was carrying a couple of ancient Japanese swords with her. They were all expected to wade into this fray weaponless—well, *they* were the weapons, right?—that was what all that training had been about. Well. Training had also been about the use of all the various weapons one could use—rifles, pistols, silencers, brass knuckles, swords, knives, garroting wires. The usual. But still, their whole philosophy being: Train the person to be a weapon and they won't need to carry extra weapons with them, with a secondary philosophy in: Don't be above using whatever potential weapon might be at hand if you want. And she'd seen it—when the bookshelf began rocking—she'd noticed an ornamental kind of sword on a stand on the very top shelf. It looked like some Ren Faire knockoff, but any thinnish piece of metal with enough of a blade coupled with the power of her mighty fucking punch should do the trick.

Let's be honest: If she couldn't cut a sword—even the cheapest of swords—clean through a guy's wrist, she should just turn in her Trained Assassin Badge and Assassin Gear and open up a quilting shoppe.

Tired of this tumbling-around bullshit and with the beginnings of an idea for a plan in mind, she charged right at him, hoping to get close enough to him to a) get by him and to the sword, and then b) cut off his fucking hand.

He lit into her with some fierce blue crackling power shit. She spun into and then out of it and stumbled straight into him, tripping on half a desk drawer on her way. She grabbed for him as she fell forward, snagged the cuff of the glove—the wrist of the former hand?—and then, falling, falling, she yanked it clean off.

# 35.

Rose crept for a hundred or so feet toward the camp where they were holding the girls, then paused long enough to pick up a medium-sized branch and throw it in a high arc over the heads of the guards and over the large tent, waiting for it to crash into something on the other side, grab the guards' attention just long enough so that she could skitter across the flat, bright expanse separating her from the guards and the tent.

She had three of them off their feet and flat on their backs— the Spindletop move—before the fourth knew she was even there. He lunged, she slipped through his lunge—that one was Thread the Needle—caught him in his solar plexus with her knee as she passed by him, an afterthought really, then, pivoting, threw her weight, in the form of her elbow, onto his back, heard the cough, the whoof escape his mouth, but heard, too, the charge coming from her blind side, shifted her weight right, spun low—the Revolving Door (Crouching)—and swept the fifth guard off his feet, heard the action of a semiautomatic, from behind her again (next time, she would make sure there weren't so many different angles to attack her from), and without thinking performed a zigzagging series of back handsprings, aerials, and flips, suddenly so fast, so much faster than she thought she could be, that when she stopped and realized she was standing just inches away from the guard with the gun, she swooned a little from the head rush, but not so much she couldn't grab the rifle by its butt and shove it hard into the guy's nose and then take it from him.

She spun around with the rifle ready to fire some too-close-for-comfort warning shots at the others, but they were gone.

Well.

Two of them were gone, the other three were on the ground, breathing but knocked out. The last one, the one with the now-broken nose and no longer the rifle in his hands, stood up behind her, his right hand cupping the blood coming out of his nose, his left hand raised as if he were giving up, but she couldn't trust him, Rose decided, so she brained him again with the butt of the rifle.

All in all, she figured it'd taken her five minutes.

She looked around the campsite. Looked at the four men knocked out and on the ground at her feet. She looked at the rifle in her hands.

Then she fainted.

# 36.

It had been a test, of course. Everything with these people was all about tests. Project-based learning, the other girls told her. All the rage in Europe.

"How did they know?" Rose asked. "How did they know I'd try to leave tonight?"

Colleen shrugged. "They know," she said. "They know just about everything."

She had passed, of course. With flying colors, in fact. Better than anyone had expected, in fact. When she came to, Colleen had been there, picking pine needles and dirt from her hair. "Don't worry," Colleen had said. "They don't deduct points for fainting at the end." Then she smiled and then she laughed and explained the test, the fact that they were given strict orders to keep their distance until she passed, that for whatever ineffable Emma reason, this had been all part of Rose's training.

"I mean," Colleen said, "we all had to pass this test, but we did it as a team and with more training under our belts. None of us had to do what you just did, all alone."

Then Emma and Henry stepped into view and Emma helped Rose to her feet and told her how impressed she'd been, and for a long time, the whole thing made Rose so fucking mad that she could barely speak. Even when she could speak and she could smile at it and laugh it off and pretend that none of it bothered her, the thought of the whole thing pissed her off all over again whenever it came up.

But now. Now she was part of the team. She was an integral part of the team. She knew fuck-all about what they were going to be doing as a team, but that could wait. She didn't care about that now that she was a piece of a whole, and not just any whole, but a superpowered, kick-ass, girl-team whole. And now, all she cared about was which fake trail Colleen came down and how awesome it was going to be that she beat them.

Except, Colleen should have found at least one of the trails by now. First Wendy and then one of the trails, maybe both of the trails, but certainly not all three of the trails. But where was she?

Rose's instinct was to rabbit, but she tamped that down. Her trails, her booby traps, were good, very good. So good, in fact, that she wished it was Henry on her trail and not Colleen. And then she would watch him as the net tripped him up and yanked him into the trees overhead or as the trip wire loosed the branches and covering below his feet, sent him falling into the deep ditch she'd found and made deeper earlier that morning. Then she would climb up or down and help get him free, or maybe, if he fell into the ditch, she would just stay down there with him. She wouldn't lord it over him all triumphantly because that seemed unbecoming, even to her, but she would make him admit to her that she'd done good, better than he'd have expected, that she'd gotten to him. Once he'd admitted all of that, she'd admit that he'd gotten to her. She'd hit him, gently but firmly in the shoulder or the chest, and call him a dumbass, tell him his stupid fucking plan to stay away from her didn't work, that all it had done was make her think about him more, and that he was an idiot. He'd say, I know, or maybe he'd say, I was a fool, and then they'd kiss again. The hole was deep enough to keep prying eyes out of it all, whatever happened in her booby trap, and she'd kiss him but for real this time, and then? Who the fuck cared about And then? And then would take care of its own damn self.

But it wasn't Henry on her trail. It was Colleen, who hadn't found the dummy trail or the fake dummy trail, who had, in fact, found Rose's third trail, and who had crouched herself down behind Rose—how? how had she crept up on her so fucking quietly?—and whispered, finally, into Rose's ear, "Nice work, kid. You almost had me fooled." Then she said, "Wendy's going to kill you for those boots, you know."

And then, grabbing Colleen swiftly by her weak-side arm, Rose flipped her up and over and onto her backside. "Yeah, maybe," Rose said, "but she's going to have to find me first." And then she ran, laughing as she disappeared back into the woods.

# 37.

The director shoved Rose back and scrambled to grab the glove, which she had flung across the room. She grabbed him by the ankle and tripped him to his face. He kicked wildly to make her let go and somersaulted himself closer to the glove and onto his feet. She kicked the bookshelf hard enough to drop the sword into her lap.

It was sharper and finer wrought than she'd expected.

She stood and held it loose at her side.

Sweaty and his shirt untucked and his own shirtsleeve scorched from the glove or from her pulling off the glove, the director looked almost as worse for wear as she felt.

Not that it mattered. He'd grabbed the glove. He stood up with it and turned to look at her and he sighed a heavy sigh and looked almost sad.

Maybe he hadn't had a chance before to really see her, to see how young she was, to see how much she resembled the very women he had brought to the Regional Office and helped to train, the women (and girls) he had guided and loved, or maybe he was feeling sad about what was to come—cleaning up the mess of this assault, checking in on the families of those who'd been lost today, picking up the pieces and moving forward. She didn't know. All she knew was that he must have been feeling pretty fucking confident to already be looking sad about what he was going to have to do to her, how he was going to have to move forward with all of this.

But then he wasn't putting on the glove and then she looked at the glove, looked more closely, saw that it had ripped—or she had ripped it—from the bottom of its wrist/cuff to the point where the middle finger met the palm, and it hung there limp and unnerving but powerless, even she could sense its powerlessness.

He dropped the glove. He closed his eyes. The fight had all come to an end so quickly Rose wasn't sure what she should do next.

According to the protocol, she was supposed to tell him Emma sends her best, but Jesus, that seemed just cruel at this point, after all that had happened. As far as Rose could tell, he believed his own friend and partner had sent her to kill him, and so she couldn't say whether it would be better to die with the wrong understanding of why, but also she didn't think Emma was the kind of person you could lie to about a thing you hadn't done.

She lifted the sword. She said, not too loud but loud enough: "Emma sends her best."

He opened his eyes. "Wait, what? Who?"

"You heard me," she said, and then felt bad about how short her tone had been. "Emma. She sends her best."

"Emma? Emma's dead."

"Apparently not dead enough," she said, and then she lunged

at him, lunged past him, lunged as hard as she could lunge, the sword held in both hands and flush with the horizon, and before he could say anything else, before he could even know for certain he was dead, the top half of him toppled one way, and a second later, the bottom half fell the other.

From *The Regional Office Is Under Attack:*
*Tracking the Rise and Fall of an American Institution*

While what is known about Oyemi, both before and after her transformation, is limited, often obfuscated by competing accounts and flimsy theories, many of them posited or spread by Oyemi herself, the life of Mr. Niles is much more accessible. Books could be written on the life and times of Mr. Niles, though this paper will only account for what is germane to the purpose of offering a brief history of the rise and fall of the Regional Office, the events that brought Mr. Niles and Oyemi together, what worked to break them apart, and how these events conspired to destroy the thing they'd worked so hard to build.

Once he and Oyemi abducted the woman named Nell, it stands to reason that Mr. Niles became nervous, apprehensive. Stands to reason that he paced the office more than usual, even for him. That he woke often throughout the night—sensitive to every sound from the street below, every creak on the stairway above—woke so often that he might as well have not slept at all. He had involved himself in a kidnapping. Anyone not a sociopath and not Oyemi would have become nervous and apprehensive once the act of kidnapping happened.

Let us first clarify: The future Operative Recruits were never kidnapped. Oyemi and Mr. Niles, and later, Henry, made each Recruit an offer: remain in this quotidian life or train to fight the forces of darkness.

Not so the Oracles.

Nell and the other two (whose names have been lost to history) were not made offers, were not given choices, were simply kidnapped and then altered.

It stands to reason that this unnerved Mr. Niles.

In college, he had majored in economics. Before that, sure, he had dropped out of high school and engaged in some small-time robberies to get by. Nonetheless, nothing in his life had prepared him for this, for aiding and abetting the physical and mental and supernatural transformation of strangers, young women no less. And, to be perfectly honest, there is extensive evidence that Mr. Niles never cared for nor wanted to involve oracles, or soothsayers, or palm readers, or fortune-tellers of any stripe, in his plans for the Regional Office.

Mr. Niles, in fact, harbored strong feelings against the desire for foreknowledge of this sort. Mr. Niles, in fact, very much did not want to believe in oracles, a desire made more difficult to fulfill if Oyemi planned to surround herself—and him—with them.

His father believed in oracles, specifically in a prophecy that his life would be cut short by a fire, something he learned, no doubt, from some sideshow carny. But his father was devoted to this prophecy; it was his favorite story to tell, the story of his future demise. Mr. Niles would listen to his father and his father would tell him how he was going to die and Mr. Niles would ask his father how he knew this and his father would claim that it was all in the prophecy, clear as day, that it was straight from the oracle's mouth. Mr. Niles would ask his father why he simply didn't do something about this prophecy to prevent it from coming true, and his father told him, "Well, son, I've thought about it, I have, but that's what the Greeks did, you know."

His father said, "You know the Greeks, son? Great people, the Greeks. But the ancient Greeks, not like that Greek son of a bitch who runs the gas station."

He said, "Smart people, the Greeks. Inventors of the wheel and time, but dumb about prophecies.

"Take Oedipus, for example," he said. "The king heard a prophecy that his son would murder him and marry his wife and so the king, he tried to get smart, he tried to fix things so the prophecy wouldn't come true, like leave his firstborn son on a hilltop to die, or in the woods to be eaten by wolves, or something like that, it doesn't matter what, because in the end, whatever he did, this king, it didn't matter."

He said, "Whatever they fixed, the Greeks? It only worked to make the prophecy come true. No matter what you do, a prophecy is a prophecy is a prophecy, and you can't do anything to change it that won't make it happen."

"So what are you going to do?" Mr. Niles asked his father.

"Nothing, son," he said. He smiled at his own brilliance. "Don't you get it? You do nothing and the prophecy doesn't even matter. Do nothing and you've beaten the system."

"Does that mean you're not going to die in a fire, then?" Mr. Niles asked.

"Nah," his father said. "It's just a theory. I'll probably die just like the oracle said I would."

All of which confused Mr. Niles, made him feel a heavy sadness when he was a boy, and then pity for his father as he grew older. But the idea of prophecies and fate's hand controlling a person's life wormed its way into his head, and soon he came to the decision that someone or something held the knowledge of his future, too, and that there was nothing he could do to change any of it. It was all preordained, whether he'd been told about it or not, and no matter what he did, the secretly held prophecy about his own life couldn't be altered. And this led him from one bad decision to another, so that by the time he was supposed to be graduating from high school he was instead spending his nights standing outside in the dark parking lot of a twenty-four-hour grocery store mugging people.

Mr. Niles tried to be fair about the muggings.

Mr. Niles had always believed in fairness.

By his own admission, he targeted the beer-bellied

middle-aged bachelors who shopped early in the morning, at two or three a.m., approached them as they were walking out with two grocery carts full of cereal boxes and Top Ramen and dollar bags of moldy apples. These were men, he thought, who could have avoided the whole mess—being robbed, that is—if only they'd have gotten married, settled down, made a few kids, and started shopping at the normal hours of the day when normal people shopped.

He waited outside until a guy came out of the store, until he walked through the parking lot in between his two shopping carts, until he was just reaching his car. And that was when Mr. Niles would step out of the shadows with a gun he'd found in his father's locked file cabinet, moving so quickly that by the time he had his gun pressed up to the guy's fleshy stomach, pressed into all of that fat until the tip of the barrel was right under the guy's rib cage, pressed hard so that the guy would know he wasn't fooling around, the guy was too surprised to do much else but what Mr. Niles told him to do, which was usually to lie down in the trunk.

He thought about his father whenever he shut the trunk on the guy and took the keys out and dropped them into his own pocket. He thought about his father and the Greeks. He placed his ear to the trunk and listened for whimpering or heavy breathing or all-out sobbing. He wondered whether the guy had once heard a prophecy about how one night he would find himself locked inside a trunk and if then he had taken steps to remove all trunks from his life. Like Sleeping Beauty with all the spinning wheels. And then if the guy, forgetting there was a trunk attached to his car, thought he had fixed it by removing all trunks and all possibilities of trunks from his life. By avoiding all flea markets or specialty import stores or antique shops. Thinking the whole time he had fixed it, tricked the prophecy, won the game, but instead he had somehow led himself to this moment. Instead, he had led himself to the parking lot of this grocery store, to a life that was loveless, childless, and that necessitated shopping at odd hours of the night only to wind up, finally, locked inside his own trunk.

"You should've not done anything," the young Mr. Niles would yell through the hood of the trunk. He'd bang real hard on the top of the car. "You should've just left it well enough alone," he would yell, louder, banging even more, banging to punctuate each word.

After a while, when Mr. Niles became tired of robbing these men, and when the date of his father's prophesied death came and went, leaving his father still very much alive, he gave up on oracles and the preordained nature of life. He tested for his GED and enrolled in a junior college; transferred, at Oyemi's insistence, to Rutgers; and then left New Jersey after graduation and moved to the city. By then, the stirrings of the Regional Office were stirred and then they kidnapped the woman named Nell, transformed her, and held her captive.

*an interlude:*

# THE HOSTAGE SITUATION

We were already at a loss—tired and scared and confused—when they grabbed Harrison by the collar, sharp enough we could hear the seams of his shirt rip, and then stood him up and then shot him in the head. They did this and we wilted, the bunch of us, like lilies in high heat. Some of us screamed or sobbed, but the rest of us looked on in silent shock.

Then they shuffled us out of the conference room, where they'd been holding us, and into a smaller office—Laura's—which made Laura feel better at first, to be in a familiar setting, until one of us reminded her that she'd probably die there, and while a lot of us used to joke about how we spent so much of our time at work we'd probably die at our desks, too, none of us—Laura least of all—liked how this joke was playing out in real life.

All of us were frightened at this point but a lot of us were confused, too. A lot of us still thought that we were nothing more than agents for an exclusive travel concern catering to the ultra-rich and famous and didn't know that our jobs, our physical bodies, even, were a cover for what really went on here, went on downstairs, nearly a mile below us. When we split into two factions—those who wanted to devise a plan of escape or attack and those of us willing to wait until they let us go or shot us like they shot Harrison, whichever came first—we were also split, though not all of us realized it, by what we knew and what we didn't know. Those of us who knew the truth about our jobs, about the travel agency and the real agency below us, were willing to wait. Maybe we didn't know exactly what was in store for us, but we had a good general idea, and for us, knowing what we were up against, there seemed to be little else to do but to wait. While one half of us were thinking about our families, our friends, and what we were going to do when we got out of there, the other half were wondering how long it would be, really, before they shot us all or simply piped some noxious gas into Laura's office through the vent.

Were thinking, in other words, only of ourselves, and how long we had to be ourselves.

Still. We didn't do anything to stop those of us who wanted to escape. In fact, we decided, why not just tell them the truth? We would have wanted to know, right, that the men we were fighting against were part of some dark, evil force bent on the total destruction of the planet and all its innocent peoples, that if we were going to die, we were going to die for something important, something bigger than us. Sure, we had been sworn to secrecy, but we decided in the end, What's the harm?

What's the harm in telling them? What's the harm in planning our escape?

We'll probably be shot anyway. Might as well be shot for planning a foolhardy and imperfect escape as for anything else, right?

We made an announcement. Those who knew, who maybe were still uncertain about the rightness of what we were doing, shuffled uncomfortably, refused to make eye contact. The others, well, they laughed, they clapped their hands together like we'd just made a funny joke, said, "You're funny. Why didn't I know how funny you are?" And that was that. Maybe they believed us, maybe they thought we were keeping things light, keeping spirits up. Regardless, we got to work.

We ransacked Laura's desk and cabinets and collected three boxes of paper clips; a number of dull pencils; two staplers; a gauzy blue-colored rock Laura used as a paperweight; two pair of scissors, one of which we noticed she had stolen from Larry in accounting; and a key-ring pepper-spray canister.

We considered the paper clips and made a joke about chewing gum and MacGyver, but then we were stumped.

Someone picked up the pepper spray and tapped the nozzle, which must have broken after so many years bouncing around inside Laura's desk, and a wide expanse of pepper water spat out in all directions, and for a moment, we were coughing and wheezing, our eyes were red and blurred by tears, and we swore at whoever used the goddamn pepper spray, but the swearing, our anger, didn't last. We were too spent to shout or swear or rail for too long.

Too spent from our morning commutes and the drudgery of booking yearly world tours for snarky, overprivileged douchebags who owned yachts big enough to contain every one of the possessions we'd crammed into our shitty apartments in Queens. Too spent from the pain in our lower backs and the false promise of lumbar support, from the soreness in our hands, the carpal tunnel syndrome that made it impossible to open mayonnaise jars, and from, finally, this. This last worst insult. Not just the men in black with their guns and their shoving and pushing, the bullet through Harrison's skull, the strong urge to piss ourselves, the sore dryness of our throats, the drips of sweat running down our backs to pool at the waistbands of our underwear, the meager tools for our escape, the small chance that we'd make it out of this alive. Too spent from not just all of this but now the pepper spray, too, which had left us winded and undone, and all discussion of escape fell away as we sat in a huddle, gasping and rubbing our eyes.

They had taken away our cell phones, our watches, too, and shot the crap out of Laura's computer, and for an excruciating eternity, none of us knew what time it was. Then Milo remembered his pedometer, which was surreptitiously clipped to the inside of his belt, and which doubled as a watch. What was more surprising than the fact that Milo's pedometer was overlooked was that Milo, a truly fat fuck, had a pedometer at all, the poor thing clipped inside his pants—who knew he could have fit anything inside his pants?—and he was proud of it, we could tell, even though we made him explain what it was a couple of times and why he had it. We asked him, What time is it? and Milo looked at the pedometer and then he shook it and he pressed a couple of buttons and we figured he'd never really used the thing, figured it had been giving him false readings this whole time because he hadn't set it up, had just clipped it to himself and figured that was that, but then he let out this deep, heavy sigh.

It's five till, Milo said, and, groaning, we demanded, Five till what, asshole?, and he sighed again and said, Ten, and we were dumbfounded.

Hours had passed, we had thought. Many, many hours must have passed. We knew this, were certain of this. Our stomachs growled because we'd missed not just lunch but that break in the middle of the afternoon that we all looked forward to when we sent Jenny across the street to pick up some coffees and bags of chips. It had to have been late afternoon, at least. We were sleepy and worn out because the day was coming to a close, and we'd been thinking to ourselves, What will our families think, what will our friends around the city think when we don't show up at home, at that great little bar in Red Hook, at our dinner date; we had been thinking, When will demands be made, what will the nightly news cover about us, when will our loved ones receive the phone calls asking for the interesting details of our lives, for recent photos?

But no. It had only been forty-five minutes and already we'd grown restless and irritable, and it would be hours and hours still before anyone missed us, before anyone even noticed we were gone.

Holly suggested we play a game, to pass the time better. The rest of us ignored her or made faces behind her back. We considered the idea of escape again, and with nothing better to do, no recourse, no e-mail or Internet or smartphones to pass the time with, with only each other and nothing much in common—how many more times would we have to listen to Carl go on about the square-dancing class he'd started taking in Bushwick, really?—even those of us who had been against planning an escape were on board now, and with the earnest resolve of the truly desperate.

William took charge because he was that guy, the guy who took charge but to whom no one paid the slightest attention.

He snapped his fingers at Laura and demanded a legal pad and pencil, even though they were right there on the desk in front of him. He drew a map of the office and stared at it. He said things like, So what we need to do first is, and Okay, okay, this is good, this is great because, and, I wonder if maybe instead we should. He obviously had no fucking clue what to do next but was trying to make it sound like he was unknotting some thorny but brilliant plan. We let him at it with the sad understanding that this delusional activity was all the glue holding poor William together.

In the meantime, Jackson, who played shortstop in our softball league, and whose batting average was consistently in the high .300s, and who, it was once rumored, could have gone pro, and whom some of us called Action Jackson, though never right to his face because we didn't want to come on too strong, huddled a group of us together and said, stage-whispering, So, what do you think? How about we tell them that one of us is sick and when one of the guards comes in to investigate we smash him over the head with that blue paperweight Laura's got on her desk? Take his gun, go from there?

We looked at each other and then at Laura's paperweight and then back at Action Jackson and then nodded and said, Sure, why not?

The thing was this: We all knew the plan was doomed to fail. Most of us didn't think it would work even so far as to get someone to come into Laura's office to investigate. It was such an obvious ploy. The men in black outside Laura's office, if they were even within earshot, would know exactly what we were up to. If they had seen any kind of hostage-situation movie clip made in the past thirty years, they would ignore us once Jackson started yelling through the door.

But still. We tried it anyway. Michael was on the floor doing a decent job, we thought, of having a heart attack, and some of us wondered—what with all the double-bacon cheeseburgers he ate for lunch—if he'd had some experience in this role.

Jackson, too, good old Action Jackson, was a surprisingly good actor. There was a timbre of real fear and anxiety and concern in his voice. His eyes showed the fear, too, which spoke to a true devotion to this role since no one but us saw his eyes as he was standing on this side of the door with Laura's blue paperweight hefted over his head.

In any case, none of us, not even Jackson, thought there was more than a slim chance that one of the goons would come through Laura's office door, so it was a bit of a shock when the door opened, that it opened as fast as it did, as if the guys were just waiting for us to pull some kind of stunt like this. And it was more of a shock—to all of us but to Jackson especially—when the guard caught Jackson's arm midswing, how cleanly and quickly the guard broke Jackson's wrist, and then pulled him—him, the strongest and most athletic of all of us—into a tight hug as if he were some kind of rag doll and then snapped him, snapped Jackson like he was that cookie part of a Twix in a Twix commercial. Jackson's eyes widened when this happened but that was all. It happened so fast that there wasn't any pain to speak of, not in his eyes, anyway. Not in his face. No grimace, no groan. Maybe he was dead or maybe he was simply paralyzed, but when the guard let go of him, he landed on the ground like a cardboard box would, or not like a cardboard box but like a side of beef would, or not that either. He wasn't a side of beef. He was Jackson. He was Action Jackson. He landed the way Action Jackson would have if Action Jackson were possibly dead.

Michael scrambled to his knees and stumbled against the desk and pulled himself shakily to his feet and the guard, finished with Jackson, pulled his gun and aimed it at Michael's head. We held our breath. We didn't even look at Jackson, crumpled on the floor. We wanted to rush to him, to throw ourselves prostrate over him, to sob uncontrollably, but the gun pointed at Michael shut us all up, made us keep perfectly still.

Then the guard smiled and then the guard left and we didn't understand what had just happened and we didn't know what was going to happen next and we had no fucking clue as to what we should do.

A long time passed and we didn't move. We didn't rush to Jackson's side, didn't sob over his prone form, didn't do much but stare at the door, at the space where the guard had stood and aimed his gun at one of us after having ruined another of us. Michael was breathing hard and Laura—poor Laura—whimpered to herself. Jenny sat heavily into Laura's office chair. But otherwise, we were quiet and still. Even William, who normally might have taken this opportunity to make some sort of speech—a disappointed-in-our-poor-efforts speech or a stern but encouraging father-figure speech or a rallying-the-troops speech—even William was quiet.

He was the first to move. He dropped to his knees and then lowered his ear to Jackson's face. Jackson's eyes were open and wide still, as if his face, his expression, had become stuck. We couldn't see any up-and-down movement in his chest. His body didn't look comfortable lying as it was. William was there for some time, his ear pressed to Jackson's chest and then to his face and then back to his chest.

Then he looked up and shook his head, which was the wrong thing to do considering what he said, which was, I don't know how, but he's still breathing.

We were so relieved by this we didn't even bother to tell William that the sad and wistful headshake wasn't proper head-movement protocol for when someone you thought was dead turned out to be alive. Instead, we rushed to Jackson's side, where we quibbled immediately: lift him, leave him, set his head at an incline, cover him with a jacket, don't let him fall asleep, no, if he wants to sleep, let him sleep? What we agreed on though was the need for a doctor.

And also, to be honest, there were those of us who wished, secretly, that he was dead outright.

We weren't cruel. We understood he was in some way better off not being dead, but how much better off?

We thought about his wife and his son, who was eight and who would bat-boy for us at games. We thought about the change waiting for them when we got out of this. Their once strong and handsome husband and father now irrevocably broken. Doctor's bills. Physical therapy, wheelchairs, feeding tubes, an elaborate blinking system with which to communicate. She would cheat on him, or would leave him entirely. We'd met her enough times to suspect she was that kind of woman. The son would grow up weak and servile, or a bully. Jackson would become a burden they would come to despise and one day he'd wish that he'd just died and would regret that his condition, which prevented him from living life, also made suicide a near impossibility. We considered his life laid out for him and shook our heads at the travesty of it and wondered at the thin line between being dead now and the life waiting for him in the future.

But mostly, those of us who wished he'd died did so because we dreaded the idea of spending the next few hours in here with Action Jackson—God, what a stupid name—incapacitated and possibly dying, but certainly not being helped by lack of proper medical administration. We imagined good odds on his dying before all this ended. And if he didn't die, if he regained consciousness, we imagined his making demands we couldn't fulfill. Or even if he were to lie there stoic and strong, how depressing would that be, the constant reminder of him? How bad for team morale? And while we didn't have a good plan for what to do next, whatever plan we came up with would surely involve leaving him behind, and wouldn't that be easier, we thought to ourselves, with him already dead?

We kept this to ourselves, though. We touched him gently on the shoulder or the cheek, careful not to move him or make him worse.

Then we moved away from him and by unspoken consent, we stayed as far away from that part of the room as we could for the rest of the time we were trapped there.

Then we heard loud laughter coming from the other side of the door.

This unnerved us, made us feel uncertain and more frightened than before. It was the kind of laughter you heard at a party or a bar or a reunion.

We couldn't imagine, in other words, what had made them laugh so hard. Or maybe we could but would rather not have. And maybe this was what made Karen—quiet, unassuming, prudish Karen—say, Guess they found Richard's monkey video. And this. This made us laugh, laugh so hard. Maybe because it was Karen who brought it up after making such a fuss over the video in the first place. Or maybe it was the idea of those goons huddled around one of the computers in the cubicles watching that video on YouTube. Or maybe it was just the stress of our situation, the urgent need for some kind of release. Whatever the reason, Richard's monkey video had never been as funny to us as it was then. The video showed a chimp, a trained chimp, taunting a baby, first with a bottle and then with a squeaky giraffe and then the baby's blankie, coaxing the baby to it each time with this thing or that, only to snatch the item away at the last second just before thumping the baby hard on the forehead. The baby fell for it every time and then wailed and screamed and cried this big openmouthed, toothless cry after the chimp thumped him on the forehead. It was a cruel but really, really funny video. Karen, who'd just had a baby four months ago, and was maybe a bit bitter coming back to work so soon, made a number of complaints about the video. She complained enough and to enough of the right people that we had to attend a seminar. Control software was installed onto our computers. Every minute of every workday was tracked. No more social networking. No more personal e-mail. No more porn. Was it surprising that none of us really liked Karen all that much? She knew that we didn't like her much, but she thought it was because of what she did, when really, and it is a nuanced argument, we admit, but we already hadn't liked her because we'd already decided that she would turn out to be the kind of person who would do what she did.

So her joke here, in the middle of all of this, surprised us, made us reconsider her and our dislike of her, though the more honest of us knew that if we all got out of this alive, or even if only some of us did, including Karen, it wouldn't be long before we shifted back into our established and familiar office roles.

But still. In that small, brief moment, each of us loved Karen.

Then the door opened and we shut up, afraid they were coming in there to make us shut up.

Hostages, we figured, weren't supposed to break out in spontaneous, raucous laughter.

But they weren't there for us. They were there to add to our numbers. Two men marched into the office holding a woman between them and then they threw her into the lot of us and left, shutting the door behind them.

William moved to help her up but stopped. He looked back at us, his face white. She'd been beaten up badly, we could all see that, but we couldn't see what had freaked William out until he stepped back and then we saw what was utterly, horribly wrong with her, which wasn't that she was black-eyed and bloody-browed, wasn't even the long, thick gash down her arm that extended from her shoulder almost to her elbow, but rather that her other arm was missing entirely. Her blouse had been ripped off at the shoulder of the missing arm. We could see the seams and the jagged edge of the material. We couldn't see what was underneath the material, but it was in the shape of a shoulder, a truncated shoulder.

Then we got a glimpse of her, got a look at her face, and we realized who she was.

Sarah O'Hara.

We knew her, but the way she looked now, her eyes downcast, her face bruised, her shoulders slumped, jerking with silent sobs, we couldn't believe how afraid of her we'd been, and we were once very, very afraid of her.

For one, she was generally very mean. She arrived out of the blue on occasion, stormed through our offices, yelled at our various managers, and stood haughtily over our shoulders as we made our calls, as we coaxed our clients into ever-bigger vacation packages, as we tried to up-sell the sixth Sherpa since no one, not since the Krakauer book, attempted Everest with fewer than six Sherpas. No matter what we said or how much we sold, we could never seem to do enough for Sarah O'Hara.

Once, she hung up Kelly's phone, Kelly who shortly thereafter succumbed to a nervous breakdown and quit. Hung up Kelly's phone in the middle of a sales call with one of her biggest clients. No one knew why. Not Kelly, not our manager, Benjamin, also no longer with the agency. None of us could figure it out. The call was going well. Before that hang-up, Kelly was our best salesperson. She had convinced her client that there really was nothing more spectacular than to travel with one's own hot-air balloon and hot-air balloon crew. You never know, she was in the middle of saying, You never know when you might want to go up in a hot-air balloon. Say you are casting about in the Antarctic waters south of Argentina and you want to take a hot-air balloon over the Perito Moreno Glacier. Unless you bring your own, she continued, and that was when Sarah O'Hara pressed her index finger down on the phone and hung up the call. Then she looked at Kelly, who had turned abruptly around to see what the fuck had just happened, and she waited. She waited to see if Kelly would say or do anything, waited for an outburst or tears, or something. With Sarah O'Hara, no one ever knew. Kelly turned back to the phone, not a word or a look, and redialed the number, which none of the rest of us would have had the balls to do, not with Sarah O'Hara standing right behind us. She redialed and then, with a smile on her face, she apologized, a mechanical issue, she had moved to another phone, wouldn't happen again, and what did they decide about that balloon? And sure, credit where credit is due, she made the sale, but those of us who knew her best could hear the slight hitch in her voice. Just a tremor. A blip. Nothing at all. Sarah O'Hara made a note on her clipboard and then walked away. We consoled Kelly. Patted her gamely on the shoulder. She smiled and shook her head and gave out a long, relieved sigh. And then the next day the tremor had become a trill, and then a shake, and soon enough, she couldn't talk on the phone without stammering or stuttering. She lost her clients. Had her breakdown. Quit and moved back to Kansas to live with her folks.

The week before all of that happened, she'd won a trip to Costa Rica for having the best monthly sales record three months running. She never claimed it.

What had poor Kelly done to deserve any of this? What, other than stand out as a brilliant sales associate? Kind and generous and glowing? Nothing. Nothing that we could see. Some of us speculated—she had made some cruel joke at Sarah's expense (a lot of us had, but we couldn't remember hearing anything of the sort from Kelly), or she had discovered the real agency below the fake agency (though she never let on anything of the sort), or she had e-mailed Sarah one too many times asking for a new order of Post-it notes or copier toner or a new mouse pad—but really, none of this made sense, and in the end, most of us decided it was all arbitrary, that Kelly was offered up as a sacrifice, an example to remind us how replaceable we all were, how powerful Sarah was, how unnerved we should be around her.

And we were. Unnerved. But the real reason, or maybe the other reason, some of us—not all of us, but those of us who knew something about what really went on there—had once been very, very afraid of her was because of a rumored mechanical arm, one she could use, the rumors went, with fearsome and deadly force.

Which seemed to us now both less of a rumor and less of an arm, having been indelicately removed.

She pulled herself up enough to push herself across the carpet and to the wall. She sat there, her knees against her chest, her arm draped over her knees, her head, sobbing and weeping, cradled in the crook of the only elbow she had left to her. We were at a loss. Even William, who never missed an opportunity to unsuccessfully try to comfort someone. Even Karen, who believed her faith could heal all wounds. None of us knew what to say or do in a situation in which we were tasked with comforting a woman we hated about her superpowerful mechanical arm, which had been torn from her body.

We were surprised, then, when Laura took the lead in this. She moved past us and we caught a strange and unsettling look in her eye. This whole time, she'd hardly been there at all. But now she was back, mentally back among us, and had come back with a strange, some of us would say ferocious, look in her eye. She bee-lined for Sarah and who knew what she would have said or done, but she didn't make it there before Sarah's sobs came to a halt. She then whipped her head up to look at the closed door and then back to us—her long ponytail swinging all the way around so that stray hairs batted against her nose and lips. She then stood in one fluid and dangerous motion. She took a quick look at Jackson on the floor. Then she gave the lot of us another once-over and was clearly disappointed in what she saw. She recovered and resigned herself to us.

Wiring of some kind hung loose and useless from where her arm should have been.

Laura was about to say something, maybe William and Karen, too, but she stopped them with a look.

Then she said, "No time for chitchat." Then she pulled a gun—a handgun, maybe a Beretta, maybe something else because we weren't well versed on handguns—pulled this gun out of no-where. She didn't smile. She didn't grimace. She didn't look down at where her arm used to be. Her face was smooth and unburdened and, suddenly, quite lovely.

Then she said, "I've got a plan."

We all agreed it was a shitty plan but we also all agreed that we couldn't say as much to the woman with the gun and the one arm and the entrails of another (mechanical) arm hanging from her shoulder socket. We couldn't tell her how it was just like Action Jackson's plan and look at what had happened to him, think of what might happen to us. She told us the plan and how we would charge out of here, overwhelming the big, strong, heartless men with guns by the sheer number of us pouring out of the office, and William, God bless him, asked her, "What about Action Jackson?" and then flinched when she said, "What the fuck are you talking about?" because who wouldn't have flinched? But then, because William was William and William didn't know when or how to stop himself, he pointed to Jackson on the floor and said, "Sorry, I meant Jackson. I meant him. What about him?"

She looked at Jackson on the floor and then said, with disgust and with the implication that he must have been some kind of idiot to be on the floor broken the way he was, said in a way that made us all hope that Jackson was dead or, at the very least, unconscious and unable to hear any of this: "What? The dead guy? We fucking leave the dead guy. That's pretty standard, friend."

Maybe we should have pulled together, let bygones be bygones, become a stronger unit in the face of outside adversity, but Sarah was just so mean and angry, and maybe she had the right to be angry, what with her whole life coming under assault and her mechanical arm stripped from her body, but we couldn't bring ourselves to do it, couldn't bring ourselves to play along. And so when Michael—poor Michael—called out to the guard that we needed help, that the one-armed woman they'd brought in here was having some kind of fit, and the guard opened the door, opened it but didn't step inside, we did not rush him, did not overwhelm him with our underwhelming numbers. We stood there and, we're ashamed to admit, a couple of us nodded with our eyes at Sarah standing with her gun on the other side of the door. It wasn't unlikely that we saw the guard roll his eyes at us, at the situation, at the foolishness of this foolish plan, and he swiveled around the open door, his body inconceivably lowered and small, out of range of the gun she was aiming where his head should've been but wasn't, swiveled around the door and up close to and behind her, grabbing her with his larger, strong hand in the shoulder socket where once there had been an arm, and he squeezed.

When she screamed, we felt maybe the worst about what we'd done, or not done.

We were impressed, though, by her ability, amidst all this pain and what we assumed must be deep-rooted sorrow, her ability to break the guard's knee with a swift kick, and then his nose with a balled, backhanded fist. We also felt like dummies for not helping her out because, judging by her skilled performance, by how quickly she dispatched the one guard who knew where she was and what she was waiting to do, we might have stood some chance of escaping if we'd helped. And sure, those of us who were just travel-agency schmucks, we didn't know what to make of her "plan," but those of us from the Regional Office, we should have known, did know that she was supposedly some fearsome fighting dynamo, but we'd never seen her in action and had always chalked her reputation up to the mechanical arm, which we weren't entirely sure even existed, and if it had once existed, it certainly wasn't a part of her anymore. By the time we realized our mistake, it was too late, as three more men streamed into Laura's office, batons swinging at Sarah, poor, one-armed Sarah, who did not give up, who was not the kind to give up, even as they dragged her away and hit her. She screamed and bit and flailed, and three men weren't enough, but then two more swept in, and, for what it was worth, five, five men was what it took to carry Sarah out of the office, and two more men to help the first man, who was covered in blood and seemed to be in serious pain, and then, at the last minute, at the last possible minute, not all of us, but a few of us ran.

Finally, we ran.

And when we chanced a look back over our shoulders at the others still in Laura's office, looking a bit dumbfounded at what we'd just done, we thought to ourselves, See you folks on the other side, and suddenly, amidst all the confusion, we were free.

Once we broke free of the chaos right outside of Laura's office, we made our way to the copy room. We figured there'd be a map there—a fire exit map in any case—something, anyway, to help steer us around where we thought the men with guns might be, that might help us plan some strategy to escape unnoticed. Plus, Carl said he'd heard rumor of a secret passage we could find, which none of us believed, and even if it had existed, there was no way it would have been marked on a fire exit map, but we let him think what he was going to think.

The copy room turned out to be kind of a coup on our parts. We were right about that map, which marked out a clear path to the exit with little, uneven dashes, (and, sadly for Carl, no secret passageway) but also someone had left a box of doughnuts there. We did our best, as we passed over the crullers and grabbed for a jelly or a cream-filled, we did our best to try to coddle ourselves with the idea that this stroke of good luck was only the beginning. Or not even the beginning but just one more sign in a long line of good-luck signs, beginning with the fact that we weren't killed right off, that we shoved our way out of that small office when we had the chance. This was just one more sign, we decided, that things from here on out would be smooth sailing, that, with bellies full of jellies, there was nothing we couldn't do or survive. It was a foolish thought, but right now all we seemed to have room for were foolish thoughts, since there was no thought more foolish, really, than that we would get out of there at all.

As we left the copy room, we congratulated ourselves on not just our escape but on how in sync we were with each other, and how good our instincts were, how we should've been spies or special agents ourselves, and, busy congratulating ourselves, we were surprised when one of the goons grabbed one of us—Carl from accounting—and socked him over the head with the butt of a pistol, and only because Carl was so wide and the hallway so narrow were the rest of us able to keep running despite the two other guys with the guy who brained Carl.

We ran and turned and turned and turned again, hoping that our haphazard movements made it more difficult for anyone to find us or catch up to us, and then, because we weren't spies or special agents but were desk jockeys and horribly out of shape, we had to stop, catch our breath.

After that, we decided it wasn't so much fun. We had lost Carl and the fire map since Carl was the one carrying it when they took him. We thought we'd been heading left for a while. We didn't know directions, though—east, west, north, south—and mostly our only hope was that we weren't going to land back at Laura's office.

There were five of us left and one of us was an intern, so really, there were four of us left, since in these situations the intern was always one of the first to go.

We found ourselves in a wide hallway, maybe near accounting, but we would have to have asked Carl about that but we couldn't and so we stopped and leaned against the wall and placed our hands on our knees and breathed in as deeply as we could. We stood there and the intern said, joking but not joking, too, "I'm too old for this shit," and then Frank said, "I only had two days till retirement," and then the intern said, "Really?" and we said, everyone but the intern, "Shut the fuck up, kid," and we stood ourselves up straight and we stretched our necks and pushed out our chests to stretch our backs. The intern started stretching out his hamstrings or his quads and we shook our heads at him, and as we stood there, an arm, a mechanical arm, came around the corner at the far end of the hall and began to snake its way past us.

Or didn't snake.

Snake is not what it did.

It was an unsettling sight, that bodiless monstrosity, half-covered in tattered pieces of skin, coming toward us. Not that any of us had ever spent considerable time pondering the way an arm might move itself—maybe humping itself forward like some kind of legless caterpillar—but seeing an arm move itself toward us made each of us realize that we probably would have imagined it wrong. Its fingers dug into the floor, gouging out hunks of carpet and the foam padding underneath it and the concrete slab beneath that with each grab, and then it threw itself forward, by what leverage or law of physical motion we didn't know, but it was oddly reminiscent, to at least one of us, of a cheetah, but without the cheetah attached.

We stood there quiet and still as the arm came up even with us and Frank moved to touch it or grab it, none of us were sure why, but the intern touched Frank lightly on the shoulder and shook his head and said quietly, "I wouldn't if I were you."

We weren't sure if Frank's moving or the intern's speaking or neither of those made that arm stop, but it stopped, and the hand swiveled around on the wrist, but not the way a hand should swivel, and it turned to look at us, as if the hand were the thing's head, the fingers some kind of antennae or feelers. We flinched back, thinking maybe the tips of the fingers would be electronic eyes or something worse, but the tips were just tips, with bits of carpet sloughing free and dusting the floor.

And then it turned back and resumed its strange, gouging push forward, and then it was gone, and for a moment, we looked at each other, unsure what to say about what the hell had just happened, and this was too much, too patently absurd, and the only response to the patently absurd is hysterical laughter, which lasted maybe five full minutes. Our faces were sore from the strain of laughing and the grime on our faces was cut through by tear streaks. And then the laughter petered out and we moved onward, ever onward, one of us chuckling on occasion, the bunch of us thinking to ourselves, What strange and thrilling times we live in. Thinking: How amazing that we are alive and part of such a unique world. A world you felt, at one point, might be full of nothing more than reality singing competitions and Donald Trumps and Kardashians and Angelina Jolie's cute ethnic kids, and Carson Daly, a world that hardly seemed worth saving, worth all of this effort, and then, and then.

"That was fucking incredible," Frank said.

And then we turned the corner and found five men dressed all in black, all of them dead. Their rifles broken into pieces, their necks snapped, their eyes gouged out, one with his tongue torn from his mouth.

We stood there over the dead for less than a minute, remarking on the number of bullet holes in the walls and the floor and the ceiling, making note of how fucking lucky we were just now, lucky that the hand didn't murder us, too, when a second team of men arrived, turning around the opposite corner, catching sight of their dead comrades and the five of us standing over their dead comrades but not registering exactly what had happened, and then one of the guys straightened up and looked at us and said, Holy fuck, which made the others stop and take stock of this tableau, and then there were rifles, maybe seven of them, pointed at us.

There was a pause. We could see it in their faces, the disbelief and the confusion. The scene seemed to point in one direction— that our motley crew had dispatched these soldiers—while the look of us seemed to point in the exact opposite direction, and our first instinct was to throw our hands up and surrender ourselves, to assure them that we had had no hand in any of this (ha, ha), that we had once been hostages, that he was on the sales team and that one, too, and that one over there was a project manager or something, and this one, this one right here, with the cheap haircut and the ill-fitting pleated khakis, was an intern, a fucking intern for Christ's sake. Of course, there was no way we could have done any of this. Except that before we could even raise our hands or open our mouths, the intern dove for one of the bodies, dove more quickly, more fluidly, than any of us would have expected possible, and came back up with the dead guy's rifle in his hands and managed to squeeze off a couple of rounds.

Which would have been amazing, if he hadn't missed. If he hadn't severely missed. We wouldn't have been surprised if he hadn't just missed those guys but the walls behind those guys, too, was how badly he missed. He was a goddamn intern.

Then they recovered and then they started to shoot, and they—they did not miss.

We lost Larry, who might have been just shot or who might've been shot dead, but who wasn't, regardless, following after us as we ran away. We felt sorry for him, but not sorry enough to stop. And we abandoned the intern. Fuck that guy, we thought. And fuck whoever was in charge of hiring the fucking interns, we thought.

We found an open utility closet and hid ourselves there. We took stock. We had been shot, in the calf and in the shoulder, and one of us, nicked in the ear, the earlobe sheared off and smelling of cordite, which we made a point of saying out loud because we hoped the naming of the things that were tearing us apart might make those things less frightening. We huffed and bent over in pain and tried our damnedest not to collapse into a blubbering mess, but it was hard. It was very hard, and then we decided it was too hard, and one by one, we crumpled into ourselves and sobbed and cried out for our mothers, our wives, but quietly, because they might've been close enough to hear us, and that's how we waited it out. We rode out the mess of our meltdowns and waited until we'd completely disintegrated, hoping that once that had happened, we could pull ourselves back together again because we were men, and being men, it was what was expected of us.

After we pulled ourselves together, we didn't talk about what had just happened between the three of us. None of us mentioned the sad truth of the matter: that we were surely going to die there, if not there in that utility closet, then there, somewhere there at the Regional Office.

We didn't say anything about the long hours we had devoted to this organization, to the fact that it was maybe our first real job, our first job that hadn't been a temp job or a job our fathers had gotten for us or a college work-study job or a job as someone's assistant, that while we were here we'd felt close to something great and powerful and mysterious, and now that it was falling down around our ears, we didn't say anything like, I should have worked for H&R Block, or, I should have left the city years ago. We didn't talk about our families, nor did we talk about the fact that we might not have had families yet, that we were still young enough to not have families on the radar yet, but that there had been a girl we'd seen walking by us the other day, a girl with shoulder-length brown hair, deep-brown, chestnut-brown hair, and how she'd been wearing a light blue blouse and a dark blue skirt, and how she'd smiled at us, how she seemed to have been smiling at everyone, but she had smiled at us, which was a thing that had never happened to us, had never happened to us in this city, in any case, and so we turned, couldn't help but turn around, or how we'd watched the movement of her hips and ass underneath the skirt fabric and that we'd also watched the way her arms swung as she walked, and had noticed the way she smiled at people and that they smiled back at her, and they did, they all smiled back at her, and we couldn't stop thinking about her smile, about her face when she smiled, that we'd watched her until she'd been lost in the crowd, and how we'd stopped and looked around and for the first time, maybe, we saw the city, we actually saw the city we were living in and working in and for the first time saw ourselves making a real life here, saw ourselves one day building a family here.

None of us mentioned that. None of us mentioned this or anything like this. We didn't bemoan the fact that we had tickets to see a movie tonight or a table at Peter Luger's we'd been waiting on for almost a month.

We didn't bother confessing to the fact that we had all, secretly, long harbored a deep and unsettling love for Jessica, and that the thought of her, shot through the head maybe, was more than we could bear.

Instead, we debated among the three of us whether to stay in the utility closet or to risk going back out there again. Which was what we were engaged in—a heated argument about being killed in this utility closet or being killed out in the hallways and under the fluorescent lights—when the door yanked open and Frank was dragged out by the collar by what looked to us at first like the disembodied arm, and so we all screamed, Frank maybe the loudest, but then another arm shifted into the frame, this one holding a gun pointed at Frank's head, which was subsequently fired, which made a mess of the utility closet and us and Frank's head, and we all screamed again, except not Frank, not this time, and then, panicked, we shoved Frank, poor Frank, we shoved his dead body into the guy who'd made him dead, and then we tried to run.

Sometimes a person who is very experienced at a thing—tennis, bowling, poker, killing—will be undone by a person who has no experience at a thing at all because the inexperienced guy will do things that no experienced guy would do, or would expect anyone with even half a brain to do, which is the only explanation we could offer for how we managed to get not just out of the utility closet but past the three guys standing in front of the utility closet waiting to do to us what they'd just done to Frank.

We ran in opposite directions, which they maybe suspected we would do, and then we realized we'd done this and then each turned to run in the direction of the other, which was maybe unexpected, and then ran into each other, knocked each other down, which was certainly unexpected, which would certainly have been considered far from best business practice when trying to flee a scene of imminent execution, but knocking each other down saved the two of us since both of us were shot at by one of the guys trying to shoot at us, but we fell just in time and he shot one of his coworkers in the shoulder, or that was how it looked anyway as we scrambled to our feet and shoved our way past the guy who'd just shot his buddy and who was more than a little surprised by that and by the fact that we were up and still moving and weren't quite dead yet.

We were lucky and stupid and unpredictable and for a minute, for maybe two minutes, that gave us a fighting chance, gave us hope, but then we turned that first corner and ran into another team, and then one of us was caught in the leg with something painful and sharp. We couldn't hear anything now, couldn't hear anything but the roar of panic and adrenaline and fear and pain inside our own heads, and so we didn't know if we'd been shot or stabbed with a knife, but then one of us fell, and the other one stopped because we weren't going to be alone in this, couldn't bear now to be finally alone, and we helped each other up, bolstered each other up even as the bullets whizzed by us and then through us, and then one of us fell again but fell for good, and this time the other one of us, me, the other one of us didn't.

I mean me.

I mean I.

I didn't go down.

I didn't stop.

I kept running.

And then I was the last one left.

I was the last one left and I'd pissed my pants and I had a long gash on my thigh, and there was blood on my hands and my face, but I didn't know whose because it couldn't all be mine, it couldn't all be my blood, and I was shaking, which was funny, because I didn't even know those guys, but I wasn't—

I didn't feel like what I was shaking out of was fear. I wasn't worried anymore so much about what would happen to me. That wasn't why I shook. I shook because of what had already happened and because they were gone, all four of them, and I tried to stop thinking about this because it was a dumb thing to think about, a dumb, pointless thing to think about at that moment, when they were after me, I was sure they were still after me, not to mention that I didn't know where the hell I was or how I would get the fuck out. But my thigh hurt and my body hurt and if I tried to clear my head, there was nothing there but the pain, but if I thought about these things, there were these things, too, at least, and not just the pain.

I stumbled into an office that I thought was going to be a door to a stairwell or something, and then heard sounds of men talking and searching, but I didn't know where they were coming from, and I said, Fuck it, and burst out of the office at a screaming charge, though how I charged anywhere with that gash in my leg, I couldn't have said, but there was no one there and I stumbled down the next hallway.

I could hear them behind me. I could hear their voices and their footsteps behind me. Closer and closer. I was just so tired, though. I just wanted to stop and say, Okay, guys, you got me. I wanted to stop with my hands up over my head if only so I could take a minute or two to not move any piece of me anymore. Just when I was about to do that, when I had stopped running and was simply walking quickly and then not so quickly, had slowed myself down like you sometimes will at the end of a long run, and was waiting for them to catch up to me, I turned one final corner and there I saw a door, an emergency exit door, and I shoved myself through it because at that moment I could not think of anything I would have described as an emergency moment more than that moment right then. And through the door was an elevator, and in that elevator was one button, just one, and the door closed, and I sank to the floor, and the elevator didn't seem to move, and I waited, and then the doors opened, and on the other side there could have been a huddle of them, masked and armed and waiting for me, but it wasn't them. It was the outside world, and it had never looked so fucking beautiful as it did right then, and then I ran and I didn't look back.

I never looked back.

BOOK III

From *The Regional Office Is Under Attack:*
*Tracking the Rise and Fall of an American Institution*

When other scholars try to pin onto the first Oracle the blame for the fall of the Regional Office, these scholars often point to a moment that occurred early into her tenure as Oracle. Or they try to trace a link from the discovery of the first Oracle to the discovery of that first Oracle's daughter to the fall of the Regional Office, a specious argument, at best.

Anyone foolish enough to assign blame for either the rise or the fall of an organization as complex as the Regional Office to one source proves himself little able to understand the nuance of history, an understanding of nuance necessary for strong scholarship. History and complex systems cannot be boiled down to mere sound bites or taglines, but sadly recent published (and peer-reviewed) research demonstrates the current and dangerous trend of encapsulation that this paper hopes to speak against. The very people who will lay blame at the feet of the Oracle once known as Nell are no better than those who make illogical and obstreperous claims that Mr. Niles might be blamed for the spectacular failings of the overall Regional Office.

After her transformation, the Oracle in question, the first Oracle, once known as Nell, remained in the office. She sat out front. She stared out the windows. She didn't speak. She didn't sleep, either. If she ate, Mr. Niles had never been a witness to that spectacle.

Slowly, Oyemi gathered the materials she needed to build the Oracle a space where she could prognosticate in the time-honored manner of oracles littered all over B movies and pulp science-fiction and fantasy novels. A shallow pool of milky-blue water (check), a darkly lit room imbued with an eerie, sourceless blue-white glow (check), a bald and trembling and ageless woman connected by hoses or cables to a futuristic melding of computer and man (eh, more or less, if that's what you'd call a few orange first-generation iMacs Oyemi bought secondhand and jerry-rigged herself). She gave up her office for the Oracle, set the turtle-shaped kiddie pool on a platform in the middle of the room so that the Oracle would still be able to look out the window at the traffic on the street and the buildings on the other side. The computers—there were four in all—were attached to a couple of printers. It was all still a trial-and-error sort of game, as far as Niles could tell. The few times he walked in on Oyemi, she was digging into the back of one of the computers or testing the cables out on other computers and the Oracle was seated quietly in a chair at the window.

Mr. Niles did little to hide how little he thought of all this.

He asked Oyemi if the Oracle had given them the Powerball numbers yet. He once walked into the office wearing gauze wrapped around his head and over his eyes, gauze he'd made to look cheaply bloody with red Magic Marker. When Oyemi didn't notice, or noticed but ignored him, he pretended to stumble around the office blind and said, "Could you give me a hand here? I've stabbed my eyes out because I killed my father and fucked my mother." And then, "Oh, if only I'd been warned of my horrific fate!"

He knew he wasn't being helpful or a good friend or a good business partner. He knew that he was slowly sabotaging their plans of saving the world, of rescuing and training at-risk but powerful, oh so powerful, young women, everything they had talked about, but he couldn't help himself. He didn't want an Oracle. He didn't want to believe in or rely on the Oracle, didn't trust her or whatever machinations Oyemi had performed on her. And if he had been more honest with himself maybe he would have understood that what he had been against wasn't the Oracle herself, but anyone or anything stepping in between him and Oyemi. Instead, he latched on to a lingering sense of unease about the fact that they had abducted the Oracle, though this had become dulled by the quiet, unsettling presence of her sitting unvaryingly at that window, and to this, he attributed his distaste for what was going on.

Not that she seemed unhappy—or happy, for that matter—nor that she seemed to harbor any intentions of escape, and he was sure that no one who had known her would recognize her, or her them, and truth be told, the people who had once laid claim to her probably wouldn't want her back, not anymore. Regardless, he felt that they—he and Oyemi—had moved too far afield from their original intentions. They'd made plans. After they had understood more fully the scope of Oyemi's transformation, they had conjured together beautiful, brilliant plans. The world was in need of their help—it was clear—and they wouldn't let the world down. They would build an army of superwomen. (There had been an unspoken agreement that they would only seek out women.) They would recruit and train these women to fight the evil forces of darkness. Together, they would root out evil, become an all-knowing and all-powerful force. And maybe, if they made some money along the way, what was the harm in that?

They had all of this to do. They had a world—or worlds, even—to explore and exploit and make their own, and none of this Oracle business, none of this kidnapping rigmarole, seemed to fit in with any of that.

But mostly, he felt jealous. Jealous of the attention Oyemi was devoting to this woman. Jealous of this strange, wordless connection they shared. And this jealousy needed an outlet. The fact that Oyemi had brought this person into their plans needed some reckoning. That she had done so without consulting him needed some reckoning. He needed to remind her, for his own cruel purposes, that this Oracle had once been a woman, had once had a life that Oyemi had diverted to her own agenda.

To get back at Oyemi, then, he went in search of the girl in the photograph, the photograph he had found in Nell's wallet the day they'd abducted her. He didn't know who she was or where she might be, but he knew her name.

Nell had written it on the back of the picture.

Sarah. Her name was Sarah.

Judging by the photograph, Sarah had been young. Five or six, maybe. She had dark hair and big eyes and a pretty face. He assumed she was the Oracle's daughter. He went to the address on the driver's license first, which turned up little more than Missing Person posters of Nell, which he tried to inconspicuously pull down, even though they were old and weathered and torn. Nell's apartment was empty but the landlord told Niles not to get his hopes up, as it had already been rented, and thank God, since the last tenants had skipped out on the place almost two months ago, a woman and her kid, and who the hell knew where they'd gone off to.

That had been his only lead. Once he'd found out that there had been no real effort to find Nell, he should have given up on the girl, gone back to Oyemi or moved forward to a new life, but he found his thoughts returning to Sarah whenever his mind was left to its own devices. He began to seek her out in newspapers, looking for mentions of the daughter of a woman named Nell gone missing now for eight weeks, twelve weeks, but there was nothing.

By this time, Oyemi had finished building out her office space for the Oracle. She seemed reluctant to show it to Mr. Niles, though, which made him feel guilty. Ever since he'd started looking for the girl in earnest, he had barely stopped by the office, had said no more than ten words to Oyemi. Caught up in their own projects, they were growing apart, and Mr. Niles didn't doubt that this would continue to an unsatisfying and regretful final split, but in hopes of making up for all of this, he expressed a keen and overindulgent interest in seeing the Oracle's room when Oyemi told him it was finally finished.

Little about the room had changed. It was warmer in there because of the bank of humming computers, Niles assumed. It was dark inside, dimly lit by some ethereal glow. Something about it all left him unsettled. Perhaps the hum of the computers or the heat or the strange way the room dampened their voices when they spoke or the fact that the Oracle still didn't speak, that he didn't realize she was even there at first, lingering just under the surface of the water, or maybe it was the connections, thick black cables running from the computers to the pool, disappearing into the underside of the pool, and into the

Oracle herself, so he assumed, half-submerged in the pool. Mr. Niles couldn't say. Or maybe it was the crown of diodes or neural connectors wrapped around her bald head or the blue and red and gray USB cables jacked, somehow, into her pronated hands, which hung limp over the pool's edge. Or maybe it was all of it. Or maybe it was simply that the not-rightness of Oyemi and her plans had finally been writ large, made so undeniably clear that all that was left for Mr. Niles to do was to mourn what had been his best friend.

He glanced at Oyemi, only to find her looking at him. She was waiting for him to say something. Did you catch the Mets game last night? he wanted to say. Or, Affleck's got a new movie out, want to go? Anything, really, that might bring reality, life outside, crashing down into this weird space she'd built, as if the presence of an outside world complete with a piss-poor Mets team and so-so Affleck movies would make Oyemi see the ridiculousness, or the wrongness, of it all.

Maybe he could have tried harder. Redirected her, maybe. When she'd first asked him more than a year ago if he'd wanted to have some fun—with her new discovered powers, with her great-uncle's money—maybe he could have suggested a ski vacation or a road trip to Mexico instead.

"We can do whatever we want," she'd told him. "We can change the world, can make it better, can change so many lives."

And he'd lied. He'd said, "I don't know what I want yet," when he knew, or believed, that what he'd wanted was her. This want of her had been with him for so long, in fact, since the sixth or seventh grade, that it had seemed eternal or like an extension of him. That it remained with him, even after the accident, even after the physical change, the revelation of her new special traits, only made it seem that much more permanent, so that when it slipped away from him, when he looked at her one day and she said to him, "We should do this," and he realized the wanting had completely gone, he felt guilty, as if he'd betrayed not just her but some simple and necessary part of himself. So he said, "Yes, yes we should."

From that point forward, to practically everything she asked or suggested, no matter how insane or possibly evil, he said, "Yes, of course we should."

But faced with this bald and enigmatic figure floating in a turtle pool, he felt forming on his lips for the first time the word *no*.

Then Oyemi left. A phone call or something, although later Mr. Niles figured out this had been a ruse, that Oyemi had simply wanted to leave Niles by himself with the Oracle. He waited, unsure of what to do or where to look. He wanted to sit down but there were no seats in the room. He considered sitting on the edge of her pool, tracing lazy eights in the water with his fingertips, but that thought made him shudder.

He tried to think of different things to say to her, pithy, unconcerned remarks in case Oyemi was standing nearby listening in, if only to prove to them both—Oyemi, the Oracle—that he wasn't bothered by any of this and that he didn't buy any of it either. But the best he could come up with were the blandest of statements—how's it going, how's the view, what's new in the Oracle business—and so he kept quiet, stuffed his hands in his pockets, and waited.

After a minute she spoke.

He was so unprepared for her to speak, so unprepared for what her voice might sound like, he didn't hear what she said at all and dumbly said, "Did you say something?"

Her voice had a property to it, distant and echoing, as if she were plugged into an amplifier with the reverb set to high, or as if she were more than one person talking at once. She hadn't turned to look at him but it seemed as if her voice filled the room and he wondered if Oyemi had set the Oracle up with speakers or something.

"Brooklyn," she said again. "What you're looking for will be in Brooklyn," she said, and before he could say anything, before he could contest her, tell her that there was no way in hell that she would know a good goddamn thing about what he was looking for, she said, "You'll find what you seek in Brooklyn." Then the printer began to warm up and then it took a sheet of paper and printed out an address at the top of it, a map underneath. He took the sheet and looked at the address. He looked at the Oracle.

"I know what this is," he said. Then, louder: "I know what you're doing." Then, yelling: "Don't think that I don't know what the fuck you're trying to pull here." Not at the Oracle. He didn't say a word to the Oracle. Not that it would have mattered. She stared out the window and ignored him. Oyemi still hadn't come back, but Niles took the slip of paper, folded it a few times, and stuffed it into his jeans pocket and left before Oyemi could return.

It took him nearly a week to go to the address the Oracle had given him. In that week, he didn't once call Oyemi or drop by the office. He kept the slip of paper in his pants pocket at all times. He worried his fingers over it when he was nervous or when his mind was preoccupied, and not a few times he pulled it out of his pocket forgetting what it was, thinking maybe it was an old receipt, something he should throw away. Seeing the address printed across the top, he would fold it back again and stuff it quickly away. He did this so often that the paper was soft and smudgy from his attention.

When he finally went to the address that the Oracle had given him, he found himself at the corner of Avenue M and East Thirteenth, one of the many parts of Brooklyn wholly unfamiliar to him and where there was nothing more than a bodega. Inside, he asked about the address, which he couldn't find, because the clerk claimed the street number didn't exist.

Of course, Niles thought. And what had he expected, really?

He was about to leave, then, when the bell over the door chimed and in walked the girl, the one from the photograph. Sarah.

Seeing her there, he panicked for no good reason. His first instinct was to run off before she could see him. Then he remembered she didn't know him, didn't know he had been looking for her, didn't know he'd taken her mother from her and had turned her—or had been party to the turning of her—into the very same creature that had sent him here to find her, even though how the girl's mother had known he was looking for the girl in the first place he couldn't have said. Then he took a deep breath and pulled his shit together and stepped into one of the aisles and pretended to look like he was shopping, and he watched the girl. She was two or three years older than in the photo, but it was her, he was certain of it.

When he was feeling good about himself, confident in his convictions, he would look back at this moment in the bodega and convince himself it was dumb luck that the girl happened into the store when he wasn't even technically looking for her. The only other possibility—that the Oracle had known not just where the girl would be but that she had known where she would be when Niles would be there, had known that Niles would sit on the address for a week before seeking it out, or had not actually known any of this, had simply had a premonition that spat out an address that happened to lead him right to the girl—undermined too many firm beliefs he held about this world, his control over his own life.

At the moment, though, seeing Sarah for the first time, he didn't consider any of this. He watched and listened and waited and when she left, he followed after.

For a long time, he followed after her.

She was living with her aunt in a neighborhood deeper into Brooklyn. Her father had been absent for her entire life.

She was not just a pretty girl, but was smart and could be funny.

She was a third-grader at a middling elementary school in Sheepshead Bay.

She had few friends, and just as few enemies, and despite being a rather pretty little girl, she moved through her life mostly unnoticed.

She did not like bologna, or, at the very least, didn't like it enough to keep for herself but instead fed it to stray cats whenever it was given to her for lunch.

He found out all of this and he found out a number of other things and he found that he didn't have the first clue what to do with everything he found out about her. But mostly he found that he couldn't stop thinking about her, couldn't stop worrying over the life he and Oyemi had boxed her into when they ran off with her mother. Thoughts of her kept him up at night—her crying herself to sleep or naming one of her dolls after her mother or lashing out at her aunt or cutting herself with tiny razors or turning to drugs and drinking or seeking out ways to slip through the cracks of a normal, healthy childhood. So it made him laugh once, long after he'd brought her to Regional, after he'd made her into a new kind of woman, when he asked her about her childhood, and she described for him as bland and normal and dully happy a childhood as he could have imagined. But at the time, as he waited for her to run out of school with the rest of the kids, as he followed her on her way back home, as he stood outside her apartment or tracked her to Coney Island or into the city, he imagined for her a wretched and untenable life.

Looking back on it all, it was difficult for him to understand how he managed to spend so much of his day in pursuit of this girl, watching her, making sure that she was, on the surface at least, okay. He would set up a trust for her, he decided, find some way to make it seem like a prize or award she'd won. He would make himself somehow a silent part of her life, dub himself her Magwitch.

In the meantime, he resigned himself to watching over her, as if the simple act of keeping an eye on her were enough to keep her out of trouble, keep her safe, help her to become happy.

After nearly two months, Mr. Niles went back to Oyemi, the office, the Oracle. He didn't know what to expect. He had long ago found an apartment of his own. He had lost contact with her, and she had left him to himself. No phone calls, no late-night arrivals on his doorstep. Either Oyemi had given up on Mr. Niles or she was so mad at him for ducking out, and for so long, that she'd cut him off entirely.

The front door was unlocked and he steeled himself to face her, but Oyemi wasn't there. Instead, there was a note, folded over with his name written across the top of it. His name and the date. Maybe she wrote this sort of note every day, he thought. Maybe she expected him to show up unannounced any day of the week, and she left him a newly dated note every day. Unlikely, but maybe. The note was short, simple. "Back tomorrow. Oyemi." Mr. Niles looked around the front office and then his own smaller office. Not much had changed. Then he went in to see the Oracle.

The room was dark, as the sun had begun to set, and everything in it was bathed in blues and greens and reds from the computers and printers, the glowing water. She stared out the window, even though there was less and less for her to see there, and for the first time he wondered what she was looking at, what she was looking for. He wondered if she even saw what was right in front of her, or if Oyemi's administrations had taken that away from her, had made any kind of present sight impossible.

He cleared his throat. She didn't move. He began to speak and then stopped and then started again, feeling self-conscious and like a boy in trouble, or in love.

"I found her," he said.

"Sarah," he said, though barely loudly enough to hear himself over the fans and motors running in the room. "Just so you know," he said.

"Not that you wouldn't have known anyway, I guess.

"Not that you need me to tell you what happened."

She hadn't moved. She didn't look as if she could hear him, or as if she cared, or as if she had any sense of anything going on in this world. She looked as if she were trapped inside a world maybe not of her own choosing and that no matter what he said or did, she wouldn't hear or recognize him, and so he turned to leave. And then the printer kicked into gear.

A small slip of paper fell into the tray.

Mr. Niles, unsure what else he should do, picked it up, read it.

*How is she?*

He should leave, he knew. He should open the door behind him and leave and take the slip of paper with him and never speak to the Oracle again; he knew all of this. Instead, he said, "Fine. I suppose."

He said, "Not great, of course. I mean. Confused, maybe. Sad? But she's with family, or. She's making it."

He looked at the slip in his hands. He felt he should say more. He had come to her, after all. The air between them begged for him to say something more.

"I'm going to help her," he said. "I don't know how, yet. But I'm going to take care of her. Keep an eye on her for you."

He waited for the printer to start up again. It didn't. He coughed and cleared his throat. He didn't know how to finish things up here, so he moved to leave again, deciding that an, Okay, well, thanks for the assist, or whatever else he could come up with to say would feel like the worst thing he could say, worse than saying nothing at all.

Then she sat up.

Not all the way up. The cables, the cords, the diodes or neural monitors, whatever was attached, however they were attached, wouldn't let her sit all the way up. She struggled to pull herself higher out of the water and he worried that she would pull something out, break something, short the building, electrocute herself.

She turned. Again, not all the way. But she turned from her window and she looked right at him, not through him or past him or at the world or worlds she could see around him. She was pale and trembling and covered in a thin sheen of sweat, and she was crying, had been crying.

"Can I see her?" she said, not through the printer, but with her voice, and not her Oracle voice, full of thrumming portent and hidden wells of power, but with the soft, mousy, simple voice he remembered from the unassuming girl he'd spoken to outside of Duane Reade.

He shook his head, but just barely, slight enough you could have missed it.

"Can you let me go to her, go to see her, can you let me go, please?"

He moved now, slowly but deliberately, for the door. He inched his way there, avoiding sudden movements, as if she were a pack of wild dogs or a bear. He didn't shake his head or nod or tell her soothing lies. He hoped that if he simply stopped responding, she would stop talking.

She didn't.

Two months before, three months before, if she'd asked him to set her free like this, if she'd made even the slightest movement toward escape, he would have helped her. Oyemi be damned, he would have let her go. But not anymore. She had suddenly proved herself to Mr. Niles, had maneuvered him to Sarah and shown him how powerful she could be, and maybe she hadn't known that this was going to happen, maybe she had printed out that address with no knowledge of what was going to happen, but she had given him that address, had made herself seem far too real, and as much as it pained him to say so, and as often as he would, in the future, deny to himself the validity of her predictions, Oyemi was right. They needed her. They had her. He wasn't going to be the one to let her go.

She didn't raise her voice or try to pull herself out of the pool. She simply sat there, halfway out of the water, halfway turned to look at him, connected in her unsettling way to the computers and printers and who knew what else, and spoke her plea to him with soft, unending persistence: Please, please let me see her, let me go to her, let me see her, please, just to see her, just to hold her, please, let me go, can't I go see her, can't I go be with her.

He opened the door, stepped out of the room, and closed the door. Oyemi had done something to the doors and the walls because it seemed as if he had stepped into a vacuum. All the sound from the other room cut off, and the sudden silence made him nervous. He pressed his ear to the door to listen, to see if the Oracle had stopped pleading with him when the door had closed, but he couldn't tell. He couldn't hear anything at all but his own shallow, labored breath. His neck hurt and his shoulders felt sluggish and sore. He needed to sit down, to sit and catch his breath, let his body, which wouldn't stop shaking, recover, but he couldn't stand to be there, afraid she might try to disconnect herself and come tumbling after him from the pool, wet and naked.

He went home. He waited up all night. He couldn't sleep, couldn't get her voice out of his head, but mostly couldn't stop thinking of what ramifications this might have, what consequences he might suffer at Oyemi's hands if he'd somehow damaged the Oracle, broken her, made her unusable.

She might kill him when she found out. Kill him or worse.

When Oyemi called him the next morning, though, it was simply to tell him about a lead on a girl outside of

Chicago. She acted as if they hadn't just lost two months between them. She didn't ask him what he'd been doing all this time, didn't yell or guilt-trip or threaten or beg. And when he asked her about this later, Oyemi confided in him: She had known. The Oracle had told her that very first day they'd brought her back to the office, had told her that Mr. Niles would seem to be lost, but that he would return, that she should let him be lost for a while, confident that he would return.

That morning, though, she only told him the Oracle was already hard at work, had already found a girl. "She's in Peoria," Oyemi told him. "I've got the details on her at the office. Pick them up on your way to the airport. I've got you on the ten forty-five out of Newark."

After that night, Nell faded away. Maybe, Niles thought, that night had been her last gasp. For a while, he worried that she might resurface, might ask him again about her daughter, but she never did. From that moment forward, she was an Oracle and nothing else, and was soon joined by the others, and there were days when Niles forgot entirely who she had once been.

As for Sarah, she grew older. She moved effortlessly from elementary school to middle school, excelled in science and math, was accepted into Bronx Science, the prestigious magnet school. She played volleyball and ran track. She made the National Honor Society and won a small prize for a robotics competition when she was fifteen, and by the time she entered her senior year of high school, she'd been accepted at Caltech. The very real possibility that she would leave the city, would leave Mr. Niles's sphere of influence, loomed over him and frightened and saddened him. This was when he first tried to work her into the list of credible Recruits for the Regional Office. When that didn't work, he came up with the idea of feeding her information about her mother's disappearance. He varied this just slightly from the truth, namely in that in his new version, Nell was abducted by someone else and was eventually killed. Then he left Sarah a trail to follow that led her, finally, and just as she turned twenty, back to him.

He took her in. He made her promises. He made her strong and powerful and tied her to him. He gave her a mechanical arm. It was the only way he could think of to bring her into the fold, to make her as much like the Operatives as possible, to give her power and control over her own life. He trained her in deadly arts. He entrusted his organization to her and convinced her to entrust her future to him, and when her mother and the two other Oracles made their prophecies, he and Oyemi paid attention.

When the Oracles singled out a girl imbued with latent mystical properties that, when honed, when unleashed, would make her powerful, they paid attention. Every single time, every single girl, he and Oyemi paid attention.

When the Oracles pointed them to Henry, living in Buffalo, working as an underpaid, overworked bike courier, they paid attention. They collected him, brought him to the Regional Office, though they had no idea what they were supposed to do with him. (They gave him a job in the mail room, where he stayed for almost a year, underworked and overpaid, and Mr. Niles and Oyemi remained in the dark about what to do with him until one day Mr. Niles discovered him sitting in the stairwell sharing a cigarette with one of the new Recruits. The new Recruit showed great promise, according to the Oracles, but Mr. Niles had made little headway in her training. She abused the other Recruits and belittled the martial arts trainer and no one liked her and she lied and cheated and stole from the other girls, even the other Operatives. And until Mr. Niles found her sitting in the stairwell with Henry, he and Oyemi had assumed she hated everyone in the entire office. Her name was Jasmine. Afterward, Mr. Niles found Henry and asked him what they had been talking about and Henry told him, "Not much, really, just stuff." Then Mr. Niles watched Henry and Jasmine more closely under the suspicion that Henry was hoping to become romantically involved with Jasmine. Instead, what he found was a remarkably improved Jasmine: in her training, in her attitudes. What he also found was that Henry spent time chatting with all of the Recruits, and the Operatives, too. But. They came to him. They found him. In the mail room or in the break room or as he was getting out of his car or as he was riding the elevator down to B4. They found him and talked to him and asked his advice and showed him what they had learned and he showed them how to do what they had learned even better. "Do you have experience with martial arts or weapons training?" Mr. Niles asked him, and Henry shook his head and said, "Not really, no," and he took Henry to meet Oyemi, and Oyemi, who had never been as strong when reading men as she was when reading women, shook her head, too, and shrugged her shoulders, and said, afterward, "If you think it's the best move, Mr. Niles, then, by all means, take it." And so Mr. Niles did, and the next day, Henry was moved out of the mail room and into an office, and that afternoon, he flew with Mr. Niles to Shreveport, where Mr. Niles was to collect a new Recruit, a girl who knew nothing of the latent powers within her, knew nothing of the evil forces of darkness surrounding her, and at the last moment, he turned to Henry and said, "You take it from here," said, "All you need to do is get her to the Regional Office," and Henry shrugged and said, "Sure," and he said, "Any words of advice?" and Mr. Niles said, "Try not to scare her," and Henry laughed and said, "Me? I don't scare anyone," and within ten minutes, they were back in the rental car on their way to the airport on their way back to the Regional Office, the girl sitting close to Henry in the backseat, the two of them joking as if they'd been best friends since preschool. It had been the smoothest recruitment Mr. Niles had ever witnessed, and after that, Henry was given control of recruitment and outreach.)

When the Oracles sent message after message to Mr. Niles and Oyemi leading them time and time again to a building on Park and Fifty-Seventh, they paid attention, and moved their offices to that very spot.

When the Oracles offered cryptic messages concerning a dark power rising in Budapest or Akron or Cape Town, they paid attention.

And the Oracles had not once, never once, steered them wrong.

So when the Oracles began to make noise about the demise of the Regional Office, when they spoke of the death of Oyemi herself, when they spoke of betrayal from within, they paid attention.

When the Oracles singled out Emma, their brightest Operative, their fastest and smartest and strongest, they paid attention. When the woman who was once Nell singled out Henry as the one to kill her, they listened to Nell then, too.

A commonly held theory posits that the Oracle formerly Nell was misunderstood. That Mr. Niles and Oyemi believed incorrectly that Henry was being singled out as a solution to the problem, when in fact he was part of the problem. It seems reasonable to assume that Mr. Niles and Oyemi were so caught up in the larger picture of the Regional Office that they did not know about the romantic relationship that had evolved between Emma and Henry. All of the Recruits and Operatives had a relationship with Henry, brotherly, or fatherly, but platonic, always platonic, so it did not strike them as out of the ordinary that he would be close to Emma, too. He was close to all of them. That was part of his job.

Surely, if they had known, they would not have assigned him as her executioner, would have more simply killed her while on assignment, made it to look an accident. Evidence exists that Mr. Niles pushed for such a solution to the very end, in fact, but Oyemi, in her misreading, would not stray from the plan to use Henry as the Oracles had instructed.

Had Oyemi and Mr. Niles better understood the prophecy, might they have escaped it? Many believe so, since it has since been proven that Henry, over two years, and some believe Emma at his side (or rather, as she lay in hiding), planned and executed the assault on the Regional Office that resulted in the deaths of Mr. Niles and Oyemi, in the destruction of Oyemi's compound and the consequential destruction of the Oracles, too.

There is another theory, one that extrapolates unreasonably from this reasonable hypothesis. This theory often bandied about and gaining traction even among those who should know better is that the Oracle formerly named Nell intentionally introduced Oyemi and Mr. Niles to information—not necessarily untrue information—of an event that would never have come to pass had the information remained unrevealed. Furthermore, that this Oracle acted specifically to enact vengeance on Oyemi and Mr. Niles for making her an Oracle at all. As implausible and ridiculous as this theory is, let us take a moment to disassemble it.

Set aside for the moment the plain and simple fact that Oracles do not control the future they see or report on— i.e., they do not control the future, nor do they control what they see of the future—set aside this universally acknowledged truth and the argument remains as easily undermined as ever.

Consider these questions, which remain unanswered by those who would argue in favor of the agency of an Oracle:

1. When would the Oracle have first conceived of this plan, and why would it have waited nearly fifteen years to set it in motion?

2. What do we make of the Oracle's own sense of self-preservation, of its desire to protect its daughter? Would the Oracle not have foreseen not just Oyemi's and Mr. Niles's downfall but also the horrific transformation lying in wait for its daughter? Would it not have been simpler and safer and more humane to subvert the actions of the two who formed the Regional Office at its outset, when the Oracle's daughter was still just a girl, hurt and saddened, certainly, by life's early traumas, but comparatively unchanged, unharmed?

And, finally:

3. How could the Oracle know the exact consequences of
   its own actions when general theory holds that Oracles have little to no specific foreknowledge or understanding of their own personal timelines?

These questions fail to address even the most simple
matters of logistics—how did the Oracle, for instance,
convince her other two cohorts that this would indeed
become the future? Those who argue in favor of a righ-
teously vengeful Oracle puppet-stringing the likes of Mr.
Niles and Oyemi and the whole of the Regional Office
to its own demise fail to respond to these and the numer-
ous other questions posed to them, arguing that since
the Oracles were destroyed in the fire that destroyed
Oyemi's compound and, presumably, Oyemi herself, the
same day the Regional Office came under attack, scholars will never know for sure the intentions underlying the
actions of the Oracles, a position that will no doubt be
argued until there remains no breath left for argument,
but which fails to convince the authors of this paper, who
consider the case closed.

# 38.

Sarah wasn't actually asleep. She was only pretending to be asleep.

She had become quite good at pretending to be asleep. At pretending to be other things, too.

Unconscious, for instance.

Sobbing uncontrollably was also a thing she had become good at pretending to do.

Horrified into a state of catatonia by the constant reminder that someone had launched an assault on the Regional Office. Horrified that in the meantime, someone had also wrenched her mechanical arm from her body.

That.

She had become quite good at pretending to be that.

It helped—if *helped* was the right word—that they helped by repeatedly hitting her in the face or the back of the head or shocking her with electrodes and asking her if she was so tough now, now that she didn't have her mechanical arm.

Hitting her without questioning her. Hitting her just to hit her.

That is to say: Some of the times she might not have been pretending.

But right now, she pretended to be asleep. She'd closed her eyes. She'd done her best to relax and deepen her breathing, make it regular. Her chin had fallen so that it just barely touched her chest. She was doing her best to convince the people who had her hostage that she was asleep, not because that might keep them from stomping up to her to wake her, hit her more, but because through the cracked office door she could hear their radios and she wanted to listen without their knowing she was listening because listening gave her hope, because what she could hear was not good, not good for them, not good for them at all.

There were shouts and screams and gun bursts of a violent but confused and frightened nature. Someone shouted out of the walkie-talkie something along the lines of, Blue Team! Blue Team! Report in! Report!, with little success. Someone else suggested sending Emerald Team to go check in with Blue Team but before panic could take firm hold of these panicky mercenaries, Wendy—that asshole intern Wendy—told everyone to shut the fuck up and calm the fuck down because no one was going to check on Blue Team and don't you idiots watch television, watch movies? Don't you idiots know that sending team after team after team is like throwing good money after bad? Everyone sticks to the plan, she told them, and that's that.

Sarah pretended she was sleeping but in her sleep, she smiled. Not a big smile, not a triumphant smile, but a sly and knowing, tiny, barely perceptible smile.

# 39.

"No one respects me," Sarah told Mr. Niles, shortly after he'd appointed her his right-hand man, no pun intended.

"They will," he'd said. "Give it time," he'd said. "Show them the you I know, and they will fall in line, and they will respect you," he'd said.

Hearing this, she'd wondered, in the far back of her mind, But will they like me?

And slightly farther back than that she'd wondered, Who is the real me?

Because she didn't know. Before, she'd been a certain kind of person—who went to college, whose childhood had been scarred by personal tragedy—and after that, she'd become a different sort of person, the kind of person who possessed a mechanical arm and had been given the opportunity to exact formidable vengeance on those who'd caused her childhood tragedy.

But now, and outside of that, who was she?

Not that it mattered. For all the efforts she made to be the kind of boss that would make them feel respect, or awe, or fearful regard, the people who worked for her, the people she was in charge of, didn't fall in line, respect her, or like her.

Except Henry.

Henry seemed to like her, or to not dislike her, anyway. They acted like friends, or close acquaintances.

He listened to her, that is, when it seemed that Mr. Niles had stopped.

"No one respects me," she would tell Henry over lunch or a drink. "No one likes me."

And he would take a bite of salad or a sip of beer and say, "You're kind of an asshole sometimes." Or he would say, "You're an easy target."

"They act like I'm an office manager," she would tell him. "They tell me when the copier needs new toner. Or when they need new Post-it notes. Or when the water cooler bottle needs to be changed. Or when the interns fuck up. They tell me these things and then walk away and then laugh, I can hear them laugh. All those nine-to-fivers, laughing at me."

And inevitably, he'd say: "You're not the office manager?" Or, "Wait, who is the office manager?"

And every time, even though she knew what he was doing, she'd say: "Carol. Carol's the fucking office manager."

And he'd laugh and he'd tell her, "See? You're too sensitive," or, "They know this pisses you off," or, "You have to ignore it," or, "You can't let them get to you."

Easy enough for Henry to say, though. People liked Henry. People waited for Henry to speak before offering their own opinions, which often closely mirrored Henry's. They went to him for advice about things he knew nothing about and listened to him even more attentively when he claimed—truthfully—that he didn't have the answers.

Henry never had to ignore the things she couldn't ignore. These jokes and pranks and personal slights always got to her. And why shouldn't they have? She'd laid waste to an entire secret black-ops organization that had been terrorizing the Western world for going on thirty years. When a few office drones called her into the break room because they couldn't open a jar of pickles and they needed her with her mechanical arm to loosen the top up for them, except that the top had already been loosened, or manipulated in such a way that by giving it a good twist, the whole jar exploded, throwing pickle juice all over her and the floor and the walls and the ceiling, even though she'd used her nonmechanical arm against this very eventuality, when a thing like that happened, she couldn't very well let them get away with that.

She had pickle juice in her hair for fuck's sake.

Henry had told her to laugh it off, to let it go, that to address it only fueled it.

But as far as she could see, Henry wasn't the one with pickle juice in his hair.

# 40.

The truth of the matter was, Sarah wouldn't have cared as much about the nine-to-fivers ("They know you call them that," Henry had told her) if she'd had a better track record with the Operatives, who were, in her own mind, more closely aligned with her and her hybrid position at the office.

Sarah met her first Operative for the Regional Office a month after she recovered from obtaining a new arm. Before then, Mr. Niles had kept Sarah mostly to himself and to the doctor, whose leg was healing nicely. For most of a month, she spent her days in the lab or recovering in her room.

"Soon enough," Mr. Niles told her, "you'll meet everyone else. Henry, our Recruiter. The Operatives."

"Is that what I am?" she asked. "An Operative?"

Mr. Niles laughed and said, "No, no, Sarah. You're a client. We work for you. All of this," he said, gesturing at her room, her mechanical arm, the file full of information about her mother's disappearance, "is for you."

The training, too, or so he explained it. Because she was not the type of woman to be satisfied to know others had avenged her mother on her behalf. No. Mr. Niles could tell. She would only be satisfied if the vengeance was hers. The arm, the training, the recon and support—these were offered to her by the Regional Office. All of that, and the wisdom and experience of the Regional Office's own Operatives.

The first Operative she met was Jasmine, and she was tall and statuesque and dark-complected and the most striking woman Sarah had ever seen except that standing behind Jasmine, waiting for Jasmine's cue, were four or five more of the most striking women Sarah had ever seen. She didn't know the names of the others but she knew Jasmine's name because Jasmine was the loudest and brashest of the Operatives she'd seen on campus since she'd arrived, since she'd begun her own training session. She laughed the loudest, often at her own jokes, and in the training room, she screamed the loudest when she attacked, loud enough that Sarah could hear her scream even through the sealed door, the protected viewing windows.

"Hi," Sarah said, holding out her hand for Jasmine to shake. "I'm Sarah."

Jasmine stared at the hand and then threw a brief glance back at the girls standing behind her.

"You're Jasmine, right?" Sarah said, trying to keep any emotions out of her voice. She was wondering how long she would keep her hand held out like that, how long before Jasmine either took it or acknowledged it, or before Sarah let it drop back to her side.

"I don't shake robot hands," Jasmine said, the beginnings of a smirk creeping into her lips.

"It's not," Sarah began, about to share the secret of which hand was which, but then she remembered and shifted, seamlessly, she hoped. "A problem," she finished, and brought her hand back down to her side and then put it inside her other hand, and then let it drop to her side again, feeling self-conscious suddenly about what to do with her hands.

"I'm supposed to train with you guys this morning," she said. Jasmine shook her head and frowned and turned and started walking, the others falling in step behind her. Sarah hated herself for doing this, but she did a half-jog to keep up with Jasmine, who must have been at least seven feet tall. Sarah smiled up at Jasmine as if any of this behavior were normal behavior and continued, "I've been doing a lot of one-on-one work with Robert, martial arts Robert? You know, Robert? Of course you know Robert." She could feel all of the words, every single word ever, tumbling out of her mouth and she couldn't stop them. "I mean, you know, a lot of hand-to-hand combat training, which has been great, but Mr. Niles? He wants me to get in some group training, too."

Jasmine stopped and Sarah turned and saw they were standing at the door to the training room, which Sarah couldn't help but think of as the Danger Room, even though she made sure not to say this out loud for fear of being made fun of. Ever since she'd arrived, she'd been afraid of being made fun of, or being pitied, or being ignored, and something about Jasmine, about her posture, about her eyes, made Sarah feel like all three were happening simultaneously.

"After you," Jasmine said, opening the door.

Sarah stepped inside and then Jasmine closed the door behind her and sealed it shut. Then Jasmine's voice came through the intercom speaker. "But first, let's see what you've learned so far."

Sarah had hoped this would happen, had daydreamed it a number of times in the cafeteria, eating by herself, and in her dorm room, had pictured herself somehow trapped in the Danger Room alone or even with a few others, but with the attention on her, on her mechanical arm, the scenario thrown into high alert, attacks and obstacles coming at her too fast to see, too fast, even, for the Operatives. But not too fast for her, for her arm, her beautiful mechanical arm. And then the scenario would run its course, and the smoke and rubble and haze would clear as the room righted itself, and standing there in the middle of it all, not even breathing heavily, would be Sarah, untouched, unscathed, triumphant.

Which wasn't exactly how everything happened when Jasmine locked her in the training room by herself.

More, what happened was this:

The floor shifted under her, unexpectedly. She slipped, she scrambled to keep herself up, and so distracted by the shifting flooring, she failed to notice the swinging, padded mallets that lowered down from the ceiling. Not just those, but also the small gun turrets firing paint balls that slid out from openings in the walls. She failed to notice these too, and the tackling dummies running along rails in zigzagging patterns around the room. Watching the video repeatedly and in slow motion after the system was shut down by Mr. Niles, who had happened by to check in on everyone, Sarah could barely make out that it was the paint ball that first tagged her in her left shoulder, throwing her back in anger and surprise and right into one of the swinging mallets that clipped her right ear, that spun her around into a tackling dummy, which carried her for a few yards before another mallet knocked her out from the dummy's tenuous grasp, by which time the guns had locked her position pretty well and set up a barrage of paint pellets at her.

Less than two minutes had passed and she was curled up on the floor trying her best to cover her ears, her face, pelted by paint balls, covered in so much paint it had all run together and turned brown, her arm useless except to protect her head.

# 41.

Waiting, held hostage in the Regional Office, beaten and ridiculed, Sarah curbed her despair with a theory. One that explained the screaming and shouting going on over the radios, the loss of Blue Team and, if she wasn't mistaken, Emerald Team, too.

Someone had slipped through. When these assholes had stormed inside, rounded everyone up, someone had slipped through the cracks and was mounting a counteroffensive, not unlike the counteroffensive she had planned.

She wondered who it was.

She had someone in mind but still, she liked to play the game of wondering who it was out there in the building wreaking havoc on Blue Team and Emerald Team and whatever other goddamn teams were out there. Worming his way through the air ducts and back stairwells and through empty offices, laying waste to everyone in his path, John McClane–style.

From what she could tell, the girls, their girls, seemed to be off on a mission—she didn't know how but these bastards had tapped into the Regional Office protocols, had sent them all on bogus missions all across the globe. And if what she had seen was accurate, they'd sent Jasmine, their best, to a whole different, alternate universe. And the Recruits? Where were they? Trapped, probably, inside their dorm on the Upper West Side. Trapped and fighting their own fight. She didn't know for sure.

Which told her two things: Whoever was behind this wasn't after the girls, or rather, might have been after the girls but not to destroy them, and whoever was out there playing *Die Hard*, in the stairwells and air ducts, wasn't one of the girls, either.

And it sure as hell wasn't one of the hostages, any of her dumb regular colleagues.

She'd had enough experience with the hostages, was full of enough pain and bruising and blood and broken bits of her, that she could attest for certain that it wasn't any one of the goddamn hostages, frightened little sheep who had just sat idly by while those goddamn mercenaries kicked her ass and who couldn't follow a simple plan, not even to save their own lives.

She hadn't seen the first sign of the security director all day and was beginning to suspect he'd been behind the security breach and also probably the protocol breach that sent the girls away, and even if he wasn't, even if he wasn't one of "them" and he had somehow managed to slip into work unnoticed by her or the bastards mounting this assault on the Regional Office, that didn't change the fact that the security director was a fat-fuck computer jockey who in no uncertain terms would have been unable to sneak around the building via the moderately sized air ducts or effect any change in this situation whatsoever.

In her mind, that left one person.

Well. Two people. That left two people.

It could be Henry. Sure. Henry was a possibility. Logic pointed to Henry. Field trained. Smart, capable.

If someone were to have asked her: Say an assault is mounted on the Regional Office and you're taken out of the equation and the Operatives are taken out of the equation too, and one rogue agent is maneuvering through the building slowly decimating the ranks of mercenaries who've attempted this assault, who do you think that rogue agent might be? Of course, she would have said, Henry.

Henry would have been that rogue agent. Everyone would know the answer would have been Henry, which was why it couldn't be Henry. Aside from the simple fact that she knew too much about Henry's crisis of faith, it couldn't be Henry because the people mounting this assault would have also known the answer would've been Henry. They would've known just as well as she did that if anyone were to become a rogue agent operating to save Regional, it would've had to have been Henry, and so they would've done one of two things before the assault even started: bring Henry on board, or kill him.

So it couldn't be Henry out there John McClane–style because Henry was dead. And if he wasn't dead, he was one of them, in which case he was still dead, and he simply didn't know it yet because she would be the one to kill him.

And so, by sound, logical reasoning, that left only one man in all of the Regional Office capable of all of this.

If her hunch was right, that left only Mr. Niles.

Not that her hunches had been right, or even close to right, so far that day, but if it's any consolation to Sarah—which it probably isn't—she would have been just as wrong thinking it was Henry.

# 42.

Two months into her training, Sarah came out of hand-to-hand combat class and a man of entirely average-sized good looks, aside from a nose a touch too wide for his face and curly hair that had grown too long, was standing outside waiting for her. Or so it seemed by the casual way he leaned against the wall, by the way he perked up and smiled and pushed off the wall when he saw her come out of the gym. She'd seen him around but hadn't met him and didn't know his name yet. He opened his mouth to say something but then was distracted by a group of Operatives, or maybe they were trainees, it was hard for Sarah to tell the difference. They all held themselves up with the same sort of haughty self-confidence, even the new ones.

"Hi, Henry," the gaggle of them said, and though none of them giggled, there was a hint of giggle in their voices. He smiled at them and gave them a little wave and as they were turning the corner, one of them looked at Sarah and said in a Stephen Hawking kind of voice, "Hi. Ro-bot." And this made the others laugh and then they were gone, but she could hear them laughing still.

She felt her face flush and she clenched her fists at her sides, then remembered herself and remembered the man standing in front of her, and she closed her eyes and relaxed her arms, both of them.

"Don't let them get to you," he said once she had opened her eyes and looked at him again. Then he smiled and said, "Man, that sounded pretty dumb. It always sounds better in a movie or something, doesn't it." He smiled again and held out his hand and said, "Henry. My name is Henry. Heard you've had a rough go of it."

"Well," Sarah began, reaching for his hand.

"Is it your left?" Henry interrupted. "Arm, that is. I've got a guy who bet me it was your right arm, but that seems just way too obvious." She pulled her hand back. He laughed an awkward but disarming laugh and said, "I'm kidding. I don't have a guy, or a bet. It's just easier for me to get the awkward thing out right away because I'm going to say it eventually. I know I am. But this way, I say it, and there's a weird moment, and then it's over, and then I'm not spending the whole conversation thinking about when I'm going to accidentally say the thing I'm not supposed to say." He held his hand out for a moment longer, then pulled it back, too. He shrugged and frowned. "It's a quirk. Now. How's training going? Pretty shitty, huh?"

"It can only go up from here, right?" Sarah said, and she felt like crying. She'd managed to contain all of the emotions that she should have been feeling about her arm, about being in the city and not with her aunt, about discovering the truth about her mother, about the way the other women had been treating her, and would have kept them all in check so long as no one asked her about any of it. But as soon as anyone said the first nice thing to her, all of it threatened to come out.

"Let's go get a drink," he said, doing a fine job of ignoring the tears welling in her eyes, which gave her a moment to wipe them away and shove the feelings that caused them back deep down inside herself. "Because, frankly, there's still down. Sorry to be the one to tell you this, but . . . Things can always go down.

"Your problem," Henry said, "and it's not just your problem, but your problem is you have this sense about you that there's something different about you."

Henry had taken her to a hotel bar not far from the travel agency. It wasn't yet two in the afternoon. They'd taken the elevator back up to the travel agency, had walked through the travel agency, had crossed Park and walked a few blocks, had come into this bar, and not once had Henry stopped talking. Henry hadn't given her time to change out of her training outfit and Sarah felt self-conscious, or she would have if anyone had been in the bar but the two of them and the bartender.

"There is something different about me," Sarah said, almost frustrated by how much she needed to talk to someone about all of this.

"Right. I know. Trust me, we all know. But there's something different about all of the women here. All the Operatives and trainee Recruits, anyway. They're all different from the rest of us, and from each other. But the difference between their difference and your difference—do you want to know the difference between their difference and your difference?" he asked. He knew she did, otherwise why would they be here talking about any of this? He liked to hear himself talk, Sarah could tell, and since he was the first person not Mr. Niles she'd found any sort of connection with, she humored him. She nodded and even went so far as to say, "What's the difference between their difference and my difference?"

He nodded back at her and took another drink of his beer, his third, but Sarah was trying not to judge him by it. "The difference," he said, "is how they carry that difference. Even the Recruits, even before they're recruited, even before we've sought them out, they carry what makes them different in an open and, I don't know, kind of loud way. You've seen them around the office, you can't not see them around the office. They're bigger than life, these women."

"But they are bigger," Sarah said, interrupting him. "Jesus, have you seen Jasmine? She's like a hundred feet tall."

Henry shook his head and paused to take another drink and then dropped his empty glass too heavily onto the table and said, "No, no she's not. You know how tall Jasmine is? It's in her file. I measured her myself."

"You measured Jasmine?"

"S'my job. Stop interrupting. I measured her myself and I kid you not. Five feet three inches."

"No she isn't."

"S'true. I'm going to get another drink. You want another drink? It's entirely true. You're what? Five four? Five five? You're taller than Jasmine. But. It's part of her power, or the mystical property of her. Or who knows what the fuck it's about, I just find them and train them. I'm no expert. But! I've watched them, I've observed them all, and they each have different strengths and different—but not many—weaknesses, and they all have this one thing in common. Every. Single. One of them."

Henry picked up his empty glass and tried to take a drink from it and looked a little perplexed and said, "I drank that one way too fast."

Sarah considered telling him that he'd never gotten his next drink but thought better of it.

"What?" she asked. "What do they have in common?"

Henry rubbed his face and his eyes and then looked at her and said, "Haven't you been listening to anything I've said?" He waited for her to say something and when she didn't he sighed. "They carry their difference, the way they carry their difference. They have differences, see, they each are very different from the rest of us, and the way they carry this difference, well, it's like their difference, they carry it with a sense of pride. Like it makes them better. And it does. It makes them stronger and faster and smarter and more powerful. They know it and they make sure everyone else knows it, too. That's the difference between their difference and your difference."

"That their difference makes them better than my difference?"

"Christ," he said. "You're smarter than this, you know." He took her hand and squeezed it tightly, his fingers pulsing against her fingers and her palm with every syllable, and said, "No. They act like it makes them better. You don't."

"But," she began, and he let go of her hand and grabbed her other hand.

"But nothing," he said. "You've got a mechanical fucking arm, right? That's not nothing, right? A mechanical fucking arm that—Jesus, which one is it?" He held up her hand and pressed his fingers deep into her own and pulsed them again and studied it through squinted eyes. "I mean, it's remarkable, isn't it? Your hands. Exactly the same." He dropped her hand and sighed and said, "I can't tell. Weird. I thought I'd be able to tell." Then he looked at his watch. "Ah well, we should get back to work. I've got a Recruits meeting in twenty."

He paid. Sarah was surprised walking out of the dark bar into the bright afternoon sun. They didn't say much of anything else walking back to the travel agency and riding down the elevator to the Regional Office, even though she wanted to say more. As they stepped off the elevator, he told her, "I'm around, you know. If you want to chat or get another drink."

"Thanks," she said.

"It'll get better," he said. "I mean, first, it'll probably get worse, but then it will get better. If you remember what I told you, that is." Then he turned and then, walking to the men's room, he said, "Or not."

# 43.

Jasmine threw the first punch.

But before that, Sarah had been swimming for almost an hour. She'd had the pool all to herself. None of the others thought swimming offered enough impact. The Operatives and the Recruits were all about impact. Sarah liked the smooth motion of herself through the water. She had been a decent swimmer before, but since coming to the Regional Office and the new arm and really getting it together generally, she had become sleek and natural in the water, slipping through with almost no effort. She had assumed that with her mechanical arm, she would feel lopsided, not necessarily because of the weight of it, though the weight of it had entered her mind, but because of its strength and her normal arm's lack thereof, but somehow her body had adjusted and her strokes were even and strong and while her normal arm did eventually tire out, she had found herself able to swim at a strong pace for hours on end before that happened.

She had asked the doctor about this, about how her normal arm managed to keep up with her mechanical arm, and jokingly had asked him if they had in fact given her two mechanical arms, and the look of horror that crossed his face was so horrific that she quickly laughed and assured him she was only kidding, that she knew he'd given her only the one arm.

Ever since she broke his femur, he had been touchy and a bit twitchy around her.

"I'm not sure," he said, once he'd regained his composure. "Perhaps the hyperadvanced nanotechnology we used in the mechanical arm is sending signals to the rest of your body, has somehow found a way to boost, even just a little, your own strength and endurance?"

This idea struck her as both fascinating and a little unsettling, and so she'd brought it up to Mr. Niles, who shook his head and laughed and said, "He's a kook, that old man. Hey, when he's right, he's right. I mean, look at your arm, look at the amazing work he did with your arm. But listen, the reason your body is stronger is because we've been strengthening it. Remember? You've been training every day for four months now. Of course the rest of you can keep up better for an hour, for two hours, and if you keep it up, maybe four or six hours, which is when you'll be ready for the thing. But your body has limits. Your arm doesn't. So don't push it too hard."

And so, an hour, sometimes an hour and a half, was all she would let herself swim at one time before giving herself a rest.

She stopped at the edge of the pool and held herself there, her eyes closed, her nose just below the surface, the waves rising and falling against her ears, so that the echo of them against the indoor pool became muffled and then clear and then muffled. Hanging there in the water, she felt she could swim across the Atlantic if she wanted.

When she pulled her head above water, she saw Jasmine standing at the edge of her lane and two others standing behind her.

Jasmine squatted down and smiled at Sarah a mean kind of smile and then said, "Look. The robot knows how to swim."

And Sarah didn't know why that—more than anything else—set her off, but set her off it did, and there were words said and feelings felt, and Sarah climbed out of the water, and there were more words and more feelings, and, well, Jasmine threw the first punch, but still . . .

She threw it so fast no one saw it, not even Sarah, who only barely felt it, felt the wake of it, the soft touch of air against her cheek, her earlobe, the ripple of her hair. In the moment, or immediately after the moment, Sarah thought she must have moved out of the way of Jasmine's punch, ever so slightly out of the way. Maybe her arm had given her a sixth sense about these things or maybe she was in possession of some kind of mystical property, had always been so, a power buried too deep for anyone to detect it, but protective and powerful enough to shift her an inch to the left just before she was punched, but no. In hindsight, Sarah would understand that Jasmine threw that punch so fast that no one could see it and so close that only Sarah could feel it, but missed all the same, on purpose. Namely, to make it look like Sarah threw the first punch—or kick, as it turned out—like Sarah was the instigator, and it worked.

Sarah was quicker than any of them expected her to be, she could tell by the looks on their faces and by the fact that she swept her leg under Jasmine's to sweep Jasmine off her feet.

Jasmine recovered quickly enough, though, and was up and skipping behind Sarah even as Sarah landed her mechanical fist on the floor where Jasmine's head had been. She cracked the deck and heard a small chorus of sarcastic oooohs.

Sarah was outmatched, of course.

Of course, Sarah was outmatched.

Jasmine had been around a long time. She'd outlived Gemini, who had been one of the first Recruits and legendarily strong. Chances were, she would outlive the entire crop of new Recruits, too, judging by the sorry looks of them. She wasn't the strongest. That was Lucy. She wasn't the fastest, that was clearly Celia, and Dominic was by far the smartest—the shit that girl knew baffled even Oyemi—but Jasmine was by far the shrewdest, the most observant, the best able to look for and then exploit even the tiniest movement, the smallest tell. Of all the Operatives—except for maybe Emma, who had just arrived and was still a bit of a mystery—Jasmine put the mystical properties of her existence to work best. Which was how she'd known exactly how close and how fast to punch. Which was how she'd known to skip behind Sarah on her right because she knew which arm was the strong arm and which arm was more than just strong. Which was how she knew that in two minutes Henry and Mr. Niles would arrive to break everything up. Which was how she knew that to kill this girl, this one-armed freak, all she'd have to do was slide up behind her, crack her neck—done!—and let her fall, not that she wanted to kill her, per se, just put her in her place. How she knew where to hit her—pop, pop, pop, kidney, kidney, lower back—and how hard—hard enough to make a point but just shy of leaving a deep mark. Which was how she knew she had ten seconds left to get in one more good punch, to the nose, nobody can ignore a broken nose, which she threw with maybe a little more juice on it because why not, one last good punch, why not give it more of the juice, but which—to her surprise—didn't connect because the girl got lucky. The one-armed freak's one arm caught the punch midpunch and wouldn't let go, no matter how strongly Jasmine wrenched, no matter that she practically flung Sarah across the room. The arm— that fucking mechanical arm—wouldn't let go of her arm. Who knows how long it would have held on if Mr. Niles and Henry hadn't shown up, shut everything down, separated Jasmine and Sarah, pulled them away. Even Sarah didn't know. The last Sarah heard from Jasmine, as Henry pulled her down the hall, was, "You got lucky, freak, but not next time. Not so lucky next time."

But it wasn't luck.

Watching the video of it all later while in bed, feeling sore and trampled, Sarah saw just how well Jasmine had set her up. She saw, or didn't see, the punch that started it all, saw her own leg-sweep that came out of nowhere, seemingly unprovoked, saw how quick and fluid Jasmine was, and realized how much she'd under-estimated these women.

All of this was secondary information, though, was back-ground noise to what she couldn't figure out no matter how many times she rewatched the video.

How had she caught that punch?

Jasmine had hit her three times, had thrown her forward onto her knees with those punches, and she had a clear shot at Sarah's face, Sarah too dazed and winded and in pain to even think of defending herself, but despite what Jasmine thought or said, catching that punch had had nothing to do with luck, had had nothing to do with her, had had everything to do with her mechanical arm, which had moved on its own, had surprised Sarah as much as it had surprised Jasmine.

Had surprised her and, now that she had watched it happen again and again, frightened her, too.

Frightened her not a little bit.

# 44.

Sarah waited for something to happen, for anything to happen. For Mr. Niles to bust in and save her. For Wendy to come in and ridicule her. Anything would have been better than sitting tied up in this chair, with all these men with guns outside the door, and wondering just how many bones of hers were broken. A lot of bones. A lot of things must have been broken about her, she thought, for her to feel the way she felt, which was not good.

She wondered what they planned to do with her. She wondered why they hadn't simply killed her yet. Any hope that they'd be able to use her to their own ends or that they'd be able to turn her to their side should have been well done away with by now.

What with the hostage situation and how she had handled all of that.

What with how she had screamed out over and over again as they dragged her away that she would find who was behind all of this and destroy that person and then find every single last one of them, too, find them no matter where they hid, no matter what they tried to do to escape, that she would have her vengeance on their very souls if necessary.

She had screamed a lot of things. None of them very pleasant.

She wondered when they'd come back in here and whether it

would be the small quiet one who came in here, who was methodical and almost tender about his painful administrations, or the loud, big one, who was brash energy and uncaring force. She wondered what it meant that she was trying to decide between the two of them, which one she liked more (the big one).

If she had her mechanical arm, she thought, she would be out of these ropes in seconds, in nanoseconds.

If she were one of the girls, one of the Operatives, she thought.

But this thought, futile as it was, was interrupted when Wendy stepped into the office.

Fucking Wendy, the fucking intern.

# 45.

A week after the fight with Jasmine, Henry stopped Sarah in the hallway, took her gently but firmly by the elbow. Her body was still sore from her scrape with Jasmine and she flinched at his touch and he let her go, an apology in his eyes.

"I know what you're going to say," Sarah said.

"I doubt it," Henry said.

"It wasn't me. I didn't start that fight."

Henry gave her scoffing eyes. "Of course you didn't." He shook his head. "The flip of your hair, the look in your eyes. Not to mention, Jasmine fights dirty. It's what she's good at and everyone knows it."

"I didn't."

Henry shrugged. Shrugging seemed to be his default reaction to just about anything Sarah said. "Come with me," he said.

"Where are we going?" she said, and when he didn't answer and didn't let go of her arm, she said, "Where are you taking me?"

"Out," Henry said. "It's the end of the road, you're off the team, kid."

Sarah stopped; Henry reached for her wrist; she yanked her

arm free from Henry's grip. "What?" she said. "You're joking. I'm off the team?"

"Christ, O'Hara," he said, and then turned and kept walking. "Where's your sense of humor?" He stopped and turned and said, "Well? You coming or not?"

"Tell me where we're going."

He shrugged. "My office. Is that acceptable? Can we go? Can you walk a little faster?" And when he turned again, she jogged to catch up.

Henry's office looked like the office of a crazy person.

"This isn't your office," Sarah said.

"And by the way," Henry said, ignoring her. "You're not on the team. You're a client."

Henry barely glanced at her as he stepped over and around piles and stacks of papers and files, empty printer boxes, pieces of gray Styrofoam, an old tube TV set with a VCR embedded in the front of it, to get to the only free chair, which might have been behind the desk or on the other side of the desk, Sarah couldn't tell, because she wasn't even sure it was a desk.

"This is the office of a crazy person," she said.

"No arguments there." He reached under his desk and lifted— with some effort—a battered and heavily taped cardboard box labeled "Lamps, Kitchen Supplies, Plunger," and set it, tilting to the left, on top of the stacks of paper and files and photographs on his desk.

"Has anyone else seen this office?" Sarah said. "I mean, like, Mr. Niles? He doesn't mind that this is an office?"

Henry opened the box and nodded at it. "Well," he said. "There you go. Have a look, go ahead, take your time."

Sarah stood in the doorway, mostly because she didn't see many places she could go.

"Oh, for Christ's sake, just move shit around," he said.

Sarah scanned the area right in front of her but couldn't see what was movable and what should be left in place.

"Jesus," Henry said. Then he shoved his desk forward and there followed a chain reaction of shifting masses that toppled piles left and right, a slip-slide of paper off chairs and the desk. Sarah thought of domino chains cascading down but then reconsidered. Domino chains are exacting and deliberate, are meticulous, which Henry's office was anything but. Instead, she thought of a mudslide, like the kind that threatened Los Angeles, everything full of sensitive and unpredictable threat.

Somehow, he cleared a patch of floor in front of his desk and then tipped one of the other chairs—which she hadn't seen the first time around—back just enough to let the folders and books slide off it, and he dropped that chair in the almost cleared spot, its two back legs wobbly on a half-empty box of Pendaflex folders, and then he patted the seat and said, "There."

Then he stood up to better look inside his box and flipped through folders, pulling them out and tossing them into Sarah's lap once she had sat down.

"This isn't all of them, but you don't need all of them."

"What are they?"

He sighed, stopped, looked up at her. "Don't ask me questions you can easily answer for yourself. You're smarter than that." Then he went back to his box.

Sarah opened the folder on top and then held it above her lap, since Henry hadn't stopped tossing new folders onto the pile growing there.

On the first folder was a name—Jasmine—followed by: "Weaknesses & Threats."

# 46.

Even with her eyes closed, even pretending to sleep, Sarah could tell it was Wendy by her perfume. Not that she knew what kind of perfume Wendy wore but by the simple fact that there was perfume and that it was so strong.

"We know you're awake," Wendy said in the voice she had once reserved for intern Jacob. "You can stop pretending because we know."

Sarah wasn't surprised it had been Wendy when it turned out to be Wendy.

Okay, so maybe she had been very surprised, but she shouldn't have been, and that was just as close, right?

The thing was, she had liked Wendy.

Sarah wished she hadn't liked Wendy, who had tried so hard to be Sarah's friend, had tried to get into her good graces. And maybe Sarah shouldn't have fallen for this kind of thing, maybe she had let herself believe that Wendy wanted her as a mentor and potentially, long-term speaking, a friend. Maybe Mr. Niles had been less attentive, less present, and maybe Henry had been acting weird since Emma was killed in the field, and maybe Sarah had been tired of being left out by the other girls. Nobody could blame her for being susceptible to the flattery and attentions of a pretty, intelligent, hardworking intern who, sure, maybe wanted a leg up in the hiring process after her internship, but that hadn't meant she wasn't also sincere in her desire to be Sarah's friend.

And so, yes, maybe Sarah had made efforts to take Wendy "under her wing" so to speak, offered her special attention, commended her on a job well done when it had been a job well done and sometimes even when it had been a job done only so-so, had offered her advice and brown-bag lunch dates in her office, practiced writing her letters of recommendation.

In hindsight, Sarah felt foolish. Even Sarah, desperate-for-human-contact Sarah, should have seen how naked these machinations were. Making a connection with Wendy had been too easy, way too easy, and Sarah knew herself well enough to know that she didn't make connections that easily. Even in college, even with other difficult-to-connect-with mathematicians and physicists, she didn't make connections, and so, connecting as easily as she had with Wendy, Sarah should have realized the wrongness of the connection and should have stopped liking Wendy, stopped offering her praise for her work, stopped thinking of her as a protégé, a future friend.

Well, Sarah had stopped now.

Sarah kept her eyes closed. She continued to pretend to be asleep. This infuriated Wendy, Sarah knew it did.

She could hear it in Wendy's sigh.

"I'll just have someone come in here and cut your eyelids off," she said, disgusted that it had come to such threats. "I mean, for Christ's sake, we took your arm off. What's a pair of eyelids?"

Sarah threw in a snuffle and a hitching half snore for good measure.

"Funny," Wendy said.

Then she said, "We all thought it was fake, you know."

Sarah imagined Wendy's face as she said this. Imagined her pouty face, which, in Sarah's mind, wouldn't be so pouty when it was smashed with her mechanical arm.

If only she'd had her mechanical arm.

"Not that the real thing did you any good, I suppose," she said. "But we had a pool going, did you know that? We all made bets and we all lost."

Wendy knocked something hard against the office desk. "It's heavier than I thought it'd be."

Sarah knew she was lying, knew that no matter what, Wendy was a lying bitch who would never, ever, not in a million years, bring the mechanical arm with her to interrogate or harass her.

Sarah knew this. She'd have been a fool to think otherwise, and Sarah—despite what people might have thought or said—was no fool.

"Simpler on the inside, once we took off all the skin. Simpler than I imagined it would be." She rapped it against the desk again. "Whoops," she said. "Fragile, too."

Sarah opened her eyes.

She was the biggest fool she knew.

Wendy was holding a broomstick in her hand, rapping it against the desk. She smiled.

"Made you look," she said. She laughed at her own joke, despite how sad and lame and unfunny it was.

Or maybe it wasn't the joke Wendy was laughing at.

Then Wendy's face changed. Like a ripple, the face shifted into a serious, very serious, face, but not pouty serious, which was a kind of face Sarah was accustomed to seeing on Wendy, not that, but something else, a dangerous kind of serious, which was a look Sarah had seen a number of times but never on Wendy. Never on Wendy or Henry or Mr. Niles or the Oracles, either, who were generally blank faced or smiling in their bald, creepy oracular way.

No. Wendy had a face all of a sudden that she shouldn't have had.

She had the face of an Operative, not one of their own Operatives, obviously, but the same kind of very dangerous face of one of the very dangerous Operatives.

"We gave you a choice," she said. "We made a reasonable— a more than reasonable—offer to you," she said. She said this softly and almost as much to herself as to Sarah. She was trying to make it seem like there was something regrettable in what had happened so far, what was about to happen. Sarah couldn't tell with Wendy what was real and what was an act, not anymore.

Then the face, that look, was gone and the pouty serious face was back, but Sarah couldn't get the other face out of her head and she knew that Wendy had just done something, something deliberate to frighten Sarah, and Sarah wished she could tell herself that it hadn't worked, but it had.

"Okay," Wendy said, in a way that might have been the way a head cheerleader said it when her other cheerleaders had been goofing off or talking for too long about boys or had been on a bathroom break and it was time to get back to the hard work of cheerleading again. "Fun time's over." Said it in that bright, chipper high school girlish way, and then she closed the office door and lowered the office blinds and she waded into the deep end of Sarah's despair, waded in there and did her best to make it deeper.

# 47.

Jasmine wore glasses and was only five feet three inches tall, and her right arm was slower than her left and she was dyslexic.

Corrine suffered from painful and unpredictable and lengthy periods, arbitrary and violent, lasting weeks at a time.

Joan refused to brush her teeth or visit the staff dentist and chewed gum incessantly.

Veronica spooned two bites of food into her mouth at every meal before drenching her plate in salt while no one was looking.

Maddie drank a bottle of whiskey each night after returning home from assignment.

Erin took pills. Every kind of pill.

Eden cut herself with whatever sharp piece of metal she could find, literally, carrying in her mouth a tiny blade stripped from a razor or a thumbtack swiped from the office or the coiled jagged spring from a ballpoint pen, worming it deeper and deeper into her cheek, her tongue, the soft tissue connecting her tongue to her jaw.

These girls, Sarah thought. These poor girls and their powers and what their powers did to them.

Teri bound herself into her bed. Thick, leather, medical, insane-asylum straps bound.

Ruby punched her fist through piles of cinder blocks after each assignment, punched until her knuckles bled.

Rebecca had killed herself.

Serena and Hazel and the other Rebecca and Camille and Alyssa and Hannah and Anne-Michelle died, died, died, died, were killed in action, were killed in the field long before the Regional Office, before Henry had a chance to figure out what secrets they hid, what instabilities they manifested.

Henry had given her more files, more folders for her to read, but she stopped. She just stopped.

# 48.

After the pool incident, a final confrontation between her and Jasmine was bound to happen. Sarah knew. She'd seen enough movies, read enough Gossip Girl novels to know that sooner or later, she and Jasmine would lock horns again. And, well, she'd rather have had it happen on her own terms, by her own doing, and would rather have stopped feeling so tense and anxious about when it would happen. So Sarah made it happen on her own.

She watched Jasmine's comings and goings, waited for a moment when she would be by herself, and then Sarah jumped her.

That had been ten minutes ago. Their fight had lasted now for ten full minutes. It wasn't going well.

It wasn't going as badly as anyone who was not Sarah might have expected, considering.

But it wasn't going as well as Sarah had hoped it would.

Sarah pulled her fist back to punch or counterpunch—she'd lost track by then who was punching, who was countering—but Jasmine was too fast, always too fast, and she bobbed under Sarah's punch and slipped in close and grabbed Sarah with both hands, trapping Sarah's arms at her sides, and lifted her off her feet, but instead of throwing her or cracking her head into the ceiling tiles, Jasmine pulled her down and held her so they were eye to eye. A thin trickle of blood ran down Jasmine's temple. Sarah's breath was huffed and squeezed out of her. Jasmine grimaced and Sarah struggled against Jasmine's grip, and Jasmine smiled, and Sarah winced her eyes closed, expected the worst. And Jasmine pulled her in for a kiss.

A deep one.

It was almost painful, this kiss, full of a force that Sarah couldn't have said for certain was passion or anger or whether in that moment there was even a difference, but there it was, a kiss, unexpected and not altogether unpleasant but not exactly pleasant, either.

Then Jasmine broke the kiss and Sarah had a hitch in her chest, had to scramble to get herself breathing.

Jasmine butted her in the head and threw her backward and Sarah landed hard on her ass.

And then Jasmine was laughing, but Sarah couldn't tell if it was real laughter, and she said, "Hey, okay, all right, okay, I get it, I get it, and maybe if you weren't a robot, maybe something, maybe we could have had something here, but it can't be. I'm sorry. It just can't." She turned and started walking away. "I mean, a girl and a robot who might also be a girl?" She turned down another hall but Sarah could still hear her. "Nobody would accept us, we'd have to live alone together in the woods, it would be too hard, just. Too. Damn. Hard." And then either she stopped with her joke or she had finally walked far enough away that Sarah couldn't hear her anymore.

But after that, Jasmine and the rest of them just kind of ignored her. They didn't accept her, but they left her alone, and that was something, right?

# 49.

Sarah had lost hope. After the assault, after her arm, after the hostages, after Wendy. What else could she do but let go of hope?

It was one thing to hold on to hope in the face of great danger and an uncertain future, but in the face of great danger and a fairly certain future? A fairly certain future and an already painful present?

In the face of all that, hope slipped away.

She wasn't proud of herself, but she didn't hold it against herself, either.

Her shoulders slumped, insofar as they could slump, the ropes having been tied around her pretty tightly so that even slumping seemed a restricted activity.

Her sigh was a resigned-to-her-fate kind of sigh.

She had lost. The Regional Office had lost. If Mr. Niles wasn't yet dead, if Oyemi wasn't found and murdered, she knew that they soon would be and that there was nothing she could do for any of them or about any of it.

It was sad, the thought. Sad that it took them less than a day, less than half a day, to break her down, but break her down they had, and kudos to them for knowing exactly how.

She would never rescue Mr. Niles from the clutches of evil.

She would never sit at his desk, handed control of the Regional Office, once he stepped down as director.

She would wait here in this chair, bound by these ropes, and that was about the end of that.

A small voice in her head yelled out one last gasping, I will get free from these ropes, you motherfuckers, but she tamped that voice down, shushed it, quieted it, gently stroked its forehead until it became calm and compliant, because she'd been beaten, and having been beaten, now all she wanted was for it to end, for all of it to end.

She was tired and weepy and afraid.

And then things went black. She wasn't sure what it meant, but things going black seemed to implicate an end to things.

"Oh, good," she said. "About time," she said.

Except everything went black. Not just the office. She could see through the blinds and the cracks at the top of the blinds that the whole floor, maybe the entire building, had gone black, too.

It's a trick, she thought.

Then the screaming. Then the screaming began.

But actually, there had been shouts before, shouts when the lights had shut off, when the power had gone down, but she had figured those shouts had been part of the game, part of the trick. One more way of fucking with poor one-armed Sarah! She tried to convince herself the same about the screaming, but the screaming seemed different.

The screaming sounded urgent and fearful and full of pain.

Fake, she thought. Fake fear. Fake urgency. Fake pain.

But the sound of pain, and Sarah could attest to this in a first-

hand kind of way, the sound of pain was a sound that was difficult to adequately fake.

And for a second, Sarah considered maybe there was a chance,
a small chance, a very small chance that something was happening. That whoever (Mr. Niles?) had been maneuvering through
the building in a deadly and secret way had finally made his way
to the real action, had dispensed with enough teams to make a
play for a full-out rescue.

"I know this is a trick," she yelled. She was beyond pretending
that they weren't getting to her.

"I know you fucking assholes are just trying to fucking trick
me," she yelled. "Stop trying to trick me," she said, quieter now.
Under her breath. The only one who could hear her over the shouts
and gunshots and the screams and small explosions was her.

What was going on out there? she wondered.

# 50.

"How was it for you growing up?" Mr. Niles asked. He said this as offhandedly as he could, as if he were asking her if she'd pass him some salt or the ketchup please, but she could tell he was tense, was listening intently for her answer.

They'd just finished a lunch meet: new Recruits, operations pipeline, department budgets, typical stuff.

"It was fine," she said. But he wanted more, and she didn't know what it was.

Before, when people found out about her mother, they wanted details, wanted to hear Sarah's theories, wanted to tell her their own theories, wanted to feel part of but separate from what seemed to them an unfathomable childhood trauma. Sarah would never have accused them of being jealous of her, but there was a want there, a desire of some kind for a tragic history on that scale that they could call their own.

But that wouldn't be what Mr. Niles was after. He already knew the details of her tragedy, had known them better than she had, nor was he the type to need or want a vicarious tragedy to live through, and even if he harbored such a desire, he had at his fingertips this very thing on a whole different level, as Sarah had discovered reading through Henry's files on the Operatives.

Then, not sure if this was what he wanted to hear or not, she said, "Normal, really."

He relaxed. "Normal?"

"Sure," she said. "I mean, people always think of kids as super sensitive, or intuitive, or something like that, and they are, to a point, but also they're still people. Like, once, I tried out for drill team, I was in ninth grade? And I didn't make it, and all these friends of mine did, and I went home, and as soon as I saw my aunt, I started crying, just fell to pieces, and she tried to comfort me, told me what you tell people, you know, Sorry, I know you wanted this, you did your best, maybe next year, but then, you know, she was also like, It'll be okay, it's not the end of the world, and I took all of this in and blew up at her. She didn't understand! What did she know about it! It was the worst day of my life! And she gave me a look. She didn't say anything, just gave me this look, but I knew. I could tell what she was trying to say, and I told her, Yeah, worse than that day, and then I called her a bitch and locked myself in my bathroom, except it was the only bathroom, and I just stayed in there for hours, so long that my aunt had to go across the hall to use the neighbor's bathroom." She sighed. "So, yeah, just your typical teenage nightmare."

"Maybe you were acting out, though," he said.

"That's what my aunt said, and I let her believe that because it made her go easy on me, but, no. I was just really upset about drill team—I mean, everybody was on drill team—and then I punished her for not being as upset as me." Sarah shook her head and laughed. "My poor aunt. She didn't want kids, mostly because she didn't want teenagers, but she tried her best. I was in the bathroom for hours and I must have painted and repainted my toenails fifty times, and every time she knocked on that door, I'd pretend to sob even louder, but that was too much work after a while, so then I pretended I had fallen asleep in there."

"So. Normal," he said.

"Pretty much," she said, and he laughed, and after that he treated her with a more casual touch, seemed to need to protect her less than before, and once she realized this, she wished she had lied.

# 51.

And then the door busted open and a flash of light broke through the darkness and something in the office caught fire and by the firelight Sarah could see the thing that had busted the door open, which was one of the guys who'd been holding everyone hostage, except not anymore because he was dead. Sarah couldn't tell if he was dead because he'd been thrown hard enough into the door to bust it open, or if he had been dead even before he'd been thrown into the door.

But really, that wasn't her biggest concern.

What the hell was going on was her biggest concern. When were they going to stop fooling around and just put her out of her misery was her biggest concern.

The dead guy, though. The dead guy through the door spoke to either the team's commitment to this trick they were trying to play on her, or the more likely explanation, the explanation she'd been fighting against since the power had shut off in the first place, the one she was still fighting against now because once you had lost hope, once you had resigned yourself to things not going your way, you found yourself more than a little skeptical of the notion you'd been wrong and that things would in fact go your way, but still. The dead guy on the floor seemed to point to the notion that this was not a trick and that she was going to be saved.

Sarah closed her eyes. She opened her eyes again. The pile of papers was still on fire, though the fire was petering out. The dead guy was still dead on the floor.

She closed her eyes again. She grabbed a hunk of her cheek with her teeth, her jagged, no-longer-really-there teeth, and bit hard, and opened her eyes again, and again saw the fire, again the dead guy, and it all seemed unreal, this tableau broken occasionally by the flash of gunfire, the glow of another small fire in the distance. She stared at the guy on the floor and the fire and couldn't stop staring.

Someone charged at her through the darkness and this brought her back into the moment. Someone with evil intent in his heart, she figured, or maybe Wendy, of whom Sarah now harbored a healthy fear.

The charging became louder and more urgent and then another body was thrown forward into the office, was thrown with great and terrible force, so that it wasn't unlikely that the throw itself was the thing that killed the body that had been thrown.

But the throw wasn't what killed the body.

What killed the body was still sticking out of the body's back, which was what probably caused the blackout, too. She understood this now. The blackout, the screaming, the gunshots, the explosions, the chaos, the death and destruction of the teams who'd executed this assault on the Regional Office hadn't been the handiwork of Mr. Niles or even Henry. All of that had been the handiwork, literally, of the thing that was currently sticking painfully and awkwardly out of the back of the new dead body on the ground in the office.

Which was a mechanical arm.

Which was, not to put too fine a point on it, her fucking mechanical arm. Which unmoored itself from the goon's backside and surveyed the office and then saw—did it see?—then saw Sarah, saw her and locked itself, locked its seeing eye, wherever that might be, locked it dead onto Sarah.

And then it lunged. It lunged right for her.

From *The Regional Office Is Under Attack:*
*Tracking the Rise and Fall of an American Institution*

Then began a period of great success for the Regional Office. The first Oracle led Oyemi, within a week, to the next and then the third and final Oracle. The trio guided Oyemi to the first real Recruit—the young woman in Peoria did not pan out, though the record on why she did not pan out has been lost—a woman named Gemini (whose exploits, such as disrupting the Ring of Three and expanding her mouth into a vortex to swallow whole the swarm of bees set loose on Kansas by the warlock Harold Raines, and, ultimately, her death at the very hands of Harold Raines, can be read about to exhaustion in any number of other papers, as well as in the haphazard account of the Regional Office *The Book of Gemini*).

Soon after the recruitment of Gemini, the first full class of Recruits was brought in for training, resulting in a freshman class of Operatives that included Jasmine, the longest-standing field Operative in the history of the Regional Office. Shortly after, the Oracles led Mr. Niles to the discovery of Henry (already discussed at some length), after which Henry recruited his own class—the fifth and final class recruited under the umbrella of Oyemi and Mr. Niles—and found, hidden within that class, Emma.

By this point, the Regional Office had grown, had long since moved out of its humble offices in Queens to the building it occupied on the day of the attack in midtown Manhattan. Oyemi and Mr. Niles had enjoyed nearly unparalleled success with their venture. Certainly, the Regional Office was not the only organization of its kind. The city had long supported groups such as the Legion of Good, the Powerful Six, and Hammersmith's Men, but nothing on the scale nor with the success of the Regional Office.

During this time, Jasmine came into her own, and while the most famous of the early Operatives, Gemini, had died, other formidable Operatives had joined the ranks of the Regional Office, most notably: Juneau, Robin Cueto, Kelly Shepherd. Together, these women saved the world from destruction, from self-annihilation, from the evil forces of darkness, from interdimensional war strikes, from alien forces. And standing out from this crowd of powerful women was Emma.

Of the ten missions most often attributed to the Golden Age of the Regional Office, Emma was responsible for the successful execution of six, including the retrieval of the Tremont Hotel from interdimensional, time-traveling assassins who intended to murder a future madame president by kidnapping and murdering her great-grandmother.

(Granted, Jasmine played pivotal roles in all of these, but it is Jasmine's sad fortune to have remained with the Regional Office through good and bad, and not planned for two years the destruction of Oyemi and the Regional Office, and far too often are her history and her contributions to the Regional Office overlooked.)

By this time, Oyemi had moved her side of the operations to her secret and remote compound in the Catskills and Mr. Niles had taken over as director of the Regional Office in Manhattan. The end of the world was thwarted time and again by the Regional Office over the course of this golden age, which lasted between five and five thousand years (the count varying depending on timelines and how one considers the actions of Operatives when those actions spanned space, time, and dimension). The forces of evil threatening at every turn the survival of the planet and the innocents living on it in blissful ignorance were often foiled multiple times in the span of one week. With the assistance of the Oracles, the trust fund left Oyemi by her great-uncle quadrupled, and soon after, the travel agency was formed and, much to everyone's surprise, added its own profit to the accounts.

By practically every metric conceivable, the Regional Office had arrived, its Operatives had never been stronger, its missions never more dangerous, and the whole thing could not be stopped.

And then, almost without warning, it all came to an end.

The beginning of the end of the Regional Office can be summed up thusly:

A man fell in love with a woman.

The same can be said of almost any iconic tragedy— *The Aeneid, The Iliad, Romeo and Juliet*.

The fall of the Regional Office.

More specifically:

Henry fell in love with Emma.

Then Emma was marked for death by Oyemi via the predictions of the Oracles.

And Oyemi, either through ignorance or a cold sense of fate, told Henry to kill Emma.

More specifically still:

One day, Henry slipped into his car to drive home at the end of a normal day. He turned the key in the ignition. He switched off his stereo because sometimes he just wanted the sound of the wheels on the road, the bumps and skips of the tires rolling across the uneven pavement. He checked his rearview mirror. He shifted down to reverse, and then he passed out.

He came to in a chair in an office with a mineral water in his hand.

"Hello, Henry," Oyemi said, her voice coming from behind him. "I hope water is okay. If not, I can get you something else."

He paused, but for just a second, and then said, "Water's fine," because it was the only concrete thing he could land on. Of course he'd met Oyemi. She'd been there when Mr. Niles had hired him, and he had seen her a few other times, but those meetings had all been brief, officious, and not nearly as unsettling as this one.

Oyemi walked around and sat against the desk in front of him.

"Usually," she said, "I like to play a little game." She nodded at the water in his hand. "Make the person in that chair think they've been here for a while, have been discussing important things with me all this time, and only just woke up at the very end."

Henry looked at her but didn't know what to say or that there was anything he should say.

"You know," she said. "You're in the chair, you've got a drink in your hand, you wake up, and I'm sitting or standing across from you, saying something like"—she waved her hand and shrugged her shoulders—"'I hope you understand, the fate of the agency rests on your shoulders now.' Or, 'I'm glad we agree on this,' or, if I'm in a mood, I might say something like, 'I'm sorry to hear that's how you feel.' Something like that."

"Ah," Henry said.

"I know," she said, and sighed. "It loses something in translation. It's funny. Trust me." Then she said, "You ruined it, though. You woke up too soon."

"Sorry," he said, because whatever he might not have known about Oyemi, he was fairly certain that you didn't want to ruin anything for her.

She waved off his apology. "Just me, wasting time." She paused. "Avoiding bad news, too. That's part of it. I hate giving people bad news."

Henry cleared his throat. The glass in his hand seemed heavier all of a sudden. "News?"

"And then, too, this game, this trick, it lets me say something true, something real, and then pass it off as a joke, you know, like, 'Fate of the agency rests in your hands,' and so on, and then it feels less serious when I tell someone, 'No, in fact, what I said was true.'"

"I'm sorry," Henry said. "I'm a little lost."

She smiled. People who said Oyemi had an unsettling smile didn't know from unsettling smiles.

"The fate of the agency," she said, still smiling.

Her smile was predatory and ever widening. She contained in her mouth, as far as he could tell from various furtive glances, the normal amount of teeth, but after every meeting with her, he came away with the sense that her mouth had been full of teeth, rows and rows of teeth, sharp and blunt alike, but too many.

"The fate of the entire Regional Office and all it stands for and all it does, in fact, depends on you." Oyemi looked at her hands, now folded in front of her. "On you, Henry." Then she looked up at him and smiled again and he wished she would stop smiling. Then she said, "And here's why."

Henry knew little about the Oracles, their origin,

their design, how accurate their predictions were. They'd been moved out of the city and to Oyemi's compound shortly after he'd been hired. Their messages were cryptic, delivered from the Oracles to a team of analysts—the channelers—who ran analytics, cross-checked predictions and world events on various spreadsheets. It was a mystery to him but he hadn't ever cared how it—or the entire system—worked. He received assignments by way of a channeler from the Oracles. Girls to pick up. The wheres and whens but little else.

By whatever means, assignments landed in his inbox and that was all that mattered to him.

"They do more than just hand down your recruiting assignments," Oyemi explained. "Their first order of business, in fact, is to scan through all time and all reality for threats to the Regional Office. They're our first line of defense," she said. "And they've singled out a threat," she said. Then she paused and leaned in closer. "And that threat is right here. In the agency. Even as we speak."

Henry gauged the distance between him and Oyemi, between him and the door, tried to predict how many guards were outside this office—maybe none, Oyemi being what she was—tried to calculate the possibility and probability of the various bad scenarios laid out before him—punch Oyemi in the neck and then run for it, or just run for it, or just punch Oyemi in the neck and then try to kill her—but finally, he exhausted the options, decided none of them were good, that none of them would save him, and so he stayed in his seat.

Oyemi watched him through all of this—no more than a second or two—and then smiled when she saw him relax, resign himself, and then laughed and said, "Not you, Henry." Then she frowned and looked at her hands, her fingers. "Worse," she said. Then she looked back up at him. "One of the girls," she said. "One of our girls."

"The girls?" he asked. He stared at her for a minute, tried to picture one of his Recruits betraying the Regional Office but couldn't. "No," he said. "No." Then: "Which one?"

She knelt in front of him and placed her hands on his knees and looked earnestly into his eyes and said, "I'm glad you asked."

She didn't know. She had received some flimflam from the Oracles—it would take Henry some time to uncover exactly what the Oracles had told Oyemi, namely: *The one who once loved will one day destroy that which was once loved,* and so on—and from this, from this small ambiguous prediction, he was supposed to single out the Operative poised to destroy Oyemi and the Regional Office. That was now his job. He was supposed to help Oyemi find the girl who would betray Regional.

"How?" he asked. "How am I supposed to do that?"

"Get close to them," she told him, and he thought of Emma, and he thought, I am, I am close to them. "Learn what they're up to, their secrets, their desires."

Maybe she saw his look, a skeptical look, because she said, "You won't be alone. We'll be here to help," she said. "The Oracles. Me. Make new files for each girl. Photos, dossiers. Pass them to one of my men, and I will work with the Oracles and we will figure this out together. I promise. We will."

Only in hindsight did Henry realize there had been something pleading to her voice, her argument, as if she needed him, specifically, and as if he had any choice but to say yes.

As Oyemi instructed, he took photographs and built secret dossiers and case files for every working operative, for all the new Recruits.

He didn't like the work.

Sure, he'd made his own secret personnel files on them all, but with the express intention of making him better at his job, as their trainer, their Recruiter.

He had made first contact with these women, had performed the collection of them from foster homes or juvenile detention centers, from in-the-middle-of-nowhere town squares and suburban McMansions, from trailer homes at the edge of swamps. He had overseen and led their training, and he felt connected to these women, who were, in turn, connected to him, or so he'd long believed.

Most saw him as a brother. They told him things. They cried in his arms, and only in his arms. To cry in anyone else's arms would have risked discovery, risked the admission that inside them there still lived something frail and vulnerable and human. And so, while the betrayal of the Regional Office was as much a betrayal of him and his life's work, to suspect any of these girls felt like an even worse betrayal of a friendship, a relationship.

Henry didn't like sneaking about and taking photographs of them moving through their days just to pass this information on to Oyemi. After a few weeks, though, the new task felt like any other part of his job because that was how things worked no matter who you were, no matter what you did. Not to mention, none of what he'd done seemed to matter. He collected information and passed it on to a man working for Oyemi, but he never received any feedback, never heard anything about the files he put together, the photographs he took, and soon he forgot about the true nature of all he'd been doing.

Then, less than three months later, Henry walked into his office and found Oyemi there waiting for him, Oyemi who never came to the Manhattan office, who worked and lived in the secret compound upstate.

"You can put away your camera, Henry," she said. "We've found her."

BOOK IV

# 52.

It felt good. Sarah could admit that it felt very good to lay waste in this way, her mechanical arm taking on a life of its own, taking over in the heat of the moment.

Felt good to let go.

For once, God, to really just let go.

Not that she wasn't sad.

Seeing Mr. Niles there in his office, which was the first place she went once her arm had found her, seeing him ruined, cut in two, seeing him like that made her sad.

She'd give her sadness the time it deserved, but not now.

Right now it felt very very good to simply follow after her mechanical arm as it did things that amazed even her.

Finding her and reattaching itself to her shoulder for one. That was pretty fucking amazing.

Escaping its captors, and wending its way through the labyrinth of the Regional Office, all the while laying waste to any man, woman, or machine that stood in its way, only to seek her out as if it were some long-loved loyal pet traveling alone across the vast American landscape to find its master.

She certainly hadn't thought her mechanical arm could have done that.

She punched her fist through the face of one of the goons. Clean through it.

She heard the peripheral sound of gunshots—with all the noise and commotion, every sound seemed peripheral—and had barely a chance to turn before her mechanical arm reacted—faster than she could have ever reacted—swiveling around with the man's face still hanging from its wrist, swiveling and then moving herky-jerky style in what seemed a random pattern and she didn't know what the arm was doing until it shook loose the poor man's head and held up its open palm for her to see the bullets it had caught, to show her what it had done like a cat presenting her a mouse.

Then the mechanical fist closed and she pivoted and threw the bullets, threw them like she was an outfielder throwing from deep center, threw as hard as she could, which, because of her arm, was harder than what was humanly possible. She threw the bullets and four more men fell.

She grinned.

This is how it begins, she thought.

My life, my real life, she thought. It begins like this.

# 53.

Inside the package that had been hot-glued to the inside of her door had been a letter, but if anyone were to ask her when it was all said and done, How did you know, what clued you in, what intel had you obtained? she would say, Chatter, a lot of chatter, or, A sense, I simply had a sense, or, Mr. Niles, Mr. Niles knew something big was coming and he had set me on this weeks ago, months ago, and even still, I figured it out only as it was happening. She would say this and not worry that anyone would discover otherwise because Mr. Niles would be dead by then, because Wendy, too, Wendy would be gone, and because the letter, which she had read so many times that she had memorized it, had been destroyed. By Sarah. Sarah had burned the letter in a metal bowl in her kitchen only just before she left to come to work that same morning.

# 54.

Sarah hadn't been prepared: for the bursting forth of power, for the connectedness. She hadn't been prepared for the sense, though she wouldn't ever tell anyone this, that there had been something emotional to this connection, that there had been something almost sentient.

She had felt an explosion of joy when her arm attached itself back to her shoulder. Joy that had come not just from herself but from the arm, too, but not just joy, not something just so simple as joy.

Anyone could feel joy.

She had felt another sense. She had felt something akin to completeness, or near completeness, or the promise of one day becoming complete.

A warm, almost liquid feeling had rushed over her. It began at her neck and shoulders and cascaded down like a blanket of warm, soapy water. And it had been too much. She'd admit that—to herself if no one else—that it was all a little too much. She'd doubled over, fallen into a sobbing, hiccupping fit, as if only when the arm had come back to her had she been able to understand just how ruined and alone and incomplete she'd been without it.

In the middle of a pitched battle, in the middle of the destruction of the Regional Office, she had doubled over and wept.

And the arm had let her weep. It was as if the arm saw what she was experiencing, understood instinctively what she needed right at that moment, and told her, Go ahead.

Told her, Take a moment. That's fine. Take your moment, get it all out of your system, let yourself go.

Told her, It's okay. I've got this. It's a-okay.

She couldn't say what the arm did exactly while she was doubled over, sobbing into her shirt, but when she came to, she was surrounded by bodies, six of them, that hadn't been there just a minute ago.

# 55.

She grabbed a guy who might not even have been one of the guys, but by this point, did it matter? She grabbed this guy and threw him headfirst through a cubicle wall and maybe she heard his neck snap or maybe it was the wall that snapped, and then, it was over.

The assault on the Regional Office was over. There was no one left. He had been the last guy.

Or there were people left, but they were the women, the Operatives.

When did they get here? she wondered. Have they been here the whole time?

Later, she would learn that they'd been summoned. Someone (or something?) had summoned them all back home. They hadn't known why until they'd arrived and realized what was going on and then took up the fight.

But for now, all she knew was that they were here. They were breathing hard and were bent over, catching their breath. Katie touched her left cheek, which had a long flap of skin flapping off it. They were torn up but they were professionals. She could say that much about them. They didn't stand around in a daze, looking for someone to tell them it was over, the day had been saved. They figured it out, or they knew it instinctively, and then they started to clean up, attended to the hostages, attended to the Regional Office, or what was left of it.

Sarah told Jasmine about Mr. Niles. How she had arrived too late to save Mr. Niles. She didn't tell her how she had wanted to cry at the sight of him, split in two, how she had wanted to cry, to slide to her knees in between the two halves of him and sob in her hands, how she had started to do this, in fact, had started falling forward, stricken at the sight of him, but that her knees wouldn't bend her to the ground, no matter how hard she tried, she could only stand there, and that before she was ready, her body turned on its own, turned and began to run, run from his office and run to the floor where the fighting was going on, how her body had abandoned not just Mr. Niles there but also her own commands, had left them behind, had obeyed some other commands.

Instead, she asked Jasmine to go see to Mr. Niles, to cover him up, that at least.

She and Jasmine still did not always get on. Jasmine liked to ask questions, liked to question anything Sarah said, liked to make sure that Sarah and everyone else knew, even after all of these years, that Sarah was not her boss, liked to imply that, mechanical arm or no, right-hand man to Mr. Niles or whatever, she didn't take orders from Sarah and only rarely took requests.

Sarah didn't know what to expect, then, when she asked Jasmine to see to Mr. Niles.

But Jasmine didn't ask questions. Didn't argue or pout or roll her eyes. Didn't move around like a robot behind Sarah's back, which she had been known to do. Jasmine only nodded and placed her hand gently on Sarah's arm, and didn't say anything, and then left to see to Mr. Niles.

# 56.

*Dear Ms. O'Hara,* the letter read.

*We are writing to you out of respect, out of respect and out of a sense of some obligation, obligation to you, and maybe out of not a little guilt, guilt not for what we have done or what we are about to do, but for what we have—until now—failed to do, which is to tell you the truth about your employer, to tell you these truths, and then to offer you a way out, or not just out, because what good is it to you to simply have a way out, and so also a way forward.*

*We are offering you this: a way forward.*

# 57.

It was a confusing time, the two weeks following the assault.

Henry was still missing. The security director was dead—they found him in his apartment, executed by the looks of it. Oyemi's compound had been burned practically to its foundation. It seemed safe to say that she was dead, the Oracles, too, whose charred remains had been discovered at the bottom of their now-empty pool, the heat and power of the fire having cleared the strange blue liquid from the basin.

One of the Operatives had found them when they went up to check on the Catskills compound and had called Sarah into the chamber where their pool had been. The bodies, burned beyond recognition, all looked the same. Sarah didn't wonder which one of them had been her mother. Because of course she found the files, after all the dust settled and after she settled herself into Mr. Niles's office and looked through his files. She found the records verifying what she had learned in the envelope taped to her door that night before the attack. She knew what had really happened to her mother, and of course she felt betrayed by it all. Oddly, though, she didn't feel betrayed by Mr. Niles. She should have, on some level she knew she should have blamed him, but she didn't. He'd been a young man, a foolish and young man, when that had all happened. He had been swayed by Oyemi, and what good would it do to hold a grudge against a dead man anyway?

No good. It would do no good.

And so the betrayal she felt was aimed at whoever sent her the envelope in the first place, and no matter, standing there in front of the charred corpses of the Oracles, she certainly didn't try to imagine one of them with her mother's face. Because why would she have? What would she have gained by doing anything so sentimental and ridiculous as gently touching each corpse on its charred forehead, by whispering I love you and I'm sorry to each one in turn, by trying to picture each body, not as it had been before the fire, because the Oracles had never looked like her mother, had always looked only like Oracles, bald and tinted by the light of the milky-blue water they were submerged in, but by trying to picture each with her mother's face, her mother's smile, her mother's mousy, shoulder-length hair?

Would she have gotten her mother back?

Would the past seventeen years of her life have been any different?

"I've got it from here," Sarah told the Operative, Jennifer or Jenny or Jenn, she couldn't remember. The girl nodded and left Sarah to it and then Sarah stood there and stared at the dried-out pool and the blackened bodies, mostly skeletons now, and she waited for twenty minutes, for an hour, until finally Jasmine's soft touch on her shoulder woke Sarah from whatever waking sleep she'd fallen into.

# 58.

It was a confusing time and so no one really noticed, not the Operatives, not the remaining administrators, not the last recruitment specialist, not Sarah herself, that there was no one actually in charge of Regional anymore, or that quite by accident, being in charge of Regional had fallen to Sarah.

What do we do with Mr. Niles? Sarah had an answer.

How do we reboot the security system? Sarah knew that, too.

As the questions began to snowball, Sarah led. She put reasonable and simple plans into place. She closed the dormitory where the girls lived. "They might still be out there," she said. "The people who did this to us, they might be out there just licking their chops, waiting to take our girls out all at once." She put them in apartments spread out all over the city.

Sarah was the one who ordered biweekly check-in meetings. She brought the bagels and coffee and rugelach and juice until, after the second meeting, a woman named Jordan, who had been a low-level systems analyst before the assault, said she would bring the food for the next meeting, smiled at Sarah, and said, "You've got enough on your plate already."

Not that the others weren't helping out. Accounting gathered itself, counted its missing, and then budgeted repair costs, dug into offshore accounts, restored some financial order. Research, marketing, travel agency staff, who hadn't known it before but knew now that they not only had been a cover for Regional but had also handled all the travel for the Operatives—all were up and running again in a matter of days.

Because they understood.

There were still operations to be completed, case files to be drawn up, distributed, and then filed once the mission had been completed.

Evil to be thwarted.

Wrongs to be righted.

Operatives handled their own filing and the research. They learned computer systems. They learned the recruitment software. Candace, a fairly new girl, an Operative for less than a month before the assault, found a girl in Toronto she wanted to bring in, and so recruitment began again. Jordan handled not just the systems analysis but security as well.

They all fell into line in a way that would have made Mr. Niles proud, but what Sarah didn't see, not at first, not until it was pointed out to her, was that they all fell into line behind her.

And after some debate, after plenty of hand-wringing on Sarah's part, and questions, mostly along the lines of, Are you sure about this? But really, really sure you want me?, Sarah agreed to step in as head of the Regional Office. Legal drew up a contract. Then it was official.

Sarah was in charge.

Of everything.

From *The Regional Office Is Under Attack:*
*Tracking the Rise and Fall of an American Institution*

This study would be remiss and incomplete if it did not take a moment to delve into the two theories on how Henry managed to so effectively enact his plans against the Regional Office, theories that speak to the pivotal question of whether he worked alone and in secret, or did he have assistance?

Obviously, Henry was aided, there is no question in this matter, aided by his own team of Operatives. Of the women who worked for Henry, we know for sure there was Wendy, Colleen, Windsor, and Rose. But the question then is: Was there someone else, someone equal to Henry, planning and executing this assault?

The theory that he planned and executed this alone proceeds thusly:

Oyemi told Henry he would be the one to neutralize Emma, who the Oracles had determined was the threat. How she had decided on Emma, Henry didn't know. Still, he talked Oyemi into giving him two weeks to finish the assignment. Two weeks to kill Emma.

Of course, when he first met Emma, Henry didn't know he loved her or would love her or that she would love him.

But isn't that always the case?

You toiled in your job for year after year, training stunningly beautiful and dangerous young women to fight the encroaching forces of evil, caught up in a work life that offered satisfaction on many deep levels but that precluded any sort of real chance at long-lasting relationships. You resigned yourself to a life as a bachelor, to keeping your feelings for these amazing and powerful women on the level of friendly or brotherly love, whichever it was they needed to make it through the day, and in the process of doing all of this, you reached a bottom-level sort of contentment in life because what choice did you have, really? This was the life you'd chosen, or maybe it had been chosen for you, but it was your life after all and you'd made your peace with that, had resigned yourself to all of that when one day, along came a woman of extraordinary grace and beauty, the kind of woman you couldn't help but fall in love with, except you didn't say anything or make any moves because you were a gentleman and you were fully aware of that old saw about your pen and the company ink, not to mention, deep down you had always been a chickenshit. But still, for the first time, you could imagine how, under different circumstances, you might have had a chance with one of these women, with this one woman in particular, that she might have found some way to love you back, and for the first time, too, you began feeling the stirrings of some real and long-ignored dissatisfaction with this life you'd built for yourself. So maybe you paid her a little more attention than you did the other Recruits, the other field Operatives, and maybe she noticed and offered you sly, under-the-radar smiles, and maybe you began to share inside jokes with each other, or you brushed past each other in the narrow (but not that narrow) hallways. Or maybe one day you found yourself in the break room looking for your lunch in the fridge and she came up behind you and placed her hand on your shoulder and with that light but comfortable and unhesitating touch sent an electric jolt through you down to your very bones. She bent into the fridge next to you to see what you were looking for and even as the thought itself entered your own head, she beat you to it—she always beat you to these things—by saying, You know what, why don't we just go get lunch instead, you and me, and maybe a drink, too, or not a drink but a something else?

And maybe you should have known how it would end. Or Henry. Henry should have known.

Or maybe not known *exactly* how it would end.

Who would have known *exactly* how it would end?

The Oracles, maybe.

Not that he would have believed them. Even if they had told him, had sent him a message. One day he would fall in love (not likely) with a Recruit who would love him back (as if). One day, he would learn that the woman who had captured his heart was also the woman prophesied to betray the Regional Office and destroy Oyemi and Mr. Niles and everything they'd ever worked for.

Told him that he would be assigned the task of killing her, this woman he had come to love. Told him that he would be forced to choose between Love and Loyalty, that he would choose Love over Loyalty, and then told him that it wouldn't matter because while Love might be eternal and undying, Emma wasn't either of those and would be killed anyway.

If they had told him all of this, he wouldn't have believed them.

Not that the Oracles ever gave such explicit instructions on the future of this world. More, *The one who loved will destroy that which was once loved.* That was more their speed. That was the kind of ambiguous bullshit the Oracles yammered on about.

Of course, he was strapped for ideas on how to wrangle his way out of this plan of Oyemi's but figured an extra two weeks was an extra two weeks. Except the first week and a half he wasted by trying to come up with a plan on his own. And then Emma cornered him in the parking garage, asked him, "What the fuck, Henry, you've been acting like an idiot the past week and a half," and that was when he told her. About Oyemi. About the prophecy. About his job to do.

Emma didn't get angry or upset, didn't become unsettled or frightened. Her eyes didn't widen or even grow colder, more calculating. She listened to what he said and then she nodded once, said, "Right," and then told him an address and a time, told him to relax, act normal, placed her hand softly against his face, smiled, and then she turned and walked off.

Once she'd gone, he spent his day as if it were any normal day.

He filed reports. He read and reread case files of potential Recruits. He sat in on meetings with Sarah and her mechanical arm and Mr. Niles. He expressed serious and real concern about the news that Emma had failed to show up that day for her briefing. Then the day ended and he packed his things but no more of his things than he might normally pack, and then he drove home as he should normally have driven home. The point being: He did not once give away anything about what he'd done, what he planned to do, had not let slip his affections, his sudden and vivid daydreams, had not confided in any-one, not even (or especially not) Sarah, who seemed to him just so beholden, not just to the Regional Office, but to Mr. Niles, and therefore, someone he couldn't trust.

So it should have been a surprise when he arrived at the address Emma gave him—an abandoned, foreclosed house in White Plains—that he found her, Emma, splayed out on the ground, a pool of blood pooling up beneath and around her, a lifeless look to her lifeless face, but it wasn't. It wasn't a surprise at all.

Because here was the thing about Oyemi: The thing about Oyemi was she was no fool. She wouldn't have had Henry and only Henry on this job. She probably hadn't had only him on the job at all, in fact. Who she'd had on the job had been professionals, men or women or both, who would've known what they were doing, wouldn't have cared about the target, wouldn't have flinched at the prospect of what they were supposed to do, who would've prepared for every contingency, even and especially the contingency of his trying to warn her. Which was why, just as he moved toward her, to check her for signs of life, to take one last look, to dumbly try to staunch the bleeding, a fire was set loose on him from all sides. Not an explosion, but simply a rising wave of flames.

The room flared up, began to melt. Henry didn't care. He tried to reach Emma but the rooms, all of the rooms, had been rigged. He saw an opening, but it closed before he could take it, and he couldn't see her through the flames, so many fucking flames, and then he saw another brief opening and took it, became trapped, barreled through, and at the last minute was blown clear of the house and, landing headfirst on the walkway outside, was knocked unconscious. When he woke, he woke up in the hospice wing of the Regional Office, and every day since had regretted taking that opening, escaping the fire, leaving her behind.

# 59.

Rose hadn't been told there'd be a robot.

That hadn't been in any of the literature, hadn't been part of any Assassin Training Camp seminars or lectures, hadn't been part of any post–Regional Office debrief, not that she'd gotten any real post–Regional Office debriefing. Everyone had somehow failed to mention that one day, ten years into her future, ten years after the attack on the Regional Office, a robot would show up hell-bent on ruining her life—not to mention killing her—for all that Regional Office bullshit.

Ten fucking years.

Jesus, a long fucking time. They waited a long fucking time for revenge.

Not that she was bitter that no one had told her about there being a fucking robot.

Not that she cared that the men and women she had trained with those years ago, had assaulted the Regional Office with, had all but completely fallen off the face of the earth. But Jesus Christ, was it too much to expect a card at Christmas? A phone call on her birthday? Forwarding information and a new phone number just in case, oh, who knows, a fucking robot stomped into her fucking yarn and bead shoppe and started tearing shit all to hell?

It swung its robot arm at her. She pivoted, grabbed it by that same arm, heaved it through the wall, except that how that actually transpired went more like: It grabbed her by her face and smashed her head through the cash register.

Fucking robots.

# 60.

Rose often pictured them coming in here, Henry and Emma.

Not right at that moment, though. God, what a fucking embarrassment that would have been if those two showed up just as she was getting her ass handed to her by some two-bit-looking robot that wasn't even fully covered in synthetic skin.

No. If it were a choice between suffering a painful and brutal death at the hands of this crusher or suffering that kind of embarrassment in front of Henry or Emma? Rose would take the painful and brutal death every time, friend, and thank you very much.

Not that she hadn't pictured that moment, though, that awkward and awful reunion.

The bell over the door would tinkle. She wouldn't look up, not right away, even though she would know it was them, would sense it in her skin. Maybe Henry would clear his throat or Emma would say, "Hello, dear," the way she did, and Rose would look up and smile at them, briefly, just so they knew that she knew they were there and that something was in store for them. She would offer them something to drink, some cookies, maybe, because for whatever fucking reason, whenever she pictured this moment, she pictured herself in it having just baked a batch of chocolate-chip cookies. They would catch up on what was new and relive old times, and then, just when they were comfortable, just when the last tattered shreds of awkwardness and discomfort had fallen away, *bam,* she'd pull out the banker box of files she kept in her storage closet, throw that shit on the table in between the two of them, and then yell at them: Ten, there are ten more fucking boxes just like this one.

Then she'd pull out a file, it wouldn't matter which one, and open it up and read from the top:

Subject suffers violent and debilitating nightmares.

Subject often uses sex as a weapon.

Subject suffers from deep trust issues.

No shit, Sherlock, she would say. That's the thing about being the subject who was abducted when you were fucking sixteen and trained to be a superpowered assassin with the promise that you'll help save the world when really all you're doing is settling a fucking score.

Subject is often violent to herself and others.

She wouldn't show them the scars. She wouldn't have to.

Subject often lies for no apparent reason.

She could go on.

She would go on. She would go on and on and on.

She kept all the receipts, too. Every therapist visit, every prescription filled, ever since the attack on the Regional Office. Just in case. She had the receipts taped to individual sheets of blank paper, all professional and shit, and then tabulated in a spreadsheet—a highlighted spreadsheet. She had all of this ready for the day that one of those assholes showed up, not that they ever would, but had it just the same, neatly organized, and then, stapled to the front, a fifteen-page itemized bill, and at the bottom of that bill, in all caps and in red, next to the line "Total Due," she'd stamped: "YOU OWE ME MY LIFE BACK, YOU FUCKERS."

She'd ordered that stamp specially made online.

She had pictured this moment often—the banker's box, the invoice—but no matter how hard she tried, she couldn't make it feel as delicious a moment as she wanted it to be when she imagined it happening.

A failure of her weak imagination, perhaps, or maybe she just knew them too well, knew they wouldn't care. They wouldn't even fucking apologize. They weren't the type. There'd be no, Sorry we took you from the life that you knew, from your family, from your friends, sorry we whisked you away and made promises, so many goddamn promises, all of which we failed to keep. No, Sorry we made you cut that one dude in half, that you still think of him from time to time, wonder about his family, whether he had one, what they might've been told about him, about how he died, sorry you can't stop picturing the stunned look in his eye.

They would justify. That's who they were.

She had wanted to leave the life she had been living, they would remind her.

She had wanted to get away from her dumb and neglectful father, her overbearing and angry mother, her pitiful and untempered sister.

She had hated her friends, hated her hometown.

She had hated her life.

She had told them so herself. They came for her just when she needed them most.

And what about those promises? What about what they gave her, the training, the powers they helped her discover within herself, helped her unleash and hone? The adventure, the thrills. Not to mention, she had been paid handsomely. She had been offered work after the Regional Office job. She had been offered a new life if she'd wanted it, an apartment in Biarritz, a new name, a new way forward, and she chose. She chose the life she chose. They had done everything they said they would. They molded her, taught her a craft, and then watched her become so very, very good at it. Could she give them that, at least?

And yes, she could give them that at least.

She was very good at what they trained her to be, but so what?

So what if she was good at this thing?

It wasn't her life, wasn't the life she had thought she'd wanted, wasn't the life she was supposed to live.

Not to mention they broke her fucking heart.

# 61.

She couldn't help but think that the whole robot thing just seemed so dated.

The whole fucking enterprise just seemed so dated to her now. Coldhearted revenge, a comeuppance for crimes she'd committed in her past, etc., and so on.

Not that the robot looked dated. It looked sleek and ultramodern, and kind of feminine. Kind of like a girl.

Although every robot that wasn't sheathed in some kind of humanlike skin—and this one wasn't—reminded her of Robocop. Even the sleek, newer-looking ones. Maybe that was the new thing with robot design, though, some hipster kind of return to the retro. No more hiding the robot bits underneath synthetic skin and wigs and clothes. Less T-1000 from *Terminator* and more Maximilian from *The Black Hole,* or B-9 from *Lost in Space.* It was sad, really, she thought. This whole fucking thing would have been easier to swallow if Rutger Hauer were on the other end of this battle to the death.

Jesus. Rutger Hauer? Where the fuck was her head?

She couldn't focus on one line of pop-cultural references, much less concentrate on not being smashed by a robotic fist.

Still. It was weird to think, wasn't it, that there could be

Rutger Hauer; bad sci-fi movies like *Lost in Space;* small, quaint bead and yarn shoppes in small, quaint Texas towns; and still be towering robots hell-bent on death and destruction. Or, rather, the other way around. The robot first and still all those other normal things. She'd spent these past few years caught in a limbo between constantly thinking about and completely forgetting about all that had happened to her, but had finally begun to edge, ever so slightly, in favor of forgetting, and now this fucking robot beast showed up.

It wouldn't stop swinging at her, or throwing shit at her, or grabbing her by the shoulder or ankle or wrist and slamming her into things, for one. Then, to make matters worse, the fucking thing wouldn't shut up. It just kept talking, and in a strange voice, strange for a robot, anyway. Not the kind of voice she'd have expected a robot to have. Rose would have expected something like the robot voice of Stephen Hawking, but this was just like a person, or not even just a person but maybe like a girl's voice, and for a second, Rose wondered if the robot was a girl robot, and then if there was such a thing—a girl robot with girl robot parts— but then it wouldn't shut up or stop swinging at her and whatever it was, it was just like anybody else, just as nonstop, just as god-damn annoying.

It kept saying things like, "Leave it to them to train you just enough to get you into trouble," as it wrenched a bank of cabinets out of the floor and then hefted them over its head, finishing with, "but not enough to get you out," as it heaved the whole thing at Rose, who saw this coming, but then the robot must have seen Rose see it coming and calibrated its throw in such a way that, even though Rose jumped out of the way, it clipped her hard in the shoulder and spun her in midair like a spinning coin.

And it said things like, "Was it worth it?" while holding up a skein of yarn. "All of this?" it asked. "Is all of this worth the things you did, the lives you ruined, the people you destroyed, the work you unraveled? For this?" Said that or something just like it before shoving the cabinet of alpaca yarn (Go Alpaca, You'll Never Go Backa!) toppling to the floor. "This shitty little yarn shop in the middle of this shitty little town?"

# 62.

It was a high-quality yarn shoppe, thank you very much, in a, yes, admittedly, shitty little town, but even still. That wasn't her whole life. She had a dog, a big gray, lazy Great Dane named Birdie. And a boyfriend.

I have a boyfriend, now, too, Rose wanted to say, almost said, clamped her mouth shut just before saying.

Not that the fucking robot would want to know or care, but his name was Jason, thank you very much, and they'd begun dating just after her roof started leaking and she'd hired him to fix the leak, and sure, he kept trying to get people to call him Jace, despite all the times she told him to stop doing that, that he was making a fool of himself but also of her just by association, which she was beginning to suspect only made him want to try even harder. And sure, just this past weekend, right as shit started getting hot and heavy across the bench seat of his pickup, he'd screeched things to a halt by asking her, So, what is this, am I your boyfriend now, or what?, and she'd curbed her serious desire to head-butt him and instead told him, Christ, grow a pair, would you? Not to mention: She'd known him way back in middle school when he'd had a total crush on her then, and, God, now that she was thinking about it, could he be more pathetic?

Jesus, if she got out of this mess with the robot (*when,* she corrected herself, *when* she got out of this mess with the robot), the first thing she would do would be to break up with Jason. That was the goddamn truth.

Except he was funny and really cute and a good fuck and, what's worse, so Patty told her after she'd come back, he once cornered Akard after school—after Rose'd pulled her disappearing act—and beat the shit out of him when he heard Akard saying something the likes of how Rose had to skip town since she'd whored herself out to every man who'd take her in this town. And when it came right down to it, she couldn't get enough of that boy, even just sitting together on his couch watching DIY shit on the TV and scarfing down fucking lime-chili Cheetos, or going at it like horny fucking teenagers every chance they got, and every minute of every day she worried he'd find out who or what she was (which was what, exactly?) and when he did, he'd be the one to leave her, and, God, she thought, what if he came over now?

What if he chose now to surprise her with lunch or cookies or just to say hi?

No, no, no, no, no.

The robot swung its fucking robot arm. Rose didn't duck, didn't leap, didn't sway. She grabbed the thing and rolled back, absorbing its momentum, using it against itself, and pivoted at the last possible second, throwing it, the arm and the robot, head over ass, back into the wall.

Because fuck if this robot was going to ruin the one good thing she had.

And the robot smiled. It stood and turned and smiled, damn it.

"Well, well," it said in its non–Stephen Hawking voice. "Look who finally woke up."

# 63.

Rose came back to her hometown on a whim. It wasn't like her mother had died, there was a funeral to go to—though her mother had died, a few years before, and no one could find Rose to tell her. Her sister had set herself up in their old house and Rose couldn't think of anywhere else to go and had grown tired of drifting, drifting, drifting.

She had assumed that once all the Regional Office stuff ended, she'd get this special kind of life with special kinds of friends. Even after she'd finished her assignment, even after all that had happened in the Regional Office, she thought this.

She'd taken care of the director—even that euphemism, *taken care of,* made her stomach turn, the thought of the look of him, cut in two—and she'd busted her way out as unglamorously as she'd busted her way in, and then she'd made her way to the rendezvous, but no one else was there. Not Emma, not Henry, none of the other girls. And sure, Emma and the other girls, they were taking care of their own assignments, could have been running late, but what had happened to Henry? His whole job was to wait at the safe house and keep it, well, safe. Only later did she begin to suspect that he'd never intended to go to the rendezvous, that maybe he and Emma had never really expected there to be anyone to rendezvous with.

But that suspicion wouldn't come until much later. At first, rather than assume the others were having more trouble than she'd had, were injured or even dead, she thought back to training, to her unshakable feeling that she was on the outside of that group looking in, and began to wonder if she was still outside of it all, if she had been given different rendezvous instructions than everyone else, and if the others were all at some bar in Brooklyn eating pizza and drinking beer and having a good laugh at poor old Rose. But before this idea could take serious hold, the door crashed open, Colleen stumbled in looking roughed up—a cut across her eyebrow, her wrist held gently in her other hand looking decidedly unwristlike—and she said, "We have to go, we have to go now."

"What happened to you?" Rose said, but before Colleen could answer, she said, "What about Henry, what about the others?"

Colleen shook her head. "Fuck Henry, man. If he's not here, then we definitely shouldn't be here either."

Rose hesitated. She looked around the hotel suite, looked at the minibar she'd wanted to tear into but hadn't because she wanted to share it with the others.

She'd imagined champagne toasts and a late night recounting all the shit that had gone down. She didn't know where she'd gotten the idea there'd be champagne, but that was what she'd settled on.

"Come on, Rose," Colleen said. "There's a car downstairs. We need to go now."

"What about your wrist?" Rose asked, but by then Colleen had already grabbed Rose's go-bag and thrown it at her and then she was out the door and on her way to the elevator and Rose didn't have much choice but to follow after her.

"What about the others?" Rose asked.

They were stuck on Canal Street waiting to slip into the Holland Tunnel and out of the city.

"Are we picking up any of the others?" she asked.

Colleen shook her head, honked at a truck trying to pull out in front of them. "What others?" she said. "As far as I know, you and me are what's left, and that's it." She checked her blind spot before squeezing in behind a yellow cab. "I almost didn't even go to the hotel."

"Wendy?" Rose asked.

Colleen shook her head.

"Becka? Windsor, Jimmie?"

"Look, Rose, what do you want from me? I don't know, I wasn't with them." She let go of the steering wheel and pressed her palms into her eyes even though the car continued to idle forward, listed to the left. Rose reached for the wheel, but Colleen beat her to it. "But Wendy," she said. "Wendy's gone, I know that much."

And then they stopped talking about it and then they drove to Philadelphia.

"Why Philadelphia?" Rose asked.

"Who is going to look for us in Philadelphia?" Colleen answered.

Rose offered to drive but Colleen wouldn't let her. She drove them to the airport, then parked in the long-term parking lot. Rose hadn't asked her where she'd gotten the car. She'd just assumed Colleen had stolen it.

"Here we go," Colleen said.

"What do you mean, here we go? What do we do now?"

Colleen handed her a thick manila envelope. "Everything you need is in here. Everything you need and half of everything Wendy needed." She took a shaky breath. "Might as well, right?"

"But," Rose said.

"Whatever you want. That's what you do now. Just. Not with me." Then she smiled and gave Rose a kiss on the cheek and whispered, "See you around, okay?"

"No you won't," Rose said, and she wasn't going to cry, though no one would have blamed her for it—it had been a long day, a long two years—but she was very close to punching Colleen in her face, and Colleen probably wouldn't have blamed her for that, either.

Colleen stepped back—maybe she could sense Rose's body tense up—and laughed and said, "Probably not," and she turned and started walking. Rose followed after, waiting for Colleen to stop, to turn around, to slap her straight, to tell her to grow up, to tell her to find her own way, to stop following her like some lost little puppy, to go find her own fucking life, but she didn't. Colleen kept walking, and then, Rose didn't know how, she lost herself in the crowd.

# 64.

The envelope had money in it—cash, prepaid credit cards, securities set up in her name, or, rather, her fake name. A couple of burner phones, a new set of identification, a slip of paper with different contacts encoded on it—Mexican, European, South Asian, Australian. A few amulets and crystals—that would've been Windsor, who was all about protective amulets and shit—and a small jeweler's pouch with a plastic spider ring inside it and a note attached with "Decoder Ring" written on it in Henry's handwriting.

She slipped the spider ring on her finger just in case it had been magicked or imbued with some kind of power, but no. Just one of Henry's jokes.

Hardy-fucking-har-har, Henry.

The idea of buying a plane ticket, of locking herself in a large metal tube as it hurtled across the country in the nighttime sky, made her queasy, so she took a bus instead from the airport to a Greyhound station. She bought a ticket to Chicago from there but stepped off the bus in Cleveland, and there boarded another bus headed to Houston, where she stole a car and drove it down to Brownsville, and then, early the next morning, among all the *abuelitas* walking across the river into work, she crossed the border into Matamoros and there slipped quietly out of sight.

A month later, she made contact with a guy in Monterrey and took a freelance gig rooting out narcoterrorists but she and the guy who'd hired her had irreconcilable differences that resulted in her fist connecting with his nut sack, and she left right after that for Cuba, where she heard a rumor of some supernatural flim-flammery going on. This turned out to be a pack of werewolves, one of whom had been some kind of geneticist before and who was hard at work on not any kind of cure but a means for making the change permanent and maintaining his manly intelligence while wolfed out. But a couple of women from the new and improved Regional Office got there just as she did and Rose spent a week hiding out in an abandoned grocery store until they'd packed up and left.

Every once in a while she went hunting for anyone else from training camp and the assault, but they were either all dead or just plain better at low-profiling it than she was.

She took shit job after shit job working for some real assholes, not because she needed the money but because she didn't know what to do with herself.

Twice she filled out college applications, and once she even went as far as to mail them off but had moved—three times, in fact—before the acceptances could find her.

Then she took a job with this guy Jonathan, a straightforward heist of some mystical artifacts, she didn't know what they did or who they were stealing them for, and didn't care, frankly. She was smarter, stronger, faster, and more powerful than Jonathan, but also she wanted to sleep with him, mostly because his girlfriend—who was running technical and mystical backup on the job—didn't trust her, assumed she was some kind of physical and sexual threat, which made Rose want to be those things if only so she could shove it back in her face and tell her, Self-fulfilling prophecy, bitch. Anyway, the job was simple. Break in, grab the shit, break out again, and sure, it was a high-security place, but wasn't she the one who broke into the Fortress of Living Flame, which, before she'd shown up, had been protected by eternal, magical flames for a millennium, if not longer? She could handle the security for a simple breaking-and-entering, except she'd been distracted, had overlooked a mystical rune or two, had walked right through a mystical barrier that dropped her into the bottom of the Mariana Trench, and she had just enough time to think to herself, Oh, shit, what a fucking loser way to fucking die, except really she got only so far as, O, before blacking out, and when she woke up, it was to the face and voice of the girlfriend, who dabbed her forehead gently with a warm, wet cloth, and who, when she saw Rose open her eyes, said, "I could have left you there, I just want you to remember that. I thought about it. I thought about leaving your ass down there. Don't forget that," and Rose didn't.

In fact, that job was what drew the line for Rose, what broke the camel's back, what eventually sent her back home.

After that job, the trajectory of her life weighed heavily on her.

After that little drop in the Mariana, after that little talk from Jonathan's whiny girlfriend, Rose thought long and hard about her life choices before, during, and after her little (and unsatisfying) romp with Jonathan. She thought about it on the plane back to the States, and then on the bus from Dallas to her shitty little hometown. She thought about it every time she thought about killing her sister, who was putting her up for a little while until she found her own place, figured out the rest of her life, but who was fucking driving her insane every minute of every day. She thought about it whenever she ran into some yokel from her past who couldn't think of her as anything more than Margaret's youngest, the pretty one itching for trouble. She thought about it when she put the money down on this storefront and the inventory to stock it. She thought about it all the fucking time, if you really must know, and figured that thinking about it was enough, that thinking about it equaled change.

Her hope had been to compress her life to make it seem like it had been one straight line from childhood to this moment in her late twenties, that there might arrive a day when she could step out of her yarn and bead shoppe and look at the small downtown square of her small Texas town and believe, deep inside herself, that everything else—Emma, the training camp, Henry, all the other girls, the assault on Regional, what she'd done in Spain and Morocco, all the things she had done—must have happened to somebody else, and maybe this hadn't quite worked out as well as she'd hoped it would, but she'd been trying, damn it. She'd been trying really fucking hard. She hadn't fucked Gina's husband, had she? And she could have. Gina was as tight-assed as she had been when they were kids and she could tell that dude was itching for a good fuck, or, hell, any kind of fuck. But Rose didn't, did she? And when the quilting shop on the other side of town kept stealing customers from her, undercutting her prices, offering knitting and quilting classes—that had been *her* fucking idea—she hadn't burned that place to the fucking ground, had she? These were choices she made. Hard choices made deliberately. And look at how things were going with Jason. As much as it hurt her pride to think on it, she was in a fucking relationship with a guy who wanted to be called Jace.

That was growth. That was change.

So, yeah, this shitty life was the life she felt she deserved, a comeuppance of sorts, an off-her-high-horse sort of life, but it was life, still. She'd had plenty of opportunity to choose otherwise, but she had chosen shitty life over no life a long time ago, and damned if she was going to let some Robocop-looking robot take that away from her.

# 65.

Except she couldn't figure this robot out.

The robot, she decided, was fucking with her. Playing games with her. Hurting her, sure, beating the shit out of her, well, not quite, not yet.

But still.

It was a goddamn megarobot or whatever, so why wasn't it beating the shit out of her? Why wasn't it going in for the kill? It pained her to think this, but she thought it might have even been pulling its punches, giving it to her easy.

Rose had gotten in her shots, too. The antique, heavy register smashed down on its head. The knitting needle shoved into its ankle gear that, for a second, had made the robot limp, but then the needle was shoved out somehow, hard enough to stick into the wall, and the thing repaired itself right in front of her.

It was fast and it was smart and it was strong but she was learning, moment by moment, catching on to its rhythms, picking up on its tells. But. Rose had a sinking feeling that all of this was a game to the robot, that every punch she landed, every small bit of damage she inflicted on that thing, only made it stronger, as if whatever fueled it fed on the kinetic energy of each impact.

She stood up. The robot held bunches of yarn in its robot fists.

It was saying something, she could tell by the movement of its nonrobot lips, but there was a ringing in her ear and she couldn't hear much above that.

Maybe it was testing her.

God, she thought. This better not be another fucking test.

Her nose was bleeding. Her left eye was swelling up and soon she wouldn't be able to see out of it, not well enough to fight, anyway.

If this is another test . . . , she thought, and for a second, at the idea of someone else throwing some unbeatable monster at her as a way to test her, she wanted to give up.

She was so done with being tested.

Henry and Emma and Jonathan and that guy for that job in Spain.

It would go like this: She would figure out some way to beat this robot or get past it, or there would be some kind of switch or mechanism and if she found that and threw it or clipped it or punched it, this robot would come to a shuddering halt and then some asshole in an expensive suit that on him would look incredibly cheap would step out from the shadows, slow-clapping or maybe not. Maybe instead of the slow clap of grudging respect, she'd get a snarky bit of, "I was beginning to worry you might not ever figure that one out." But either way, there would be some dangerous job, some exorbitant payoff, some promises made. Promises, promises, promises. And her entire yarn and bead shoppe would have been crushed all to hell because some asshole with an outsized checkbook and a desire to rescue his dead wife from the bowels of hell, or who had called forth some demon horde and had lost control of them, wanted to a) test his toy out and b) make sure she was still up to the work.

Except she wasn't. Any yahoo in the shadows watching this fight go down would be able to see pretty easily that she was not up to the test, much less the job, whatever it turned out to be. She'd been fighting, what, fifteen minutes and already she was tired. Tired and out of practice. She'd become a creature of habit. Her life had become easy and predictable—work all day in her yarn and bead shoppe, dinner with Jason, back to his house for a bottle of wine or a six-pack of beer, where they'd watch some trash on the Learning Channel or the Food Network with her dog, and then she'd drift off to sleep on the couch and he'd wake her with a soft kiss on her lips and then down her neck and then they'd move things to the bedroom, or else he'd fall asleep, too— and that was how she liked it, had been what she looked forward to, the regularity of this, the simplicity of this, seven days a week.

And now she had to muster herself up for this?

# 66.

And then the robot had her by the neck.

"Says here you offer classes," the robot said, loud enough she could hear it over the ringing in her ear.

It held her pressed up against the corkboard wall near the bathroom in the back. It pulled the flyer off the corkboard. Rose had been trying to get people to take her knitting classes for a year now, but all the people who would have been interested in knitting already knew how to knit, or else they signed up for classes at that quilting shop on the other side of town. "What do you think?" it said in its voice that was still not a robot voice. Then the robot held its free hand in front of Rose's face, wiggled its thick, shiny robot fingers at her. "Are these knitting hands?"

The humor, too.

Rose didn't quite understand the humor, wouldn't have expected that from a robot. Yet here it was, making a joke, maybe making fun of her, even.

The grip around her neck was loose enough that she could say something if she wanted, and she had the uncanny sense that the robot *was* expecting her to say something. As if the robot had made a joke and she was supposed to look fear and death in the eye and say, Fuck it, and offer her own witty remark in return.

She'd never been any good at that sort of thing, and she didn't know what to say to the robot wiggling its fingers in her face, and so all she could resort to was what she knew.

"I have a number of different-sized knitting needles," Rose told it. "I'm sure we can find something that would work."

For a second, it looked like the robot was about to smile, and then it thrust her up with such force that she cracked her head against and then through the crappy drop-down ceiling tiles and she thought, not for the first time, about the original wood-beamed ceiling, and how she'd always wanted to tear away the tiles to expose those beams, and this reminded her of the director's office and the nice beaming going on there.

Exposing those beams would have made this space so much nicer.

# 67.

When she was ten, Rose's daddy had taken her to the beach. It was strange. Even Rose knew at ten how strange it was. He shook her awake while it was still dark, held his finger up to his mouth to quiet her down, and then smiled a smile that usually meant he was drunk, but this morning she couldn't smell any of the drink on him, which made his smile even more worrisome.

He wrapped his arms underneath her and started lifting her out of bed, but she was too big for him to lift out of bed that way and her legs tangled up in the covers. He struggled for a second and then he dropped her halfway out of the bed, and she landed half-assed on the side of the bed, the rest of her ass sliding off her mattress and landing hard on the hard floor, along with her wrist and ankle and everything else. She twisted her ankle but didn't sprain it. Her wrist stung. Tears welled up in her eyes, but her daddy didn't notice, had started into a fit of giggling that he was working to tamp down, clamping his mouth shut with his left hand and waving at her with his right, as if she were about to burst out into giggles, too. Then he wiped his laughing tears and then he wiped her pained tears without asking her if she was all right, and then he stood her up on her feet and grabbed her hand and pulled her out front and loaded her into the car, all without saying a word, and not until they'd passed the 7-Eleven, and then the Coca-Cola bottling plant, did he say, as if she already knew where he was taking her, as if they'd had this little trip planned for weeks: "You excited for the beach, sweet pea?"

When they got to the beach and he pulled out the bag he'd packed for the day, she half-expected him to have brought her old bathing suit, the one that didn't fit her anymore, or to have forgotten to bring a bathing suit for her at all. The other half of her, though, didn't so much as expect but hope that maybe he'd bought her a brand-new bathing suit, like the bikini she'd seen in Target a few weekends ago, the aqua-blue one with the white piping and the ruffly top.

She should have known which half was going to be the right half.

"You're just a kid," he said. "No one cares if you're out in the water in just your clothes."

What he had brought with him were a couple of inner tubes, a big, thick black one for him, and a smaller light-blue one for her. His plan was for them to sit in their respective inner tubes and let the surf and the waves do all the work. Tubing down the coast, he called it. More exciting than tubing down the river.

"Let those other chumps fight against the waves by swimming, or sit on the sand and bake in the sun," he said.

"Let those other chumps bore themselves to death inching down a swampy river," he said.

Except there weren't any other chumps. Not on the beach or in the surf. She doubted there were any chumps floating down the river, either, wherever the river was. It was October in Texas, and the beach was empty and the water cold and choppy. If she squinted, Rose thought she could see a squall forming out over the gulf in the distance.

We're the chumps, she wanted to say.

You're the chump, she really wanted to say.

Then, as she took the inner tube he held out for her, she sighed. I'm the chump.

They were supposed to anchor the tubes to the shore with a thick length of rope tied to a tree or shrub or the front bumper of the car, which her daddy would park right up at the edge of the shoreline, otherwise the current would draw them farther and farther down the coast. When she asked him about the rope, she saw in his eyes a flicker, the briefest look of Ah, shit, I forgot the rope, but he recovered quick enough and said, "You're old enough. I thought you'd like to try it the big-girl way."

He handed her a pair of goggles, to keep the salt spray out of her eyes, and a snorkel, just in case. In case of what, she didn't want to consider. He threw a diver's mask over his own face, and then a Houston Astros pith helmet on his head, the kind with the cup holders and straws meant for cans of beer, but instead of beer, her father had sloshy, melting frozen margaritas he'd poured into old Bud Light cans, the idea being that salt water, which would ruin a beer, only made a frozen margarita taste better.

At first, she was surprised to find herself having fun. The waves pulled her out and threw her back to the shore like they were rough-and-tumble friends. Sometimes she was swooped to shore under a bubbling, ruffling breaker, and sometimes she was lifted high on the crest of a wave, felt her tummy flop in on itself. The water was cold but even in October the air was hot and humid and the contrast felt warm and shivery, and against her better judgment, she found herself screaming and laughing and giggling with her father, who had finished the first set of margaritas-in-a-can and was working on finishing his second set. Where he kept them, she didn't know and never found out.

It was unexpected fun, which made it somehow even more fun, the kind of fun you had when you got away with something, but then the storm she'd seen in the distance fell onto them in a rush, and the waves, already heavy and forceful and on the verge of mean, crashed over them with real purpose. Rose became anxious. Gallons of salt water sloshed into her nose and mouth. They had moved farther and farther down the shoreline so that she couldn't see where they'd parked the car anymore. She tried to catch her daddy's attention, but he didn't care about the heavy rain, the rough waters. He thought it was all hilarious good fun, and he was drunk. Then a wave picked her up and then threw her down on the beach, where she landed face-first, cutting her skin just under her right eye against the blunt plastic of her goggles. Her cheek felt bruised and her whole body hurt and she stood up shakily and watched her daddy waving at her, yelling, "You're all right, pumpkin. I'll meet you back at the car." Except the car was locked and the rain was coming down hard and fast and she sat behind the car, leaned against the back bumper, where the wind and rain didn't hit her as hard, though they still hit her, and still pretty hard. Her father didn't come back for another hour, deep into his drunk and missing his own inner tube and pith helmet. He didn't see her, maybe, or had forgotten all about her, had jostled the driver's-side door open and jumped into the seat and started the car all before she could even stand herself up—cold and tired and sore. It took minutes of her pounding on the passenger window before he realized she was still there, the doors were still locked. She refused to speak to him the whole way home, but he was too drunk to notice or care. Typically him: sober enough to drive home, too drunk to notice his daughter. By the time he dropped her off at her mother's, the storm had passed and he blew her a kiss and gave her a smile and a wave as if they'd just finished a picture-perfect daddy-daughter day, and then he was gone.

After she'd come back to this town, after Morocco, after Spain, her father had found out and came back into town and made her sit down for lunch with him. Her mother had been dead for a few years by then, and her sister, Stacey, had become a sorry excuse, living in that old house of their mother's, the place unchanged down to the goose-themed wallpaper in the kitchen. Their father had moved off some thirty miles north where he'd found a woman who liked him enough to not care just how little he did. He looked old and haggard and small, which at once pleased and depressed her. He didn't ask where she'd been, what she had done to herself, why or how she'd left, or where she'd gone. He told her that someone—maybe someone she had known back in high school—once stopped him on his way out of the post office to tell him she'd seen Rose pole dancing at a strip club in Oklahoma, which made him laugh and say, "My Rose? With a job? I think you're mistaken." He laughed telling her this. And then when the bill came, he waited for her to pay for lunch, didn't even pretend to reach for his wallet, and then they shook hands, and even before she'd grabbed her purse, he'd gone.

Maybe he'd wanted something from her but had gotten cold feet and decided not to ask, or maybe he had some lingering sense of obligation to her as her father, but either way, she never saw him again after that.

# 68.

Her father hadn't been the only one to fail to ask her what had happened to her so long ago. No one seemed to know that she had gone, had been whisked away so many years ago, or they had known she'd gone somewhere but had assumed she'd gone to some normal kind of place in the normal kind of way. College or junior college or to a slightly larger town, maybe, to find a slightly better kind of life. No one who saw her as she maneuvered again through her small hometown, which had changed so little, could even muster surprise that she had come back, but instead made automatic assumptions that she had gotten married and came back to raise her family, or that she'd come back looking to get married before it was too late, or that she'd gotten a job teaching at the elementary school, or was going to be working at the courthouse as a paralegal or an assistant. How they formed such specific ideas about why she was back and what she was doing, she didn't know, but nobody seemed surprised, and when she told them she hadn't decided what she was going to do yet, they gave her a sweet, poor-thing look and patted her gently on her arm and told her, "You'll find something, I'm sure." And then they'd ask her about church and make sure to invite her to theirs.

Even Stacey hadn't been that surprised when Rose knocked

on the door. Rose sat on the couch and waited for fifteen, twenty minutes, listened to Stacey complain about the house; about their mother's death and all the hassle that accompanied it; about their father, who had shown up not even two days after the funeral trying to make some kind of sinister claim on this house; listened to her go on about all of this before Stacey finally, sighing heavily, asked, "So what's been up with you?"

"We just figured you went off to live with Dad," she said when Rose asked if they hadn't gone looking for her, hadn't even noticed that she'd gone.

"But I didn't," Rose said. "Did you even ask Dad?"

Stacey shrugged.

"I went away. I was taken away," Rose said. Kidnapped, she almost said. Changed.

Stacey shrugged her heavy shoulders again. "And now you're back, so what? You look fine."

"Honestly," her old friend Patty said when she saw her, "at first we kind of assumed that you'd been raped and murdered by that guy, what was his name? And we were about to say something about it, but then your sister told us your mom kicked you out of the house and sent you to live with your daddy."

She had met Patty for lunch near the end of her first week back home, when she was just beginning to think about staying. Patty hadn't stopped growing until long after Rose had left, had grown into a tall, broad-shouldered woman who wore her shiny black hair in a shoulder-length bob with bangs.

"You should definitely go see Gina," Patty had said. "It would kill her to see you, still so thin." And then, after hardly any time at all, they ran out of things to say and ate their lunches quietly but for the soft grunting sounds Patty made while she ate, and then it was time for Patty to go, shopping to do, dinner to make, laundry to fold, and she gave Rose a hug and told her how nice it was to see her again, and then she was gone, and for the first time, standing outside on the square watching the tall, hulking frame of Patty lumber down the street, for the first time in what seemed like a very long time, Rose knew what she wanted to do.

Or maybe *want* was too strong a word, or the wrong word altogether. She knew what she needed to do.

She needed to come back home. She'd left too soon, left before she'd been ready, and since leaving home, her life had gone off the rails. She'd cut a man in half, for Christ's sake. And had done other things, sure, but there's not much left after having done that. And she felt on the run, always unsettled and on the move. But coming home. Starting over. That would fix everything.

# 69.

The robot punched her, finally, but really punched her. And for the first time in her life, Rose thought, Oh, Jesus. I think I might lose.

She shot across the room and hit her back against the far wall, embedded herself there, the wind knocked out of her.

Even if she could have moved her head, she wouldn't have looked down, wouldn't have dared to look at the spot where the thing hit her, afraid there would be a hole there, a robot-fist-shaped hole passing right through her chest, where her heart should have been. That's how it felt, anyway, as if the thing punched clean through her, everything else caving in around that spot, as if that spot had obtained the gravitational property of a tiny black hole.

"I expected you to be stronger," the robot said.

"I expected you to be faster and smarter, too," it said.

"I expected this to be much more difficult than it has been, honestly. Expected you to put up at least a little bit of a fight. To be clever. To find some way to try, at least."

Rose couldn't breathe. She couldn't move. Then it grabbed her, lifted her up, a foot off the ground, maybe more, she couldn't tell.

It turned her around, its hand wrapped tightly around her throat again. Its robot head was bent toward her ear.

It's strange, she thought, that they gave a robot lips.

"I wanted this to be more interesting," it said, and then it dropped her and she landed badly on her ankle and maybe that was broken now, too.

# 70.

If she was going to be honest with herself, and what better fucking time to be honest with yourself than at the very goddamn end, it was less the fact that she never saw Emma again after the Regional Office job. That hurt, sure. She loved Emma. They all loved Emma. But she wasn't surprised, and so maybe it hurt just a little bit less.

But that bastard Henry had told her he loved her (okay, so maybe in a best-friend, brotherly kind of way, but still, she was only eighteen, she was impressionable, and he should have known better), told her that he would come find her after the job was finished, that they would have some kind of adventure when it was all said and done (and maybe when he said *they* he meant all of they and not just him and her).

And it wasn't like he was dead.

She knew for a fact that he wasn't dead.

Colleen had told her he wasn't dead.

She had run into Colleen once in Spain. Ibiza. Rose was in between jobs, hadn't yet experienced her Mariana Trench epiphany, but it wasn't far off, either.

They ran into each other in an open-air market. It was awkward, at first, and then they fell onto each other, hugging and sobbing. They spent the next two days with each other, sleeping at each other's hotel rooms, one waking early and buying coffee for the other, visiting tourist sites with each other, until finally Colleen insisted they simply stay in the same hotel, the same room, to save money, even though they both had money to burn. They didn't talk about the camp, or Emma, or their assaults, or the attack, the things they had done, the people they had lost. Colleen had enrolled in cooking classes at the hotel. This was her third time through the class. She'd been there for months and had learned how to scuba dive, had parasailed, had learned spearfishing, had gone pearl diving, had exhausted and worn out the poor activity director, had seen the sights so many times that she had considered, jokingly, applying for a job as a tour guide. She paid for a long-term rental scooter. Rose didn't have to ask her why she hadn't simply bought a scooter or let out an apartment, for that matter. Colleen made paella and brought it back to the room one night. Another night she made diver scallops with a vanilla-champagne reduction, and Rose asked her what was Spanish about it and Colleen shrugged and said, "Saffron, I guess," and the next morning, as they sat on the balcony of Colleen's hotel room, which stunned Rose every time with its view of the Sant Antoni Bay, as they sat there silent but not comfortable in their silence, having run out of everything to talk about that wasn't the operation, that wasn't Emma or the Regional Office, Rose asked her if she'd heard from anyone else.

"Becka," she said, "or anyone else, maybe? Henry, maybe?"

And maybe Colleen knew how important it was and pretended it wasn't important at all to spare Rose's feelings, or maybe she didn't know anything at all when she said, "Henry was, well, you just missed him, not more than two weeks ago." Then she said,

"I'm sure he'll be in touch with you. You were always his favorite, you know. 'The best we ever trained, blah, blah, blah.' And, 'What an amazing girl.' You know how he was."

She nodded. And then, because if she didn't leave in the next few minutes, she would burn the hotel to the ground, Rose decided it was time to move on.

"I think it's time I moved on," she said.

Colleen sipped her coffee and nodded. "Okay," she said.

And there was a moment, a soft, brief moment when it seemed one or both of them would start talking, would talk about what had happened at camp, what had happened after camp, what had happened to them since the assault on the Regional Office, what had made it so impossible for either of them to settle into any kind of new normal. But before one of them could crack, Colleen stood up, abruptly, too abruptly, knocking her knee into the table, sloshing Rose's coffee out of its mug, and Colleen said, "Sorry," and Rose shook her head and half-smiled and said, "It's okay," but not, I'm sorry, too, though she hoped it had been buried there, an I'm sorry, too, buried in the tone of her voice, maybe, or somewhere deep in the words she actually said. Then Colleen said she had to get ready for class and Rose said she'd probably be gone before she got back from class and Colleen nodded and said, "Okay, well, take care of yourself," and not, I'll see you soon, or, I'll see you later, okay? but Rose thought she could hear that somewhere in her voice, too, and after Colleen went back inside the room, Rose finished her coffee, packed her bag, and then left while Colleen was still in the shower.

She hadn't seen Colleen since, and hadn't heard from Henry, not even once.

# 71.

She shouldn't be thinking of Henry at a time like this, she knew. She shouldn't be thinking of Henry or Emma or Colleen or Windsor or Wendy or any of them. She should be thinking of herself, and aside from herself, she should be thinking of Jason, poor silly Jace. Or her sister, though her sister never thought of her. Or Gina or Patty or her asshole of a father.

But she wasn't. She was thinking of Henry.

She wished she had seen Henry, if only one more time. One time before all of this, before the robot, before the end.

She opened her eyes to look at that robot and that was when she saw the sword and then she wasn't thinking of Henry, either, and was, much to her dismay, thinking of the director and his glove and the sword and what happened with the sword.

Rose wondered where it could have come from, where the robot would have hidden it. There didn't seem to be any hiding places on that robot. But there it was, long and thin, gleaming and cold and sharp, though, really, with as much force as the robot could bring to bear, that sword didn't have to be sharp, just strong. And it was both, she knew it was both sharp and strong.

Sharp enough, strong enough, anyway, to split a man in two.

"Is this how you did it?" the robot said in its nonrobot voice.

"Did you toy with him? Did you throw him from place to place and toy with him like a doll?"

The robot didn't have to say who the "him" was. It knew she knew. With that sword in its hand, the robot didn't have to say anything at all, in fact, but it wouldn't stop. "Did you beat him bloody in the very place he felt safest? You with all your strength and power, and him just a man. Did you do all of that and then with his own sword, did you cut him down?"

The robot stopped and held the sword down at its side. "Is that how it happened?" And maybe it was waiting for Rose to say something, but she couldn't. She couldn't think of what to say and knew it wouldn't matter, though she did feel the desire to make note of the director's rather powerful glove. It seemed all so very personal, Rose thought. Strange that something so personal might come out of a robot, and she looked at its face, really looked at the robot's face, and wondered if it was even a robot at all.

No, she thought. That face, those eyes. That face is a woman's face.

And then she knew.

Oh, she thought. It's you. I always wondered about you.

Not that she spent nights awake wondering about the girl with the mechanical arm, just every so often she wondered what she looked like, if she had survived the assault, what her life must be like, what it would feel like to have a metal part of you swinging at your side. Now that she was face-to-face with the girl with the mechanical arm, she looked for that arm, but then caught herself because there wasn't a mechanical arm anymore, or rather, all of her was mechanical arm now, or rather, mechanical everything, and then she felt embarrassed for looking at her so nakedly and for a second, the only thing she wanted to do was tell her, I'm sorry. For the look, for what she'd done, for all of it, but that urge quickly passed.

The robot had the sword raised up again.

Rose wished she'd figured it out sooner.

Not that she hadn't known this thing had come for her from the Regional Office. Of course this thing had come from the Regional Office. Where else would it have come from?

Not that figuring it out sooner would have mattered very much. This thing wasn't like anything she'd ever faced, wasn't like anything she had been trained to face by Emma or Henry at the compound. This wasn't some superpowered girl like herself, or an office slouch like most of the people at Regional. Even now, she couldn't think of a move or countermove or strategy that might have disabled the thing or gotten her past it and now that goddamn sword.

But maybe—if she had known sooner, if she had figured it out sooner—maybe she would have fought differently. Fighting a thing simply on a mission is different than fighting a thing on a Mission. She would've fought differently, or maybe just harder.

From the very beginning, she would have fought harder.

But here she was, at what was most likely the very end, doing the only thing she could think of to do. Forget about the pain. Forget about the bones, broken if slowly mending. Forget about everything else and charge straight at that motherfucker, even if it would be the very last thing she'd ever do.

Which was what she did.

From *The Regional Office Is Under Attack:*
*Tracking the Rise and Fall of an American Institution*

The second theory on how Henry managed to so effectively enact his plans against the Regional Office proceeds
in almost the exact same way as the first theory, except
for the small but significant difference that Emma was
not killed, that her death had been entirely faked.

# SARAH

# 72.

The doctor wasn't sure how Sarah's shoulder and mechanical arm had come back together. He studied her, where the arm reattached itself.

"It's not a perfect fit," he said. She almost yelled at him when he said this. Nothing could have been more perfect than this fit. "I mean," he said, warily catching a look in her eye, "it's perfect now. But it's not where we put it originally. Not how we put it originally."

He was skeptical of the story she'd told him, she could tell. He thought maybe she'd had help reattaching the arm, but that seemed unlikely. Or maybe the stress of the situation, the pain and stress and instability of it all, maybe coupled with some pharmaceuticals and some neurological suggestive therapy . . .

"Maybe what?" Sarah asked.

Maybe they hadn't ever taken it off to begin with. Maybe they'd tried to take it off—hence the queer way it didn't quite line up with how it had once lined up—but failing that, they'd done their best (and had succeeded) to convince her that it had been removed.

"What better way," he said, "to neutralize the largest threat than to convince the threat that it had been neutralized?"

He floated this idea out there as if it were a bubble, hesitant and fragile. She popped it, almost violently, emphatically, jabbing her mechanical finger into his very soft and pliable chest, because she had wondered much the same thing herself, had tried to think back to the moment when she'd seen it on the gurney in front of her.

And it was a thought she would rather not think.

But what if? What if her mechanical arm had been there the entire time?

"No matter," he said, and there was something frightened in his voice and she tried to think calm thoughts, tried to remember Mr. Niles waving his arm at the destruction she had wreaked right after he had given her this mechanical arm. She smiled uncomfortably.

My, how they must have laughed at her. They must have laughed and laughed and laughed. She never even suspected, they would have said. She never even considered she might still have both her arms, they would have said. And then they would have howled. The thought of their laughing at her made her wish they were all still alive so she could kill them all again, and to settle her thoughts down, she thought of Wendy, of dead, frightened-eyed Wendy, and this made her feel better.

"The arm is in place and is still functional," he said. "That's great news."

He scheduled her for another appointment, asked her to clear her schedule so they could cover it again. They didn't have enough of her own skin to use but he could create a synthetic that would match almost perfectly. But at first she said no. She didn't know why she said no but it felt necessary to say no to covering up the mechanical arm.

Then she said, "I'm sorry. You're right. We have to cover it."

And a week later, it was covered, and for days, she couldn't pass by a mirror without staring at the mechanical arm and admiring once more how much it looked like just any normal arm would look.

For a couple of days, after she returned to the office with her new skin, people stopped and admired her arm. Just like new, they said. Or, It looks perfect. Or, Soon, we won't remember which one was the mechanical one at all. But this she knew was a lie. How could it not be a lie? They remembered, all of them remembered, and would always remember, she thought, and that was a shame.

# 73.

She was in Mr. Niles's office and his mother was cutting his hair and he was talking about the business of Regional and she couldn't stop hopping from foot to foot. Mr. Niles was about to raise his eyebrows at her and say something about this, she knew, but then he was sliding into his car in the parking garage, which was only strange in that he usually had someone drive him, but he was sliding into his car and she was there holding the door for him and she was apologizing to him for a report he'd asked for that she hadn't delivered yet and he didn't care, didn't care at all, and she was still shifting from her left foot to her right, left to right, right to left, and he was smiling and shaking his head and saying, Don't worry about it, it's fine, and she was still apologizing even as he closed the door and started the engine and she waited and watched as he pulled out of the garage and then, ending there, the dream would have been really no different than any number of other anxiety dreams she'd had about Regional, but it didn't stop there because she turned and started to walk back to her office but tripped, stubbed her toe or her whole foot on the curb and tripped, and there was suddenly a sharp and burning pain in her foot, but in her real foot, too, and she woke up.

She stumbled to the bathroom. In the light, she couldn't see anything wrong with her foot, but it hurt like holy hell, and she gritted her teeth and squeezed her mechanical fist. Then she squeezed her normal fist. She took some ibuprofen and then more and then the bottle was empty and she was in her bed and the pain was such that breathing made it worse.

Blinking. Blinking also made it worse.

The pumping of blood through her veins. That, too.

Everything. Everything made it worse.

# 74.

*In the fall of 1993,* the letter continued, *your mother was abducted.*

*This is not something you do not already know. This is not something we need to remind you of, yet while you know a story about the abduction and disappearance and ultimate fate of your mother, you do not yet know the full and accurate story.*

*Let us begin, then, with the fall of 1993. Your mother had dropped you off at school that morning and had, on her way back to your apartment, stopped at a Duane Reade. Let us say she needed to buy a new hair dryer. Really, does it matter? In the grand scheme of things, no it does not, but let us say that we know for sure that what she bought was a hair dryer, a small pack of Band-Aids, and Tylenol PM.*

*It is important to us that you understand just what and how much we know about your mother and about the man and woman who abducted her, and about you.*

*Your mother was taken just as she left the store.*

*You have been led to believe that the man and woman who took your mother were the anarchists Manuel*

Guzman and Nadja Prcic, that she was abducted by these two and returned to a secret location in Queens, where she was brainwashed, such that she forgot who she was, who you were, or that you were even a you to be forgotten about. After which, she was moved in secret to Houston, then to Managua, where she was trained to be a freedom fighter, and then, from there, was snuck across the Atlantic into West Africa, where she was given further instruction and deeper brainwashing. Then, during an operation—the attempted (and foiled) detonation of a bomb in the London Underground—your mother was killed.

You have seen the photographs.

You have read the dossiers.

You know the reports.

As far as you are aware, you have killed everyone involved in the operation but for one man who killed himself.

It is our unfortunate responsibility to inform you that in all of this, however, you are wrong, though only because you have been misled.

As of this moment—as we are penning this letter to you—your mother is still alive.

# 75.

By the end of the assault it had been a minor miracle that she was standing still, much less fighting. Much less crushing skulls with her bare hand.

Even she had known that the arm had managed all the heavy lifting, had pulled her along, had made all of the decisions, moving her left or right, punching or not punching, crushing or not crushing, according to its own mysterious rubric.

And she hadn't cared. Let the arm do what it wanted to do.

But when it was all over, she could barely stand, much less walk. Her arm held her up, propped her against one of the few remaining cubicle walls.

The doctor declared her unfit for anything but the emergency room and then stitched her up as best he could. Her busted lip. The bulging, purpling bruises on her cheek and over her eye. The cauliflower of her ear, which had been boxed again and again. He applied cream, a salve of some sort, to the places where they had placed the electrodes and the hot pokers.

Her ribs, three of them, had been broken. He couldn't do much for those.

Internal bleeding he handled as soon as he could get her into the operating room.

Then there'd been the shock of losing her arm, and then of the arm's return, the emotional and mental rigmarole that had gone hand in hand with all of that, but she kept that for herself. She could have handed that to the doctor, too, and maybe he would have handed her something back—a tranquilizer, maybe, or a hug. But that, the emotional thing that had happened back there, the weeping and sobbing into her shirt, the liquid feeling of feeling whole again—that she kept for herself.

But despite all of this, despite the pain of torture and hastily performed field surgery to remove her arm and despite the fighting and the reattachment, despite all of this, nothing had happened to her foot.

Her foot—both her feet—should have been fine.

# 76.

By the time the doctor saw her the next morning, she couldn't walk unassisted. She hobbled into the examination room using a crutch. Her breath rasped; her skin had paled. She had a fine, pungent sheen of sweat clamming to her face and neck and chest.

Not a few times during the night had she considered cutting off the foot herself, cutting it off just below the calf.

After an examination and X-ray, the doctor told her there was nothing wrong with her foot, and she considered punching him through his face.

Lately, she had been considering punching people through their faces a not-inconsiderable number of times.

So much did she want to punch him through his face, her mechanical arm had come up to punch-through-the-face level. Her fist was a closed and ready-to-punch fist.

She forced it down. She exerted a great deal of force of will to make it go down. When it did, it grabbed hold of the edge of the table in a serious and life-threatening way.

"Check," she said. "Again." She gritted her teeth. Her fist gripped the table hard enough to crumple the edge of it. She didn't care. All she could do was grit her teeth or crush the table with her fist or crush the doctor's skull.

He checked again. He didn't know what was wrong. He gave her something to take for the pain. She looked at the bottle he handed her and shoved it back at him and in the same fluid motion grabbed him by his collar, her fist cocked and ready to punch again.

He gave her something much stronger.

By the afternoon, her foot was green. The entire foot from the tip of her toe to the top of her ankle.

Not a deep green, not a green you would call forest or sea turtle or even just green, not yet, but it wasn't yellow either.

It was beyond yellow and was moving confidently into the green family of colors.

The sight of the green foot made the doctor blanch, made him stutter. He rubbed his hand through his thin hair and pulled it down tightly over his face. She grabbed him again and pulled him close and he smelled like sick, or sick and sweat, and she was desperate now.

People had to fucking carry her there, and she was now desperate.

"Cut it off," she said. "Cut the fucking thing off and do it now."

# 77.

Not only is your mother still alive, but you have seen her and she has seen you innumerable times. It is possible that you and your mother have seen each other on a near-weekly basis now for the past seven years that you have been working for the Regional Office, working for Mr. Niles and Oyemi, working for the very people who took your mother from you.

Manuel Guzman and Nadja Prcic, while not the best of people, while guilty of a number of crimes and sins, and not exactly undeserving of being hunted down and smote by your lovely mechanical arm, had nothing to do with the abduction of your mother but were simply offered up by Mr. Niles—along with the other men and women you stalked and killed, men and women the Regional Office would have gotten around to dealing with eventually if not for you, so do not blame yourself for their deaths, which were hastened, surely, but not by much. Mr. Niles has, for this long time, been working to control you and your movements, all in an attempt to hide from you the very information you came looking for.

*Your mother is much changed from how you would remember her. Have you figured it out? Have you guessed yet where your mother is, who your mother has become?*

*It is not our intention to be coy or to throw puzzles at you like obstacles in a training course, but it is simply our hope that if you can come to the conclusion on your own, if you can take the small pieces of this we have given you and pull together a full picture of what wrongs have been committed—against you, against your mother— then you will more likely believe this truth than the one you were fed by Mr. Niles.*

*It is not an easy choice we are asking you to make, we understand how hard this choice must be, the choice between a story you have told yourself again and again, that you have done right by your mother, by her spirit, have taken righteous vengeance against the men and women who stole her from you, and the story that you have done very little at all, have done less than very little in fact, have worked to advance the goals and livelihoods of the two people who deserved your vengeance most.*

*We navigate through this life with the good-faith hope that we are doing our best, that we are aimed in the right directions, that we are helping the helpless. Maybe we slip, maybe we mess up, maybe from time to time we do things that are less the right thing. Or we cut corners, or we make choices that serve our interests over the interests of those who depend on us, or we hide the consequences of the decisions we have made with the hope that those consequences will never be seen despite how often we make those same decisions. We go back to the ones we love when clearly they do not love us, or do not know how to love us, or show us their love in a way easily mistaken for hate. We are weak in the face of the hard work it sometimes takes to be strong. We convince ourselves (incorrectly) that silence is not a form of consent. We let good people die and sometimes we kill them ourselves and we hide and we hide and we hide and soon hiding becomes the thing we are best at doing, but it is time, Sarah.*

*It is time to stop hiding, Sarah O'Hara.*

*It is time to stop peeking out from behind the coattails of Mr. Niles, the flaring nostrils of Oyemi, the long reach of the Regional Office, to stop peeking out from behind your mechanical arm, to stop hiding behind your aunt and the tragedy of your childhood, time to stop hiding from what is real and painful and frustrating and all of the other emotions we find it so easy to hide from, and time to admit that you know, have known, have always known since the first time you saw her, bald and trembling and half-submerged in the milky-blue water of Oyemi's Oracle Pool with her "sisters," time to see your mother, time to stop pretending it's not her.*

# 78.

The relief she felt when she came out of the surgery, when she came out of the haze-inducing anesthetics, was an ecstasy kind of relief.

The relief in having this part of her removed was almost as strong, in fact, as the relief she felt when she'd had that other part of her reattached.

It lasted for a day, for almost two days, and she wondered how strong the anesthetic had been. She didn't take any of the painkillers the doctor had given her. She didn't need them, she felt so fucking good all of the time now. She should have cut the other foot off, too, for good measure.

The lab was working on a new foot for her. The doctor had asked her to wait two weeks, three weeks, and then the foot would've been finished and they could've removed the bad foot and replaced it all in one operation, but she couldn't wait. She wouldn't wait. She would have cut it off herself if he hadn't done it for her.

For now, it was disguised. They didn't have the prosthetic on hand, and so it was disguised with wrapping and a boot, the kind people wore when they broke their foot. She had a story to tell in which she was a klutz. People liked to hear about when you were a klutz, she decided.

But in all honesty, she didn't care what people liked to hear about or what people thought about when they saw her with her boot and her wrap because all she could think about was how good she felt now that the foot was gone.

This feeling was a fleeting feeling, however. This feeling lasted not even two full days before it was gone and was replaced first by an itch at the base of her leg, around the place where her foot would have started if her foot had still been there, and was followed, not long after, by a sharp, but not as sharp as before, kind of pain.

At first, it was like she was being touched by a sharp piece of ice. And then it was like she was being jabbed by that piece of ice, or as if the sharp piece of ice were being worked into her skin, were working to gouge out some essential part of her there in that new and raw stump.

Or, and this was what she decided, it was like the sharp piece of ice was not on the outside working its way in, but was instead on the inside trying to dig itself out.

She unclipped the boot and unraveled the wrap and looked at the place where there had been a foot, but she couldn't see what might have been going on.

She placed her fingers gently on the part of her that was still wrapped in gauze but couldn't feel anything through the gauze and so she unwrapped the gauze, too, and tested the skin, the nerves, with the soft pad of her index finger and then with the rest of her fingers, and there she felt them.

She couldn't see what they were, not yet, but she could feel them. With her fingertips, she could feel them pushing their way out of her stump, and they were sharp and cold and not ice but not unlike ice, either.

Not ice, no. Metal.

# 79.

Everyone was scared of her now. The interns, the jerks in accounting, the office staff, the travel agency staff. Even the Operatives. Oh, boy, were they scared of her now.

They were more scared of her now than she could have ever hoped or wished for. They were the kind of scared of her that surpassed even the kind of scared they had been of Oyemi.

It helped, if *helped* was the right word, that the skin they'd grafted onto her mechanical arm to redisguise it had sloughed off, simply died and peeled off, leaving the shiny interior exposed.

The doctor, who was maybe the most scared of her, had no explanation for this, didn't even correct her when she said it had just died and fallen away. The skin was synthetic. There had been nothing in it to die.

If they'd known about the other part of this, if they'd known about the way in which her own body seemed to be systematically targeted by the nanotechnologies in her arm, targeted for replacement and improvement, if they'd known about her foot, which she'd covered up with a shoe, if they'd known about any of this, they would have been the kind of scared of her that would have bled into a dangerous kind of scared.

The kind of scared that would have led them to draw up

plans, perhaps. Execution and elimination plans, maybe. Dissection and examination and for-the-betterment-of-science plans, perhaps.

And she didn't know that such plans hadn't already been drawn up, did she?

No. She did not.

It had taken less than forty-eight hours for her body to grow a new foot, except that wasn't right, considering the foot was mechanical, and her body couldn't "grow" mechanical things, but there it was, a new foot for her. It had been painful, but only in the beginning. Less than forty-eight hours, but already other pieces of her were beginning to wither and die and would need to be replaced by machine. She could tell.

The decay wasn't visible, but the post-decay replacements were. More of her than just her foot and her arm was beginning to feel inorganic. Her ankle, the lower edge of her calf. The toes on her other foot, four of them, including her big toe, were skinless and had a metallic shine to them. They smelled like pennies or nickels or maybe they just smelled like mechanical toes. When she touched them—and she couldn't stop worrying at them as if they were loose teeth—they were cold and smooth and hard.

Her shoulder.

She'd felt none of this, though. There'd been no pain since the foot. This was a thing she was grateful for but also she couldn't be sure how grateful she was or should have been. She didn't like pain. She wasn't the kind of person who sought out pain and suffering. But without the pain, what then?

Without the pain, would she wake up one day and find herself replaced, entirely replaced?

Regardless, though, the nanotechnologies—that was her only guess as to what was causing all of this—seemed to be learning, seemed to be engaged in some kind of trial-and-error process. After her foot, this—whatever this was—had developed a new process of find and replace, something less painful or intrusive or physically stressful.

She had no idea what happened to the organic material once it died. She had no idea what happened to the pieces of her that had been her and had since been replaced.

She half expected to find a bevy of toes or other patches of herself gathered at the foot of her bed, tangled in the sheets and duvet like socks kicked off during sleep, but there was never anything there.

# 80.

She showed the doctor her homegrown foot but didn't show him anything that came after. It was a shame, really. Before all of this, he had finally become a little more comfortable around her. Had apparently forgiven her for crushing his leg so long ago, for destroying his lab. Now he avoided looking right at her, and she felt each day more strongly this need to have him removed—from his position, from the Regional Office entirely.

He had been there almost from the beginning. Mr. Niles had brought him in on their second meeting together. Mr. Niles had told her, I can help you with your problem, but you'll have to be willing to help us out with ours, too, and when she had offered to pay whatever price he would charge, he had waved that away and told her, That's not exactly the kind of help we need right now. Then he'd called the doctor into the office, introduced the two of them, described for her the work the doctor had been doing—cutting-edge nanotechnologies, beyond joint or bone replacement—and then explained to her that she would have access to the entire Regional Office if she would be willing to act as a test subject for a new mechanical arm the doctor had devised.

"You won't be able to tell a thing," he'd told her. "No one will be able to tell." Then he'd held up the doctor's hand, held it by the wrist, and said, "See this, see this hand? Mechanical, the whole thing." She'd been shocked, amazed. She had seen high levels of robotic technology on campus, some of the highest, but nothing had ever pointed to something so advanced as this. She asked if she could touch it. Mr. Niles offered it to her, the doctor standing there like a living doll, and it felt warm and pliant and so very real.

"Okay," she'd said. "Yes, okay, yes, I will do this."

Only later, long after her own surgery, after being given her own mechanical arm, had the doctor told her, in whispering, confiding tones, that his hand wasn't mechanical at all. He waved his hand in front of her. Shook it, really. Told her, "Blood, bone, nerves." Then he chuckled and she barked out a chuckle of her own, and then he laughed a loud and only-barely-on-the-edges-of-sanity laugh, and she laughed with him because it was too late, by then it was way too late, and they'd been right. Mr. Niles and the doctor had taken a risk with her and her arm but it had paid off because you couldn't tell. You looked at one arm and then the other and they looked the same, exactly the same.

She hadn't always liked him, the doctor, but she had always respected him, and now she was going to have to kill him.

# 81.

*She is the one who first brought you here. Did you know that? Your mother? She brought Mr. Niles to you when you were still a girl and he brought you to the Regional Office, but it might as well have been her leading you there by your hand. Might as well have been her opening the door to Mr. Niles's office for you, moving Mr. Niles's mouth as he offered to change your life forever.*

*And she brought us to you.*

*So here we are.*

*We are at your door and we are not empty-handed. We are offering you a way out, and once out, a way forward. They have lied to you and manipulated you and for too long we have stood by silently and watched this play out, but now we are here, speaking out, reaching out to you, to tell you this:*

*Stay home. For a week, for two weeks, for a month or six. Or better yet, leave. Cape Town or Nova Scotia or Taipei. That is your way out. And when it is time, we will find you, and we will show you your way forward.*

# 82.

Sarah didn't, though. She didn't kill the doctor.

He killed himself. He left a note but it didn't say much but that he was sorry, but not what he was sorry for.

It didn't matter anyhow. Her plan to kill him had centered around her plan of keeping her transformation a secret, but now so much of her was inorganic or some strange mix that there was no way for her to hide the mechanical parts of her anymore.

It had been six months, almost seven months now, since the assault. Oyemi had not been found, and when she was honest with herself about this, Sarah would admit that Oyemi was probably dead, or had been so compromised that she might as well have been dead. No matter. The Regional Office was operating again, not at 100 percent, but not far from it, either.

And no one had asked her to step down or to begin the search for her own replacement, not even now that she was in the middle of her own replacement of sorts.

She missed Henry, would find herself some mornings seeking him out in his office or the break room, and then would wonder what had happened to him, how his cards had fallen, but she found she missed Mr. Niles most of all, and most mornings, when she came into work and made her way to his office, she forgot he was dead, that the office was hers now.

She was thinking about him now, in fact, sitting at his desk, now her desk. She couldn't make herself comfortable sitting there, so she stood up and walked around the room and then made her way to the bathroom. She turned on the light. She looked at herself in his bathroom mirror, at the two mechanical arms, at how obviously mechanical they were, and then thought about how sad that would have made him.

She pushed against the soft parts of her, but this didn't satisfy her, whatever it was she was trying to satisfy.

Pushing against the soft, organic parts of her with a mechanical forefinger, all she felt was the cold metal against her warm, squishy skin. Something inside the mechanical finger, some bit of sentient technology, sent a reading to her still-organic brain that determined for her, almost as quickly as if that finger had still been a human finger, that she had touched living skin.

A readout scrolled through her mind in a strange and unsettling way. Her brain was still her brain, but everything came in as a readout now.

Looking in the mirror, she wanted to cry because it was all so beautiful, the thing that the thing had created, the thing that the thing had made her into, all shining chromes and swooping tubes and artificial ligaments, so beautiful and flexible and powerful that if she'd seen it in a tech conference showroom, she'd have wept at the beauty of it. She wanted to cry, too, because it was her, not some showroom prototype, and she was afraid and she didn't know when it would stop.

She didn't know if it would stop.

How long? she thought. How long will this go on?

Which piece? she thought. Her very next thought: Which piece of me will go next?

She thought this thought, or rather this thought popped unbidden and unwanted into her head, and before she could whisk it away, before she could bury it deep in the darkest recesses of her mind, she felt it, she felt a soft but urgent pressure in her chest.

A twitch in her heart.

From *The Regional Office Is Under Attack:*
*Tracking the Rise and Fall of an American Institution*

One can imagine, in light of the not-unfathomable notion that Emma and Henry had conspired to fake her death and enact revenge on the Regional Office, that it would have been Emma leading the team that burned Oyemi's complex to the ground. No records can place Emma at that scene, though in all truth, any records placing any of this anywhere are difficult if not impossible to find.

But Emma—if she lived—Emma especially was a ghost at this point.

Even had Oyemi suspected Henry's actions, she would not have expected anything from the realm of Emma. And the Oracles? As far as they were concerned, Oyemi had already been duly warned of both Emma and Henry. In light of this, one can imagine the warning system that Oyemi had come to rely on almost completely—the Oracles—failing her when she needed them most.

Imagine: Emma with Windsor and maybe another of Henry's personal Recruits—Jimmie or Becka—on the Amtrak out of Penn Station. The two (or three) of them sitting in the dining car, not hashing or rehashing out their plans, because they know them by now so intimately, so completely, that to go over them even one more time might tip the scales in the other direction, might cause one or more of them to overthink and slip up.

The lot of them jumping off the train as it slows to round a curve.

The cover of darkness. Their stealth, aided by their mystical properties.

Imagine the quiet deliberation as Windsor unmoors the locks—physical and magickal—that Oyemi had set in place to protect herself, her Oracles.

Windsor's soft, quiet, consistent breaths, the care with which she works her magick—both literally and figuratively—and the softly tingling buzzing feeling this gives Emma, just under her ears, where her jawbone connects to her skull, how much this relaxes her, how much her own relaxation sets Windsor at ease.

Dogs roaming the compound that never know the three of them have slipped through the fence and are making their way to the house on the hill.

The house itself smaller than they imagined, modest, even.

The small kernel of doubt lodged deep within Emma, unretrievable and not wholly ignorable, that maybe the best course, the smartest course, would be to abort the mission, to find Henry, to set these girls free before it's too late for them, to jet off with Henry to Finland, maybe, or New Zealand, to let bygones be bygones.

Oyemi there on the porch, her eyes wild with fire and

power, her hair lifted not by wind but by the electromagnetics swirling around her.

Because she knows.

It is too late, but she has seen the necessary and pointless five minutes of her future, knows they have come for her, that the prophecy has come for her, that she read it all wrong.

Windsor falling first, struck by a fireball, incinerated before she hits the ground. Jimmie screaming, her urgent need to leap out of the way rendered inert by fear, by the sudden reality of death and magick and power and the realization that, truly, she has none, or next to none, in the face of Oyemi.

Emma uncaring. Or caring, but not yet, not now.

Emma will remember to cower in fear later. The fear will make her temporarily deaf and mute. She will cower and shake just on the other side of the fence from the still-burning compound. She will scream and scream until she is hoarse, but she won't hear herself over the crackling and violence of the fire, but she won't hear that, either. She will shiver until her whole body aches, but not yet, not now.

Now she will spin and drop and roll and lunge and throw her own magicks at Oyemi, borrowed of course, these magicks. A dagger, its blade forged in an interdimensional fire; an amulet stolen from the Regional Office itself, stored within its underground vaults, its powers never tested, unknown. She will weave a spell stolen from one of Oyemi's own books, filched by Henry when he reported back to Oyemi that Emma was dead.

She will bring these powers to bear, and these powers will fall short, and Oyemi will deflect them all, turning fire into ice, melting the tip of the blade even as it flies through the air toward her, raising a host of roots from the very earth her house stands on, but despite all of this, she will fall.

Maybe Jimmie recomposes herself, sets the fire that burns Oyemi's compound to its foundation, and the flames licking at Oyemi's heels distract her just enough. Or maybe one of the Oracles, seeing for the first time her own bleak future, the charred bodies of her brethren, tries to save herself from Oyemi's fate, and this, the sight of her Oracle, struggling to pull herself free from her pool, from the house, from this timeline, distracts Oyemi. Or maybe Emma, maybe Emma is simply that fast, that good, slipping past the roots even as they reach up to grab her, trip her, pull her into the earth and strangle her there. She slips past and cartwheels about and lands, finally, face-to-face with Oyemi, moves too quick for Oyemi to react, twists her head from her neck, and this, maybe this is what catches the world on fire.

One can imagine. This, any of this, all of this, none of this, but all one knows for sure is:

Henry made a plan.

He was a Recruiter, was good at recruiting and train-ing, and so that was where he began.

Wendy first, whom he quietly installed at the Regional Office as an intern, as a mole. And then Windsor and Jimmie and Colleen and Becka and Rose, finally Rose.

Emma had strong feelings about Rose but he wasn't certain, put off recruiting her until it was almost too late, and then he met her, and then he saw what Emma sensed in her, which was a kernel of Emma herself, lodged somewhere deep inside Rose.

And then he trained them, with Emma at his side, and then he went to work. Figuring out the location of Oyemi's compound took six months. He did other things, too, in those two years. He recruited more Operatives for the Regional Office. He organized and collected the office donations for the March of Dimes. He hired various teams of mercenaries, paid grunts, and put them under the charge of his team.

For two years, he planned, and when the day came, he walked away from the Regional Office for good.

Although, technically he didn't go into work that day.

Nor did he go to Oyemi's compound.

Burning the compound to the ground, destroying everything within it, had been Windsor and Jimmie's job.

Instead, Henry spent part of the day in the city.

The Met by the Etruscan vases, the small custom-jewelry store where he and Emma almost, as a joke, bought each other matching rings after they'd spent the day walking through Park Slope pretending to be one of those new young couples recently transplanted from

Manhattan, on that rooftop where they'd eaten Italian ices together, the roof they'd snuck onto on Mulberry. He went to a toy store. He and Emma had come there only once and only because it had been raining so hard that they'd ducked into the first open store they came upon. They browsed the toys, walked down the aisles while the rain came down outside.

"What do you think about kids?" he'd asked.

"Oh, I hate them," she said, her eyes wide and her mouth just slightly open.

He smiled and nodded and said, "Me too."

And they smiled and then they kissed.

"I do like toys, though," she said.

And he said, "Me too!" exaggerating for effect because they'd gotten into the habit of exaggerating in a way that characters sometimes do in romantic comedies or sitcoms because to think of this thing that was happening between them, whatever this thing was or would become, as anything more serious than a romantic comedy made them both nervous.

They spent an hour browsing through the toy store, stayed long past the end of the rainstorm, holding hands and looking at the toys of their youth, and then separated when she became involved with the kaleidoscope selection, began reminiscing about the kaleidoscope her father had bought for her to take as a present for a birthday party, but then her parents were killed a few days before the party and so she'd kept it, kept it for eight or nine years and through a series of foster homes, kept it until she was fourteen, when one of the boys she was living with, when she wouldn't give him a kiss, smashed it with his boot, so she smashed his jaw with her fist, and after that started sneaking out of the house, and after that started shoplifting, and then auto-thefting, and so on, so forth.

"Maybe things would've been different," she said, "if I'd never lost that kaleidoscope."

"Maybe," he said.

He said this even though he knew better, knew that the Oracles would have plucked her out of a mansion dream house just as easily as they would have picked her out of juvenile detention—it had happened before—just that more often than not the places the Oracles plucked these girls from were of the detention or psych-ward type, though you couldn't blame the girls for this. They'd been imbued with unchecked mystical strength and intelligence, and it seemed nitpicky to complain when that sometimes also led to deviant, violent, often troublesome behavior.

He had admired Oyemi for this ability to seek out these young women, troubled perhaps the way she had been troubled before she'd discovered her own powers. He admired her ability to take what everyone else saw as weaknesses, as difficulties, and transform them into cold, hard, sharp strengths. When it came right down to it, aside from the fact that she had asked him to kill the one woman he'd come to love, he had liked Oyemi.

Though, *liked* was maybe too strong a word.

After a while, he'd tired of each new kaleidoscope she picked up and gazed into and so drifted away to the models and toy engineering sets and there found a ridiculous piece of crap that he couldn't help but fall in love with.

It was a building kit and on the cover of the box was a *Tyrannosaurus rex* made from winches and girders and struts and, where there should have been clawed feet, tank treads. He pulled the box down from the shelf and looked at it. He pictured its pieces spread out over the light-gray rug in his cold, sterile living room, and for a second, he considered buying it, and then Emma came up behind him and looked over his shoulder at the box in his hand and laughed and said, "Boys and their dinosaurs."

"Damn right," he said, and looked at her and asked, "Find a dolly or something?"

She smiled and sheepishly, but not really, held up a twirling baton. "Guilty," she said. He laughed and she laughed and said, "No, but wait," and then she spun it and twirled it and threw it and spun herself and caught it.

"I used to be good at this," she said. "You know," she said. "Before."

She ran her small routine again. He wanted to clap but smiled instead.

"We should get these," she said, gripping it like a cop with his baton and then swinging it forcefully down over her head, "but, like, for all of the girls. We could put together a routine—I'd choreograph it of course—and the monsters, they'd see the bunch of us with these batons about to bash their skulls in—the fucking monsters wouldn't know what hit 'em."

She twirled it in her fingers lazily and smiled shyly, but he caught a hint of real shyness in that shy smile this time, and she said, "Right?"

"Definitely," he said, and he bought her the baton, and now, since he couldn't find here what he'd really hoped to find here, what he hoped to find everywhere he looked, he wanted to buy himself that damn *Tyrannosaurus rex,* but the store had changed. It was still a toy store, if you could call it that, but full of European toys, promising education and not a whit of fun.

He picked up yet another blocky, handmade wooden toy car and placed it back in disgust and then left.

He had a plane to catch.

Though by all accounts, he missed that plane, checked in, obtained an electronic boarding pass, but never boarded, and perhaps he purchased two tickets, boarded under an alias, but it is also easy enough to imagine a slightly different scenario.

Easy enough to imagine him stealing a car instead. Taking this car up the Hudson and across the George Washington Bridge and out of Manhattan and north.

Maybe he drove north, through Paramus and past Mahwah, north along the Hudson River. Maybe he took I-87 for nearly two hours north and then turned off toward Hunter but didn't stop in Hunter, but turned onto an unmarked, little-used road and followed it for another twenty minutes, and turned off it onto a private driveway that wound for another two miles, but even before he wound his way up the drive, maybe he felt, even if he couldn't see, the smoke in the air, thick plumes of it billowing up and out, black enough that the presence of it was palpable even against the black, moonless night, and when he arrived, maybe he wasn't surprised to find the compound ablaze, and if there was one piece of it not on fire, he could not tell by looking at what was in front of him.

And once there, maybe he waited. Waited for the fire to jump through the tall metal gate and catch hold of the woods surrounding the compound. Or waited for something else. Perhaps he sat in his car and watched the flames burn hot for as long as he could, until the smoke became too much for the car's filter. And while there, he hoped, what? To see some sign of Emma, perhaps. Some sign from her? She was dead (or if not dead, if her death was faked, they had already established their rendezvous plans). But still. Maybe this is where he had come, why he missed his first flight out of the city.

And maybe he caught a glimpse of something out of the corner of his eye. A movement, a shadow cast by the flames, he was sure, but for a second, maybe he thought it was Emma. He could picture her stepping out of the woods, mystically untouched by the flames that raged only on the other side of the gate, stepping out and rapping her knuckles on the passenger window to get him to unlock the door.

He would have liked to have had her with him then. If she were around to console him in this moment, he wouldn't need consoling in the first place. But still. Maybe he wanted to be there with someone. He wanted to have someone there to hear him say, What happened to it all? He wanted someone to hear him say, There was something special here. We had something real. The Regional Office was something real. Say, What went wrong? He wanted someone there to acknowledge that something great and singular and brilliant and wonderful was going away, had already gone, in fact. Even now, as he watched Oyemi's compound burn, he wanted there to be at least one other person watching with him who knew what was happening, one other person to be sad about it with him, to regret, not the fact that he was instrumental in its demise, but that the Regional Office had become a place where demise, where violent upheaval and near-total annihilation, seemed inevitable. Seemed the only option left.

He would have sighed. The smoke and heat would finally have been too much. He would have thrown his car in reverse, turned the thing around. He'd have checked his rearview mirror, the sky lit by the false sunset of Oyemi's compound burning out of existence, and he'd have wondered at how quiet it was, at how the road in front of him was nothing but peace and quiet and calm. Even as he drove, he would have thought about Emma, looked for her out in the woods on either side of the road. He would have wished she were there beside him, and at once, the idea that she had slipped into the trunk of his car while he was distracted by the flames would have become for a second so real that he pulled over, stepped out of the car, and opened the trunk, but, of course, she wouldn't have been there.

Maybe, then, he looked around, took a deep breath. And maybe, then, he got back into his car and kept driving, drove back into the city, back to the airport, where he should have gone to begin with.

But whatever the case: He missed his flight, and he scheduled another.

At the airport, he clutched his boarding pass and placed his shoes and his coat on the conveyor belt and walked through the detector. Something about this simple act released a tension that had been building inside of him since he left a dead Emma in a burning house, since he left the Regional Office.

It had been so long since he'd flown out of any airport but the Regional Office airport, so long since he'd had to stand in line, wait for a ticket, pass through security, wait for the boarding call, that he felt suddenly like a boy again, as if he were on some grand and mysterious adventure.

Feeling adventurous and boyish, he walked into a place called the Fuel Bar and found a seat and ordered a cocktail—a peach concoction called the High Dive—and then he leaned back in his chair and smiled.

He looked at the time.

He tried to think of what he'd be doing right now if he were at the office. He closed his eyes and tried to remember what he'd put on his calendar for the day. Meetings, meetings, a lunch meeting, and then meetings. In between all of that? Filing something, probably, or training a Recruit. But then he thought about what had actually happened at the Regional Office after he left, what might be happening still. Now that he had left in such a spectacular fashion.

How mad would Sarah be?

If she were still alive, that was.

He had let them know that he would prefer it if she didn't die, but he also let them know that ultimately it was up to them how they handled Sarah if she didn't accept their offer, their way out, their way forward.

If they hadn't killed her, then, how mad would she be?

He took a sip of his High Dive. It came in a heavy and fluted glass. It was too sweet and he should have ordered a beer or ordered nothing at all, but he didn't care.

Today was a good day.

Today was the first good day, the first good day he'd had.

Today was the first of many good, good days.

The last good day had been some time ago.

Had been the time Emma stayed with him for two weeks in his apartment. Somehow she had fooled the Oracles, fooled Sarah and Mr. Niles, had made it seem like she was on assignment in Rio when in fact she was hiding out in his apartment, reading his books, listening to his records, eating his food, and sleeping in his bed. Sleeping in his bed with him.

Since that day. Well. He could argue there had been other productive days, days where he felt he'd done some good if the days themselves hadn't been good.

The day he'd tapped into the Oracle's network—a surprisingly simple task that, in its simplicity, made Henry wonder just how complacent Oyemi and her people had become—and then, shortly after, when he'd tracked down Wendy, who'd been living in Minneapolis.

He had felt good about all of that, or not good.

Good wasn't what he'd felt.

Proud, perhaps.

Or not even proud.

As if he had accomplished a thing he needed to even if it was a thing he didn't relish or really want to do. That was how he'd felt. How he'd been feeling the past few days. The past few years.

In ten years, of course, they'll find him—Henry. They'll come for him while he is getting a shave.

He will be leaned back in the chair with a hot, steamed towel wrapped around his face, will be breathing in the slight, medicinal, clean, soapy smell of the towel, waiting to be lathered up, will be thinking of little more than what he should do for dinner after the shave when they, or rather she, will come up to him and lift the towel off his face, drop it in his lap, and say, "Hello, stranger."

At first, he won't recognize her.

His first thought, seeing her, will be, Why did they send a robot?

His second thought will be, When did they start using robots?

But it won't be a robot. It'll be Sarah, who will, by that time, only look like a robot.

By this time, he won't have seen Emma in ten years. She will have missed their rendezvous point. He will have gone searching for her in the rubble of Oyemi's compound. He won't have found her or any sign of her, or Oyemi or any sign of Oyemi. He will have placed cryptic ads in the Missed Connections sections of hundreds of weeklies across the country, will have looked for her abroad and at home. He will have come home every day expecting to find her in his apartment the same way he'd found her all those years ago, wearing one of his shirts, reading one of his books, listening to one of his records, but he never will have. In all this time, he will never have once suspected that she is dead. And then he will see Sarah, and then he'll know, or think he knows.

As soon as he figures out that Sarah herself has come for him, that she has probably already found all the others (perhaps even Emma), he will hide his feelings, or do his best to hide them, and will focus on the fact that she is part—or mostly—robot. He will glance at her arm, her left arm, which has always been the arm he's suspected is the mechanical arm, and he will think to himself, Aha! I was right! Because there it will be, her mechanical arm, naked and metallic and exposed and full of a strange, almost organic beauty, but then he will look at her other arm, her right arm, and it will be the same, almost exactly the same, and so he won't be able to say which one was the original mechanical arm. For some reason, the fact that he will continue to live his life holding on to this mystery—even if not for very much longer—will sadden him even more than the fact that he has been found out, has been caught by surprise, and that his uncertain future now seems certain to come to a short and violent end.

Although to be completely honest about it, what will upset him most of all will be that he won't be getting the massage that comes complimentary with every shave, and for a second, he will consider asking her, Can you wait, can you give me just ten minutes, can you wait ten minutes, please?

But that wouldn't be for another ten years.

A lot could happen in ten years. Almost an entire life could be lived in ten years.

And as far as Henry knew, that life started right then, at JFK International.

Or better yet, that life would start when he and Emma met, which they would do. Not right away—situations had to cool down, everything had to pass them by—but soon.

He forgot how sweet his drink was and took another sip and then grimaced and then leaned back in his chair to wait and to think or to not think at all about anything, about any of it. He didn't think about the future, and did his best to stop thinking, finally, about the past, and he worked hard to concentrate on just this moment, this moment right now, here in this airport, the freedom he felt or should have felt sitting there with the knowledge that things had gone not the way he'd wanted them to go—he'd never wanted things to go this way—but how he'd planned them to go.

He took a deep breath and looked around him at the crowds moving here and there to catch flights or grab luggage or a taxi and all he saw before him was a bright, uncluttered, simple future. A future that was spread out before him, that was waiting for him in Durham or Cape Town or Helsinki, but was waiting for him all the same.

# ACKNOWLEDGMENTS

Thanks to PJ Mark for reading this a million times and for not just helping me find the right home for the book but also helping me carve the right book out of the original jumble of words I sent you. Thanks to Megan Lynch and Laura Perciasepe for taking this book on and picking up where PJ and I left off, and to all the amazing folk at Riverhead Books for their continued support and enthusiasm and for telling everyone how much they like both my books and my pies.

Every writer needs a first reader. For years now, Bryan Dunn has been mine, and I can't thank him enough for his thoughtful readings of my work. To his name, I now add both Emily Raw and Kerry DeMunn, and thank them both as well.

Many thanks also go out to E. Tyler Lindvall, Dinaw Mengestu, Owen Egerton, Marie-Helene Bertino, and Hillery Hugg for reading or listening to portions of this and offering me unbridled encouragement to keep moving forward.

Thanks to the Institute of American Indian Arts and the University of Kentucky, my colleagues at both of these grand institutions, for their support, for great students to work with, and the time and space in which to write, test, and revise.

But most of all, thanks to my mom and dad and my sister, who put up with me and continue to put up with me for going on very many years, and for my kids, Anabel and Dashiell, who are only now realizing just how much work it takes to put up with me, and eternally—literally, for an eternity—thanks to you, Sharon. You make putting up with me seem clever and fun.

## Also by MANUEL GONZALES

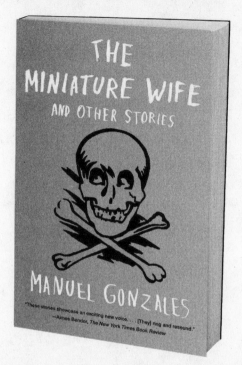

**The stories in Manuel Gonzales's exhilarating first book render the fantastic commonplace and the ordinary extraordinary.**

"It's easy to compare Manuel Gonzales to George Saunders, but it would be just as easy to compare him to Borges or Márquez or Aimee Bender. . . . He makes the extraordinary ordinary, and his playfulness is infectious." **—Benjamin Percy,** *Esquire*

"Hilarious and chilling." —*The Washington Post*

"Is there a term for something that's sad, funny, and strange all at once? Sunge? Frad? Because that would describe this imaginative debut . . . even the most absurd emotional conflicts feel familiar somehow, which only makes them more moving." —*Entertainment Weekly*